Praise for Anna Smith

'Gripping . . . a rollicking read' *The Times*

'Rosie is such a believable character . . . I had to read the whole
thing from start to finish in one sitting'
Lorraine Kelly

'As perfectly paced and neatly plotted as any Ian Rankin novel'
Daily Mail

'Strongly plotted, written in plain, punchy language, and very good
on the tensions and divided loyalties between the establishment
and the fourth estate'
Guardian

'Grabs you by the scruff of the neck and doesn't let you
go until its jaw-dropping conclusion'
Best

'Shocking and compelling, it's impossible to look away until
the last headline has been written'
Daily Record

Anna Smith has been a journalist for over twenty years and is a former chief reporter for the *Daily Record*. She has covered wars across the world as well as major investigations and news stories. *Screams in the Dark* is the third thriller in a series featuring crime journalist Rosie Gilmour. Anna lives in Scotland.

Also by Anna Smith

The Dead Won't Sleep
To Tell The Truth

SCREAMS IN THE DARK

ANNA SMITH

Quercus

First published in Great Britain in 2013 by Quercus Editions Ltd
The paperback edition published in 2013 by Quercus Editions Ltd

55 Baker Street
7th Floor, South Block
London W1U 8EW

A CIP catalogue record for this book is available
from the British Library

PB ISBN 978 1 78087 120 2
EBOOK ISBN 978 1 78087 1196

10 9 8 7 6 5 4 3

Printed and bound in Great Britain by Clays Ltd, St Ives plc

Typeset by Ellipsis Books Limited, Glasgow

For my father

'Give me your tired, your poor, your huddled masses yearning to breathe free...'

Emma Lazarus *New Colossus*

PROLOGUE

Glasgow, July 1999

The alarm didn't beep when Tanya pushed open the door and entered the building. She stood for a moment in the tiled hallway, waiting, ready to punch in the code. Nothing. She made her way up the staircase, muttering under her breath about how careless the rich were. So careless they could leave office doors open all night for burglars. At the top of the landing, she caught her reflection in the mirror. She touched her swollen cheek and winced at the pain. Bastard. The drunken beatings were worse now that Josef had been jobless for months and spent his days boozing in the flat, while she worked at cleaning offices till she came home at night dropping with exhaustion. Fuck him. One morning, she'll walk out and never come back, she promised herself.

The stench hit her first as she opened the door of her boss's office – and then she saw him. Tony Murphy was hanging from the ceiling, his chair beneath him lying on its side. Her hand went to her mouth and she steadied herself against the wall as she felt her legs buckle. She closed her eyes, but the grotesque image was still there: the face blue, one eye bulging like a gargoyle, the other slyly half open, the swollen tongue poking through blue lips and hanging to the side. Tanya gagged, feeling the sick rise in her throat.

The closed venetian blinds clanked and fluttered at the open window. She turned to look again at Tony's distorted face, shaking her head in disbelief. Then tears stung her eyes. Yesterday in the hotel room where they had their secret trysts, he'd told her again how much he loved her. Again, he promised he would leave his wife and they'd be together. Liar. She closed her eyes and pictured him turning her over in the bed in the throes of passion so he could come in his favourite position, and remembered how, afterwards, they'd lain there, spent and in each other's arms.

'Why, Tony?' she sobbed into her hands. 'Why?' She slid down the wall and sank to the floor. Tony had made her believe that life was full of so many possibilities if you loved enough. Now the dream had turned into a garish, terrifying nightmare, and the reality was there *was* no escape from the life she had.

Eventually Tanya glanced up at the clock on the wall. It was nearly 9.30. She had to compose herself, pull herself together. She got to her feet and stood sniffing, wiping her face with the back of her hands. She took a step towards the desk, where she squinted at two envelopes addressed in Tony's handwriting – one to Millie, his wife, the other to Frank, his partner in the law firm. She picked them up and shoved them under her vest, then tucked it into her trousers. She looked up at Tony's body, and the tears came again.

Tanya was backing out of the office when she heard the front door open. She staggered to the top of the stairs and started screaming as Frank Paton, startled, ran up the stairs towards her. She couldn't speak, but just pointed in the direction of the room.

'Oh Christ! Oh Christ no, Tony! Call an ambulance, Tanya. Hurry.' He covered his mouth and nose with his hand.

'He's dead, Mr Frank. You can see he's dead,' she said through sobs.

Paton looked at her, then up at Tony's body, twisting at the end of the rope. He took out his own mobile and dialled 999.

'This is Frank Paton, of Paton, Murphy Solicitors, in Renfield Street.' He took a breath. 'My partner Tony Murphy has hanged himself ... What? ... Here, in his office ... I just came in, the cleaner found him ... He's hanging from the ceiling. He's dead.'

He turned to Tanya, his eyes full of tears. 'They're on their way.' He swallowed.

Tanya watched as Paton went to Tony's desk and lifted a buff folder full of papers. It was marked 'Asylums Pending'. Underneath, written in thick black felt pen, were the names of several countries – Somalia, Rwanda, Zimbabwe, Kosovo, Albania, Iraq, Syria, Turkey.

'No note. Can't believe it. Nothing. Not even for Millie.' Paton closed his eyes, and pinched the bridge of his nose with his thumb and forefinger. 'Oh, Millie. What am I going to say to you?' He whispered to himself.

He stood for a moment, looking around the room, then bent down and went into the open safe in the corner. He took out three more bulging files and left the room.

At around the same time, across the city, Ben Gates steered his boat up the River Clyde, where a crowd had already gathered on the walkway despite the steady drizzle. People always stopped for a look when a body was found in the water. Morbid curiosity. Ben had seen it all before. He waved at the uniformed cops standing on the embankment, but he didn't need them to direct him. He could see it already, bobbing in the current. He carefully eased his boat closer to the body, but his trained eye knew straight away. He took out his mobile and called the Strathclyde cop who had phoned him twenty minutes earlier at the Glasgow Humane Society to say they needed his help.

'Jim . . . it's just a torso.'

'What? You winding me up, Benny? I'm trying to eat a fried egg roll here.'

'Seriously, Jim. Torso.'

'No legs or anything?'

'Christ sake, man. Do you not know what a torso is? You'd better get rid of the ghouls up there before I bring it in.' He hung up.

Ben pulled his boat around so it shielded the torso from the gaping crowd. Whoever belonged to the remains in front of him had been a living, breathing person at one time – recently in fact, judging by the looks of things, the colour of the raw flesh where the arms and legs had been severed. He picked up the oilskin and expertly cast it across so the body was covered and snared, enabling him to drag it towards him. When it was close enough he gripped the ropes and dragged it onto the boat, easing it over the side and gently laying it on the bottom as though he was handling a precious child. He didn't touch it, or lift the cover back. His father had always taught him that curiosity wasn't his job. His role was to preserve the dignity of the poor soul they'd recovered, and take it towards its final journey. He slowly made his way to the embankment, where he could see the cops already pushing everyone back.

Ben tossed the rope to the young cop standing at the edge, trying to keep his feet on the slippery, muddy bank, and turned off his engine as the two cops hauled the boat up the slope inch by inch. The ambulance men made their way down with a stretcher. Ben could hear the big Strathclyde Police sergeant on his radio telling them to send transport. The boat, with the torso still in it, would be taken in a low loader to the mortuary so that everything would be kept intact for the post-mortem. Not that there was much left to examine.

'Fuck me!' the sergeant said as the two officers pulled back the cover. He bent down, peering at the chest.

'What the fuck's that? Is it tattoos?'

'Tattoos?' the paramedic sniggered.

'Well, what is it?' the sergeant screwed up his eyes.

'Stitches,' the paramedic said. 'Looks like they've been

done by a blind person wearing boxing gloves. But it's stitches. Rough-looking job all right.'

'Stitches?'

'Aye.' The paramedic turned to his partner, then to the sergeant. 'Somebody's opened this guy up. Something well dodgy here. We'd better not touch it till the CID come.'

One man held the key to these two grisly scenes, but he was nowhere near them. Tam Logan was so cold he couldn't keep his eyes open. The blood on his temple where they'd hit him with the butt of the gun had congealed hard. He tried to focus on his wristwatch but it was a blur. He guessed he'd been in the back of the refrigerated van for nearly two hours.

Suddenly there was the sound of bolts being slid and someone pulled the door back. Tam tried to sit up, but his hands were tied and he slumped against the side. He heard voices outside, and shook himself, trying again to get up and this time managing to make it to his feet. Two men wearing balaclavas climbed into the back of the van and stood over him. His stomach lurched when he saw their guns. They stood in silence as another man climbed in and looked down at him. He wasn't wearing a balaclava, and Tam recognised him as the man they called Doctor Mengele – though never to his face. He'd seen him before at the plant, dressed in his white coat, and he knew he was a foreigner. They'd said he was from Bosnia and he was the boss, but nobody knew his name.

'What were you doing?' The Doc eyed him coldly.

Tam said nothing. He tried to swallow but his mouth was dry.

'Why did you steal it? Did you think we would never find you?'

Tam shook his head. 'I don't know. I'm sorry.' He could feel his knees shaking.

The Doc stared at him again, then took a deep breath and gave a bored sigh. He looked at one of the masked men.

'Kill him.' He turned and walked away.

CHAPTER 1

Rosie parked her car and walked towards the noise. It was supposed to be a protest, but it looked more like an unruly mob.

'What do we want?' bellowed the fat woman standing on the low wall.

'Equal rights,' the crowd chanted back.

'When do we want them?' She was whipping them up.

'Now!' Clenched fists punched the air for emphasis.

Equal to what, Rosie wondered, as her footsteps scrunched on the broken glass from bottles tossed by the obligatory thugs who would turn up anywhere looking for a fight.

She stopped for a moment and gazed up at the notorious Red Road flats, a bleak cluster of eight massive tower blocks scarring the skyline. It must have seemed like a good idea at the time to house families in slab-concrete blocks thirty-one storeys high. But then it *was* the sixties, so you had to assume that whoever sanctioned it was off their tits on drugs. Because in a few short years high living, as the flats were dubbed, had become low-life dens, with junkies and drug dealers on every floor. And at least twice a year some poor bastard took a swan dive from the twentieth floor, either because they'd been shoved or had simply run out of hope.

From where Rosie was standing, it was hard to see what this lot were fighting over, but she'd decided to come up to the Balornock housing scheme in the north of Glasgow and see for herself. The protest had been staged by the angry residents of the council flats who'd become incensed at what they claimed was special treatment for asylum seekers. Charity begins at home, said one of the banners. Go home foreigners, exclaimed another. She sighed. Welcome to Glasgow – the city with the big, bleeding heart.

'You fae the papers?' A lantern-jawed man sucked on a roll-up cigarette as he approached her.

Rosie looked at him and paused before she answered. On a scale of the most unwelcome guests in a place like this, number one was the cops, two was the DSS snoops, three was anyone from the papers.

'Yeah,' she took a chance. 'The *Post*. Came up to see what all the protest is about. Can I ask you exactly what's happening?' Not that she didn't know.

'What's happening?' His voice went up an octave with indignation, and Rosie got a whiff of just-drunk booze. 'What's happenin' is these fuckin' foreigners are gettin' everythin' handed to them on a plate and we get fuck all.'

'Really?' Rosie tried to look sympathetic. 'Like what?'

'Hoovers,' he said. 'And kettles. Washin' machines. Stuff like that. They come skiving in here from some foreign place and get a council house, fitted carpets, new kitchens. But if you're born and bred in Glasgow you just get in the queue behind them. We're like second-class citizens. It's pure shite, by the way.'

Rosie nodded. 'I see what you mean.'

But she didn't really. Sure, it might not have been clever to accommodate the sudden influx of asylum seekers in Balornock, one of the most socially deprived housing schemes in the city. But Rosie could bet if you did a straw poll of every Balornock council tenant who wasn't a refugee, you'd find that two in three of them had Irish grandparents. If they were to take their heads out of their backsides for a moment, they might consider that their own ancestors were themselves half-starved, impoverished refugees from Ireland who came over here on the boat with nothing but the clothes they stood in. And right now, the very people waving placards were second or third generation from those refugees who fled violence and bigotry in their own country. But if you were ten floors up and skint on a Friday, with your man on the dole and four hungry kids, you jealously guarded what little you had.

The sound of glass crashing and people screaming made them both turn towards the crowd.

'See what I mean? This could end up in a riot. Fuck them.' The man took off at speed towards the youths throwing bottles.

A police van drew up and a bunch of uniformed officers jumped out and headed towards the mob. Rosie followed close behind. Another police van arrived with reinforcements and they headed to the front of the crowd to form a human chain. Rosie weaved her way through the mob to see what had triggered the trouble.

In front of the Red Road flats, she could see two minibuses full of people, refugees by the look of fear on their faces as bottles rained down on them, bouncing off the windows. Children screamed from inside the bus.

'Get to fuck back to wherever you came from,' a skinny woman spat from the crowd.

'You don't belong here,' another screamed.

Half a dozen police officers went across to one of the minibuses and began to let the people out one by one, escorting them inside the building, while the rest of the cops stood holding back the crowd.

Rosie watched as the terrified refugees stepped out, some of them in tears, all of them with the haunted, deathly pallor she'd witnessed in conflicts all over the world. Her mind flashed back to Kosovo, still fresh and raw enough to make her stomach turn over. She'd only come back two months ago after six weeks on the frontline, and the images of the traumatised Kosovo Albanian refugees, beaten and bloodied by the Serbs, continued to haunt her sleepless nights. That was partly why she'd suggested to McGuire, her editor, she should come up to Balornock to see just what was going on with this discord over asylum seekers building up a head of steam. Already, there had been several random attacks on refugees in the scheme, apparently the work of vigilantes determined to run the foreigners out.

Now, just seeing the faces being helped out of the minibus and into the flats, Rosie was back in the muddy field in the border post in Blace, as stricken refugees staggered into Macedonia, each with a horror story of what they had suffered at the hands of Serbian soldiers who butchered their way through towns and villages. To survive all of that, and then end up here? Where you were a figure of hate because you had a fitted carpet? Christ almighty! Rosie looked back at the crowd and felt ashamed of her fellow countrymen.

Her mobile rang in her pocket and she fished it out.

'You still up in Balornock, Rosie?' It was Lamont, the news editor, whom she despised and seldom had to deal with.

'Yeah, why?'

'McGuire wants you back down here. Tony Murphy's just been found hanged in his office. Oh, and there's a torso been fished out of the Clyde. I've sent Reynolds over on that one. But McGuire wants you back.'

'Fine. What's the story with Murphy?'

'Dunno. He does mostly refugees these days. Asylum cases. Who knows?'

'I'm heading back anyway. I've seen enough here.'

Rosie didn't need to sell the news feature on refugees to Lamont. She knew he'd be negative, as he always was with every idea she put up – backstabbing bastard that he was.

The police seemed to have calmed the situation, and the crowd began to disperse, so Rosie made her way across the back court to her car. As she walked past the back entrance to the flats, she stopped when she saw a young man standing against the wall. He looked Bosnian or Kosovan, or he could have been Turkish – it was hard to tell. But he was definitely a refugee, she decided. He had that lean, lost look they all had. He stood there weeping, his lip quivering. Rosie watched him for a moment and he looked through her, tears running down his face. He was obviously in some kind of meltdown.

'What's the matter?' Rosie went over to him. 'Is there anything I can do. Are you sick ?'

He shook his head. 'English no very good. I am Kosovan.' He sniffed and wiped his face, seeming to compose himself.

'You living here?' Rosie pointed to the flats.

He nodded.

'How long you been here?'

'One month.' He started crying again. 'I alone. My mother, my father . . . ' He drew his hand across his throat. 'They killed.'

'The Serb soldiers?'

He nodded.

'Do you not have friends here? Other Kosovo refugees? There are a lot of Kosovan people here now.'

He shook his head and bit his lip. 'My friend. They take him.'

'Who?' Rosie asked. 'Who took him?'

He took a cigarette out of his jeans pocket and his hands trembled as he lit it.

'I not know.' He glanced over his shoulder.

Rosie screwed her eyes up, confused. 'What do you mean?' she asked.

'I run away. They take my friend. I not know where he is.' He wiped his tears with the palm of his hand.

Rosie automatically extended a hand of comfort, but he flinched and drew back.

'Let me take you for a cup of tea.' She pointed to the cafe across the road. 'We can talk there. Maybe I can help you.'

He shook his head, and began to back away.

'Don't be afraid. It's okay. My name is Rosie. Rosie Gilmour. I am a journalist. Do you understand? Newspaper?'

He nodded, then shook his head. 'I am frightened. I must go.' He began walking away, with Rosie pursuing him.

'Please. Wait. Hold on. Please.' She caught up with him and he stopped. She reached into her bag and pulled out her business card. 'I just want to give you this.' She held out the card. 'It's okay. I promise.' She reached out and touched his arm. 'Don't worry. I want to help you. I was in Kosovo in April. I was there. And in Blace. I saw . . . things.'

He seemed to calm down a little. He looked at her, took the card and put it in his pocket.

'What is your name?' Rosie asked.

He paused and looked around him.

'Emir,' he whispered. 'My name is Emir.'

Some of the protesters were making their way across the car park, and he glanced at them.

'I go.' He backed away.

'Emir. You can phone me. Any time. I will come.'

CHAPTER 2

'Dear oh dear! Two stiffs and it's not even lunchtime,' McGuire chuckled as Rosie walked into his office. 'This never happens when you're not involved Gilmour. Must be down to you.'

'Yeah, very funny, Mick.' Rosie plonked herself on the leather sofa opposite his desk. 'You should try and incorporate that air of sympathy the next time you've got a funeral eulogy to make.'

'Ha! That's good coming from you,' he grinned. 'By the time you got home from Spain last July, there were bodies everywhere. By the way, is that paedo Vinny Paterson still trying to climb out of the well your mates chucked him down in Morocco?'

'Touché,' Rosie half smiled, 'but I can assure you this morning's unfortunate stiffs have nothing to do with me.'

'Don't worry, Rosie. We'll soon change that.' McGuire took off his reading glasses and placed them on his desk. 'That's a real shocker about Tony Murphy. Hanging from the ceiling in his office? *Very* strange. Got to be something dodgy there. I feel a scandal coming on. What's the word on the street?'

Rosie sat back and rubbed her face with her hands. The whole protest scene up the road had somehow exhausted her.

'I talked to one of my lawyer pals on the way back from Balornock. Like everyone else, he's stunned. Murphy seemed to have it all. Married, two kids at university, big house, didn't appear to have money worries. Mostly did a lot of refugee work in the past couple of years, helping asylum seekers stay in the country, fighting for their rights. All that sort of stuff. Wasn't always like that though.'

'Yeah, I've seen his face on the telly talking about refugees. What do you mean?'

'Few years ago,' Rosie said, 'he and his partner Frank Paton were more into criminal law. They defended any hoodlum with a wedge of money, or some lowlife toerag as long as they got legal aid. You could sometimes see the pair of them in O'Brien's with a couple of well-known gangsters. I've seen them myself a few times, but not for a while. I thought it was a bit strange that they suddenly became these white knights fighting for poor bastard refugees. They never struck me as woolly-headed liberals.'

'Money, Rosie,' McGuire said. 'It's all about money. These lawyers fighting asylum cases make a fortune in legal aid fees. It's all appeals, fights against deportation, long drawn-out hearings. Every time some asylum seeker turns up at a lawyer's office, the tills start jingling like Christmas Eve.'

'True,' Rosie agreed. 'That sounds like Paton and Murphy. Naked greed. But why hang himself? He must have been into something. I'm waiting for a few people to get back to me, in case he was into drugs or anything.'

'Any suicide note?'

'Nothing. It might not have been suicide. Maybe it was just made to look that way.'

McGuire raised an eyebrow. 'Is that just your vivid imagination, Gilmour, or are you basing it on actual evidence?'

Rosie paused. 'No, nothing really. But something drove him to suicide, Mick. I'm going to do a bit more digging.'

'Good. Nothing like a bit of intrigue to give a shape to the weekend – as long as the Sundays don't come up with any revelations about what made Murphy cash in his chips.' He turned to his computer screen. It was time to go.

'Oh, Mick,' said Rosie as she stood up. 'Talking of intrigue, something else up at the Red Road.'

McGuire was still looking at his screen.

'Never mind,' Rosie said. 'I'll tell you later.'

'What, Rosie?' He looked up. 'Don't fuck about.'

'Well, it's just that as I was about to leave the protest, I came across this refugee. A Kosovan guy, late twenties or early thirties. Always hard to tell with refugees as they're kind of old before their time. But he was crying.'

'Crying?'

'Yeah. At the back of the flats. Just standing there sobbing by himself. My heart went out to the guy. Poor bastard is probably traumatised by everything in Kosovo and just feels desperate and alone. Who knows, but I went over and spoke to him.'

'Go on.'

'He didn't speak great English, but from what I understood his parents were murdered by Serb soldiers. Then he said he was alone now, that he'd been here a month, and that his friend was taken.'

'Taken? Here or in Kosovo?'

'Here. He said "my friend they take him", and then he said that *he* ran away. But when I pressed him for more information he just backed off. The guy was absolutely terrified. Something has happened, but I don't know what. I gave him my card, and told him I'd been in Kosovo. I think he'll phone me.'

'How can you tell?'

'Sometimes you just know, Mick. I feel it. He's got something to tell and he just doesn't know how to yet, but something has scared the shit out of him. And his pal is missing.'

'You need to find him, Rosie. Can you stake out the flats? .'

'If it comes to it I will. But I'm hoping he gets in touch before I have to do that.' Rosie changed the subject. 'What about the torso? Any word on that? What's Reynolds saying?'

'Not much. All we'll get from him is what the cops want us to get. He told Lamont that cops are still trying to identify it, but they've revealed it's a male. These plods are amazing. I guess they came to that conclusion because the torso had no tits.'

Rosie chortled.

'I'll see what else we can find out as the day goes on, but I want to have a better look at Tony Murphy. Find out a bit more about his work as a refugee lawyer. I'll talk to some contacts.'

'Fine,' said McGuire, 'but I hope your weeping refugee guy phones you. He sounds interesting. Either that, or back in Kosovo they told him he was going to Madrid or somewhere exotic, and he's just depressed he ended up in Balornock in the rain.'

Tanya sat in the cafe, sipping coffee and drawing the smoke from her cigarette deep into her lungs as though her life depended on it. She ran a hand over her face and leaned back, so exhausted she could barely keep her eyes open. She ordered another coffee, black this time.

The questioning by the police when they'd descended on the offices of Paton, Murphy was much more involved than she'd imagined. While the paramedics and medical team worked in Murphy's office, two detectives had taken her to another room. They sat her down and reassured her their questions were just routine, but they needed a statement from her of exactly what she found when she'd arrived at the offices. She turned down their offer of an interpreter, telling them she'd been in Glasgow for nearly three years and understood the language. The female detective had made her a cup of tea and talked sympathetically to her, as Tanya gave them an account of what she'd found. All during the interview she could feel sweat trickling down her back and was glad she'd tucked the letters into her bag before they spoke to her. Eventually they told her she could go. As she left, she put her head around the door of Frank Paton's office, where he sat staring into space.

Now, glad the cafe was almost empty, she sat in the corner booth furthest away from the counter and took out the letter Tony had addressed to Millie. She opened it carefully, took out the single sheet of notepaper and read it slowly, her heart sinking with each line:

Dear Millie,

The picture of your lovely face, and our smiling, beautiful children, is the last image I see. Please forgive me. I could not go on any more with the lies. I love you forever, always have. I'm sorry. Tony.

There were three kisses at the end.

The knot in Tanya's stomach turned to anger. It had all been one big lie. Everything. He'd never had any intentions of leaving his family so he and she could be together. He'd promised her they would settle in Spain, somewhere in the countryside where nobody would find them, where they could live off the land and begin a whole new life. They would have a child together, he told her, their own family. Nothing of their past lives would matter as long as they had each other. She was so stupid to have fallen for it.

How naïve she'd been, believing it was so much more than just sex, given how they had met in the first place. She had been working as an escort girl in London when she came to Britain from the Ukraine – a step up from hanging around the international hotels in Kiev, where middle-aged businessmen paid well for the leggy Russian ladies who told them they were the most wonderful lovers. She had moved from London to Glasgow, and she'd met Tony at a party in a city hotel where the escort agency had sent her, assuring her that she would be mingling with the top drawer and reminding her that discretion was more important than ever in this kind of company. Tanya had been surprised to find that the party was mostly made up of thuggish men in shiny suits, snorting coke from a glass-top table along with other escort girls, half naked, and cavorting with two of them at a time.

She'd caught Tony's eye as soon as she came into the room, and he made his way across to her and offered her a drink. He wasn't like the others in this party, he told her, and he could see she was different. They went somewhere quiet, just to talk. And that's how it all began.

She finished her coffee and pushed the cup away. She brought out the other letter, addressed to Frank, and opened it:

What have we done, Frank? What happened to us? We were the wide-eyed law students who were going to change the world. Remember? I told you we should have stopped. See you in hell . . . Tony.

CHAPTER 3

Rosie looked at her watch while she was agreeing to meet Don Elliot, her Strathclyde Police CID contact and friend. She had time for a quick coffee, she told him and no, she didn't want to go to O'Brien's tonight. She ignored Don's digs asking her if she had a hot date. She had, but that was her business.

She smiled to herself as she drove up Byres Road towards the cafe in Ashton Lane, feeling that little rush in her stomach because later she was going to TJ's flat where he was cooking dinner. Happy Friday. Rosie checked herself for behaving like a lovestruck teenager of late, waiting for TJ's call, anxious if it didn't come, stressing out that perhaps he'd disappeared again. Get a grip woman. Her mind drifted to the moment six months ago when he'd turned up on her doorstep, but she pushed it away in case the memory would become diminished by reliving it. She wanted to cherish the moment so she could call it up now and again like a treasure. On the way to the cafe she called TJ to let him know she'd be a little late, but he pre-empted her before she spoke, joking, 'Yeah, Rosie. I know. You'll be late. Don't worry, I won't start cooking till you come.'

'So, whatever happened to a few stiff gin and tonics when you finish work on a Friday?' said Don, sidling into the booth opposite Rosie. 'What's got into you, Gilmour?'

'Health kick,' Rosie replied. 'Skinny lattes.' She held up her frothy coffee. 'Decaf, by the way.'

'What a faggot you turned out to be.'

'You should try it some time.'

'What, being a faggot?'

'No. The decaf latte.' Rosie sipped her coffee.

'No thanks, I'll have a beer.' He looked up at the waitress. 'You got Peroni, sweetheart? Might as well join the yuppies.'

Rosie watched as Don poured the lager into the frosted glass and took a long, thirsty slug.

'I needed that,' he sighed. 'Long day.'

Rosie raised her eyebrows, knowing he was bursting to tell her.

'So, Don. What's the craic with the torso? Grisly stuff, I dare say.'

'Too right. I was in at the post-mortem. Didn't take very long, as you can imagine, given that there wasn't much left of it.' He shook his head and downed another mouthful of lager. 'Tell you what, Rosie. Something very strange going on here. Very fucking strange.'

'Yeah,' Rosie said. 'What kind of psycho cuts someone's arms and legs off? Shades of Dennis Neilson, remember him from Aberdeen? Cutting up his victims and cooking their limbs in a big pot. Some very weird people out there.'

'You bet,' Don said. He waved the waitress over and ordered another Peroni. 'But hey, it gets worse, Rosie.' He lowered his voice and beckoned her closer. 'Somebody took this fucker's heart and lungs out. Kidneys and all. The lot.' His eyes widened. 'Aye. And his . . . er . . . tackle. I mean, they even took the poor bastard's tackle!'

'Jesus! You're kidding.'

'Seriously. The pathologist couldn't believe it when they opened it up.'

'What's the thinking? Is it some kind of ritualistic killing? Any ideas where the body is from or anything like that? White? Black? Brit?'

'White,' he said. 'And yeah, there was something interesting. Some tiny wee tattoo up above the groin. Looked like a flag of some description. Green with a yellow half moon and a star. How's your knowledge on flags?'

'About as good as your stamp collection.'

Don sniggered. 'Well, good job we have forensics then. Me neither. The boss just got a call an hour ago to say it's some kind of ancient Bosnian flag. Dates back to the Middle Ages.'

'So it's a Bosnian. Who chops up Bosnians? I mean, in this country?' But Rosie's mind was already doing double time.

'You know, Don, I was up in Balornock this morning and there were some real angry scenes with the locals protesting about refugees getting so many handouts.'

'I know. I heard about it.'

'There's been vigilantes attacking refugees. You don't suppose they could have done something like this, do you? Chopping people up?'

Don looked at Rosie, then lit a cigarette and blew smoke slowly into the air.

'Like the Shankhill Butchers, you mean?' he said. 'Remember the nutters in Belfast back in the seventies? Picking Catholics at random off the street and butchering them?' He raised an eyebrow. 'The Balornock Butchers . . . '

Rosie nodded. 'Anything's possible, I suppose.'

'It is. Actually, a vigilante mob was mentioned, but I'm not sure they're seriously thinking in that direction right now. And you see, just because the torso had a tattoo like that, it doesn't mean he was from Bosnia. Loads of people these days get tattoos in everything from Arabic to Chinese – it's all very trendy to have some ancient proverb or shite written in Egyptian or Hebrew or some crap. Doesn't mean the guy was Bosnian. He could be from Govan.'

'Yeah, but Bosnia's not a bad place to start though,' Rosie said, keen to pursue her line. 'There was certainly enough anger up at Balornock, and there's plenty of nutjobs there and anywhere else capable of mutilating a body.'

Don shrugged. 'Suppose so. Might just be a one-off though. Might not be a refugee. And even if he was, he could have been into anything, might have got mixed up in the drug scene here. There's a few psychos working

for any one of the drug bosses who would chop somebody up if they needed to pass on a lesson to the rest of
the troops. Or if they got paid enough. That's a more
likely scenario.'

'So what happens now?'

Don finished off his drink. 'They're keeping an open
mind. Still doing more tests. All that crap. Will be a few
days yet before anyone knows what's what.' He got to his
feet as Rosie drained her coffee cup. 'We'll have a drink
after the weekend and I'll keep you posted. A proper
drink. I'll give you a bell Monday.'

'Great,' Rosie looked at her watch as they walked out
of the cafe together.

'Enjoy your hot date.' Don squeezed her shoulder and
they went off in opposite directions along the cobblestone road.

'Good evening, madam.' TJ did a maitre d' bow as he
opened the door, a teatowel folded over his arm.

'Evening sir.' Rosie smiled and stepped into the hallway.

TJ slipped off her jacket and dropped it on the floor.
He wrapped his arms around her and kissed her on the
lips long and hard. She caught the freshness of his skin,
and ran her hand over the back of his hair, still damp
from the shower. Slow jazz music drifted from the living
room.

'Goodness me, sir.' Rosie patted her chest theatrically.
'I hope you don't welcome all your guests like this.'

'Only the ones with money and influence.' TJ put his
arm around her shoulder as they walked to the kitchen.

Various dishes and ingredients were strewn across the worktop. Plump fresh scallops on a dish topped with breadcrumbs, and salmon fillets with some kind of sauce in an oven dish. Vegetables, herbs and bags of salad were stacked up on a chopping board next to the sink.

'Don't worry,' TJ said. 'It's not as disorganised as it looks. I'll have this restaurant up and running in no time, but I didn't want to start until you were actually here and I had your full attention.' He dropped some cut limes into tall glasses with ice and reached for a bottle of gin. 'Let's have a drink.'

'All looks great to me, TJ,' Rosie said. 'But first, I'd like to jump into your shower if you don't mind. It's been a long day.'

'Be my guest.'

Rosie closed her eyes and stood under the shower, enjoying the surge of warm water on her face. But almost immediately her mind flashed up the picture of the refugee at the Balornock flats, his face pale and haunted. It triggered a rush of the disturbing images from Kosovo that often woke her in the night since she'd come back. Her head flicked through them.

So many bewildered people on the move. The bruised faces of men and women, battered and burned out of their homes. Before the conflict, they'd been farmers, teachers, tradesmen, shopkeepers, housewives. Now they were collapsing in front of her after trekking across the mountains, huddling together in the open as they'd fled from Serb soldiers. Some had no shoes and festering blisters on their feet. And always, always the picture of the old woman with the broken hip slumped in the bucket of a dumper that was being used to ferry her down the rocky hillside to safety, her husband limping at her side, his face grey with worry. On a daily basis since she had come home, when Rosie passed a building site she still couldn't look at a dumper without seeing the image of the old woman in the bucket. So many flashbacks like that. She didn't need the doctor to tell her she had post-traumatic stress. She'd been there before in horror stories across the world, and she'd always told herself to get it into perspective. She was only the witness, after all. None of the shit she saw was actually happening to her. It was happening to others. That helped her deal with the pictures, but it couldn't make them go away.

'Come on Gilmour. Scallops are in the oven, and there's a G and T here with your name on it.' TJ's voice from the other side of the door broke Rosie from her reverie, and she was glad.

'Two minutes.' She stepped out of the shower, trying to shake herself out of the gloom.

After dinner they sat in the kitchen sipping red wine and smoking TJ's cigarettes, listening to the sudden thunderstorm. Rosie gazed through the large open window as torrential rain made the tenement buildings opposite look dark and eerie.

'You okay, Rosie?' TJ reached his hand across and ruffled her hair. 'You suddenly looked a bit dark a little while ago. What's happening?'

Rosie took his hand. 'I'm okay.' She shrugged. 'You know me, usual stuff. There's always something lurking in the background. I felt a bit sad today up at that Red Road protest I told you about. I saw this guy crying. Reminded me about a lot of stuff.'

'Tell me about it.'

Rosie told him about the protest, and about the intrigue over the torso, and the vigilantes. TJ listened as she set out the various scenarios of refugees going missing, lawyers hanging themselves.

'So you think it's all connected, but you've got nothing really to go on.' TJ sat back watching her. 'Don't get ahead of yourself. You know how you are, Rosie. You're choking to wade right in there.'

She took his packet of cigarettes and handed one to him.

'Gee thanks, sweetheart.' TJ gave her a sarcastic look.

Rosie smiled and held his hand while he gave her a light. 'Well, maybe I am getting ahead of myself here,' she said, 'but I'm just trying to lay out all the possibilities. I'm not really connecting it all, but I can't stop thinking about that refugee in tears today.' She blew smoke. 'Wish to hell now I'd been able to hold onto him for just a minute longer.'

'That'll drive you nuts now, till he gets in touch.' He poured the remains of the wine into their glasses. 'But hey. It's Friday night. Forget about all that. Let's open another bottle. I've got some news too.'

'Yeah? What's happening?'

'I've been offered a steady gig two nights a week in

that jazz club I took you to – The Blue Note. This guy, Gerry, really good jazz guitarist, and a singer, woman called Kat. Amazing voice. Really soulful. I played with them a few times in New York in a couple of gigs and one or two sessions. They're good.'

'American?'

'No. Scottish. Kat studied there for a while, but most of the work they do is session work. She's trying to make it as a singer. She's good enough, but it's tough out there.'

'Are they together?' Rosie asked, annoyed at the twinge of jealousy she felt.

TJ looked at her as though he could see out of the back of her head. She felt herself blush.

'No.' He drew on his cigarette. 'Why?'

'Nothing,' Rosie looked away. 'Just wondered.'

'Yeah.' TJ studied her face. 'Sure you did.' He sighed, reached over and took her hand. 'Rosie. What's with the insecurity? You never used to be like this.'

Rosie swallowed and looked at the table.

'I never cared this much before.' She got up and moved over to the sink. 'Come on. I'll help clean up this mess. It's like a car crash in here.' She started scraping leftovers into the bin, and rinsing plates under the tap before placing them in the dishwasher. Her stomach was in knots. What the hell was happening to her? All TJ did was mention that he was going to be working with some dame he'd met in New York and it was enough to set off a rush of paranoia. This has got to stop, she told herself. Suddenly she felt TJ's arms around her waist and he buried his face in her hair.

'Leave that, sweetheart,' he said. 'Time enough for that.' He ran his hands over her breasts and down her thighs, pushing her against the sink.

Rosie ran the water over the cutlery as TJ nuzzled her neck and put his hand between her legs, gently squeezing her. He took her hand and turned off the tap. Rosie could hear his breathing quicken.

'Leave it, Rosie,' he said again, turning her around and easing her T-shirt over her head. They kissed hard and emphatically, then TJ stopped suddenly and for a few seconds their eyes locked in silence. He took her by the hand and led her to the bedroom.

Their sleep was broken by Rosie's mobile ringing on TJ's bedside table. For a moment, she couldn't work out where she was, until she blinked two or three times and took in her surroundings, the morning sunlight streaming through the blinds. She groaned as she reached over and lifted the phone. No name, and a number she didn't recognise.

'Hello?' Rosie cleared her throat, gravelly from too many cigarettes.

'Hello? Is Rosie?'

'Yes. It's Rosie.'

'Is Emir. I am Emir. I meet you yesterday.'

Rosie sat up and shook herself awake.

'Emir! Hello. Yes. How are you? You okay?'

Silence.

'Emir? You there?'

'Yes. You can meet me? You come?'

'Yes, Emir, I'll come. To Balornock?'

'No. Not there. In city, in Central Station. Starbuck cafe.'

'Yes. Okay. When?'

'In one hour. Is okay? You be there?'

'Yes, Emir, I'll be there. Wait for me. Please.' The line went dead. Rosie sank back into the pillow. She was glad they hadn't drunk the second bottle of wine last night. She may not have had much sleep, but at least she wasn't hung over. She felt TJ's arms around her; he pulled her towards him.

'C'mon, Rosie. It's Saturday morning.'

'I know.' She put her arms around him, but she looked at her watch. She needed to be up, showered and ready to talk to Emir within an hour. She didn't have time for this.

TJ pulled her close and kissed her.

'You're not concentrating, Gilmour.'

'I am,' Rosie laughed.

TJ rolled onto his back, shaking his head.

'You'll never change. Get to work. You drive me nuts.'

CHAPTER 4

Rosie was perched on a stool at a podium near the window of Starbucks, a perfect vantage point where she could people-watch while she waited for Emir at Central Station. She sipped from a cardboard cup of frothy latte and picked at a warm croissant, enjoying the melted butter and strawberry jam. What the heck, she would get back on her diet tomorrow – again.

She lapsed into daydream mode, watching the bustle and wondering what stories lay behind the people meeting and greeting, or those parting with bear hugs and tears in their eyes. A dishevelled middle-aged woman with a drinker's bloated face shuffled along pushing a supermarket shopping trolley with various plastic bags filled with what looked like all her worldly goods. She plonked herself wearily on a bench next to a slim, well-dressed woman around the same age, who instantly bristled and shifted up a little. The trolley-pusher took a can of strong lager from her bags, put it to her mouth and swigged it. Then she turned to the lady. 'Y'all right?

Roastin' innit?' She wiped her mouth with the back of her hand.

The thin-faced woman nodded, her nose turning up a little.

'Want a drink?' The drunk shoved the can of lager towards her.

The woman shook her head and looked away.

Rosie wondered what their stories were, what had reduced the drunken woman to this. She remembered, as a little girl, shopping in the city centre on a winter's day with her mother, when they came across a woman lying in a drunken sleep over the warm air vent outside Central Station. Rosie had been aghast and sad at the sight. She kept saying to her mother to look at the state of her. 'We should pray for her, Rosie,' her mum had said. 'She's a poor soul. And she's somebody's mother.' Even as a child, the words had struck a chord with Rosie, and for months she was haunted by the moment, quietly living in dread that one day her mum would end up like that, sleeping over an air vent at Central Station, with people saying, 'She's somebody's mother.'

She was relieved when she saw Emir coming towards the Starbucks. She watched him standing outside, looking nervously around him. He was tall and slim, his dark hair unkempt and his pale face unshaven. His black leather jacket was zipped up even though it was sweltering hot in the bright sunshine that had followed last night's thunderstorm. She waited for him to turn around; when he did, she waved and he caught her eye.

'Hi Emir.' Rosie spoke quietly as she eased herself off the stool to greet him.

'Hello,' Emir nodded, his dark eyes bloodshot.

'Let me get you a coffee. You want something to eat? You hungry?' Rosie motioned him to a table in a quiet corner.

He shook his head. 'Coffee please. Black. Thank you.'

Rosie returned with coffee and a croissant. She figured he was hungry but was too polite or nervous to say.

'You might eat something, Emir,' Rosie smiled. She scanned his face. 'Don't be frightened, Emir. I will be your friend. I want to help you.'

He took a sip of his coffee, then tore off a piece of the croissant and ate it.

'So, Emir. You want to talk to me a little of what you were saying yesterday?'

'I can't find my friend. You can help?' There was desperation in his voice.

'I hope so.' Rosie touched his arm. 'Tell me, Emir. Can you tell me a little about where you come from . . . what happened to you?' She spoke slowly, hoping he would understand. 'You know, back in Kosovo.'

He nodded. 'My English not so good. Only a bit in school.' He tore off another piece of croissant and ate it, sipping his coffee. 'In my village, my mother, father and sister killed. My friend Jetmir the same for him. His father die when he was boy, and his mother killed by Serbs. They burned her house and she die.'

Rosie shook her head. 'So bad, what the Serbs did over there. I know. Go on.'

'Jetmir and me, we come together to Macedonia, to the border. We there many days with many people hungry and sick. Some die in the mud. People walked for days to get across border. We have nothing. Was very bad. Then they put us on buses and say we will be going away. Safe they say. And they bring us here. To Scotland.'

'And how have you been since you came?'

'Is okay in the beginning. They put us in a big place for two days – like a camp – and then they give us apartment. Where you saw me.'

Rosie nodded, watching him pick nervously at the napkin.

'You were very upset. Tell me what happened.'

'I tell you.' His eyes grew dark. 'The woman from Refugee Council. She come and take all our names. She tell us we will get food and some clothes. They give us things. They tell us the lawyers will look after us and help us and work on our case so we can stay here. We like living here. Is bad now in the apartments because the people from Glasgow they hate us. They fight with us because they want our things, but we have nothing.' He shook his head. 'I will give them anything. I want to be free. Just to live here. Me and Jetmir to start again maybe. So we go to the lawyer and he ask our details. He want to know where we come from, who we live with, who is our friends. We tell them we have nobody. Only us – like brothers. We want make new friends. New life here. He tell us to come back the next week. He said to trust him, we must not to tell Refugee Council. He say he can find us jobs but we must not tell. He tell us to come back, and we did.'

'Do you mean the day your friend was taken. Is that the day you went back?'

Emir nodded. 'We speak to the lawyer.'

'What lawyer?' Rosie asked. 'Do you know the name of the lawyer?'

'Yes,' Emir said. 'His name Murphy. Mr Murphy. I think they called Paton Murphy. I show you. Is close by.'

Rosie felt a little punch in her stomach.

'Tony Murphy? Was the lawyer called Tony Murphy?'

'Yes. That him, Rosie. You know him?'

'I know him, yes. Well, I know the law firm. So what happened then?' Rosie hoped her face showed nothing.

'That day, we come down from his office, and in the street at the door, two men say our names. They say they are taking us back to our apartment. They say Mr Murphy told them take us back to flats. So we go in their car, very happy because Mr Murphy is good man, but then I see after some time we are not in the city. They are talking to us and trying to understand what we are saying. Then I see no big city any more. We are going to the country. More trees. Not so many houses. I ask them. They tell me we are going to see about jobs.'

'Jobs?'

'Yes. They say Mr Murphy has tell them to take us for the jobs. We are in the back seat of the car. My friend Jetmir is nervous and he push his elbow to me to make a face that he is not happy. But we don't know what to do. I am frightened also. They keep driving. Then they come to a place not in the big road, but in another road.

It is in the woods. A big building. Not big like a factory but big. Like a place to keep things.'

'Like a warehouse?' Rosie said. 'You know. Like you would have a big storage place?'

'Yes, like that. I see two big trucks with fridges. Like I see before in Kosovo. They use them to take food to towns and villages, and keep cold. You understand?'

'Yes,' Rosie said. 'Then what happened?'

'Then it happen fast. One of the men he hit Jetmir on back of the head and he fall to the ground. The other comes to me, but I hit him hard. Then the man who hit Jetmir hit me with a stick, but I hit him hard too and he fell. I took the stick from him and I hit him on the head twice, but someone else come and they hit me on the head and I fell down. Then Jetmir tries to get up, and they start to beat him on the head with a stick. A baseball bat. I cannot watch.' Tears came to his eyes. 'I can see them taking Jetmir away. They are dragging him by his feet. They think I am dead or unconscious. But I am not. When they go inside the building, I run away.' He shook his head. 'I don't know if Jetmir is alive, because he was breathing and making noises when they take him away. I don't know where they take him. I think they will kill him. They want to kill both us.' He looked at Rosie with pleading eyes. 'But why? Why to kill us?'

Rosie had seen that pitiful look before on the faces of so many desperate refugees, from Kosovo to Rwanda, fleeing terror and murder. In the far-flung lands where factions had squabbled for generations and villages were being brutally ethnically cleansed, someone could always provide an answer to why people turn on each other. But these people had come here to escape. She had no answers.

'I don't know, Emir,' Rosie said, squeezing his arm. 'But I promise you one thing, I will find the answer. Trust me.' She lowered her voice. 'Did you go to the police? The Refugee Council? Have you told anyone what happened?'

Emir shook his head. 'I am afraid. I not know who I can trust. Maybe they don't believe me. Do you believe me?'

'Of course I do, but I think you should go to the police, or go to the Refugee Council and tell them what happened. They will have records of your friend and you, when you came here. They will investigate.'

'But how can I tell them what happened? I don't know where is the place. They won't believe me. Maybe they think I make it up and I have done something to my friend.' He put his hand to his mouth, shaking his head. 'I never do anything to hurt Jetmir. We are friends since we are children.' Again, tears filled his eyes.

They sat in silence. Rosie watched him. It crossed her mind that he might be making the story up because she knew that's the first thing McGuire would ask her. She dismissed the thought. Her gut instinct told her he was telling the truth, but she could see how far-fetched his story would seem if he turned up at a police station. The only thing on his side was that he'd been to Tony Murphy's office the day they were kidnapped. If police were investigating Murphy's death and hadn't already written it off as 'not suspicious', then they would have to listen to Emir's story. She would call Don and run it past him. So what if it was Saturday morning and he was having the weekend off.

'Let me make a phone call, Emir. Don't worry.'

Don's phone rang out and went onto message. Then Rosie remembered that he was going fishing with his mates and probably had his phone switched off at least until the evening. She dismissed the idea of contacting some out-of-hours number at the Refugee Council. It would be wrong to throw Emir into a confusing mire of red tape and officialdom.

'I want to talk to a friend of mine, Emir,' she said. 'He's a detective, and I'm sure he'll be able to help, but he's not answering his phone.' Rosie glanced at her watch. 'Listen. I don't think there's a lot we can do over the weekend. I'll take you to the police station now if you want, but it might be better for you to leave it until I can get my detective friend. But can you give me your phone number and the exact address of your flat, so I can keep in touch?'

Emir nodded, and gave her the details which she wrote down. 'Okay. I wait for you to call me.' He stood up. 'I go back to now and stay in my apartment.'

'I'll drive you there, if you want.'

'No,' he said. 'I go by myself.' He stretched out a hand. 'Thank you. I know you will help me.' He clasped her hand tightly.

'I will, Emir.' Rosie saw the desperation in his eyes. 'I'll do everything I can.' She watched as he turned and left the cafe, walking briskly across the station, and disappeared through the archway into the street.

CHAPTER 5

Tanya was a discreet distance away from the overspill of mourners standing in the drizzle outside the Catholic church, waiting for the end of Tony Murphy's funeral mass. Looking around at the smartly dressed people who had turned up to pay their respects, she wondered if they really knew who their friend was, if they had any idea of the double life he'd led. Whatever he was to them, he was more to her. She was his secret. But even as she tried to convince herself, the words of his suicide note to his wife kept coming back. *I love you forever, always have ...* That's what had brought her to the funeral, to catch a glimpse of his other life, the family he'd adored.

As the heavy church doors opened, the strains of the organ and the congregation singing swelled out and up into the leaden sky. The priest and altar boys emerged, and behind them Tony's dark oak coffin, carried on the shoulders of half a dozen men. At the front was Frank Paton, and the sight of his face flushed and tear-stained as he carried his friend brought tears to Tanya's eyes. *We were the wide-eyed students who were going to change the world* . . . Tony had written in his letter to Frank. He had told her how Frank and him had been friends since university – closer than brothers, he'd said.

Tanya watched as they came down the steps, her heart in turmoil. Then she saw his wife, sobbing as she was supported by a beautiful young girl, and a teenage boy so much the image of Tony that it took her breath away. And for the very first time, the truth cut through her like a knife. These three people, their faces etched with grief, their lives changed forever: *they* were what Tony was all about. She was nothing. She was sex in the afternoon in a cheap hotel room.

Suddenly it hit home to her that all the promises, all the plans they'd made were nothing. Shame washed over her. She had kidded herself that she'd moved on from an escort girl to a woman who was loved and cherished. She'd imagined Tony's wife was dowdy and boring, that he'd grown tired of her and only stayed with her for the children. But now she was confronted by this beautiful, elegant woman in black, her eyes puffy from crying, sobbing as her husband's coffin was placed into the hearse. This was all that mattered. And Tanya had robbed her of the final words from her husband before he took his life. She had to make amends. She knew where Tony lived, having sneaked there a long time ago for a fleeting glance at the big turreted house in a wealthy suburb of the city, where she now realised he belonged. She slunk away as the church emptied.

*

Tanya could hear the televison blaring as she got to the top step of her block of flats in Maryhill. She knew even before she put the key in her door what she would find. She let herself in and there he was, snoring, surrounded by three or four empty lager cans and a quarter bottle of vodka. She switched off the television, went straight into the kitchen with her bags of shopping, and began preparing dinner.

Half an hour later, as Tanya strained a pot of potatoes into the sink she heard the television blaring again. He was up. She braced herself, waiting to hear what he was going to moan about tonight so he could pick a fight.

'Where were you?' Josef stood leaning on the doorframe, smoking. 'Thought you weren't working today.'

'I was just walking in the city. I went to the library.' Tanya glanced at him as she set the table. She could see his simmering rage and her stomach knotted.

'The library?' Josef snorted. 'Walking in the city I can understand – that's what whores like you do – but the library? What the fuck you do in the library? Looking for books about whores?'

Tanya didn't answer. She turned away from him and went to the cooker. She took sausages from the frying pan and put them on the plates along with potatoes and beans. She placed them on the table and sat down without looking at him.

'What the fuck is this?' He sat down.

Tanya put down her knife and fork. 'It's all we have, Josef.' She looked at him. 'I told you, I haven't worked this week. The lawyer's office is closed since . . . since the death. Mr Frank said he will pay me, but it won't be until later this week. I go back to work tomorrow.'

Josef sat back and folded his arms.

'You think I can eat this shit?'

'It's not shit,' Tanya said, trying to control her anger. 'In Ukraine you would have been glad of it. You'd have been glad to eat at all.'

'Well, I am not in fucking Ukraine. I'm here.' He sneered. 'We ate better when you made your wages on your back. Maybe you get on your back for Mr fucking Frank and we eat better.'

Silence. Tanya froze, terrified he suspected her and Tony.

'You hear me, Tanya?' He slammed the table with his fist, making her jump. 'When you made money from fucking, we used to eat steak. Now you clean offices and we eat this kind of shit.' He pushed the plate away.

Tanya tried to stay calm, but the words were out before she could stop herself. 'If we eat shit, it's because you drink every penny I make and you won't even look for a job.'

She didn't even see the slap coming, but it almost knocked her off her chair. Her cheek burned. Tears sprung to her eyes.

'You bastard, Josef. Fuck you.' Tanya jumped up clutching her face and headed for the door.

He was after her in a flash.

'Where do you think you're going, you cheap whore?' He caught her by the arm and swung her round so hard she knocked into the table and sent the glasses flying. He slapped her twice on the face and she tasted blood in her mouth.

'Stop,' She screamed. 'Leave me alone, you drunk, useless fuck of a man.' She tried to spit at him but nothing came out.

He let go of her, his eyes blazing.

She wiped blood from her mouth with the back of her hand as she wept. Then she couldn't stop herself.

'I hate you. I wish I'd never met you. All you've ever done is bully and beat me and take everything from me. Can't you even look at yourself in the mirror and see how repulsive you are? My flesh creeps every time you touch me.' She tried to push past him, but he stood in front of her, pinning her against the sink. He smelled of sweat and stale booze.

His face reddened and he grabbed her by the wrists, and turned her around, forcing her arms behind her back.

'Stop. You're hurting me.'

'You never complained when some fat old bastard was hurting you as long as he was paying, you bitch. He dragged her towards the table and bent her over, slamming her face onto the wood, holding her down with one hand.

'Fuck you, woman. This is all you are. And these days, you're not even much good at that. So shut the fuck up and I teach you who is boss in this house.'

'Stop.' Tanya screamed and struggled as he pulled up her skirt and tore her pants off.

Through her tears, Tanya could see the blood from her mouth smear the table as he held her down and raped her.

It was just gone six when Tanya slipped out of the single bed in the spare room. She moved softly around the house, creeping into the bedroom where Josef lay snoring like a bull. It crossed her mind to go into the kitchen and grab a knife and stab him to death while he slept. She'd read enough in the papers about rape, that she could claim self defence. The bruises on her swollen face and an internal examination by a doctor would back up her story of last night's brutality. But it was easier just to walk out on him.

She closed the door quietly, crept down the three flights of stairs with her small suitcase and opened the door, walking out into the bright, fresh morning. It was over. Whatever it had been with Josef in the beginning had died a long time ago. The beatings had begun before she had started her affair with Tony, and once he had made her know what it was like to be treated with love and respect, her revulsion for Josef grew. She was on her own now, the same as she was when she arrived here from Ukraine four years ago. She didn't starve then and she wouldn't starve now. Josef wouldn't come after her. He would know that last night he had crossed a line.

Tanya took nearly an hour to walk from Maryhill Road into the city centre, stopping everywhere she could for a rest from carrying her suitcase. By the time she got into the city, she was just in time for the Post Office opening.

She went inside and bought an envelope and stamp. Then she addressed it to Mrs Millie Murphy, carefully printing it so it wasn't in her handwriting. She had considered the consequences of what she was doing, that police would become involved because a suicide note was now arriving at the Murphy home almost a week after Tony died. Of course they might suspect that someone swiped the note from his desk, and she was the first one on the scene. But they could prove nothing. They would prove nothing.

She went for a coffee in the cafe close to the lawyer's office before she started work. She took out the letter from Tony to Frank Paton. *I told you we should stop. See you in hell, Frank* . . . What did it mean, she wondered? She sat back, recalling how Frank had come into Tony's office and removed files from his desk and the safe. He had something to hide. And that made him vulnerable.

Arriving at the law firm earlier than usual, Tanya was surprised to hear voices coming from upstairs in Frank Paton's office. She put her suitcase in a cupboard and climbed the stairs quietly. She stood outside and held her breath, listening hard.

'It can't go on like this, Billy,' Frank said. 'Tony's dead. He killed himself over this. It changes everything.'

'No it doesn't,' another voice said. 'It doesn't change a thing. You just carry on as normal.'

'I don't think I can.' Frank's voice was shaking.

'You don't have a choice, Frankie boy. You're in this up to your fucking neck.'

Silence. Tanya waited.

'Look, Frank, you know the score here. You know what you agreed to do, and you've made plenty of money out of it, so you just keep going. You just provide the details and stuff, we'll do the rest. Don't start developing a fucking conscience now.'

More silence.

'By the way, there's a bit of a problem. These two dickheads you gave us last week. One of them got away.'

'Aw, fuck me, Billy!'

'Don't sweat man. It's no big deal. It's getting sorted.'

Tanya could hear movement in the room and she scurried downstairs in time for the door of Frank's office opening. He looked shocked to see her.

'Hello Tanya,' he said. 'You're early.'

'Not really, Mr Frank. Only a few minutes. You are very early. Will I make some coffee for you?'

'Yes, thanks Tanya.' Frank stood at the top of the stairs as the two men came down. They walked past Tanya without even looking in her direction as they left.

CHAPTER 6

As she drove out of the city and up towards the Red Road flats, Rosie kept ringing Emir's mobile number, but there was no answer. It had been that way since Sunday night when she'd called him after she finally got Don and told him the Kosovan's story. As predicted, he'd said the story was far-fetched, but wanted to meet Emir before he ran it past the bosses. He suggested a couple of detectives go to Emir's flat to talk to him, but Rosie thought it would spook him and volunteered to bring him to the police station herself before she went into work.

She was surprised to see two police cars and several uniformed officers outside one of the blocks of flats when she pulled into the car park. She got out of the car and approached a couple of young mums standing smoking, their toddlers asleep in pushchairs.

'What's happening?' Rosie said.

'Vigilantes,' one of the young girls puffed on her cigarette.

'Vigilantes?' Rosie's stomach sank.

'Aye. They got another one of the refugees last night. A boy. Stabbed.' The other girl looked at Rosie. 'It's not right that. Doesn't matter what they're getting from the council and stuff. Nobody deserves that. I mean some of these people have got weans and everything. They're just like us.'

'I know,' the other girl said. 'You can't go about stabbing folk. The thing that annoys me is the fucking vigilantes are just neds from round here who'd stab anybody. They're all wasters.'

'Do you know what age the guy was?' Rosie asked. 'Is he alive?'

'Dunno. He's in the hospital. Heard he was quite far through.'

'Where did he come from?' Rosie said. 'I mean what block of flats?'

'That one.' The girl pointed. 'I heard he was Turkish. He's been here for a few months. The vigilantes attacked him and stabbed him out in the street last night. Just picked on him. I heard the commotion – the ambulance and stuff.'

Rosie watched as the girls walked off in the direction of the city. She felt a pang of guilt at her relief that the stabbed refugee was Turkish, then quickly realised that with Emir's looks he could quite easily have been mistaken for Turkish.

She crossed the car park towards the block where she'd first seen Emir standing in tears that day. Rosie got into the tiny lift just before the doors closed and stood alongside two women who looked like refugees. They stood bunched together in the rickety aluminium box that smelled of piss, and she prayed it wouldn't break down between floors. She gave the women a friendly smile, but they looked intimidated just by her presence. Nobody spoke, and as the lift shuddered slowly towards the twelfth floor, Rosie read the graffiti scrawled in front of them. 'Go home' it said in thick black letters. She glanced at the refugee women who were staring flatly at the walls and wondered where home was for them and how it must have felt when they fled, knowing that all their tomorrows would be filled with uncertainty and fear. And to come here, tired and wretched, only to be a victim of some lowlife vigilantes who hadn't the wit or compassion to comprehend just how much these people had lost.

They all got out of the lift together, and walked along the corridor, Rosie checking the door numbers until she came to number nine. The two women passed her, but glanced back suspiciously as she knocked on Emir's door. She watched as the others went into a flat three doors down. She stood and waited. No answer. She knocked again, this time louder and for longer. Still no answer. She bent down and looked through the letter box and into the stillness of the long hallway. It looked chilly and dismal, but from what she could see at the edge of the living room it was furnished and clean. And, crucially, no smell. It wouldn't be the first time she'd peered through a letter box to be hit by the stench of a dead body.

'Emir?' Rosie shouted through the letter box. 'Emir? Are you there?' Nothing.

She stood for a few moments, not quite knowing what to do. Her mobile rang. It was Don.

'Where's this guy, Rosie? I thought you were bringing him down?'

'I was, Don, but I can't get him on his mobile. Tried all night and this morning, but no answer, so I'm up here now at his door. There's no sign of him.' Rosie spoke quietly.

'You up at the Red Road? I was going to buzz you on that. Some Turkish guy got stabbed last night by these nut-job vigilantes. That's three attacks in the past month.'

'Is the victim definitely Turkish?' Rosie said.

'Yep. Definitely a Turk. He was here with his parents.'

'What is it with these thugs who are doing this?'

'Just scumbags, Rosie. Pure pond-life.' He paused. 'So what you going to do if you can't find him. Not much I can do this end if he's done a runner.'

'I know. But it's a real bastard. I know he was telling the truth, Don. The guy was terrified. Maybe he just got off his mark. But tell you what, Don, my worry is that somebody got to him.'

'You mean the guys who took his mate? None of his story makes sense, Rosie. You do know that, don't you? I mean, why would anyone lift two guys off the street and take them outside of the city and beat them up? Why?'

'You're the detective, Don. All I know is that this guy was terrified and I believe that something happened to his pal. I don't think it was this vigilante mob, but it could have been, and I want to find out. I want to find

Emir. I feel for the guy. I think something has happened to him. I'm going to ask around here – some of the other refugees – see if they know him or have seen him.'

'Okay, Rosie. Give me a shout when you're free and we'll have a chat.' He hung up.

Rosie went along the corridor and knocked at the door where the two refugees had gone in. No answer. She knocked again, louder, and listened for any activity inside. Eventually she heard bolts being slid on the door and the key turning. The door opened only a few inches and the face of the older woman in the lift peered through silently.

'Hello,' Rosie said. 'Sorry. I'm looking for Emir' – she pointed towards his flat – 'The man who lives there? I'm his friend. I've tried to phone him, but no answer. Have you seen him?'

The woman shook her head.

Rosie looked at her. 'Please. Could you open the door for a moment? I'd like to talk to you. I promise I won't harm anybody. I'm Emir's friend.'

Rosie heard footsteps in the hall and a man's voice, then the door opened a little more when he removed the chain. The man's expression was flat and his unshaven pale face looked grubby and pock-marked. He was smoking a roll-up cigarette.

'What you want with us?' He looked frightened.

'Nothing,' Rosie put her hands up, apologetically. 'Sorry. I'm trying to find Emir, from the flat next to here. I need to talk to him. Have you seen him?'

He shrugged. 'We not know this boy. Not his name. But we not see him for . . .' he shook his head, 'some days.'

Rosie watched the man and woman and as she looked past them she could see a toddler coming up the hall.

'Can you tell me, did this boy live in the house by himself or with someone?'

The man nodded. 'Another boy. But I not see him for few days. We don't know them. Just hello is all. They are from Kosovo. Only came last month. Not say much. We think they are brothers, but they say friends.'

'Okay,' Rosie said. 'Thanks for your help. Have you not seen any of them all weekend?'

The man shook his head. 'No. I see one boy on Saturday morning. He go out in the morning, but I never see him after that.'

Rosie's head swam with alarming possibilities. What if they'd been watching him come into the station to meet her? Surely they wouldn't snatch someone from the street in broad daylight, whoever they were ... She should have driven him home. Perhaps Don was right and Emir must have done a runner, she consoled herself.

It was after ten in the evening by the time Rosie arrived at The Blue Note, and there was already a decent enough crowd from what she could see as she walked into the dimly lit basement bar. The jazz club, downstairs from Enzo's Italian restaurant in Bath Street, was more for the purists than the boozed-up punters looking for a bit of late-night live music. The burst velvet sofas and old table-cloths gave it a kind of tatty, shabby-chic look that told you people who pitched up here didn't come for the classy decor. The Blue Note was the in place to go if you knew your jazz. It wouldn't have been a usual haunt of Rosie's, mostly because it was trad jazz. To her un-educated musical palate, that involved nervous break-down-inducing continuous guitar plucking accompanied by a guy rattling a snare drum with brush drumsticks she'd have used to paint the skirting. TJ had laughed at her narrow view, but convinced her she had much to learn by bringing her on nights when the jazz was more akin to what she'd seen in the movie, *The Cotton Club*. And now, there was TJ, up there with his sax, playing a solo number under the spotlight, behind a cloud of cigarette smoke.

Rosie didn't think he saw her come in, and she sat in the corner at one of the few little round tables available. The waiter came and she ordered a glass of red wine, knowing she shouldn't, since she'd already had two gin and tonics at O'Brien's with Don and still hadn't eaten. She was glad when the waiter told her they were still serving food and ordered some chicken wings and bread to soak up the booze.

Rosie reflected on her conversation with Don, and was disappointed that he had offered no positives on how she could find what happened to Emir. If he'd done a runner, as Don suspected, then she just had to wait and see if he got in touch. With so little information and nobody to talk to, there was absolutely nothing the cops could do, he told her. Rosie accepted that, but it didn't make it any less frustrating. She would talk to the Refugee

Council tomorrow to see just what goes on with refugees and how they keep track of them.

Don also told her that some well-known Glasgow ned, Tam Logan, had disappeared and cops were looking into it. He said Tam was a grass who he'd worked with down the years, and even though he was a vicious little bastard who would slash anyone if the money was right, he was useful enough. Now he hadn't been seen for the past five days, and that was not how Tam operated. His wife had already reported him missing, but to most cops he was just another toe-rag who had disappeared off the radar. The general consensus was that he would turn up, and if he turned up dead, nobody would give a damn. Rosie told Don she might have a word with the wife just to see if there was a story in it, but it wasn't a priority. She tried to switch off and sipped her glass of wine.

'Thank you TJ,' the guy with the guitar proclaimed to a ripple of applause as TJ finished his solo spot. 'And now, let's give a good old Blue Note welcome to the lovely, the supremely talented Kat Shaughnessy . . .'

Rosie didn't hear the last part of the announcement. Her eyes were fixed on the redhead in the skin-tight jade-green satin dress, sashaying from the darkness onto the stage. She almost spluttered her wine. She hoped she hadn't said 'Christ!' out loud. So this was Kat, tousled, titian hair tumbling onto her shoulders like a lion's mane, and now winking sexily at TJ who shot her a warm smile back. Rosie swallowed hard as TJ's sax blew out the slow dreamy intro while Kat stood eyeing the audience. Full red lips pouted without even trying. It wouldn't matter a damn if she sounded like Lucille Ball on speed. Everyone was knocked out even before she opened her mouth.

Then came the voice, all husky and oozing sex – as if it would be any other way.

'It's that old devil, called love again . . . Gets behind me . . . and givin' me that shove again . . .'

Christ. Rosie's stomach hit the floor. This was Kat, the woman TJ had gigged with in New York while she was at home pining for him. No wonder he didn't get in touch. She was struck as much by Kat's voice as her beauty, and all through the song, she told herself to get a grip before the number ended; she had to be all smiles to her when the band had a break. She took another gulp of wine in a bid to snuff out the rabid jealousy coursing through her veins.

TJ spotted Rosie as the break came up and he gave her a wave and a smile. Was it as warm as the one he just gave to Kat? Rosie slapped herself to behave. TJ was coming over, and behind him, Kat and the guy who played the guitar. A threesome in Manhattan. Don't even go there.

'Hey, sweetheart. You're late – again!' TJ pulled Rosie to her feet and kissed her on the lips, giving her a little squeeze.

'I know. I was in O'Brien's with a cop contact.'

He smiled, and half turned to the redhead and the guitar man.

'Rosie, this is Kat and Gerry I told you about.' He stepped to the side to let them through.

Rosie stood as tall as she could and stuck out her hand to Kat who shook it warmly.

'How you doing, Kat? Some voice you've got there.' Rosie turned to TJ and touched his arm. 'And hey – you weren't so bad yourself in that solo.'

'Gerry.' The guitarist shook her hand. 'So this is the famous Rosie?' He gave TJ a playful punch on the arm. 'You've kept her under wraps, you rascal.'

'She doesn't get out much,' TJ joked. 'She's always working. You know what these hacks are like.'

'True,' Rosie said. 'I wouldn't normally be in here. But tell you what, it's got a great atmosphere tonight. And the jazz trio are not half bad either,' she said, smiling as they all sat down.

The waiter came over and they ordered drinks. Rosie ordered another glass of red wine and some bottled water. The owner of the bar shouted across to TJ, and he excused himself and went to see him. Then he beckoned Gerry, leaving Rosie and Kat alone.

'So, it must be a fascinating life you have as a journalist,' Kat said, drawing on her cigarette, her voice laced with transatlantic tones. She tossed her fringe away from her forehead, and her bright-green eyes sparkled like gems. 'TJ told us some of the scrapes you've been in to get a story. Sounds amazing, but a bit dangerous, I'll bet.'

'Yeah. It's great,' Rosie said, finding it hard to concentrate. 'It's tough sometimes. You work funny hours, and you get to see a lot of things other people don't. A lot of it bad. I mean, it's good in a lot of ways, but hard too.

But I wouldn't trade it for anything else . . . Don't think I could hold down a steady job.'

'Yeah. I can imagine. Must make you a bit crazy.'

Rosie glanced at the piercing eyes and a little paranoia kicked in. She couldn't make her mind up if Kat was mocking or patronising her, or if TJ had actually told his singing partner how nuts she was. Either way, she didn't like it.

'So how is it with you?' Rosie changed the subject. 'You were really good up there. It must be hard to crack though – I mean in terms of making it big. Is that what you want to do?'

Kat looked at her and then stared at the table for a second. She took a deep breath.

'Yeah. Like everyone else bashing their brains out in clubs like this all over the world – I'd love to really make it. But I'm not stupid. Things like this, I make a living, and I can get a fair bit of travel out of it. But to be honest, unless someone walks in here and signs me up to a record label, this might be as good as it gets.' She stubbed out her cigarette.

Rosie felt a little twinge of sympathy for her, even though she wanted to dislike her.

'Yeah,' she said, 'but there's worse ways to earn a living.'

TJ came back and they sat for a few minutes chatting about work and telling some stories about clubs in New York where they'd played together. Rosie felt a little out of the loop with their jokes and tales, and she could see TJ watching her. Now and again, he brushed his hand against her arm or ruffled her hair, and Rosie could see

Kat glancing at them and looking away. As they went back up to start the second set, TJ kissed Rosie again.

'You coming back to mine?' he whispered.

'I shouldn't,' Rosie whispered back. 'But you've sweet-talked me into it.'

'Good.' He went back onto the stage.

CHAPTER 7

Frank Paton took a swig of the Jack Daniels and felt it burn all the way down. He hoped the alcohol would numb his gut to the constant nervous churning. He drained his glass and ordered another from the barman, then climbed onto a bar stool and swivelled round to watch the floor show, where the skinny blonde in the G-string was now wrapping her thighs around a pole.

Time was when Frank wouldn't have been seen dead in a place like Glitz – the city's newest lap-dancing club where you could live out your wildest fantasies, and still be home in time for tea. Glitz promised you thrills and anonymity amid the glamour of its sensuous surroundings. In reality, it was a sticky-carpet basement dive, where saddos got their rocks off watching strippers writhe on a tiny stage, or stuffed a tenner into the pants of some scantily clad bird while she shoved her tits in their face. You could look and you could slaver, but you mustn't ever touch. If you did, one of the gorillas would emerge from the shadows and throw you out, blinking into the sunlight of a back alley in the Merchant City – probably minus your wallet.

And yet here Frank was, now catching a glimpse of himself in the mirror and feeling a stab of disgust at just what he'd become. How in the name of Christ had it come to this? he asked himself, not for the first time in recent months. How did it get this far? He swallowed another mouthful of his drink, looked at his watch and hoped big Al Howie would turn up soon.

Frank had been jittery enough since Tony's suicide and the subsequent questions by cops probing why a successful lawyer like Murphy would do himself in. But now he felt as if the walls were beginning to close in. He had managed to hold it together for the hour before he came here while Tony's widow Millie wept on his shoulder over some letter that had arrived in the morning post. It was almost a week since he'd killed himself, so how could a suicide note turn up now? Frank had had a skinful of booze at Tony's funeral yesterday and was nursing a hangover when Millie called him, bawling down the phone. He'd gone straight out to Murphy's house, where he found her weeping on the sofa, clutching a letter. He was as baffled as she was he told her, while he read the few short lines ... *I couldn't go on with any more of the lies* ...

The words had swum in front of him on the page and he had to sit on the sofa to steady himself. It was definitely Tony's handwriting.

'What lies?' Millie had sobbed. 'What lies, Frank? He must have been having an affair.'

Frank had spread his hands out, apologetically.

'I don't think so, Millie. Look, I don't know. I honestly don't know, but I don't think so.'

Millie was inconsolable. 'Then why, Frank? What does he mean? What lies? He must have had a woman.'

Frank had held her as she cried on his shoulder. He didn't know what to say. If Tony had a bit on the side that was more serious than the occasional illicit shags the pair of them had got up to down the years, then he didn't know about it. But what the hell: Let Millie think he had a woman. As long as she thought her husband had been betraying her, she wouldn't suspect anything else, but she'd insisted on phoning the police despite his protests that bringing the cops in would only prolong the anguish. If he *was* having an affair, the woman might be out there, and even if she was tracked down and found, what would be the point of dragging it all up, Frank told her. It wouldn't bring Tony back, and it might just pile on the agony for Millie and the kids. But she was having none of it.

She phoned the cops, and he had to sit there and listen while the two detectives who had been at his office that morning quizzed him again about exactly what he saw when he arrived at the office. He told them again. Only the cleaner Tanya was in the office when he arrived. It was she who found Tony hanging. There was nothing on his desk, because the first thing he had looked for was a suicide note, but there was nothing. He had even said to Tanya at the time that he didn't know what he was going to tell Millie. He was as bewildered as the cops as to where the note had come from. They asked him if the Tanya woman could have taken the note, and Frank dismissed it. She was just the cleaning lady who came in for an hour in the morning. And no, Tony was not having an affair with the Ukrainian office cleaner. He was certain of that much.

He ordered another Jack Daniels. It wasn't whether or not Tony was having an affair that made his guts churn, but the idea that there was a letter from Tony at all. What if there were more letters? He wondered if one would arrive at his house or office – if it did, he certainly wouldn't be calling in the cops. But right now there was an even more pressing matter: striding towards him with a face like thunder was big Al Howie, flanked by two of his henchmen.

'Frank.' Big Al looked down his nose at him, his eyes narrow with contempt. 'Give me five minutes and I'll see you up in the office. Got a phone call to make first.'

Frank nodded, and opened his mouth to speak, but Al – cocky bastard that he was – was gone before he had time.

Al Howie was always tipped to be the man who would take over Big Jake Cox's mob if it ever came to the crunch. He'd grown up under Jake's watchful eye, coming into the family as a tearaway teenager with balls like coconuts, who was as handy with a knife as he was with a gun. After the statutory stints in young offenders' institutions and graduation to a stretch in jail, Jake had used him as an enforcer for drug debts and watched with pride as his protégé carved out a reputation for violence that even he would struggle to match. But Al was an even bigger psycho than Big Jake, and with Jake now more on the sidelines since his near-fatal shooting in Spain last year, the word on the street was that there would be a blood-bath if Al were left to run Jake's turf. He wasn't old school like Jake. Frank shuddered involuntarily. He knew exactly what Howie was. Big Al had no boundaries, no lines he wouldn't cross; he was one of the most chilling bastards he'd ever encountered. Added to that he was a total coke-head, and since he wasn't yet forty, he still had a lot of damage to do.

Frank waited and looked at his watch. Fifteen minutes and still no call to go upstairs. He watched another stripper and sipped his drink.

'Nice tits.' Clock Buchanan, one of Al's henchmen came up beside him. 'You've to go up.' He stood facing Frank, with one hand in his jacket pocket.

Frank looked at him, and glanced at the hand in his jacket. Clock's real name was Billy, but the nickname came from a birth deformity that had left him with a withered left hand, much smaller than the right. In the Glasgow housing scheme where he grew up, they weren't big on sympathy towards anyone who stood out from the crowd, even if it was because of a physical handicap. So they nicknamed him Clock, on account of his big hand and wee hand. Clock had told Frank the story himself, and said that as long as his good hand could pull the trigger of a gun and handle a knife that was all that mattered.

'Come on,' Clock said. 'I'll take you up, but I've got to go out to get something for Al.'

Frank got off his stool and followed Clock along the front of the stage into the darkness of the musty hallway and up the tight stairway.

'What's this pish I'm hearing, Frank, that you don't want to work with us any more?'

From behind his desk, Big Al motioned him to sit down. 'By the way, sorry about Tony. Fuck's sake, man.'

He sniffed and touched his nose. 'Got to be better ways to top yourself than hanging from the ceiling.'

Frank didn't answer. His mouth was dry. He sat down.

Al looked at him and folded his arms. 'So,' he said. 'What's going on?'

Frank could feel the damp on the palms of his hands. 'I'm just worried, Al. It's not that I don't want to work with you. Not that at all. But this business . . . this refugee business . . . I just don't think it can go on indefinitely.' Frank shifted in his seat. 'What if something comes out.'

Al looked impatient. 'How the fuck is it going to come out, Frank? Tell me. How? Nobody gives a toss about these bastards. It's not as if they're doing a head count every day, making sure they're all there.' He snorted. 'It's working for the boys down south and they're not having a problem with it – London, Liverpool, Manchester – they're doing it and making big money. That's why we're in it. We're all getting a share of it, but we've got to provide our share, Frank. That's the deal. This is the future.'

Al took a wrap of cocaine out of his drawer and opened it. 'You knew that from the start, Frank. You knew the deal. You can't back out now.' He emptied the contents onto to the polished tabletop and chopped it into two lines. He looked up at Frank and raised his eyebrows.

'Want a wee toot, Frank? It'll make you feel better.'

Frank shook his head and swallowed as he watched Al roll up a twenty-pound note and snort a line, then sit back.

'Good stuff that. The fucking business.' He sniffed, studying Frank.

'That bloke,' Frank said. 'The one last week, from the two guys I gave you. One got away, your boys said. Did you get him yet?'

'It's under control, Frank,' Al said. 'You don't need to know shit like that.'

'But that's what I mean, Al. It's not under control if suddenly there's some guy out there who can talk about what happened.'

Al said nothing. He lit a cigarette.

Frank sat forward. 'And what about that body in the Clyde? That torso? I read in the *Post* it was a torso. There's all sorts of speculation about it – ritual killing, drug murder. Then I heard something about organs being removed or something. Might even be a refugee, the paper said.' Frank was trying to keep calm. 'That was one of your guys wasn't it, Al? How the fuck did it end up in the Clyde?'

Al burst out laughing. But it was more the manic laughter that unnerves you than the kind you want to join in with.

'I know. I asked the same question myself. Fucking hell. Try explaining that one away – a fucking headless torso with no lungs or heart. No baws either.'

'What happened, Al? How did it get there?'

Suddenly the door opened and Clock, along with the other sidekick came in, both of them dragging along a skinny guy with a badly bruised face. He was filthy and smelling.

Al got up from his desk.

'You want to know how it got there, Frank? Ask this cunt.'

The skinny guy could barely stand up. His face was puffy and bloodstained, but Frank recognised him as Tam Logan, a small-time hood who worked for Big Jake.

Frank looked at Tam, who winced in pain as his arms were being pinned behind his back.

'He got greedy, Frank. Wee Tam got greedy. Simple as that,' Al said.

Frank looked from Al to Tam. His stomach was in knots. He was afraid to speak.

'He didn't just get greedy, he got *brave*.' Al's mouth curled a little. 'This wee fuckwit even thought he could blackmail us. Can you imagine that? Fucker was going to blackmail me. *Me!*' He shook his head and his voice went up an octave.

'What do you mean?' Frank ventured.

'He stole the fucking torso.' Al said.

'Stole it?'

'Aye, stole it.' He sniffed. 'You know something, Frank? I gave Tam a break from the run-of-the mill jobs. Paid him big money to drive the van up and down to Manchester with the containers. You'd think he'd be grateful wouldn't you?' Al looked at Frank, who said nothing.

'Aye,' Al went on. 'He should have been grateful. He wasn't getting asked to shoot or slash anyone, or steal fuck all. No drugs involved, just drive the van and drop the stuff off. But no. Tam had to get nosy. He went on a wee spying mission like James fucking Bond and saw what was going on. Then he gets brave and decides he can make big money by blackmailing me.'

Frank could see the beads of sweat beginning to appear on Al's top lip, the more he was winding himself up.

'I wouldn't have done it, Al,' Tam squeaked. 'Honest, big man. I just went a bit crazy. I'd never have done it. I'm sorry. I'm sorry, big man.'

'A bit late to be sorry, Tam.' Al turned to Frank, his eyes glassy. 'You see what I'm up against Frank. You were saying what if things get out. Well, as long as you have wee arseholes like Tam among us – people who might open their trap – there's always that chance.'

He went back to his desk and opened a drawer. He took out a gun. Frank felt his head swim. He thought he was going to pass out. Al walked across the room towards Tam.

'So, you have to get rid of the traitors.'

By the time the last word was out, he had fired the gun into Tam Logan's chest at point-blank range. Tam slumped, his mouth open in a protest he didn't get the chance to make.

'Oh, fuck, Al.' Frank put his hands to his face. 'Jesus Christ man. You've killed him.'

'That was the idea, Frank. Christ, you're good.' Al walked back to his desk and put the gun in the drawer. He snorted the other line of coke and sat back, looking at Frank, his pale-grey eyes narrowed. 'Anyway,' he half smiled. 'You're a bit pale. Don't worry, Frank, did you think you were next?' He chuckled.

Frank felt sick. He watched in silence as Clock and the sidekick dragged Tam out of the door, the blood bubbling out of his chest and onto the floor. Al sat staring, his face cold and expressionless. He's completely fucking mad, Frank thought. Insane.

'Right,' Al said, eventually. 'You might as well go now, Frank. I just brought you along so you could witness that wee situation there.' He looked him in the eye. 'Know what I mean, pal? Just in case you get some kind of crisis of conscience and feel like turning us all in.' He sniggered. 'Not that any fucker would believe you anyway.'

Frank stood up and felt his legs weak under him.

'Just keep up the good work, Frank,' Al said. 'And stop worrying.'

Frank said nothing. He nodded his head slightly, then turned and left the room.

CHAPTER 8

Tanya glanced back at the wall clock in the hallway as she pushed open the door of Frank Paton's office. At the most she had half an hour to see what she could find. She had no real idea what she was looking for, but she hoped there would be something, some tiny bit of information that would give her an idea what it was that was making Frank Paton so edgy these days. Ever since that day she'd overheard the men seeming to threaten him in his office, Tanya had been watching him closely. She could have put his mood down to grief over the suicide of his best friend, but the dark shadows under his eyes and the redness of his face from booze had got worse since those men told him he couldn't back out of whatever it was he was involved in. And now, since the visit from the police over the suicide note, he looked even more wrecked.

Last night, as Tanya had sat in her tiny flat planning her next move, she'd asked herself why she was even bothering to find out what Frank was involved in. What was it to her? It should mean nothing. Because even though whatever it was probably involved Tony, it had been made crystal clear to her from the suicide letter and what she saw at Tony's funeral, that she'd played no real part in his life. She was nothing. But still, she couldn't let it go.

She had surprised herself at how calm she'd been when the detectives arrived at the office to go back over again exactly what she saw when she discovered Tony's body. Tanya had been expecting them after she'd sent the letter to Millie, and she was prepared. She'd looked suitably bewildered when they asked if there was any note on his desk. She'd shrugged. She would never look on Mr Murphy's desk she told them. He had always told her to leave his desk as it was and never touch it, because he had his own system where he knew where everything was. So she didn't even pay any attention to his desk. She'd been so shocked when she saw him hanging from the ceiling, that was all she could see. Tanya had filled up as she spoke about her ordeal that morning. It had been a convincing performance, and she'd found herself feeling quite proud later as she walked back to her flat.

Now she sat in Frank's chair and cast her eyes over the various letters and papers scattered across his desk. They meant nothing to her. Letters from the Scottish Refugee Council, the Department of Immigration, Social Services and other government bodies, as well as forms and case histories. There was no way she could plough through all this when she didn't know what she was looking for. She glanced at the safe in the corner, and before she could stop herself she went across, crouched down and turned the handle. To her surprise it was open. Her heart skipped a little.

She had to be careful. She opened the safe slowly and peered in. The buff folder that had been marked Asylum Cases, which she'd seen Frank take from Tony's desk that fateful morning, was piled on top of other papers and folders. She carefully removed it, making sure she knew the exact place she had to put it back, then knelt on the floor and opened it. She flicked through the papers. It seemed to be individual cases, with translations of their accounts of where they came from. She began to read them, quickly scanning them, the words jumping out at her ... *brutality ... rape ... murder ... beatings ... death threats*. All told the same story of fear. She sat back and sighed. Horror stories. Pictures flooded her mind from television news reports of wars and conflicts all over the world. She had never really seen much of the refugees who came and went at the lawyers' office. Mostly by the time she'd finished cleaning in the morning, the waiting room was beginning to get busy with them arriving, some men or women on their own, others with children – all of them, she noticed, with that look of apprehension, of being out of place, the way she had been when she came here The way she still was and probably always would be.

Tanya shook her head. It was hopeless. She didn't even know where to start. She gathered the papers together and was about to put them back in the file, when a sheet of paper dropped out of the back of the folder onto the floor. On it was a printed list of names of refugees and addresses in Glasgow. At the side of each name were the words printed in capitals – ALONE, NO FAMILY. Next to that was a date of interview and then a tick. The names had been gone through with a pencil, as if they were being scrubbed out. Tanya reread the dozen or so names, and the places they were from: Kosovo, Rwanda, Zimbabwe, Iraq. The lines through them didn't make sense. She thought of the words of the men in Frank's office, telling him he was in it up to his neck and that he had made money. Had he sold these people to work for someone, she wondered? It was all she had to go on. She had read in the newspapers about the people-trafficking and how some refugees ended up working as slaves, being run by gangmasters. She glanced up at the photocopier. She had about five minutes left if she hurried.

She was getting her jacket and bag together to leave the office by the time Frank came in the front door. It was after 9.30 and he was late. He was tired and dishev-elled, and she couldn't hide her surprise at how shat-tered he looked.

'Hello Tanya.' Frank attempted a smile. 'You off then? I'm a bit late this morning.' He ran his hand across his stubbly chin. 'Late night. Didn't even get a chance to shave.' He puffed out his cheeks. 'Better get myself sorted before I get any clients.'

'Can I get you something, Mr Frank?' Tanya put her bag down. 'Will I make some coffee? You want I go out and get you some breakfast?'

Frank hesitated and looked at her. 'Maybe you could make a quick coffee Tanya, if you don't mind.' He walked towards his office, then turned back. 'And, Tanya. I think you should call me Frank.' He looked a little embarrassed. 'I mean, well, the "mister" that you always call me? It makes me feel very old-fashioned and old!' He smiled. 'Been meaning to say that to you for a while. Frank will do.'

Tanya nodded as she went into the kitchen.

It was getting close to nine in the evening when Tanya took the call from the escort agency telling her she had a client. She protested at the short notice, but was told the original girl had called off and they couldn't afford to let the client down as he was a regular when he was in town. It was easy, they told her. He was an older guy, it would be fairly straightforward. She didn't want to turn it down since she had only just started back with the agency and didn't want to rock the boat.

She knew that at this time of night she wasn't getting invited for dinner. She'd be lucky if she got a drink at the hotel bar, but most likely it would be a glass of wine in the client's bedroom. She had walked from her flat in the Merchant City to the Holiday Inn at the end of Argyle Street, partly to save on the taxi fare and partly to clear her head. This was only the second client she'd had since she'd called the escort agency to say she wanted to work again. They'd told her they'd be glad to take her back, and that some of their clients had asked for her since she left. She stressed it was only for a few weeks until she got herself sorted. Sure, they'd told her. But that's what she said when she first started with them, and she had continued working for eighteen months. That's how it was when you were running out of options.

Later, on her way home, Tanya stopped for a coffee in the all-night cafe close to her house. It was warm and comfortable, with fat leather sofas you could sink into while watching the world go by from the window. Here she could be like anyone else – a student, a late-shift worker, any ordinary woman on her way home – instead of the woman she'd just been in the third-floor hotel room. She sipped her steaming mug of coffee and tried to blot out the images of the man in his sixties, grunting and heaving on top of her while she lay there with tears in her eyes for what her life had become.

She picked up a copy of the *Post*, and a headline on a story at the foot of page one caught her eye: *Cops probe refugee link to grisly torso find* . . . She flicked to page five to read more. It said detectives investigating the mystery of the torso found in the River Clyde were not ruling out that it could have been the body of an asylum seeker. They still had no identification, but police said the body had a tiny tattoo above the groin and appealed for witnesses who might know of someone who had gone missing. The story said they were also cracking down on the vigilante attacks on refugees in Balornock, but would not comment on whether this was linked to the torso. Tanya looked at the name of the reporter on the story – Rosie Gilmour. She slipped the newspaper into her bag and finished her coffee.

CHAPTER 9

Rosie looked at her watch as she waited outside the baker's shop for Jan Logan to finish her shift. She'd been here for nearly half an hour, and it wasn't the kind of place you sat in your car too long without the jungle drums beating. The only people who sat longer than ten minutes in a hole like Saracen were the drug dealers who waited at the edge of the scheme, like some kind of warped Mr Whippy ice cream man, supplying the stream of junkies who bounced towards them in search of their next fix. Even the snoops from the social had the good sense not to hang around. But Rosie didn't want to miss her woman. Of course, it was a long shot that Tam Logan's wife could shed any light on her man's disappearance, and Rosie wasn't even sure if there was any point in pursuing her. But the call from Don had been cryptic enough to spark her curiosity. She wondered if perhaps Howie was involved in refugee-trafficking. Don told her the word was that Logan had been doing some top secret driving job for Big Al Howie, but had opened his trap and stepped out of line. It didn't look like Tam was coming home for dinner – ever.

Eventually, she saw Jan come out of the shop and light up a fag before walking up Saracen Street in the direction of Springburn. Rosie started her engine and followed her at a distance. She didn't want to go knocking on the door of Jan's council flat in case it was being watched. After a few hundred yards, Rosie went ahead of her, then pulled into the kerb and waited. As she approached, Rosie got out of the car.

'Jan?' Rosie said, walking towards her. 'Jan Logan?'

The woman looked at her suspiciously. 'Who's asking?'

'My name is Rosie Gilmour. I'm from the *Post*.' Rosie stood in front of her.

'Aye. Well you can fuck off.' Jan side-stepped her then walked ahead.

Rosie pursued her. 'Look Jan, It's about Tam. Your man. I want to talk to you, Maybe try to help you. Can you just give me a minute?'

Jan stopped in her tracks and turned around to face Rosie. 'And how the fuck you going to help? Eh? Tell me that.' Her eyes blazed.

'We can write about it, Jan. Maybe he's out there . . . somewhere.' Rosie was on the backfoot.

'Aye. Somewhere over the fucking rainbow.' Jan looked Rosie in the eye and drew on her cigarette. 'You think my Tam's a missing person and maybe if I say in the paper how much we want him back, he's going to come running up Springburn Road in slow motion?' She snorted.

Rosie had to think on her feet.

'No. I don't, Jan. But I've got a feeling maybe he's being held somewhere against his will. Perhaps he's got himself involved in something and he's in trouble. If we can highlight the story, it might put pressure on people to let him go ... if that's the situation. Listen, Tam's not the worst guy in the world.'

Rosie could see that Jan was processing what she'd said.

'Listen, can we go and have a cup of tea somewhere?' She pointed to her car. 'Come on, Jan. I've got my car. We can get out of here for ten minutes while I talk to you.'

Rosie knew she was winning. Jan looked at her and her lip twitched a little. She put her hand to her mouth and to Rosie's surprise her eyes filled with tears.

'I don't know what I'm going to do,' she began to break down. 'I've got three weans.'

Rosie motioned her towards the car. They got in and Rosie started the engine.

'Look, I can't go anywhere,' Jan said, her voice quivering. 'I've no time. My weans will be in from school. I need to get home and make their dinner.' She looked over her shoulder. 'Just drive up here, where it's a bit quiet and we can talk for a minute, then you can drop me nearer my house.'

Rosie drove up towards a derelict industrial estate and turned in, taking one of the smaller roads where the place was deserted. She stopped the car.

'Jan,' Rosie turned to her. 'Listen to me. Do you have any idea what's happened to Tam? I mean, is there anything in the last few months that he's been doing different? Has he been behaving different because of his work?'

Jan said nothing. She shook her head and bit her lip.

'I've told the police everything.' Jan fell silent, then sniffed.

'Have you, Jan?' Rosie touched her arm. 'Did you really tell the police everything? Or did you keep stuff back.'

Jan looked at her and wiped the tears spilling out of her eyes.

'Tell me, Jan. What's happened to Tam? What was he doing?'

Suddenly Jan put her hands to her face, sobbing.

'I told him. I told him.' She buried her face.

Rosie waited, listening to Jan's sobbing and looking out of the windscreen at the steady drizzle.

'Jan,' she ventured. 'I want to ask you something, because I'm working on an investigation. Was Tam mixed up in something to do with refugees? Is that what's happened here?'

Jan took her hands away from her face and wiped her tears. She took a deep breath, and spoke between sobs.

'Tam's dead.' She swallowed and sniffed.

'How do you know that?'

'They told me. He's dead.' She wiped her face. 'Oh God! What am I going to tell my weans?'

'Who told you?'

'That polecat Howie's sidekick Clock Buchanan. He told me. He was sent to sort me out. Keep me quiet.'

'Keep you quiet? How?'

Jan turned to face Rosie, her eyes bloodshot and her cheeks and neck blotchy from nerves and emotion.

'Fuck sake! How do you think? They know my weans are more important to me than anything else in the world.' She paused. 'They sorted me out with money.' She put her hand to her mouth and shook her head.

Rosie said nothing.

'I know what you're thinking,' Jan went on. 'They bought my silence. They killed my man, then paid me to keep quiet. They gave me money so the weans will be all right.' She paused. 'You got any kids?'

'No, I haven't.'

'Well, maybe you'll not understand then. Maybe you won't know that when you've got a wean you'll do anything to make sure they're all right.'

They sat in awkward silence.

'I do understand.' Rosie touched her arm. She remembered the men her mother had sex with at their home for money. It had never been mentioned, but even as a kid she always knew. 'I understand what people do for their kids.'

'It's not right though,' Jan said.

'What's not right? You have to look after your kids, Jan. I can see that.'

'No, that's not what I mean. What they're doing isn't right.'

'Who?'

'Howie and that mob.' She shook her head. 'Them poor people.'

'What people?'

'Them refugees. Asylum seekers.'

Rosie's pulse quickened.

'What, Jan? What are they doing?'

Jan looked at Rosie then put her head back and her hands went to her face again. 'I'm scared. I'm so fucking scared.'

Rosie watched her. She knew it would come.

'They're killing them, Rosie,' Jan said. 'They're kidnapping them and killing them.'

Rosie tried hard to say nothing. She was almost scared to breathe in case she'd break the moment.

Jan wiped her nose. She seemed to compose herself, then spoke again. 'They steal them off the street and take them away somewhere in the countryside and kill them.'

'What?' Rosie said. 'The vigilantes?'

'No. Not vigilantes. That's just shite. I mean there's vigilantes as well, but they're just hooligans. No. This is different.'

'But why do they do it?'

Jan paused, then took a deep breath.

'I think they sell their body parts. Bones, eyes, skin. Every fucking thing. That's what Tam told me.' She shook her head. 'Oh, Christ. I can't believe my Tam would be mixed up in that.'

Rosie looked at her in disbelief. 'Christ almighty! You mean Tam was actually part of that, Jan? That just doesn't sound like him. From what I hear about Tam, he wasn't that big a player in Howie's mob.'

'No,' she said. 'He was just driving the . . . the stuff, in the van down to Manchester. That's where it's all organised from. Tam was just driving the van, one of them refrigerated vans with the stuff inside it all packed in metal containers and bottles. They took it to some factory.' She closed her eyes tight. 'Christ, I don't even want to think about it.'

Rosie was trying to process the information – body parts, tissue, vans to Manchester. She couldn't even imagine telling McGuire this one.

'Did Tam tell you all this?'

'Aye. He told me. He's only been doing it for three months. He didn't know what it was at first, thought it was just gear – drugs or something. Then he got curious. He looked in the van one time and saw stuff.'

'What stuff?'

'I don't know. He said containers and things. Then one time, he saw a torso. He said it was all frozen stiff, like a side of beef. I don't know what the fuck they were going to do with that. I mean who wants to buy a fucking torso?'

'So how did they find out he knew? Why did they kill him?'

'Because he was trying to blackmail them. I told him not to be so stupid, but he said this was bigger than drugs and bigger than anything he'd ever done. He thought he could blackmail them by threatening to expose them. I mean how fucking stupid is that? I told him not to.'

Rosie shook her head slowly.

'Jesus. What was he thinking about? You can't blackmail a guy like Al Howie or Jake Cox. Tam would know that.'

'I know.'

'So,' Rosie said quietly, 'that torso in the Clyde. Is that something to do with Tam?'

'Aye. He phoned me to say he stole it and was going to hide it, that he'd made a phone call to Big Al Howie. I told him not to be so stupid. His phone went dead in the middle of the conversation, and that's the last I heard from him.'

They sat in silence.

'What do you want to do, Jan, with all this information? Don't you think you should be going to the police?'

'What? And leave my weans orphans?'

'Doesn't have to be like that. They could get you away somewhere. Witness protection.'

Jan shook her head.

'No way.' She looked at the clock on the dashboard. 'I've got to go now, Rosie. Can you drop me up the road a bit?'

'Of course.' They drove out of the industrial estate in silence. As Rosie got close to where Jan had asked to be dropped off, she turned to her and asked, 'Jan, do you have any idea where this place is? You know – where they take the refugees?'

'I'm not sure,' Jan said. 'Tam said it was on the outside of Glasgow – out towards Drymen or something. Off the main road in the countryside. He might have it written down somewhere. I'll look in the house.'

Rosie needed more.

'Do you know who does all the stuff, you know, the operations on the bodies? I mean, cuts them up. They must have somebody who knows what they're doing.'

Jan nodded. She looked at Rosie.

'Some foreigner. He runs the place. They call him Doctor Mengele after that Nazi. I think he's from Yugoslavia or Russia or Kosovo – one of them places. Tam said he was a scary bastard.'

'Any name, Jan? Can you remember anything more about him?'

'No,' she said. 'If I find anything, I'll let you know. Phone you or something.'

Rosie stopped the car, and Jan moved to get out.

'Jan,' Rosie said, touching her arm. 'You do know that I'm going to investigate what you've told me. I won't go to the cops, I promise. But I *will* find out what's going on, and what happened to Tam.' She paused, giving Jan her business card. 'And obviously I'll never tell anyone I spoke to you.'

'I know what I've done by talking to you, Rosie. I'm doing it for Tam, even though it's too late for him. And I'm doing it for them refugees. Howie and that mob are rotten. They should get what's coming to them.' She paused. 'But give me two days before you do anything, till I leave the country. I'm out of here. The weans don't even know yet. I'm taking them out of school and I'm going to Spain, out of the way. I was going anyway, even before I met you.' She shook her head. 'I just don't know what I'm going to do. My Tam didn't deserve this.'

She got out of the car and closed the door.

CHAPTER 10

In the crowded waiting room of the Scottish Refugee Council, Rosie watched the black woman whose eyes stared blankly, seemingly oblivious to the racket of noisy kids playing with toys on the floor. She'd been motionless in the same position for the past twenty minutes, her baby asleep in a garish coloured shawl at her bosom. She was the only black person among the half dozen other refugees, each here with their stories of lives torn apart by war and ethnic cleansing. Each of them with their own separate nightmare, but all of them united by fear and apprehension of what tomorrow could bring. Rosie had heard the woman say she was from Rwanda, which probably explained the catatonic expression in her eyes. No matter where the troubled young mother would go, no matter how far away from her homeland she fled, she would forever be in Rwanda. That much Rosie knew for sure. She watched her, recollecting her own brief stint in the Congo border town of Goma, where Rwandan refugees had flooded in after the genocide. She'd been there at the height of the cholera epidemic as it swept through the sprawling tented camp. The images had stayed with her. The sickly stench of the stiff dead bodies piled up on the pick-up trucks, the refugees crawling in the baking sun to the makeshift hospital tent to die among babies too weak to fight. And always, for Rosie, the memory of a little abandoned toddler, hunkered down, tear-stained and screaming for help that never came. Rosie shuddered.

'Rosie Gilmour?'

She blinked away the flashbacks and looked up at the tall, gangly young man in the spectacles standing before her.

'Hi. I'm Christy Larkin. Can you come this way please? Margaret Bradshaw will see you now.'

Rosie got up and exchanged glances with a few of the refugees as she left the room. The Rwandan woman stared straight ahead.

'You've got your hands full here,' Rosie said, making conversation with the young man as they walked along the corridor.

'Yeah, not half,' he said, squeezing past metal filing cabinets stuffed with folders. 'There's so much to do – between people fighting deportation, and always more and more refugees arriving. Huge workload, as you can see.'

'How do you find it – the nature of the work? Must kind of wear you down a bit, all the stories.'

Christy stopped and looked at her.

'Yeah, it does, Rosie. But you must know that yourself

– having seen a lot of it at first hand in the camps and stuff.' He smiled, his eyes soft behind big tortoiseshell, geeky glasses. 'I've read a lot of your reports – Rwanda, Kosovo, Bosnia. Must have been tough.'

'Yeah. It was sometimes. But it wasn't happening to me, Christy.' Rosie gave her stock answer. 'I got to go to a hotel at night.'

Christy studied her face.

'Yeah, suppose so. But you still told the stories. That matters.'

'Thanks, Christy,' Rosie felt a little embarrassed, but touched by his youthful honesty. 'I appreciate you saying that.' She changed the subject. 'So are you with the press office?'

'No. Not really,' he replied. 'I'm a kind of investigator. I gather all the information from the refugees. Do a lot of the one-to-one interviews and collate information and background. I help identify with the press office what we should be doing to highlight certain cases.'

'Sounds like a lot of work.'

'Yeah. It's hard sometimes. Trying to get the right story across.'

Rosie scanned his face as they stood in the corridor. She sensed some underlying frustration in his demeanour.

'What do you mean, the right message? Like the refugee stories that are going to make the papers sit up and take notice?'

Christy hesitated. He shrugged. 'Hmmm . . . Sometimes. But other times you find things out that people don't want to know.'

'Who doesn't want to know? The press?'

Christy sighed. 'No. Not really.' He looked like he was bursting to talk.

'We should have a drink sometime, Christy.' Rosie took a card out of her pocket and handed it to him. 'Just you and me. Away from here and off the record.'

He put the card in his pocket and looked Rosie in the eye.

'Yeah.' He smiled. 'I'd like that. I'll give you a call.' He put his finger to his lips as he was about to open the office door.

'Margaret – Rosie Gilmour,' Christy said, announcing her as he walked into the office.

As Rosie followed him in, a pale and tired-looking woman, with mousy brown hair that needed a wash, came from behind her desk. She gave Rosie a limp, clammy handshake and introduced herself.

'I deal with the press enquiries here, Rosie. You know, organising one-on-one interviews with refugees for features. All of that stuff. Facts and figures.' She motioned her to a small sitting area with a coffee table and four soft chairs.

'You must be up to your eyes, Margaret,' Rosie said as they sat down. She declined the offer of a coffee and sat for a second watching the press officer. She looked nervy, Rosie thought. Probably snowed under with work and the strain of trying to get the right spin across to the public at a time when refugees were suddenly unpopular in Glasgow. The city had opened its heart many years ago when the Vietnamese boat people arrived, and after that, the Bosnians. But lately, with the influx of Iraqis, Kurds and now Kosovan Albanians, it was clearly getting refugee fatigue.

'Yeah. It's tough some days.' She sighed.

'This is a terrible business up the road in Balornock,' Rosie said. 'The way locals are turning on refugees, I think it's disgusting.'

Margaret crossed her legs and leaned forward. 'It is. But it's all part of a bigger picture of poverty and social problems, Rosie . . .'

Rosie didn't want to listen to a lecture on the effects of the mushrooming underclass. She'd been in that movie many times. So she got to the point.

'Margaret,' she interrupted. 'I've a couple of things I wanted to ask you – facts and figures – if that's ok.'

Margaret looked irritated at the interruption.

'Of course.' Her mouth tightened.

From the corner of her eye, Rosie could see Christy was watching her.

'You see,' she began, 'I'm wondering how you keep track of the refugees who are here. You know, once they are housed and you have records of them, so they can get social welfare and the things they need. How *do* you keep track of them?'

Silence. Rosie tried not to look at Christy. Margaret got up and went to a filing cabinet and opened a drawer. She took out a file and sat down behind her desk. Rosie could sense she was rattled. No more Mr Nice Guy.

'Well,' she said, opening the file without looking up,

'there's a procedure and a protocol. Once they are receiving benefits, the details are passed on to social work and then it becomes a multi-agency approach. We pull all the resources together to make sure the people are looked after, whether it's schools, registering them with doctors – all of the things that we need to do.'

'Yeah, I can see that.' Margaret wasn't answering the question. She had obviously found the standard civil servant doublespeak phrasebook. 'But how do you keep track?' Rosie persisted.

'What do you mean "keep track"?' Margaret's fingers clenched her pencil as she gave Rosie an impatient look. 'We don't stand guard – obviously.'

'No, of course not,' Rosie said, looking her in the eye. 'What I mean, Margaret, is this: for example, if a refugee comes here and then suddenly drops off the radar screen after say, a couple of months, what happens? How can you keep track of them is what I'm asking. And I suppose I'm asking whether you can actually keep track of them at all. If some guy from Afghanistan, for example, decides to disappear into the black economy and go and work with his mates, illegally, in a restaurant or warehouse down south, what I mean is, can you keep track of that?'

Rosie's words hung in the air, and she shot a glance at Christy, who kept his head down.

Margaret looked like she was swallowing anger.

'Well, no, not if that's what you're asking, Rosie,' she bristled. 'If what you're saying is do we control people every day, then the answer is no. If someone disappears like that and goes off into the black economy we have no control over that.' She put the pen down, folded her arms and looked at Rosie. 'Can I ask you, Rosie, has your paper got an agenda here with the refugees? At the Scottish Refugee Council we're trying to do our best for these poor people. I don't think hammering on about them disappearing into the black economy is helpful, to be candid.'

Rosie took a deep breath. 'No, of course, Margaret. I agree. No, no. We don't have an agenda, and please don't think I'm here to put the boot into refugees. Believe me I'm not.' She glanced at Christy. 'I've reported from enough trouble spots in my life and listened to the stories of enough refugees to be nothing but totally sympathetic to their cause – whether or not they stay here or disappear into the black economy. I'm just asking the question as part of an overall picture of the refugee situation here.'

Rosie's explanation seemed to take the heat out of the conversation and Margaret seemed less defensive. The remainder of the meeting went well with Margaret explaining some facts about how many people had come to Glasgow and various success stories over the years. She even volunteered that refugees did disappear from time to time and it happened in all of the cities where they'd been placed. She was honest enough to say – off the record – that they didn't even have an accurate figure of people who had gone missing.

Rosie feigned interest, but she didn't need to hear it all. She'd already got what she came here for. All she wanted to know was did they keep track of people, and the answer was no they didn't. It was all she needed.

When they finished, Rosie stood up and shook hands with Margaret as she left, aware that the press officer was glad to see the back of her.

As Christy walked her along the corridor towards the door, he stopped. 'I don't think you'll be invited to the Christmas party,' he said with an impish grin.

'I don't like parties anyway,' Rosie smiled back. 'All that laughing and enjoying yourself,' she joked, feeling she had met a kindred spirit in him. Then she looked him in the eye. 'There's something dodgy going on, Christy. Refugees disappearing.'

Christy made a face that agreed with her and they stood for a moment in silence.

'I'll call you.' He turned and went back up the corridor.

As Rosie left, she glanced into the waiting room where the Rwandan woman still sat with the same expression.

Rosie waited at the main door to the flats in the Merchant City in the hope someone would come out so she could slip through the secured entrance. She assumed if she buzzed the number Don had given her for the Ukrainian office cleaner, Tanya, she'd get a knock-back. She might only get one shot to talk to her, so she didn't want to blow it on an intercom conversation that might get lost in translation. Eventually she heard the buzz from inside, and as the main door opened, she slipped in, grimacing at the young man coming out as though she'd forgotten her keys.

She climbed the staircase to the second floor. There was no name on the door, so she checked her notebook again, took a deep breath and braced herself.

She pressed the doorbell and heard it chime inside. She waited. No answer. After a few seconds, she pressed it again, but still no answer. Instinctively she bent down and peered through the letter box. She could hear music coming from somewhere down the hall and the sound of running water. She waited a while then rang the bell again.

'Hello? Who is it please?' The voice from behind the door.

'My name is Rosie Gilmour. Could you open the door please?'

Silence.

'Hello? . . . Tanya? . . . I'm from the *Post*. The newspaper. I have something to talk to you about. It's about the law firm Murphy & Paton.'

Silence.

'Are you there, Tanya?' Rosie persisted. 'Please. Won't you open the door for just a moment? I want to talk to you about something specific.' She paused. 'It's about refugees.'

Rosie waited. The music stopped. Then she heard the key being turned and the door opened.

Tanya stood inside the hallway, rubbing her blonde hair with a towel. Her skin was slightly flushed from the shower and she looked skinny in a clingy vest and baggy tracksuit bottoms. She looked at Rosie from big, ice-blue eyes.

'What do you want with me? Why you come here?' She screwed up her face, confused. 'I only clean the office. Why you here?'

She looked like she was faking.

'Sorry, Tanya,' Rosie said, looking her in the eye. 'But can I possibly have five minutes of your time to tell you some things.' She paused keeping her eyes fixed on Tanya. 'I understand it was you who found Tony Murphy that morning. You were the first to see him?'

Tanya nodded, then looked away.

'I found him. He was already dead.'

'Tanya. I want to talk to you about Tony Murphy and Frank Paton.'

'I only clean the office. What can I say?'

'Can I come in?'

Tanya shook her head. She took a step back as though she was going to close the door.

'Tanya . . .' Rosie sensed time was running out. 'Please. Give me a minute. I want to tell you something about the law firm.' The door was beginning to close. 'Tanya. They may have been mixed up in something with refugees. Something dangerous, Tanya. Serious.' The door closed. 'You might be able to help . . . to stop bad things happening.'

Rosie cursed under her breath. It was too optimistic to hope that Tanya would talk, even if she had something to say. She'd only come to the flat as a long shot after Don had called her to say that the cops were sure it was Tanya who had sent Murphy's suicide note to his wife. They believed she stole the letter, but they had no proof so could do nothing about it. They'd questioned her, but she had just given them blank looks when they asked if she'd removed a letter from Murphy's desk. Don was convinced Murphy was having a fling with her, but he had nothing to go on but his instinct. He'd admitted to Rosie his hunch was really based on the fact that he thought Tanya was, as he'd said, 'very shaggable indeed'.

Rosie was about to give up and leave when the door opened.

'Come in,' Tanya said.

Rosie followed her down the narrow hall and into the cramped living room. She glanced around at the sofa, the one armchair, and the open kitchen, all squeezed into a tiny area. You wouldn't be swinging many cats in here, she thought.

'I just moved in,' Tanya said, as though she sensed Rosie judging. 'Is very small. I left my husband, so now I am trying to be on my own.'

'It's okay,' Rosie said, slightly embarrassed in case Tanya had read her mind. 'It's good to be in the city centre. Handy.' She changed the subject. 'Look, Tanya. As I said, I'm from the *Post* and I'm looking into the death of Tony Murphy, but on a wider picture. Because . . .'

'I know who you are,' Tanya interrupted. 'I saw your name in the newspaper. You were writing a story about refugees. About vigilantes? And a body in the water.'

'Oh, you read that?' Rosie said surprised.

Tanya sat on the sofa and motioned her to sit down.

'Yes,' she said. 'I read. I was thinking maybe to phone the newspaper and talk to you.'

'Really?' Rosie was astonished at the change in Tanya's demeanour. She was a lucky reporter, but she wasn't this lucky.

'Yes,' Tanya looked at the floor, then at Rosie. 'Do you pay for information?'

Terrific. Another hustler on the make. Whatever life the Ukrainians had led in the old Communist Soviet Union, it didn't take them long to embrace the free market when the shackles were off.

'Sometimes we pay for information,' Rosie said, deadpan. She shot Tanya a look of mild disgust. 'But to be honest, I don't know that I'm ready to pay money for a story about refugees who may be in trouble, Tanya. Kind of sticks in my throat.' She hoped she was getting through.

Tanya pushed her hair back from her face and Rosie could see the dark shadows under her eyes, and traces of a bruise on her cheek. But she was still very beautiful, pale, translucent skin, high cheekbones and an easy elegance about her.

'I'm sorry.' Tanya sighed. 'But I have no money. I was looking for some help is all.'

'Do you have any information that you think would be important for refugees?' Rosie didn't want to let it go.

Tanya got up and went to the kitchen. She took a cigarette out of a packet on the worktop and lit it, and stood watching Rosie for a moment. Then she went into her handbag and pulled out a piece of paper. She came back and sat down on the sofa.

'I have this,' she said, unfolding the paper and handing it to Rosie.

Rosie's eyes quickly scanned the sheet of paper which had a list of foreign names on it, possibly refugees, and addresses in Glasgow. Each of them had the words, 'alone, no family' written at the side, and she could see that some of them had been scored through with a pen. It could have been a random list of refugees, and it wouldn't have meant much to Rosie, had one name not jumped out at her. Emir Marishta. She remembered the surname he'd given her at the station. Next to it was Jetmir Hasani, his friend who'd gone missing, and the address of the door she had knocked on in Balornock. Her heart skipped a beat.

'It's a list,' Rosie said. 'Refugees I suppose. Where did you get it, Tanya?'

Tanya looked at her with a sort of cold defiance.

'I took it,' she said. 'From the file in Frank Paton's office. It was the file he took from Tony's desk when he came in that morning and found he was dead. He took the file away before the police came.'

Rosie took a deep breath. 'Do you want to talk to me, Tanya?'

Tanya nodded, looking at the floor.

CHAPTER 11

Rosie was at her desk trying to make small talk with Reynolds, the crime reporter who was so far out of the loop he might as well still be in the pub. And that's how it would stay as far as she was concerned. Reynolds was running down the clock on his final month's notice after McGuire made sure the redundancy deal was an offer he couldn't refuse. He may still officially have been the crime reporter, but he was kept completely out of any big investigations because the editor considered him a spy for the police.

'So what are you hearing on the Murphy suicide, Rosie?' Reynolds sat back, sticking his pen behind his ear.

'Nothing much, Bob, that's the problem,' she lied. 'I can't get a damn thing on him – no reason why he would top himself.' Rosie shrugged. 'That's the problem with suicide. No warning. It just happens. I reckon there was some personal trauma in his life, but the wife is saying nothing and neither is Frank Paton.'

'Weird though, with that suicide note arriving nearly a week after he died.' Reynolds looked smug. 'I had a tip from one of my guys. I've passed it on to Lamont.'

'Yeah.' Rosie hoped her surprise didn't show on her face. 'I heard that too, but the cops have absolutely nothing to say on it. It's up to McGuire if he wants to run it.'

Rosie kept one eye on the conference room at the end of the editorial floor. Any minute now the door would open and the various editorial heads would spill out of the room, armed with their schedules and plans for tomorrow's paper. Some would emerge flushed and agitated, having been given a good kicking by McGuire who could be a monster in conference, knocking back their stories, panning their opinions, or warning them they'd be out of a job by the end of the day if they didn't buck up their ideas. Lately, Rosie had seldom attended the twice-daily conferences, even though she was officially an assistant editor in charge of investigations. When she was working on an investigation herself, everything she did had to be kept tight as a drum – usually just between her, McGuire and the picture editor. She'd managed to convince McGuire that Lamont should be kept in the dark on every investigation until the last minute, because he was a slippery bastard who couldn't be trusted. Now she was champing at the bit, desperate to offload her latest information to McGuire. The door opened and out they came. Less than a minute later, Rosie's phone rang.

'You've to come through, Rosie.'

'Thanks, Marion.'

Rosie said nothing to Reynolds as she got up and headed for McGuire's office.

'Gilmour,' McGuire said. 'I feel as though you've been missing for days. You're such a ray of sunshine.'

'That's touching, Mick. Not days, actually. Just yesterday. I was out all day seeing people.'

'Right. Well I hope it's paid off, because I don't want this refugee story to go cold.'

'Cold?' Rosie said, sitting on the leather sofa opposite his desk. 'You must be joking. This is so hot now, Mick, it's burning a hole in my notebook.'

'Christ, Rosie, when you say things like that I can hear the lawyers gasping for air.'

'Well, I don't think we should even go near the lawyers with this stuff, Mick. At least not yet.'

'Now I am nervous.' He took his feet of the desk and sat forward. 'Come on. I'm all ears.'

'Okay. Brace yourself.' She fiddled with a pencil. 'Here's the scenario, Mick. Hold on to your pants for this. Refugees are being kidnapped and killed for the illegal trade in body tissue.' Rosie put her hands out theatrically. 'You know, a line like that should really have had a drum roll.'

McGuire looked at her, his face serious. 'Don't fuck about, Rosie.'

'I'm not, Mick. I'm absolutely not fucking about. I'm telling you. That's what I'm hearing.'

McGuire got up from his desk and came around to sit on the armchair opposite her.

'Tell me. Chapter and verse.'

Rosie began with the story from Tam Logan's widow Jan, of how she'd spilled it all out to her that day before she disappeared to Spain. Rosie really hadn't expected to hear any more from Jan, even though she felt she was holding out, but last night she'd called Rosie on her mobile with more information. She had found a piece of paper in the pocket of Tam's denim shirt he sometimes wore to work.

'She told me the name of the guy they called Doctor Mengele.' McGuire shot her a come-off-it glance. Rosie put up a hand. 'No, I'm *not* kidding! She gave me his name – Milosh Subacic. She says Tam told her he was Bosnian, but she isn't sure. And she told me where the place is where they're doing all this cutting up bodies stuff. When I spoke to her at first she said it was somewhere outside of Glasgow, but last night she was more specific. Said it was a disused slaughterhouse out near Drymen. But I think she's given quite a good location, or area at least, so I'd say it's findable. We need to go there, but I'll come to that in a minute.' She took a deep breath, ready to continue.

'Fuck me, Rosie,' McGuire interrupted. 'Are you asking me to believe that some Bosnian guy is over in Drymen cutting people up like Josef Mengele?'

'So it would seem, Mick.'

He shook his head. 'I don't believe this.'

'Wait. It gets better.' Rosie uncrossed her legs and sat forward.

'I also tracked down the office cleaner at Paton, Murphy, the Ukrainian bird, Tanya. My cop pal swears it was her who sent the suicide note to Murphy's wife – thinks she swiped it from his desk when she found him swinging that morning. But of course they've no way of proving it. I mean who else could it have been? Apart from Frank Paton, and I don't think it was him.'

McGuire's eyebrows knitted.

'Why not?'

'Well why would he?'

McGuire shrugged. 'Well, if they were involved in something together . . .'

'I suppppose that's possible.' Rosie conceded.

'Right. Okay. Carry on.'

'Well,' Rosie continued, 'I went to see her and she wasn't going to play at all at first, shut the door in my face. Then to my surprise she invites me into her flat.'

'How much?'

'Nothing, Mick. She asked if we'd pay for information and I put her right about my feelings about making money out of stricken refugees, and suddenly she changed her mind.'

'You're a class act, Gilmour. I'll give you that.'

Rosie smiled. 'Wait till you hear. Next thing is she opens up. She's been having an affair with Murphy – hotel rooms in the afternoon – and she made the mistake of falling in love, daft woman. He said he'd leave his wife . . . same old same old.'

'Yeah. And?'

'Well, she says on the morning he was found, she did take the suicide note meant for his wife, and also another one for Frank Paton. She showed me it.'

'Oh fuck, Rosie.' McGuire put his head in his hands. 'You've looked at something which is evidence that's been stolen from what may have been a crime scene.'

'It was a suicide, Mick. Not a crime scene.'

'Well, maybe not when she took it. But I've got a sneaky suspicion you're about to tell me something that will guarantee that Murphy was up to his arse in some kind of crime. That means everything they were doing was a crime scene.'

Rosie put her hands up.

'You got it in one, Mick.'

'Christ! Go on.' He rubbed his face. 'I almost don't want to hear what the suicide notes said.'

Rosie told him the contents of both notes.

'Fuck! Murphy and Paton! So you think they're actually behind this, providing the refugees?'

'So it would seem,' Rosie said.

'Go on.' McGuire was on his feet now, walking around the office, concentrating, hands dug deep into his trouser pockets.

'So Tanya told me she went into the office early one morning before Paton came in and looked in a file. A piece of paper dropped out and she photocopied it.' Rosie went into her bag and took it out. She handed it to McGuire and he looked at it.

'Names of refugees, I guess. Scrubbed out some of them.'

'Yeah, exactly. Scrubbed out. And you see the name of my man Emir? Him and his mate Jetmir – the one he told me about – they're also scrubbed out. Maybe, in Jetmir's case, in more ways than one.'

'So you really think Murphy and Paton have been hand-picking these people?'

'Yes, it's possible, Mick. Maybe they identify the ones who nobody will even report as missing – the ones who are all alone with no family. Sound plausible? Who's going to give a damn about people like that who end up in a foreign country. They're just a number in some filing cabinet at the Home Office.'

McGuire took a deep breath and pursed his lips as he exhaled slowly. He scratched his chin. 'But why? How the fuck does something like illegal trade in body tissue spring up in Glasgow. This just doesn't happen here.' He paused, then asked, 'And what exactly *is* body tissue?'

'I checked this out a bit. Body tissue is anything from skin to eyeballs to bone and veins. In other words, anything that isn't an organ.'

'Right,' McGuire nodded. 'So why Glasgow?'

'Don't know that yet. But it looks like the lawyers are working with Al Howie and Jake Cox's mob. Except Cox isn't around now – he's mostly still in Spain, but you can bet he'll be pulling the strings. In fact that's probably where he hooked up with the Eastern Europe connection. This is about the gangsters broadening out to new ways to make money. I've had a brief look in cuttings and on the internet at the organ harvesting and body-tissue trade. It's a billion-pound business and it's world-wide – particularly in Eastern Europe – places like Macedonia, Ukraine, Russia. In fact everywhere – the Philippines, USA. It's huge. If these gangsters are working with the hoods in the UK then they're all at it. They'll have identified that refugees are easy pickings, with so many of them coming and going. Nobody watches them. Nobody cares, actually. I've already been up at the Scottish Refugee Council and established that there's no stringent check on refugees, so it's easy to disappear – or be made to disappear. And it looks like that is what's happening.'

'Fuck me!' McGuire sighed. 'Unbelievable, Rosie! It really is.' He sat down. 'I want this story, Rosie.'

'We've a long way to go, Mick.'

'So what's your thinking?'

'First up, I want to get Matt involved. I like working with him. He's the best. We can take a run out to the this place and see what we can see. And I need to find more about this Milosh character, what he looks like. I'm going to get my private eye friend on that. It's obviously going to be tight and secret in whatever location they do it, so we need to tread very carefully.'

'Goes without saying.' McGuire almost smiled. 'I wouldn't want you to end up with someone ripping out yout liver and selling it on the open market.'

Rosie laughed. 'If it was my liver, it might not be worth much.'

They both sat in silence for a moment, pondering the enormity of the story.

'Cops?'

'No, Mick. Definitely not yet.'

'Rosie. People are being kidnapped and having their bits cut off and sold. Can you imagine where we'll be if it comes out we're withholding stuff?'

'I'm just saying not yet Mick. Let's have a look for a few days. Maybe the cops already know. If they do, why are they not doing anything about it? Let me just look at it.'

Mick sighed.' All right, Gilmour. You can have a look from a safe distance, but don't go rattling any cages.' He went back behind his desk and wagged a warning finger at her. 'And I mean that this time, Rosie. After that Moroccan shit last year, where you nearly got killed. No more of that.'

There was a little moment between them and Rosie looked away.

'Don't worry, Mick. I'm not going to do anything daft.' She left.

The Irish pub O'Flaherty's in Buchanan Lane was filling up with office workers dropping off for a quick drink on their way to nearby Queen Street train station. It was the kind of typical Irish theme pub you could find these days in any big city from Bucharest to Bangkok, and all of them were about as Irish as the Rev. Iain Paisley. At least that was the standard view of the purists. But Rosie liked all of them, no matter where they were, and no matter if the battered old suitcase and trinkets on the dusty shelves were purely for show, they still made her feel at home. It felt Irish to her. Rosie hadn't been to Ireland until she was twenty-five, though she knew her ancestors on both sides had been part of the wave of immigrants who'd crossed the water fleeing persecution.

She'd never really felt Irish until she found herself on a freebie press trip to Dublin and discovered that so many of the mannerisms and ways of the Irish people were exactly like all people she'd grown up with who were of Irish descent. Call it genetic memory, but it had occurred to her that this was where she should have been all her life. She fitted. Maybe that's what was wrong with her, she'd joked to anyone who would listen when she came back. She should have been living in Ireland. And it was true. The Scots, largely Presbyterian and a little buttoned-up by nature, somehow didn't get the Irish. Though with so much crossing of the water and intermarrying over the generations all of that was becoming more and more diluted. But wherever Rosie was in the world, she always liked to sample a little bit of Irish – even if the bar did look like something out of a Disney movie.

She took her drink from the barman and went to a corner with the evening newspaper to wait for Christy Larkin. The earnest young man from the Scottish Refugee Council had called her as she was about to leave the office and asked if they could meet. She was up here like a shot.

She watched as Christy came into the gloomy bar and looked around. He smiled broadly when he caught her eye and strode across the room, a big, rangy kind of guy, pushing his hair back from his face.

'Hi Rosie. Can I get you a drink?'

'No thanks, Christy, you sit down. Let me get it.'

'If you're sure, pint of Guinness,' he said, and sat down.

Rosie brought back his drink and settled into the corner, clinking her gin and tonic with his pint.

'Our press officer was a wee bit rattled by you, Rosie.' Christy grinned. 'I was loving it. She's a bossy bastard.' He took a mouthful of stout.

Rosie smiled. 'I could see she wasn't used to people being persistent with their questions. She must surround herself with yes men.' She glanced at Christy. 'Present company excepted, of course.'

Christy shrugged. 'She doesn't like me much actually. Not that I give a fuck, I'm leaving in a couple of months. Taking a year out. Going travelling.'

'Good for you, Christy. Best time to do it when you're young.' Rosie flicked a glance across his face, noticing how handsome he was behind his big specs.

'You sound like an old person saying that, Rosie.' He smiled and cheekily looked her up and down. 'And you're not old.'

'No flirting. I could nearly be your mammy.' Rosie gave him a reproachful look but half smiled.

'Well, why not? You're not old at all.'

Rosie laughed. She liked his cheek. 'Come on, Christy. Let's talk. I got the feeling when we were in the office you wanted to talk to me – not ask me out.'

'Yes,' Christy nodded, and his expression grew more serious. 'I do want to talk to you, Rosie.' He looked her in the eye. 'Can I trust you? *Really* trust you?'

Rosie put her drink down and gave him a perplexed look. 'If you didn't think you could trust me, Christy, you wouldn't be here.'

'True.'

'So, let's talk. I've also got something I want to ask you about, so trust goes both ways.'

'Of course.'

Christy moved a little closer to her. 'You know when you were asking about the tabs that were kept on refugees and if some of them disappear into the black economy? Why were you asking that? Are you investigating them working illegally?'

Rosie watched him as he took a long drink of his pint.

'No, I'm not actually. I was asking because I was wondering what happens when they disappear, how many go missing. How many have gone missing.'

'Why?'

Rosie looked at him. He knew something. He was fishing.

'Why do *you* think, Christy? Tell me.'

He didn't reply immediately, but took his glasses off and rubbed his eyes. Then he said, 'I think there's something going on Rosie. Something bad.' He took a deep breath and lowered his voice. 'There *are* refugees going missing. I've been looking back over the lists and checking addresses and stuff. There's been quite a lot in the past year, and it's been quite sudden. I've been working there for three years and it never used to happen, but now people are disappearing. The thing is, though, nobody knows if they've gone off to work illegally or whether something else is happening. There are just so *many* refugees. I've checked with colleagues down south and they're going missing there too. It's not right.' He sipped his pint. 'But nobody wants to make a big public thing about it because it's bad for the government if there's a perception that refugees are just coming over here and disappearing into the black economy.'

'So what do you think could be happening?'

He shook his head. 'I don't know. I really don't. I was thinking maybe the refugees are being kidnapped and sold to gangmasters – people-trafficking, that kind of thing – but I've got no evidence. All I know is every time I flag it up that someone's gone missing, nobody reacts. So I just stopped flagging it. Everyone's so busy processing the ones that are coming in and stuff, that nobody wants to know anything complicated. To be honest, I don't think anybody cares that much.'

They sat in silence for a moment. Rosie drank her gin, but turned down an offer of another from Christy. She felt he was someone she could take into her confidence, but not enough to tell him everything she knew. But she did need his help.

'Listen, Christy,' Rosie said. 'If I give you a name of somebody, a refugee – Bosnian, I think – could you maybe run a check on him for me? Find out who he is? Maybe even get me a photograph?' She paused. 'I don't want to say at this stage why I need that, so I hope you'll respect that. I'm working on something, having a look at one or two individuals, and this guy's name has come up. Could you help me?'

Christy nodded. 'Of course I will, if I can. Shouldn't be a problem for me to check a name. If he's not from here, then I can put his name into the computer and see what comes up nationally. Who is he?'

Rosie handed him a piece of paper.

'Milosh Subacic,' he said. 'Any age?'

Rosie shook her head. 'Nothing. Just the name. But I don't think he's young somehow.'

Christy put it in his pocket and finished his drink. They both stood up and walked towards the door.

'I'll give you a shout as soon as I have the information. Shouldn't be long.' He smiled. 'Maybe we can have another drink sometime, and I can chat you up a bit more?'

'Yeah,' Rosie laughed. 'I love a bit of chatting up by a handsome young man.' She patted his shoulder as they went their separate ways.

Rosie looked at her watch. It was nearly seven. She punched in TJ's number on her mobile, wondering if he fancied a quick bite to eat. It rang out, but she hung up when it went on to his voicemail. I'll surprise him, she decided, as she got into her car and drove towards his flat. But as she was just about fifty yards from the door she slammed the breaks on, stopping the car abruptly. Her heart stopped too. Unless she was mistaken, the woman coming out of the main door of TJ's flat was Kat. She felt as though someone had kicked her square in the guts. Kat walked confidently along the road towards her. Rosie quickly turned her car into a sidestreet like a fugitive and found herself dipping her head below the dashboard, ridiculously, and waited until she passed. She caught a glimpse of herself in the rear-view mirror. She was white to the lips.

CHAPTER 12

It had been a sleepless night, and Rosie woke up groggy. She stared at the ceiling, listening to the sound of the Charing Cross traffic drifting through her open bedroom window. By the level of noise it must be nearly eight. The world was up and about, a thousand stories playing out in the streets below. She gave herself twenty seconds to be fully awake. It was her golden rule – because any longer could give you too much time to ponder on what the day could bring and you might end up just lying there, afraid to face it. Rosie had known the utter blackness of that feeling, and she'd battened down the hatches on it a long time ago. At least she hoped she had.

She sat up on the bed and swung her feet onto the floor, rubbing her face gently. Her eyelashes were still wet from crying in her sleep again, yet the troubled dream seemed like hours ago. They say you actually only dream for a few seconds before you wake up, but it never felt that way in Rosie's dreams. Hers were powerful protracted dramas buried somewhere deep in her psyche, lying in wait for her to sleep so they could torment her. Rosie's dreams were big stories in full Technicolor, but the end was always the same. Always the tears, and the phone ringing and ringing, the way it had that day.

She hadn't had the dream about her mother for nearly a month now, though since she'd returned from Kosovo she'd been plagued by other nightmares. But last night her sleep took her somewhere different, standing under a streetlamp in the rain, shivering in the cold, and waiting for TJ to come out of his flat as darkness fell. Eventually he emerged, with his arm around a pretty girl who was giggling as they walked along the street together. They'd been so engrossed in each other, they didn't even notice her as they strolled past her. But further down the road she could hear their shrill laughter, and when eventually they looked over their shoulders, their faces turned into her mother and father. She'd woken herself up shouting for them to wait, not to leave her alone.

Rosie threw a towelling robe around her nakedness and padded into the kitchen to prepare breakfast. Hopefully the jag of strong coffee would make her mind so busy she could push last night away. She switched on her mobile phone and saw there were four missed calls from TJ, and one message. Last night she'd sat watching the mobile shudder and ring on the sofa beside her, but she couldn't answer it. She couldn't trust herself to speak to him until she dealt in her head with the shock of seeing Kat coming out of his flat. Get it in perspective, she told herself. What did you actually see? she asked herself. There could be any simple explanation. She knew they were friends, they'd worked together in New York. Christ! They worked together now. Maybe TJ was helping her with her vocals for a new song she was learning. Any simple explanation could be made as to why she saw her there last night. But it didn't make the pain and the paranoia any easier.

She picked up the mobile and listened to TJ's message, her stomach tweaking at the sound of his voice. 'Rosie, 'Where the hell are you, woman? I got a missed call from you and been calling you since. Thought you might fancy a bite to eat. Give me a bell when you get this, sweetheart.'

Paranoia. Insecurity. That's all it was. She settled down on the sofa with her breakfast and plonked on Sky News. She would phone TJ later and meet him tonight. By then, she hoped she'd have got her head around it. Her mobile rang, and Matt's name came up on the screen.

'Hi pet,' she said.

'Rosita. Howsit going, darling? I hear we're off out this morning.'

'We are Matt. We're going on an adventure. A wee spying mission.'

'Shit. I'm still traumatised after the last one.'

'Yeah, but it was a lot of fun though. I mean who else has got dinner-party patter like you and can rattle off stories like that?'

'True. As long as we keep on living to tell the tale. Where we off to?'

'Out of the city. Will tell you when I see you. Listen

Matt, I'm not going into the office. Can you pick me up here? I just have to jump into the shower and get sorted. Give me forty minutes.'

'No worries, Rosie. If you need me to scrub your back give me a shout.'

'I think I can manage. Text me when you're outside.' She hung up.

To Rosie's surprise, the location Jan Logan had given her wasn't that far out of the city, but what did surprise her was the building itself – if they were at the right place.

'I can't believe they're actually doing this in a slaughter-house.' Rosie looked out of the windscreen at the flat-roofed, long, low building in the distance.

'I know,' Matt said, firing off some shots with his zoom lens. 'But if we can knock this off, it's a great headline in itself. Slaughterhouse of Horror . . . Slaughter of the Innocents . . . Nazi-Style Slaughter of Asylum Seekers.'

'You're in the wrong job, pal,' Rosie chuckled. 'You should be on the back bench.'

'No end to my talents, darlin'. I'm not just your ordinary monkey pushing buttons you know.' He rested his camera on his lap.

They'd been sitting at the edge of the farm road where they hoped they wouldn't be seen by traffic, but could still see at a distance any movement at the sprawling building a few hundred yards away. In the past two hours, there had been nothing except one small delivery van going in.

Rosie had been astonished when Jan phoned her from Spain and told her that the place where Tam had made the pick-ups was actually a slaughterhouse on the outskirts of the city, on the road towards Loch Lomond. It had been out of commission for over a year, and to the outside world it was closed. There were padlocks and chains on the main gates and the high wire fences were topped with razor wire. From where Rosie and Matt were sitting it looked as if nobody got through the gates without prior arrangement. There was no one guarding the front gates, but when the delivery van had arrived, someone came out from the building and let them in just far enough to take the package. Matt had taken pictures with his long lens of the package being handed over and the van leaving. There were only three vehicles parked out in front of the building, inside the gates. One looked like a big refrigerated van, the other was a jeep, and the third looked like a big luxury saloon car – a Vauxhall Carlton, Matt had said, when he zoomed his camera in. He'd managed to capture an image of its number plates.

'I should be able to get someone to run them through for me,' Rosie said. 'That'll give us a handle on who owns what.'

'But if they *are* doing grisly operations in there,' Matt said, 'it must be almost impossible to keep it tight just among the few people involved. How do they do that? It's so horrific, there's always the danger of someone who might blab. Look at Tam Logan, for instance.'

'Yeah,' Rosie said, 'but look what happened to him. This mob don't mess about with traitors.' She opened a packet of peanuts and gave Matt a handful. 'The thing is though, the building itself might be a front for something else. If it's an abattoir, then there could quite easily be areas of it that are under lock and key that nobody else goes into. I don't know the set-up in these slaughterhouses, but maybe there's an area that only certain people can go into, where they prepare the meat for the butchers' shops. Maybe that's where they do the cutting up.' She shrugged. 'Just thinking.'

'Yeah. Makes you wonder what might be in your pies though,' Matt grinned.

'Thanks for that, Matt. I think I'll just have the fish fingers for lunch.'

'Or you could have just the fingers, madam. They come in all sizes. And I'm told the braised thumbs are particularly tasty, not to mention the poached penis sweetbreads . . .'

'Right, Matt,' Rosie stopped him. 'I get the picture, you sick bastard.'

'Just saying, that's all.' Matt chucked a peanut into his mouth.

'But I do get your point,' Rosie said. 'It must be hard to keep everyone quiet – though if it's only the trusted foot soldiers from big Al Howie's mob, then I think they'll know to keep it really tight. Especially after they've been told what happened to Tam.' She turned to him. 'How the hell are we going to get inside that place?'

'Well, other than go to the Refugee Council and declare yourself as an asylum seeker who's lost the will to live, I'd say it's impossible.'

They needed some luck, Rosie thought. Although the breaks had come, there was a long way to go. She already had Tanya revealing the details of her affair with Murphy, but that in itself was a story more for titillation than a major revelation. Tanya had given her a lead with that list of names and addresses of refugees, and Rosie had already been around most of them, managing to glean from neighbours roughly when they disappeared. All of them had vanished without trace – not even a word to neighbours that they were moving out. But in the world of refugees, keeping quiet about yourself was how they lived – just in case they did decide to slip off the radar and go to work illegally. There was no way of telling why they'd vanished. Her mobile rang and she pulled it out of her pocket. No name or number.

'Rosie?'

'Yes?' She didn't recognise the voice.

'Hey, Rosie. Christy Larkin. Howsit going?'

'Fine, Christy, thanks. Working away. You okay? Did you manage to make that wee enquiry I asked you about?'

'I did, Rosie,' he said. 'That's why I'm phoning you. Can you talk at the moment? I've come out of the office to speak to you.'

'Sure. Fire away.'

'Okay. I looked up that name – Milosh Subacic, the one you gave me. I checked it for refugees coming in here to

Glasgow and there's nothing. No trace. I even checked over the past three years, but nothing.'

'Really? That's a bit strange, isn't it?'

'Well, not really, Rosie. If he didn't come through Scotland or Glasgow, then we wouldn't have him on our register, unless he'd come to us later, got registered and was living here.' He paused. 'Well, I checked with one of my colleagues down in London. I've got a mate down there who kind of thinks along the same lines as me. He's a good guy, so I asked him to check, and he did.'

'And?'

'He found him. Milosh Subacic. He came in here about five years ago, towards the end of the Bosnian war. A Bosnian Muslim apparently, arrived like a lot of others at the time, during all that ethnic cleansing. He came in through London and was living somewhere in Hackney.' He paused. 'But the thing is, Rosie, that's all there is on him. Just basic details of when he came in and stuff, then his file seems to stop dead. But my mate knows other ways to track people through the system, so he tried to find his file through another means. But when he got it, the name came up with this no access red line through it.'

'No access?' Rosie asked.

'Yep. No access. It's a kind of flag that means everything from there on is shut down on him. When you come across a no access on a refugee it usually means something dodgy. Like maybe they've discovered something about his background, or he's a criminal on the run, and he's disappeared. They like to keep that quiet.'

'Christ.' Rosie could see all sorts of possibilities. 'Maybe that's not even his real name.'

'Took the words out of my mouth, Rosie,' Christy said. 'He came here as Milosh Subacic, but I suppose he could be anyone. Or he could be who he says he is, but they've found he's a thief or something, or a rapist – anything.'

'But why no access, Christy?'

'Can't know for sure, Rosie, but it could be because he's gone missing and they have something on him and are trying to find him. Could be something like that. But it's not right. My mate says he can't go into the file any more because if you hit on someone like that and it comes up no access and you do it any more than once, then it registers somewhere and you get your collar felt by one of the suits.'

'I see. That's a pity,' Rosie said. 'But you did brilliant anyway, Christy. What you've found is great and is definitely a help.' It wasn't really, Rosie thought, it was inconclusive, but it was useful. And it deepened the mystery over who this Milosh character was.

'No problems, Rosie. But hey, do you want the good news?'

'Oh, yeah,' she said. 'From where I'm sitting right now, I'd love some good news.'

'Okay. But it will cost you a drink – maybe even dinner?'

Rosie could picture his cheeky grin. 'Depends on what you've got.'

'I've got a picture of him.'

Rosie made a little triumphant clenched fist.

'You have? What a star! How did you manage that if the file was closed?'

'There are ways. My mate says there was one on his early file that he was able to access. It was obviously somebody's mistake and the picture should have been removed before they made the file no access – but it's a result for us. The pic is about maybe five years old. He emailed it to me. So what's your email? I'll send you it right now.'

Rosie gave him her email. 'That's absolutely brilliant, Christy. Really. You are definitely getting a good dinner.'

'I'll be looking forward to that Rosie. You bet I will. Listen, I have to go now. I'll nip round to a friend's office and email it from there, as I don't want to do it from work.'

'Thanks, Christy.'

'And, Rosie, I take it there's something well dodgy about this character Milosh?'

'I'm looking at him, Christy. It's part of the investigation. But it's all very top secret at the moment, so if you can just forget this conversation?'

'What conversation? See you.' The line went dead.

Rosie turned to Matt. 'We need to get to the nearest hotel where I can get to the internet.'

'So let's go.'

It was nearly seven, and only the Vauxhall Carlton remained parked outside the building. The jeep had gone an hour earlier with two thirty-something men who had locked the gate behind them as they left. Rosie and Matt waited.

'I wish he would hurry up,' Matt said, 'I'm starving.' He kept the lens fixed on the area.

'I think we should follow him at a distance, if it's at all possible, when he does come out. See if we can find where he lives.'

'Might be difficult in this road, but once we get out onto the main drag, if we can keep him in our sights, that's if he's our man, we—' Matt straightened up. 'Someone's coming out, Rosie.' He zoomed in. 'Looks like it's him. Come on my son . . . Game on. It's him!' He kept clicking away.

Rosie sat up and shook herself to life.

'Brilliant.'

They waited until the car was well down the road before they sped out of the farm road and followed. There were two cars in front of them, but Matt could still keep his eye on the Carlton, as they tailed him all the way into the city centre.

'It's too busy in here for him to even think anyone's behind him,' Matt said. 'Doesn't look like he's going to the West End though, he's heading down towards the Clydeside.'

'Yeah,' Rosie said. 'My money's on the quayside flats. You can just disappear in there and nobody knows what you're up to. A lot of the hookers work out of there.'

Rosie's hunch was right. There were two cars in front of the Carlton, and both turned into the car park on the River Clyde. They watched as he parked close to the front entrance.

'I'm going to see if I can nip in along with him,' Matt said, unbuckling his seatbelt. 'See if I can see what flat he goes into.'

'That's dodgy, Matt. He might be suspicious.'

'No he won't,' Matt said. 'People always forget their keys and get through the main entrance. I'm going to wing it.'

'Be careful.'

Rosie felt it was a little reckless, but she didn't stop him. She watched as Matt went up to the front door just a second or two behind their man. Now that she had a full view of him, she knew from the picture Christy had sent her that this was definitely Milosh – or whoever he was. She saw him glance at Matt, his face without expression, as Matt seemed to be telling him he'd forgotten his key. They went in together. Rosie waited, her heart in her mouth. She breathed a sigh of relief as Matt came out of the front door and headed towards the car.

'Got him,' he said, clenching his fist as though he'd scored a goal. 'Second floor, number five. I went up to the second floor along with him and the flat was just as you go into the main hall, So I carried on up the stairs until the next floor.' He smiled at Rosie. 'So now we know where he lives.'

'Well done, Matt. What did he seem like when you were trying to get in?'

'Hard-looking bastard,' Matt said. 'Pale, but kind of well built. Looks quite tough. I'd put him at around about forty-something.'

'I wonder if he's really who he says he is.'

'C'mon I'm starving, Rosie. Fancy a curry?'

'No thanks, Matt,' she said, looking at her watch. 'I've got to be somewhere.'

'Knocked back again,' he shook his head. 'One of these days you'll take up my offer and I'll not turn up.'

'Sure,' Rosie laughed. 'Can you just drop me in the city centre.

CHAPTER 13

Rosie was wishing she hadn't arranged to meet TJ for a quick drink on the way home. She'd expected him to suggest they have dinner, but he told her he'd arranged to meet Gerry and Kat for a practice session to go over some numbers they'd been working on. She was already smouldering with resentment by the time TJ came through the door, his sax case over his shoulder. A smile spread across his face when he saw her.

'Hey Rosie,' he bent down and kissed her on the lips. 'You all right darlin'?'

'Yeah. Long day. Staking a place out since ten this morning. Gets really tedious.'

'Ah, you love it, Gilmour,' TJ teased her. 'All that sneaking around.' He ordered a beer when the waitress appeared at the table, then sat back stretching out his long legs.

Rosie had hardly touched her wine. She felt awkward. Sitting anywhere with TJ had always been the most natural thing in the world, but right now she had no conversation, because the only thing that was burning her up she couldn't talk about.

'What's up, Rosie?' TJ's eyes scanned her face, as he leaned across and ran his hand over her hair.

'Nothing,' Rosie lied, but she knew she wasn't good at it. She puffed. 'Just tired, TJ. This story. I think it's going to be a tough one to crack.'

'Want to tell me about it?'

Rosie told him everything over the last few days, and the latest information that had come from Christy.

He lit a cigarette and blew out a trail of smoke.

'Bit of intrigue there all right, Rosie.' He gave her a warning look. 'Of course I know you won't listen to me, you never do, but I'll tell you this, Rosie. You go digging too deeply into these people – this dodgy Bosnian and the likes of Al Howie, then it's just going to get crazy. You know that. It might be *your* lungs they're pulling out.'

'I know, I know.' Rosie gave a bored sigh. This wasn't what she wanted to hear – even if he was right.

'Yeah, you know, Rosie, but you keep on doing it.' He shook his head, half smiling. 'Christ. You'd think after that stuff in Spain and Morocco last year, you'd be glad to have survived. You know, you might not actually have nine lives. You don't need to do all this crap, Rosie. I mean, you're just back from Kosovo. Give yourself a break, woman.'

Rosie sipped her wine and looked at the table. 'I can't, TJ.' She looked at him. 'What can I tell you?' She shrugged. 'It's what I do. I can't walk away from things like this.'

TJ smiled and touched her face.

'Same old Gilmour. You'll never change.'

'Anyway, enough about me,' Rosie said changing the subject. 'What you been up to?'

'Nothing. Just chilling. I don't live on the edge like you, Rosie.' He gave her a sideways glance.

Rosie was quiet, but she was simmering inside. They sat in silence, and she was aware TJ was watching her.

'Okay. What's up, Rosie?' He stubbed his cigarette out in the ashtray and leaned forward.

Rosie examined her fingernails, knowing he wouldn't let it go.

'Look at me, Rosie.'

'TJ, I . . .' She looked at him, then away. 'Last night, after I saw the guy at the Refugee Council, I called you.'

'Yeah, I got a missed call from you. I was calling your mobile all night, but you didn't answer. Didn't you get my message?'

Rosie nodded and took a deep breath. 'Well, I was in town and when I didn't get you on the phone I was going to pop round and see if you fancied going out for dinner. Surprise you. So I drove towards your flat.' She paused, feeling her face flushed. 'And . . . Well, er . . . and then I saw Kat coming out of the building.' She swallowed and waited, her heart racing.

TJ said nothing. He looked through her and they sat in heavy silence.

'And?' Finally he spoke, raising his eyebrows.

Rosie said nothing. She squirmed a little in her seat.

'Well, I . . . I just wondered. I mean . . . I wondered . . .'

TJ shot her a look that was a mixture of disappointment, hurt and anger.

'Yeah, Rosie, I know. You just wondered. The way you've been wondering ever since you clapped eyes on Kat.' He shook his head. 'I know what you wondered, Rosie, and you're wrong. Okay? Understand that and forget about it.'

'But you didn't say she was at your house. That's all. I was surprised to see her.'

'Rosie, she was at my house, and we were going over some songs. We are friends. You know that, for Christ's sake. We worked together in New York and we became friends.'

'Friends?' Rosie looked at him. 'Is that all?'

TJ shook his head and sighed. 'Aw, Rosie. Don't do this, sweetheart.' He looked at her. 'Don't do this to yourself, and don't do this to me.' He turned away.

Rosie wanted to speak, but her throat was tight. She looked at the floor.

'I was just asking,' she said eventually.

'You can't know everything about everybody, Rosie. You can't allow yourself to be consumed with stuff like that. I don't ask you about every friend in your life. You spend more time with guys than I do with women. Do I get paranoid?'

'I don't know. Do you?'

He shrugged. 'I can't run your life for you, Rosie. Apart from anything else you wouldn't let me. You're your own woman. You only let me so far into your life. Always have.'

Again, the silence.

'You went away, TJ.' The words were out before she could stop herself.

'Christ! I pleaded with you to come with me.' He snapped back, his hands held out. 'I waited for you.'

'Well. If I could have phoned you I would, but I was in the bloody hospital with my face wasted.' Tears sprang to her eyes. She got up. 'Look, TJ, I'm sorry. I think I should go. I'm saying all the wrong things.'

'Wait, Rosie.'

'No,' she shook her head. 'I have to go.' She lifted her bag and left, the image of his hurt look making the tears come as she rushed out of the door and hailed a taxi.

'Well played, Rosie,' she said aloud to herself as she slung her bag on the sofa when she got into her house. 'The one good thing to happen to you in your life, and you screw it up.' She was still berating herself as she poured a glass of red wine and went out onto the balcony. She took a long gulp and swallowed, then let out a long sigh, suddenly reflecting on that first moment when TJ had turned up.

Rosie had just held the hand of her father as he died in hospital, and was sat in a cafe where she always seemed to end up. She felt like the loneliest person in the world. Then the phone call. TJ was back. There were no questions or explanations on the phone – he just asked, where are you? She told him to come to her flat.

When he'd turned up on the doorstep, Rosie took one look at him and they fell into each other's arms. He was so sorry, he told her. But he'd been too hurt to get in contact because by her not turning up at the airport, he knew they could never make it together. He was close to tears when she told him what had happened to her. They would never allow anything to come between them again, they promised each other.

And so it had been for the past six months, not moving in together – Rosie always resisting it, because she needed some space and believed that deep down TJ needed his own space too. But it had been just about perfect. Then came Kosovo and Rosie volunteered to go. She knew it meant being away for at least two months, but she wanted to be there.

When she returned, she felt worse than ever before. She hadn't been prepared for the level of human suffering she witnessed when she got there. Back home, there had been nightmares, and when she'd woken up crying, TJ had been there to hold her. They'd spent great weekends together getting drunk, having a laugh and lots of sex. Everything was fine until last week at the Blue Note when this redhead walked onto the stage. Rosie knew that this was *her* problem, not TJ's, and that even if they had been lovers in New York, she wasn't there, so she had no rights. They weren't together. She'd had a bit of a fling in Kosovo with a doctor anyway, so who was she to judge? But she did, and that was always Rosie's problem. She told herself she should try to find some place in her head where she could deal with it, or she should walk away. She was going to be up to her eyes in the next few weeks, and every time she'd have to cancel dinner she would be paranoid he was with Kat.

Take it or leave it, she berated herself. She went into the house and ran a bath, soaking for a while, planning how to end it. She cried.

Sitting on the sofa watching some stupid old movie she was on the verge of tears again, when she heard the door buzz and got up to answer it.

'It's me, Rosie,' TJ said.

Rosie pressed the buzzer to let him in. She caught a glimpse of herself in the hall mirror, eyes puffy and face red. She wrapped the robe around her and waited until he knocked on the door. When she opened it, he stood there with that way of looking at her that completely disarmed her.

'I'm sorry, Rosie. Truce?' He produced a bottle of red wine and a takeaway from behind his back.

Rosie shook her head and smiled, choking the tears back.

'Look at the state of me.' She opened the door and stepped back as he came in.

He walked behind her into the kitchen and put the takeaway on the worktop.

Then they stood looking at each other.

'I'm sorry too.' Rosie said.

He wrapped his arms around her and hugged her tight. Then he kissed her neck and cheek, easing the robe back a little to kiss her shoulder. TJ let her go and took her face in his hands, kissing her passionately on the lips. Rosie could feel her legs weak as he opened her robe and ran his hands across her breasts.

'I love you, Rosie,' he whispered. 'Please believe me.

I never stopped loving you.' He put his arms around her lifting her up, pushing her against the wall. 'I love you.'

In the morning, Rosie was up and showered while TJ lay sleeping in her bed. She watched him as she got dressed, promising herself that from now on things would change.

She didn't even know herself how much she wanted from the relationship. They were friends first before they were anything else. All she knew was the gut-wrenching feeling that had washed over her last year when she suddenly realised he could be gone forever, and the torment she'd been in since she saw Kat outside his flat. She'd told TJ all of this last night while they ate the takeaway a couple of hours after he'd arrived. He pointed out that it was she who had said no when he asked her to move in with him a few months ago. She wanted it both ways, he told her, even though she knew it was unreasonable. That was her style. He accepted her the way she was.

Her mobile rang.

'I don't suppose that will be for me,' TJ said sleepily.

'Don't think so,' Rosie said, going over to the bed and running her hand across his head. She put the phone to her ear as she walked out of the bedroom.

'Hey, Mickey. How the devil are you?' It was her old friend Mickey Kavanagh, the ex-cop private eye she'd called for help the other night.

'I'm good, Rosie, but I'll tell you this, pal. You don't half get mixed up with some dodgy characters.'

'All part of the fun, Mickey.'

'Aye right. You'll not have much fun if you cross this particular bastard – this Milosh Subacic, as you called him.'

'Yeah?' Rosie was impressed. She'd only given him the brief information after Jan had told her the name.

'Oh, yeah,' Mickey said. 'Listen, Rosie. I spent some time on this yesterday, talked to a couple of mates in London about this guy. So I've got a few things to tell you. Best we meet for a drink or something later?'

'Sure, Mick. I can't wait.'

'Great. One thing though, Rosie. This guy is not who he says he is. His name's not Milosh Subacic.'

'Really? Come on, spill it. I'm dying here, Mickey.'

'Okay, I'll tell you one thing. He's a Serb. Former army officer. As bad a bastard as they come.'

'Christ! What time are you free for a meet?'

'Not till early evening. I'm waiting for some more intelligence to come up on him today. You can buy me a bowl of pasta later.'

'Sure,' Rosie said, glancing into her bedroom guiltily, knowing that she'd already arranged to have dinner with TJ.

CHAPTER 14

Frank Paton was hung over – big time. He hadn't even made it home, and his mobile had already been red hot with angry messages from his wife, Sally, about how he'd missed the school run, among other things. Dropping his daughter at school was the least of his worries, he felt like telling her, but he knew he couldn't. He had to keep up the front that the reason he'd been hitting the booze was because he was grieving for his best friend. He'd phone her, he decided, and attempt to make the peace once he got his first cup of coffee down him. He lifted the cup, but his hands trembled so much, he put it back down on his desk and sat back, staring darkly out of the window.

'What the fuck are you doing to yourself, Frank?' he murmured to himself as he rubbed his face vigorously. 'This can't go on, man.'

He was tired and frazzled from the bender which had begun at O'Brien's over a few drinks with some of his lawyer pals. They'd been talking about Tony and reminiscing about the old days when they'd all been at university together. As they downed bottles of expensive champagne they laughed about their youthful high ideals and how they'd been going to change the world, plotting revolution at the smoky bar in the students' union over pints of beer and cannabis joints. Look at us now, Frank had said to them, as the high of the champagne somehow began to dip, turning him morose and moody. They'd scoffed at him for thinking too much, and told him what he needed was a few lines of coke to perk him up. He didn't need much coaxing and followed one of his pals to the toilet at O'Brien's. By the time they spilled out of the bar at nine o'clock, he was high as a kite again. He knew it could only ever go downhill from there, but by that time it didn't matter. Once they'd got to the lap-dancing club it was a case of anything goes, and they ended up with a couple of slappers back at one of the guys' flats. It had been a waste of time and money, because Frank couldn't even raise a smile, and the girl had disappeared in a taxi, leaving him to sleep it off.

He stood up and paced the office, then sat back down again and puffed as he made another attempt to drink the coffee. This time he was successful and managed a mouthful. He felt the walls were closing in on him, and realised that was how Tony must have felt as he was rigging up the rope to the beam in his office.

The pair of them had already been in too deep by the time Al Howie pitched up to their office nearly a year ago and told them what he wanted them to do. They'd been horrified at the very idea of it. Handing over refugees to a monster like Al Howie? It was business, Al told them. Refugees were big business, and not just for lawyers like him and Tony to milk the system in legal fees while fighting their deportation orders and asylum cases. Refugees meant money. Nobody gave a fuck about them, Al had said. Who's counting them? he'd shrugged. It was happening in all the big cities, from London to Liverpool, and was probably also going on in Europe. All they'd have to do was provide two or three a month. Like weeding the garden, Al had said. It's not as if they wouldn't be replaced by other weeds. Al's parting shot was that it wasn't a request. He left a hold-all full of money on their desk.

They could have done something about it there and then, gone to the police, the Special Branch. But they couldn't really, because it had been a long time since Paton and Murphy had been the upright bastions of the law they'd dreamed of being when they were at Glasgow University. Those principles had been ditched the first time they'd put ten grand into a coke deal set up by Al Howie. They'd double their investment, Al had promised, and they did – several times after it. They'd crossed the line. There was no going back.

The office door opened and the temp came in with a pile of mail and left it on his desk, giving him a shy smile. Tony and Frank had never employed a full-time secretary in the last few years because temps were easier to get rid of and weren't interested in anybody's business but their own. When you had staff who became part of your life at work, they knew about all your clients and all your dirty secrets, and that made them dangerous. Temps were in and out, passing through on the way to better things or just churning out a few hours for extra cash. They didn't need to know what file was what and where anything was kept. They just typed the letters and clocked off.

He opened a couple of letters, one or two from the Scottish Refugee Council informing him of the status of some asylum-seeker clients. He placed the letters in a wire tray. The junk mail he didn't even open. He was about to throw anything he didn't recognise into the bin, when he came to a large brown envelope marked 'photographs' in black felt pen. Curious, he slid his finger across and opened it, stuck his hand in and pulled out what felt like a photograph.

He only got it out half way, then dropped it on his desk as though it had just bitten him.

'Oh fuck!' he said. 'Oh fuck, no.'

His chest felt tight, and a flush rose from his toes to the roots of his hair, making his head pound. He lifted the envelope with trembling fingers and began to ease the photograph out. The wispy blonde hair and the gap-tooth smile that lit up his life: his daughter, Louise. He had to put the snapshot down on the desk because his trembling hands couldn't hold it.

'Oh fucking hell.' His hand went to his mouth.

It was obvious the picture had been taken by someone opposite the school gates as the kids were coming out. There were other kids in the picture, but the way it had been blown up, Frank could only glimpse them. Whoever had done this had pulled up the picture of Louise for effect. He looked in the envelope for a message, but there was nothing. Before he even got time to think what he was going to say, he had already rung his home number.

'Sally,' he said when he heard his wife's voice.

'Where the hell have you been, Frank? What the fuck do you think this is?'

'I'm sorry, Sally, I'm really sorry.' He could feel the tremor in his voice.

'Sorry, Frank? Sorry's not enough. You said that last week when you didn't come home. I was on the verge of phoning the police when I couldn't get hold of you on the mobile.' Her voice was shrill in his fragile ears. 'I've just about had it with this, Frank. I've told you before, I don't need this any more. No. Actually, Frank, I don't want it any more. I don't want this for Louise.'

'I'm sorry, Sally. Listen, where *is* Louise?' His throat tightened with emotion.

'What do you mean, where is Louise? Christ, Frank, are you still pissed? You've got a bloody problem, you have. Louise is in school. Where do you think she is at this time of the day?'

He breathed a sigh of relief. 'Did you take her, Sally? Did you see her go in?'

'What? What do you mean, did I see her go in? She got out of the car and went in the way she always does. You take her most days, you know the drill. Why are you asking a stupid question like that?'

'Nothing,' Frank said quickly. 'I . . . I just hate missing the school run. I love taking her in the mornings and listening to her patter.' He put his hand over the receiver and uttered a desperate 'Oh God' to himself.

'What?'

'Nothing Sally. Nothing. I'm just so . . . so down about Tony. I feel my life has almost stood still since this happened.'

'Look, Frank,' she said, her voice a little softer. 'I know you're struggling with what happened to Tony. I know he was your best friend and your partner at work for years. But we are your family, Frank. Get your priorities right.' She paused. 'Get them right, Frank, or lose them.'

'Yes,' he said sheepishly. 'I'm sorry. Things are going to change, Sally. I promise.' His mobile rang, and his stomach dropped when he saw the name on the screen.

'Look, I've got a call coming in. I'll see you tonight.' He put the phone down and lifted his mobile.

'Al.' Frank said, his heart thumping in his chest.

'Frankie boy. You all right?'

'Yeah . . . well, bit rough, actually. Overdid the drink last night.'

'Aye. I heard you were down in the club with a few mates.'

'All got a bit late.'

'You want to watch that, Frank,' Al said, slowly. 'After all, you're a family man aren't you. It's a daughter you've got, isn't it.'

Frank felt sick. With effort he managed a 'yes'.

'Lovely wee thing, I'm told. About ten is she?'

'Nearly eleven.' He thought he was going to burst into tears.

'Well, Frankie boy. You want to look after a wee beauty like that. You want to give her the best don't you, Frank? A girl always loves her daddy.'

Silence.

'Listen mate, you know the score. You need to get some of your clients off your list. We need some spare parts. Get my drift? Get it sorted, Frank. I've got too much on my plate to think about people not pulling their weight. Just get it done.' He hung up.

Frank put the mobile down and picked up the photograph of Louise. Suddenly his mind was flooded with images of his little girl. He remembered her first steps, how he taught her to swim on holiday in Portugal, how she still climbed on top of him on his chair at night and cuddled into him. Tears stung his eyes.

'Oh Christ,' he said, sniffing, afraid to let the floodgates open. He got up and went across to the safe in the corner and pulled out the file. He sat back down and went through the papers, reading backgrounds, establishing how long people had been here, who was with them, who they had back home in whatever country they had fled from.

He came across a couple of refugees that looked perfect. One was in his twenties, from Somalia. He checked the background again and rang the mobile number that was on the list and a voice answered. Frank told him to come to the office, that he had some part-time work for him. The Somali man sounded really pleased. Frank put the phone down and looked at his daughter's picture. He did the same with another refugee, a woman from Afghanistan. Then he made another call. This time to Al. He had no choice.

Rosie and Mickey Kavanagh sat in semi-darkness in the corner of La Lanterna restaurant, sipping wine, deep in conversation. Rosie glanced around, thinking anyone who didn't know them would have assumed they were a couple out for a romantic candlelit dinner because they looked so easy in each other's company. Though if diners at the nearby tables had eavesdropped, they'd have found the conversation was far from romantic.

Rosie covered her half-empty glass of wine to stop Mickey filling it up. She knew she could never keep up with him in the red wine stakes, so she wasn't about to try. Apart from anything else, she had a lot of work to do in the next few weeks and getting wellied with Mickey wasn't an option.

'You know what, Rosie,' Mickey took a long, slow drink, his eyes twinkling. 'You're looking a million dollars. What's going on? You in love or something?'

Rosie gave a little laugh. 'Don't ask, Mickey. You know my life. Always the complications.'

'Well, something's agreeing with you. Whatever it is, hold onto it.'

Rosie raised her eyebrows indignantly. 'Oh, cheers Mickey.' She lifted her glass. 'So are you trying to tell me that all the time you've known me I look like shit or something?'

'I was paying you a compliment,' he shrugged.

'Well you need to go to charm school.'

Mickey smiled. 'No, you know what I mean, Rosie. Sometimes you've looked a bit wrecked. I don't mean that in a bad way. I mean you've always been easy on the eye.'

Rosie put her hand up. 'I think we might change the subject, pet. You're digging a hole for yourself. If I look wrecked when I'm with you, it's probably because I've been trying to keep up with you at the drink.' She laughed. 'Anyway, enough of that. Talk to me, Mickey, about this Milosh duker.'

The waiter arrived with the food and set it down. Before Mickey started to talk he sliced off a chunk of lasagne and shoved it in his mouth.

'Christ, that's burning!' He gulped some wine.

'That's the idea, eejit,' Rosie giggled. 'It's just out the bloody oven.'

Mickey put down the fork. 'Okay, Rosie,' he said, lowering his voice, 'here's the lowdown. This Milosh guy, as I said to you on the phone, he's a Serbian. His real name is Boris Raznatovic. Captain Boris Raznatovic, to give him his correct title – or at least that's who they think he is. In fact, they're more or less sure that's who he is. He was a soldier in the Serbian army, and a big player in the siege of Sarajevo during the Bosnian war and some pretty sickening stuff that went on after that. He was right in there at the forefront when they were shelling the towns and villages, getting rid of all the Muslims.

You know the story. You were there for a while, were you not?'

'Briefly,' Rosie said. 'I wasn't there long. It was an aid convoy I went on, and to be honest we didn't get to see much of the conflict. Just getting food and help to people. Kind of in and out.'

'Yeah, but you know what they were doing. The ethnic cleansing.'

'Of course. It was awful. Villages and towns just cleaned out, and all those people just going missing. The time I was there was in the aftermath of Srebrenica. It was heartbreaking.'

Mickey chanced another forkful of lasagne and washed it down with wine. 'Good scran in here by the way.'

Rosie nodded. 'Go on, Mickey.'

'So,' he said. 'He's on the run. Raznatovic is a war criminal.'

'Christ!' Rosie could see that splashed all over the front page.

'Yep,' Mickey continued, 'there are loads of them. We always only hear about the main players, the ones who were running the show, but the authorities are still looking for dozens, maybe even more, of Serb soldiers who burned and mutilated and massacred their way through places. Loads of them have just disappeared off the radar screen. Same way the Nazi soldiers did after the war. But some of the things these Serbs did – Christ almighty!'

'I know,' Rosie said. 'It was a terrible time. Even neighbours turning on each other. I wonder if they even knew the things they were capable of doing to each other before the Bosnian war started.'

'Yeah,' Mickey said. 'Anyway, this Boris Raznatovic. He's from some village near Sarajevo and is actually a qualified doctor. But according to my pal down at Scotland Yard, he was corrupt for years, doing deals with different government bodies and organisations. Always on the make. You know what these communist countries are like – everyone equal but some more equal than others. Well, he was part of that web of corrupt officials.'

'So he joined up when the war was looming?'

'He got involved in this political party, the Serbian National Liberation. They were set up after Tito to try to establish a greater Serbia. It's just the Nazis under a different name though.'

'Exactly,' Rosie said between mouthfuls of food. 'In some cases the Serbs were even worse than the Nazis.'

Mickey nodded and ate his lasagne. He tore off a chunk of garlic bread and scoffed it, dabbing his mouth with his napkin.

'So what happened to him? Did he just do a runner after the peace broke out?'

'Looks like it,' Mickey said. 'My mate tells me he seemed to disappear just before the end of it. They don't know where he went, but it's looking like at some stage he just pretended he was a Bosnian Muslim and managed to get out of the country as a refugee. That's how he ended up in London.'

'But you said they *think* that's who he is. How come they don't know for sure? And how come it took so long to come out? He must have been in London by the time they discovered it.'

'I think so. There was so much confusion at the end of the war with families getting reunited and people going back to what was left of their towns and villages. So much emphasis on the peace and chasing the major war criminals who were in charge. It was only as time went on that people who had witnessed things began to tell the stories of the ordinary soldiers who were involved in the atrocities. By that time, a lot of them had gone to ground and most of them have never been caught. They could be anywhere.'

'So did someone tip him off that they were on to him? Is that why he disappeared?'

'I suppose so. My mate tells me it was quite an embarrassment, and it was all kept quiet. He was actually working in a hospital in London at one point. He wouldn't have a proper practising licence, but he was there, and working as this Milosh Subacic the Bosnian Muslim refugee. So they'd make use of him as a doctor, particularly with the short staffing. And apparently he also worked as a GP locum, because there are very little proper checks done on these people.' Mickey let out a sardonic little laugh. 'Can you imagine that? Bad enough that he didn't have the credentials to work in this country, but how embarrassing for the authorities that a Serbian war criminal is out visiting old ladies or children who take ill in the middle of the night.'

'Jesus. Does nobody really make detailed checks on these things?'

'Evidently not. Maybe he got some documents forged. Don't know really.'

'So what happened to him?'

Mickey shrugged. 'Nobody knows. He just disappeared and they tried to track him, but the trail went cold very quickly. Absolutely nothing. Now you suddenly come along and mention his name.' He cocked his head to the side. 'By the way, you haven't told me why?'

'I know, Mick. I haven't.' She looked at him pleadingly. 'And I know you'll bear with me on this, because you know what it's like when you're on an investigation. I want a chance to look into this before I can pass anything on.'

Mickey swigged from his glass. 'No problem, sweetheart. I'm not a cop any more.' He paused. 'But you'd want to be careful if this guy is mixed up with the mob here and he's up to something. You really don't want to be around it. Some things are best left to the cops, Rosie.'

'I know,' Rosie sighed, 'but not yet, Mickey. Not yet. And anyway, what exactly are *they* doing about trying to find him now? Have they just left it because the trail went cold?'

'I don't know, I'm still digging around. Maybe they don't want to make a noise about hunting him down because they haven't got a clue where he is, and they don't want to look stupid for allowing him to disappear in the first place.'

'Sounds credible.'

'Okay,' he said, lifting the empty bottle. 'Fancy another, or will we go straight to the liqueurs, madam?'

'Let's get some coffee, Mickey. I might have a small brandy, but I've got a busy day.' She smiled at him. 'But hey, don't let me hold you back.'

The waiter appeared at the table.

'Large brandy please ... And for the lady?' Mickey looked at Rosie. 'Two large brandies thank you.' He gave her a mischievous grin.

CHAPTER 15

'You do realise we could be following a delivery of Scotch pies to a supermarket in England,' Matt said, as they crossed the border.

Rosie and Matt had been heading south on the motorway for nearly two hours, following the refrigerated van at a safe distance. It had been a spur of the moment decision, made as they watched a crate of metal containers being loaded into the truck. From their vantage point in the farm road nearby, they decided that the only way to find out where this thing was going was to follow it.

Rosie looked out at the sun streaming down onto the open fields. 'At least we've got a nice day for it.' She smiled at Matt.

'Maybe we'll go to Blackpool. Get a shot on the big dipper,' said Matt, taking a swig from a bottle of Coke.

'Great idea.' Rosie opened a packet of crisps and offered him the bag. 'But my gut feeling,' she said, 'tells me we're doing the right thing. Let's just see where it takes us. Remember, Jan said that Tam Logan took the stuff to

Manchester and that's where the action was. So let's hope that's where we're headed.'

'I'm cool with that, Rosie.' He glanced at her. 'So tell me. You were saying you'd researched this Serbian character, this Ratzarsovic or whatever he's called.'

'Raznatovic.' Rosie smiled.

She told him what she found through the internet and the newspaper cuttings she'd spent the day trawling through.

Raznatovic had been a captain in the Serb army during the early unrest after Tito died. His name was mentioned as one of the commanders in a massacre at a place called Paklenik Gorge in the north of Bosnia. Back in June 1991, at least fifty Bosnians were executed by Serb soldiers and thrown down the four hundred-foot ravine at Paklenik. The gorge was known to this day as Hell. Raznatovic's name also cropped up during the lengthy siege of Sarajevo, and again in the massacre at Srebrenica – a name that would haunt the Balkans for generations to come. When Rosie had been over there, she had spoken to the families of people who had lost sons and fathers – marched away to be executed.

When she'd told McGuire initially about Milosh he was dumbfounded. But once she relayed what she'd found in her research, he was like a dog with a bone. He wanted to put someone in to work with her, help run the story to ground, but Rosie had convinced him that if any information leaked out it would put everyone in danger. He'd stressed that she had to be ultra-careful. She knew better than to tell him they were now following a refrigerated van from the slaughterhouse. She was hoping McGuire didn't phone her any time soon to tell her to pop in and see him.

'Christ, Rosie,' Matt said. 'That's amazing stuff. I hope we get to nail this bastard.'

'You and me both.'

'Look,' Matt said suddenly. 'They're pulling into a motorway caff. We'll go with them.'

'Good,' Rosie said. 'That'll give us a chance to have a closer look at who's who. These places are always really busy and nobody even looks at each other.'

They parked the car far enough away from the refrigerated van, and watched as the guys jumped out and headed inside.

'Let's go,' Rosie opened her door. 'Just in case we can hear anything they say to each other.'

They sat at a table close enough to the two men, but in a busy enough area so they wouldn't be noticed. They could hear the conversation, but it was mostly about football. When Rosie and Matt finished their coffee they went out to their car and waited for the men. When they arrived at their van, they followed them back onto the M6.

They were about thirty miles from the outskirts of Manchester when the van indicated it was leaving the motorway. Matt followed, three cars behind. They drove onto a smaller road and through a town centre that looked a little run-down, then onto the edge and past an industrial estate. A couple of miles up the road there was a sign for PD Pharmaceuticals.

Matt glanced at Rosie. 'Game on, I'd say.'

'You think so?' Rosie felt a little buzz of adrenalin. 'Tell you what though. If they go in here, then it opens up a whole new ball game, Matt. This isn't a disused slaughterhouse in the middle of nowhere. If they're taking what we think they're taking in *there*, then that's totally another story.' Rosie was already dialling the number of the library back at the office.

'Christ.' Matt said. 'They're going in here.'

Rosie spoke to the librarian and asked her to check the name of the company to see what came up. They told her they'd phone her back in five minutes. Matt pulled the car up a little away from the entrance and they sat watching as the van approached the security barrier at the gatehouse and waited for it to be raised.

'It's some size of a place,' Matt said.

Outside the plant a huge sign with the company name was on a billboard, but nothing else. No information about what they made or what went on here. That wasn't unusual in itself, because many of these giant pharmaceutical companies made several brand-name drugs for various retail companies. The building looked like it was spread as far as the eye could see, and most of it appeared to have been built in recent years. The car park was full and, as they sat, every now and again a van with the company name would come out of the gate and head away.

Rosie's mobile rang. 'What kind of research?' Rosie was asking as she took notes. 'Right . . . right. When was that? . . . How much? . . . Okay. Can you stick all that into my email address so I can have a better look? Thanks, Joanne.'

'Hurry up Rosie, I'm getting excited here,' Matt said.

'Okay, here's the deal.' Rosie flicked the pages of her notebook. 'PD Pharmaceuticals is a multinational drug company, and they make principally heart and blood pressure pills – beta blockers, that kind of thing – for hypertension. They're a German company, but only came here three years ago. And guess what Matt?' Rosie gave him a look. 'They were given a government grant to come here and create jobs. Millions of pounds they got and, even better, you remember the deposed Environment Secretary Tim Hayman? Who quit after getting his student researcher pregnant? Well, he's only a member of the bloody board of directors. Apparently only in some advisory capacity, but I like the sound of that all right.'

'Beauty! Me too.'

'Other thing is, there were protests from time to time from this animal rights mob because they do tests on animals in here. The cuttings say they've got quite a menagerie and that's who they test their heart pills on. Monkeys, rabbits and stuff. Library said there's a lot of stuff on them.'

'So what the fuck is a refrigerated van coming from that slaughterhouse in Glasgow doing here?'

Rosie shook her head. 'Christ knows, Matt. I don't know how we're going to find that out. Maybe the place is so vast there's a little corner of it they don't know what's happening, but I'd doubt it.'

'You don't think a company as big as this could be

involved in something like trading body tissue, do you? That would be just mental. Why would they do that?'

'I don't know. You'd think it would be crazy and you'd have to ask why they'd even get involved in it. There must be lots of scrutiny of these places by government bodies.'

'Exactly,' Matt said.

'Unless there's some rogue element involved in this and nobody at the top of the tree knows. It's anybody's guess.'

They watched as the barrier lifted and the van went in and headed along the road.

'Let's just drive around the edge of the place, see if we can get any idea where this van is going. It's all pretty open.'

They drove around the perimeter of the plant, and they could still see the van heading for what looked like the final set of buildings, slightly away from the main body of the plant.

'Just keep driving,' Rosie said. 'As far as we can go.'

They did, and when they got to what looked like the back of the plant, to their surprise the wire gates were open.

'I think we just got lucky, Rosie.'

'Don't, Matt,' Rosie said. 'There'll be CCTV. Someone will spot us.'

'But look,' he said, pointing up to the perimeter fence. 'There's nothing. This place is at the very edge of the plant. Maybe it's where they keep the animals or something. It's not like the other buildings.'

'But it's still part of it, Matt. If we get caught, we're in trouble. They might get the cops.'

'Come on, let's take a chance. We'll be in and out. There's a few cars up the road a bit. Let's park there, then maybe I can see if this van comes— Look, it's coming.'

'Well, okay.' Rosie couldn't resist it.

They drove inside the gate and parked the car about a couple of hundred yards away from the buildings where the van was now stopping. Quickly, Matt got his camera out and stuck a long lens on. He started firing off pictures as the men got out of the van. As they did, two other men came from one of the buildings. They chatted briefly with the first two, then opened the back door. They brought out the crate with the containers, and, when it was unloaded, the van men shook hands with the other two, who then disappeared into the building. The first two got back into their van and drove off.

'Got some good shots there. It looked like several smaller containers, aluminium, and one slightly bigger one. Not a lot of stuff though to come all the way down here.'

'No,' Rosie said. 'This might be a central place where they operate from and they get stuff from other areas. Jan said London and Liverpool. But the whole thing about the body-tissue market anyway is that something as simple as an elbow or an inner ear is sliced into hundreds of tiny bits and can be sold for research. You're talking minute fragments here that are either used for research or for operations. That's what makes it so lucrative, because you can make so much money from a relatively small amount of tissue. I read on the internet you can get six hundred dollars for an elbow.'

'You're kidding. For an elbow?'

'Yep.'

'Imagine what you'd get for a set of bollocks.' He put one hand protectively between his legs.

'Indeed. Especially a pair that have hardly been used.' Rosie chuckled.

The sudden loud thump on the roof of the car made them jump.

'Shit! What the fuck?' Matt looked at Rosie.

Then the fist banged on Matt's window.

'Oh Christ!' Rosie's stomach turned over.

'Shit, Rosie. We're nicked.'

The burly security man bent down and his face was at the window.

'Open the window. Now, please.'

Matt looked at Rosie.

'Open it, Matt. No choice.'

As Matt slowly rolled down the window they could hear garbled voices on the guy's walkie-talkie.

Rosie leaned across and attempted a perplexed expression.

'Sorry, but I think we've taken a wrong turn. Can you help us? We were looking for the main gate, but I think we've come up the back way by mistake. Is there a main entrance?'

'Who you looking for?' The guy stood back. 'Can you get out of the car please?'

'Of course,' Rosie said, opening the door. She jumped

out and quickly went around to the driver's side as Matt slowly got out. The security man flicked him a derisory glance. Matt gave him a 'sorry mate' shrug, and Rosie put her hands up apologetically. The security man towered above her, built like a superhero, all chiselled jaw and broad shoulders. And not unattractive.

'Thank goodness we met you.' Rosie attempted a bit of breathless charm. 'We might have ended up driving around for ages. These places are so *big*.' She gave Matt a frustrated look. 'I told you this was too quiet to be the main gate.'

Matt looked suitably reprimanded.

'What are you looking for?' He seemed to soften a little. 'You Jocks?'

'Yeah,' Rosie smiled weakly. 'We don't get out much.'

The big man unfolded his arms. 'So who you looking for?'

'Quality control,' Rosie said. 'I have to pick up some documentation.'

'Medical rep?'

'Yeah,' Rosie heard herself saying, hoping it was the correct answer.

'Well, you're totally at the wrong end of the plant.' He pointed to the gate. 'You have to go out here and follow the fence all the way round and eventually you turn right and you'll see the big sign. Don't know how you missed it.'

'We came in the other way,' Rosie said quickly. 'We got lost after the motorway.' She glowered at Matt.

'You're not as smart as the Scots I knew.' The security

guard flashed her a smile. 'I was in the army with a few Jocks. Mad bastards, but balls of steel.' He stuck out his chest. 'We saw a bit of action we did. Northern Ireland. Was in Bosnia for a while. Some real shit happening over there.'

'Really? Bosnia?' Rosie was encouraged enough to risk a bit of chat. 'It looked awful on the telly. Those poor people.'

'Yeah. Was. Lot of bad things happened.' He stared past Rosie into middle distance.

'How long you been out?'

'Two years. Invalided out in the end. Combat stress they call it.' His eyes grew dark. 'Lost a couple of good mates in Northern Ireland, then Bosnia on top of it just got to me.' He sniffed. 'That stuff changes you.'

Rosie gave him a sympathetic look, wondering why he was telling her all this. He looked lonely enough to talk to anyone.

'Must have been tough. The thing is, a lot of that stress with soldiers just gets forgotten about. I read in the papers that a lot of soldiers just get ditched when they get out. Terrible that. After everything they've given.'

'Too right,' the big man said, shaking his head. 'And after all that fighting and stuff, you end up working in a shitty job like this. Directing fucking traffic.'

Rosie let the silence hang a little. 'So is this the area you work in all the time?' She threw the line out in the hope he would grasp it.

'Not all the time. It gets rotated. But I end up here a lot.' He jerked his head in the direction of the buildings where the men had dropped their boxes off. 'They keep animals and stuff in there for their experiments. And you've to watch this gate a lot, because we get them animal rights geezers turning up, trying to break in. A couple of them chained themselves to the railings last year. Daft, tree-hugging bastards.'

Rosie laughed. She was always amazed at how much information people just volunteered without thinking.

'Yeah, a lot of them are nutters.' She glanced at the buildings. 'So what do they keep in there? Mice and rats?'

'Yeah. But more than that. Monkeys. Chimps. But it's mostly rabbits and rats. They test the drugs on them. Nobody gets to go inside. All top secret. But I heard they do all sorts of shit to the animals.'

'Yeah,' Rosie said. 'It's all very controversial stuff. No wonder it's top secret. You ever been in there?'

'Nah. It wouldn't shock me though. I've seen a bit of shit in my day.'

'I bet the papers would pay plenty for a picture inside that place.' Rosie could feel Matt staring at her in disbelief.

The big man laughed. 'Yeah, you're not kidding. Don't think me and the boys haven't talked about it.'

His walkie-talkie buzzed, and gravelly voices could be heard. He put it to his mouth and spoke into it, saying he was on his way. 'I need to go, mate.' He looked almost reluctant. 'But good talking to, you, I like the Jocks. Right. You know where you're going now, don't you?'

'Yes, thanks for your help ... er ... ?' Rosie gave him an enquiring look.

'Eddie,' he said, stretching out a hand. 'Used to be Lance Corporal Barnsley.' He shrugged. 'In another life.'

'Great to meet you, Eddie. I'm Rosie. Thanks again for your help.' She squeezed his hand. 'Good luck to you, Eddie.'

He let go of her hand and walked away, then after a few yards he turned around to face them and gave a half salute and a smile.

'Christ,' Matt said. 'Quality control? You are some chancer, Gilmour. I'll give you that. A Grade A chancer.' He shook his head and opened the driver's door. 'Come on. Let's GTF before he remembers he didn't even ask for your ID.'

Rosie's mobile rang as she opened the car door, and her eyes popped.

'Emir?'

'Rosie. It is Emir.'

He sounded breathless.

'Christ man. Where are you? I've been looking for you for days.'

'I had to run, Rosie. They came for me. Can I see you?'

'Of course, Emir. I'm on my way up from England.' She looked at her watch. It was already two in the afternoon. 'I can meet you tonight. Same place as last time? Around seven?'

'Okay. I be there.' The line went dead.

CHAPTER 16

From the window of Starbucks, Rosie sat sipping a latte, her eyes darting all across the busy concourse at Central Station. She felt suspicious of anyone who so much as looked in her direction. The paranoia was beginning to kick in, and she'd been looking over her shoulder all the time as she'd walked up from the office for her meeting with Emir. They'd come for him, he'd told her on the phone. So it was a stick-on they were still looking for him.

The phone call from Don as she and Matt drove up from Manchester hadn't helped. They'd found a corpse in a burnt-out car earlier in the morning, and they were almost certain it was Tam Logan. The charred remains were beyond recognition and they were checking dental records. But engraved jewellery taken from what was left of the body suggested it was Tam. The post-mortem was underway, Don told her, but the pathologist had given them an early heads-up that there was a bullet wound to the chest. Rosie felt a pang of sympathy as she remembered Jan Logan's angry tears a few days ago when they spoke. She wondered if they'd knocked on her door yet in Spain to give her the news she already knew – that her man was dead. Poor Jan, her children without a father, even a half-wit no-use bastard of a father like Tam. In another life, with a better start, things could have been different for a feisty, bright woman who could clearly hold her own, but you didn't get a lot of choices growing up in Springburn. Too often the only way out of there was to get deeper into the clutches of the scumbags and gangsters who ran the show.

Rosie jumped nervously as a waiter clearing tables accidentally nudged her in the passing. Jesus. She needed to calm down. She rubbed her face and took a deep breath, letting it out slowly, the way she'd learned in the yoga class. But it would take more than deep breathing and yoga chants to get her through this story. She almost smiled to herself at the thought. Things were definitely beginning to unravel though. If they'd shot Tam Logan and burned his body, that meant they were trying to close down all the doors. She wondered just how Frank Paton and Tony Murphy had featured in all of this. If what Tanya had told her was correct, then they were all over this, providing refugees for the chop. It was almost unthinkable that two leading Glasgow lawyers could be doing this. And it had all become too much for Tony Murphy. Rosie thought of Frank Paton and what must be going on in his head right now. She'd have to find a way to get to him. She tried another deep breath, but it was interrupted, as she saw Emir walk through the doorway and head towards her. His face was a mask of grey.

'Emir.' Rosie squeezed his arm and resisted the urge to hug him.

'Thank you to seeing me, Rosie,' Emir said, his eyes moistening a little. He swallowed and Rosie saw his chin tremble as he fought back tears.

'Let me get you a coffee, Emir. Go and get a seat over in that table in the corner.' She squeezed his arm again. 'You'll be all right.'

He crossed the floor and sat in the booth. Rosie watched him from the counter as he sat with his head in his hands.

'Here,' she said, returning to the table with a coffee and a sandwich which she opened and handed to him.

'Thank you. I am very hungry. No food since yesterday. No money. I sleep in a field.' He bit off a huge chunk of the sandwich and took a mouthful of steaming coffee, wincing as it burned him. He wiped his mouth and took another bite.

Rosie caught a whiff of days'-old sweat and dirty clothes from him. She waited until he had eaten the sandwich before she spoke.

'So, Emir,' – she lowered her voice to almost a whisper. 'You look shattered. I was really worried when you disappeared. I went to your house and neighbours told me they hadn't seen you since that morning you were with me. Tell me what happened.'

He nodded, swallowing the last of the sandwich and taking a swig of coffee.

'I tried to run, Rosie. They came to kill me.' He ran a trembling hand across his face.

'They came to your house?'

'When I go into my house the same morning I see they are there already. They jump out on me. Two of them. One cut me with the knife. Stab me.' He rolled up his shirt, caked with hard blood and sticking to an angry, swollen wound. He grimaced in pain.

'It's poisoned,' Rosie looked at the congealed blood and tender flesh. 'You need to get this cleaned and dressed. You should have had an injection or something, Emir. Christ!' She shook her head.

'No time to think, Rosie. I fought them, the two of them, in my house. I hit one with a bottle and the other I stabbed with the knife I took off him. Then I ran from my flat and into the lift.'

'God almighty!'

Emir nodded. 'But the lift stop at every floor. And when it come to the ground and the door open, they are waiting for me. Don't know, maybe they come down the stairs. Three more people were in the lift and they see everything, but nobody help me. The men are dragging me out and punching me. They take me to the car and put me in the boot. I see people watching, but nobody help me.' He shrugged and shook his head. 'Like if this is normal in Glasgow? I don't know.'

Rosie sighed. 'Not normal, Emir, but not that uncommon. Gangsters. Lot of areas are all run by drug dealers, so people would be too afraid to interfere.'

'Or maybe they don't care. I am just refugee. A foreigner.' He looked down at the table.

Rosie felt ashamed. He was right. The people who stood by may have stood by anyway, because you don't walk into another man's fight in the middle of a housing estate unless you want your face slashed. But most of them probably gave less of a damn if it was a refugee getting battered.

'So what happened then?'

'They take me to the same place. Remember I told you? The place out of Glasgow. As soon as I am on the road, I know where I am going. It is where they took Jetmir and me that day.'

'Then what?'

'Nothing. They drag me from the boot and put me in a room in the place and left me there. I think the place ... the building ... look like where they kill the animals. We have places like that in Kosovo, where farmers are taking their animals for killing and selling.'

'It's called an abattoir here, Emir. Or a slaughterhouse.'

He nodded. 'Okay. So I am there all day. They hit me on the head with a stick and knock me out, and leave me there. When I wake up later, I can hear outside them doing things, but I don't know what they do. I hear machines like saws and hammering. Then I see from the window that it is getting dark and there is no sound outside. I hear cars starting the engines and driving away. Then is very quiet, and very dark.'

'So how did you get out?'

'In the room I saw a metal thing. Like a pole. Maybe they didn't see it. So I found it in the dark and when I am sure everything is quiet, I use it to break open the door from the side. It worked.' He shook his head and looked bemused. 'I was surprised. Suddenly I am out there, I am free. I am in this big room like in a kitchen, or maybe a butcher place with the long metal ... I do not know the word. But where the butcher chop things.'

'Benches?' Rosie said.

'Yes. I think benches.'

Rosie pictured the scene.

'That's unbelievable, Emir.'

'Yes,' he said, 'but I am also frightened because in one minute somebody maybe come in. But there is no noise. Just quiet and dark.'

'So what did you do then?'

'I find my way along the wall and look for the door. But it is locked. Big heavy door and I cannot open, even with the metal pole. So still I am trapped. I cannot see anything because it is so dark.' He shrugged and sighed. 'So I wait until it is getting light. Then I see from the window maybe I can climb out.'

'You are very lucky, Emir.'

'Yes,' he nodded. 'But when the light comes ...' His eyes grew dark. 'Not so lucky.'

Rosie sat forward.

'What happened?'

'In the light, I can see things on the table. Blood and skin, I think. Not animal skin. Human skin. I saw like bits of the brain. Maybe animal brain, or human, I don't know. But it was brain, because my friend in Kosovo's brother was a butcher. I saw before the brain of a sheep.'

Rosie felt a clutch in her stomach.

'You see anything else, Emir?'

He nodded, swallowing. Then he shook his head, and fell silent.

'What, Emir? What did you see?'

He took a deep breath. 'In a corner, there is like a big bin. The cover is on it, but the bin is full. I was ... er ... curi? Curis?' He screwed up his eyes. 'I forget how you say the word.'

'Curious.' Rosie said.

'Yes. Curious.' He paused. 'But I wish I didn't look.'

'Why? What did you see?'

Emir puffed his cheeks out.

'Pieces,' he said, shaking his head. 'Pieces from bodies. Human. For sure. A piece of a foot. Bones. But not of animals. Bones with no flesh – like the leg here.' He pointed to his shin. 'I saw one foot.' He shook his head. 'They are killing people and cutting them up in that place. My friend Jetmir. They took him there. I know I will never see him again.' Tears came to his eyes. 'Who are these people, Rosie, who do this? Why?'

They sat in silence, Rosie watching him weeping softly and wiping his nose with the sleeve of his shirt. She reached across and touched his hand, then held it tightly while he wept.

Eventually, he spoke. 'Sorry, Rosie. I am so sad. Jetmir and me are so close friends since children. I miss him. I am so alone now and I am frightened.'

'You're not alone, Emir.' Rosie said, feeling a catch in her throat. 'I will help you. I promise you.'

He looked at her and then at the table.

'So,' he sighed. 'I climb out of the window and I run and keep on running until I am far away from that place. I slept in a field and sometimes at night in an old building, and walk in the daytime back to the city.'

Rosie watched him as he stared into space. She knew she should phone Don immediately and ask him to come and get Emir and protect him. But right now that's not what he needed. Right now, he needed some care, a bath and some sleep.

'Come on, Emir. Let's go and get your wound fixed up.' Rosie stood up.

'Where are we going?'

'To my house,' she said, knowing she was breaking every rule in the book. 'We'll deal with everything tomorrow. Come on. Let's go.'

CHAPTER 17

It was after eleven by the time Tanya came through the revolving door of the Holiday Inn and outside onto the forecourt. She glanced across at the taxi rank, then up at the clear night sky, brightened by a new moon. She stood breathing in the warm night air, trying to shake off the images of the last hour in the third-floor hotel room. Another sleazy businessman in transit, with too much money and time on his hands, sampling the discreet delights the city had to offer if you dropped the concierge at the front desk a bung for his trouble. She put her hand inside her shoulder bag and touched the notes she'd stuffed there on her way from his bedroom to the lift. He'd paid her an extra twenty for being so understanding after he'd taken so long to get an erection that Tanya had just about given up on him. She decided to walk to the Merchant City rather than spend the money on a taxi. She was looking forward to a long hot shower.

It was only after she crossed George Square and headed towards Ingram Street that she started to feel a little uneasy. No real reason for it – just a sensation of panicky edginess. She looked over her shoulder just in case anyone was following her, but there was nothing, only the odd car passing or stopped at the traffic lights – no different from any mid-week night when she might have been heading home. The streets grew quieter the further away she went from the city centre, then deserted, and more silent by the time she reached St Andrew's Square. She quickened her step, wishing now she'd taken a cab. By the time she got to the front door of her apartment block, she was a little out of breath and cursed as she dropped her keys on the ground. She bent down to pick them up. Then her blood ran cold.

'Tanya.'

It was Josef's hand on her shoulder. She stood up slowly, shock running through her as she turned to face him.

'Josef.' Her throat felt tight. She braced herself for him to strike her.

'Please, Tanya.' He put his hand out to touch her hair and she flinched. 'Please. Don't be afraid.'

Tanya felt her knees shaking. She swallowed, and opened her mouth to speak, but nothing came out.

'Please, Tanya,' Josef touched her face gently. 'I'm sorry. I'm so, so sorry.'

Tanya could smell the alcohol and cigarettes on his breath. She looked up at his face, unshaven, and his hair dishevelled. His eyes softened, and somewhere behind them, she thought she could see the man he once was when they first met in London in what now seemed like another life.

'What do you want, Josef?' she managed to say.

'My Tanya.' He whispered, shaking his head. 'My beautiful Tanya.' He stroked her face with the back of his fingers. 'Please forgive me.'

'How do you know where I live?' She turned her head away from him.

'I followed you.'

'You followed me. Tonight?'

He nodded slowly, fixing her with his gaze.

'Why? What do you want?'

'Please Tanya. I want to say I'm sorry. To prove to you I'm changed.' He stepped a little closer to her, almost pinning her back to the door.

'You . . . you raped me.' She felt trapped.

'Please Tanya. Please forgive me. I have been in hell since that day. I want to die. I cannot live without you.'

She shook her head, sniffing.

'No, Josef. It's over.'

She watched as he started to cry. Tears rolling down his face.

'Please, Tanya. Let me come in. Please. Just let me talk to you. That's all. Just to talk. Don't leave me out here.'

They stood for a moment, with only the sound of their own breathing. A couple strolled past them and into the apartment block next door.

'Okay,' Tanya looked at him coldly. 'You can come in just to talk. But we are finished, Josef. You understand?'

He nodded.

She turned around, put the key into the lock with trembling fingers, then opened the door and went inside.

Josef followed her in, and they climbed the two storeys to her door.

Tanya put the kettle on, watching from the corner of her eye as Josef glanced around him.

'Is a good place here, Tanya.' He licked his lips. 'Better than where we were.' He looked at her. 'I am still there, but not for long. Is too much money.'

'Then you should find yourself a job, Josef. That's what everyone else does.'

He sat down quietly, and Tanya could sense him watching her as she made coffee. She crossed from the small kitchen area and handed him a cup, sitting on the chair opposite him and lighting a cigarette. He reached over and took one from her packet without asking her.

'You have a good job these days, Tanya.' His expression was blank.

'If you've been following me, then you know.' She drew on her cigarette and inhaled deeply, shooting him a defiant look.

Her stomach was in knots. She'd made a mistake inviting him in. At least he was calm so far, but she knew he could flip at any minute. She desperately wanted to pour herself a vodka to settle her nerves, but she didn't dare because she couldn't risk giving him any more alcohol.

'I know you are working again. I saw you go into the hotel tonight and come out later.' He looked at the floor, then at Tanya. 'You are with the escort agency again?'

She nodded, saying nothing. They sat in silence, the air heavy with tension.

'You should go now, Josef,' Tanya said. 'I'm tired. I want to go to bed. I have to work in the office in the morning at eight.'

Josef said nothing, but he didn't move. She got up and went into the kitchen.

'Please, Josef. I think you should go. We have nothing to talk about. I want to be alone.' She turned to face him.

Josef didn't speak, but Tanya could see in his eyes the rising anger. Her legs felt weak. She leaned against the worktop for support. He got up and came towards her.

'Tanya,' he looked at the floor hesitantly, then at her. 'I need some money. I have nothing. You can see that. Can you give me some money?'

Tanya shook her head. She saw his fists clench at his side.

'Josef. I need my money.' She lifted her bag, and rummaged inside it. 'I can give you twenty pounds. But that is all. Then you must go.' She brought out a twenty-pound note and held it out to him.

He looked at it and smirked.

'Twenty pounds? You were in the hotel for over an hour. It must have been more than a blow job!' He snorted.

'Take it.' She thrust the money at him. 'Take it and go.'

In a flash, he grabbed her handbag. A menacing sneer broke over his face as Tanya reached for the bag, tried to wrest it from him. He jerked his hand back.

'Give me my bag.'

'Shut up!' he said, his eyes blazing. He stuck his hand into the bag.

He pulled out a wad of notes and made a soft whistling noise.

'You have been a busy little whore. Haven't you.'

He caught hold of Tanya's wrist and twisted it as she reached out and tried to snatch the money.

'Stop it. You're hurting me.'

Josef pushed her back against the sink, squeezing her wrist.

'You're going to break it, Josef. Let it go.' Tanya pleaded.

He pushed the money into his pocket, and slapped her face hard. Tanya felt dizzy and her legs buckled a little. She leaned on the worktop for support as he slapped her again.

'You tell me to go find a job. You think what you do is a job? Slut!'

Tanya felt her face burn and blood trickle from her mouth. She blinked, looking at the red rage in Josef's eyes, and as she did so, her hand slid along the worktop to where she kept the knives. As he came towards her, ranting, she grabbed the knife and stabbed him on the shoulder.

'Bitch!' He caught her hand and twisted her arm until the knife dropped. He touched his shoulder where the knife had nicked him. Then he punched her hard on the face. She saw the room sway as she slumped to the floor.

Tanya didn't know how long she'd been out, but when she came to she slowly lifted her head from the floor and saw that it was getting light outside. She rubbed her eyes as she began to focus, and saw that all the drawers in the kitchen units were opened and their contents emptied on the floor. She crawled along the floor, her head pounding, her wrists stiff and swollen. Slowly she got to her feet and went to the sink, splashing water onto her face. She ran her mouth under the tap and spat out blood. She staggered to the living room and saw that all the cupboards were open. He must have ransacked everything looking for her money.

Suddenly her stomach dropped: the letter. She went back into the living room and quickly opened her bag. The money was gone. So was the suicide note to Frank Paton she'd taken from Tony Murphy's desk.

'Oh God, no!' Tanya went into her bedroom and flopped onto the bed. She wept until she drifted off to sleep.

Later in the morning, she got stiffly out of bed and made her way to the kitchen. Her mobile phone was in her jacket pocket. She punched in the number and waited for the answer.

'Rosie. It's Tanya. Please, can you come here? I need to talk to you.'

Across the city Frank Paton was just walking into his office when the phone rang on his desk. He put down his briefcase and lifted the receiver, then walked around his desk and sat down.

'Mr Frank Paton? Can I speak with Mr Frank Paton?'

The foreign accent had to be a refugee. Frank was irritated at having to take the call without knowing who it was and having their file in front of him. He looked at his watch. He was early. The temp secretary wasn't due in for another ten minutes. He would have to deal with it, whoever it was.

'Yes,' he said. 'Frank Paton speaking. Who is this please?'

'It is Josef. The husband of Tanya.'

Frank was surprised. Perhaps he was phoning to tell him Tanya was ill or something and wouldn't be in. He hadn't even noticed when he arrived if she was already upstairs in another area.

'Oh, hello Josef. I don't think Tanya's in yet, if that's who you're looking for.'

'No,' Josef said. 'I want talk with you, Mr Paton.'

'Me? Okay. What's the problem?' There was no answer, though Frank could hear Josef breathing. Bewildered, he said, 'Hello? Josef?'

'I must see you,' answered Josef now. 'I have information. I have something you will want.'

'What?' Frank's mind was thrown into confusion. 'What do you mean Josef?'

Silence again, but for Josef's heavy breathing, which made Frank uneasy. Then Josef spoke. 'I have the letter. To you, from Murphy, the dead man. Your partner.'

The words exploded in Frank's head and he jumped to his feet.

'What are you talking about, Josef?' Frank felt sick.

'You know what I mean. He wrote letter to you before he kill himself. You want I read?'

Frank sat back down, his legs weak. Jesus Christ! He couldn't speak. Josef broke the silence.

'I read letter to you.'

Frank sat with his hand over his mouth as Josef read the letter in his fractured English, stumbling over some of the words. But the content was loud and clear.

'Stop.' Frank said. 'Where did you get this letter?'

'Where do you think?' Josef was sarcastic.

'Listen, you cunt. If you have something that has been stolen from this office you are in big trouble. I make one phone call and you'll be in jail by lunch time.' Frank's face burned.

'So you will call the cops? I don't think so.'

The sneer in Josef's voice put Frank into a blind rage and he gasped for breath. Slow down, he said to himself. Think clearly. He had to get this letter. Fucking Tony and his fucking guilty conscience.

'What do you want?' Frank's tone was measured.

'I want five thousand pounds.'

'*What?*'

'You hear me.' Josef said. 'Cash money. Tomorrow.'

'You're fucking joking.'

'You pay the money, or I give letter to police.'

'If you give the letter to the police, you will get arrested for stealing it.' Frank hoped his voice didn't sound as desperate as he felt.

'I didn't steal it.'

'So who did?' Frank knew the answer before he even said it.

'That is for police to prove,' Josef said. 'But they going to ask you questions first. You want them to ask you questions? I think you are a crook, Mr Paton. You and Mr Murphy. Both crooks. You want police to ask questions?'

Bastard, Frank murmured to himself. The words in the letter rung in his ears – *I told you we should have stopped. See you in hell . . . Tony*. The cops would be all over him like a rash if they got hold of that. Christ! Twenty years at the top of his game and he was being done up like a kipper by some fucking Russian thicko who could hardly write his name. That fucking Tanya. He never trusted her from the start. It was Tony who wanted to give her the job, keys to the office, the lot. He trusted her too much. Now it was all coming into sharp focus in Frank's mind. Tony must have been having an affair with her. He'd even asked him once, when he found the two of them having a laugh together in the office. But Tony always denied it. Tanya must have taken the letters. The bitch.

'Listen,' Frank said. 'I'll meet you somewhere. I need to see the letter.' He wrote down the mobile number that was on his consul.

'You call me when you have the money and we meet. The letter is not a trick, you know that for sure. You meet me, give me five thousand and I give you the letter. Then we say no more. You do this tomorrow, or I go to cops.'

'Wait!' Frank said. But the line was already dead.

CHAPTER 18

It had been two hours since Tanya had called, and Rosie knew by the sound of her voice she was in trouble. She'd wanted to go to her straight away, but she was stuck in her flat wondering what to do with Emir, who was still sound asleep. She finally woke him up and told him to stay in the flat until she got back, when she would call McGuire and talk about bringing in the cops. Emir was very grateful and said he wouldn't leave until she returned.

As she sat in the Argyle Street traffic jam, Rosie's stress levels were picking up the pace. She tapped the steering wheel nervously and glanced at her watch, reflecting on last night's row with TJ. She knew how he would react when she told him she had Emir at her flat, and she considered not telling him at all when he'd called her, suggesting they go for dinner. She decided to be honest and he was predictably furious. He couldn't believe she was being this reckless when she knew the kind of guys who were already after Emir.

'You're asking for trouble,' TJ had said. Then, before he hung up, he added, 'Actually no, Rosie. You're going out of your way to make sure you get trouble. I don't know what to do with you.'

His words had stung Rosie for the rest of the evening while she tried to clean up Emir's wound, make him a meal and give him her spare room for the night. She had much more on her plate right now than a row with TJ, but she was about to phone him when her mobile lit up and vibrated on the passenger seat.

'Gilmour. Where the hell are you?' It was McGuire.

'Oh. Hi Mick. Er, I'm just heading out to see Tanya. Got a call from her this morning, and I think she's in some sort of trouble.'

'Really? Well watch what you're doing. By the way I didn't hear from you all day yesterday. And why the fuck don't you keep in touch? Am I going to have to start tagging you?'

'Sorry, Mick. It all got a bit crazy last night.'

'What did?'

'I'll tell you in a bit. I've got a lot to tell you.'

'So tell me.'

She confessed that she and Matt had driven to Manchester behind a truck loaded with containers from the slaughterhouse. Once he stopped ranting and berating her for going without asking him, she told him about the PD Pharmaceuticals and the checks she'd made on them from library cuttings.

'So, you're not telling me they're involved in the illegal trade of body tissue? Come on, Rosie. Don't tell me you're even thinking about us taking on a bloody multinational. Do you want to give the lawyers a stroke?'

'We're a long way away from that, Mick. But all I'm saying is the stuff they took from the slaughterhouse – whatever it was – they dropped off down at this plant, in an area kind of hidden away from the mainstream operation of the place. I'm told it's the section where they test their drugs on animals. I spoke to a security guard and he said nobody ever gets inside that place and it's all top secret. Maybe it's just possible there *is* something dodgy going on and it's top secret not for the reasons people think, but because of what they're really doing. Or what they're also doing . . . if you get my drift. Maybe they've got some rogue workers who are involved in the tissue trade and nobody else knows anything about it. It's anybody's guess.'

'You're beginning to sound plausible, Gilmour. But I won't be going anywhere with this until we're totally all over it.'

'Of course.'

'So what's going on with this Tanya bird?'

'Don't know. That's where I'm headed.'

'And what happened last night? You said it all went a bit crazy.'

Rosie hesitated. But she knew she wouldn't get away with it.

'Well?'

'Tell you later, Mick. When I come in.'

'You will, and your arse. What the fuck have you done?'

'Mick . . . ' She hesitated again. 'Look. Can it not wait for a couple of hours?'

'Just give me a heads-up, Rosie. Don't fuck about. If you've done something stupid I want to know now. Come on. Out with it.'

Rosie took a deep breath, then exhaled as she turned into the street where Tanya lived. She drove along, trying to find a parking space.

'Okay. Just briefly, Mick, because I'm about to go into Tanya's flat.' She stopped the car at the kerb. 'Listen. The refugee, Emir? Remember?'

'Of course I remember. I'm the fucking editor.'

Rosie stifled a laugh. McGuire was on his high horse.

'Well, he called me yesterday. When I was on my way back up from Manchester.'

'Great. At least he's not chopped liver.' McGuire chuckled at his own wit. 'Yes. He told me the most amazing story about what happened. He's been on the run for a few days. They kidnapped him. Took him to the slaughterhouse. I think he was next in line to be ... er ... chopped liver.'

'Fucking hell,' McGuire said. 'So where is he now?'

'He's in my flat.'

'*What?*'

'Yeah. I let him stay there last night.'

'Christ almighty, Rosie! Why didn't you call me last night about this?'

'It was just a spur of the moment thing. Sorry, Mick. I knew you'd go nuts, and I felt sorry for the guy. He was terrified, and he'd been stabbed on the arm. What was I supposed to do? He had nowhere to go.'

'Rosie. When you get through with Tanya, give me a call. Then go back and make sure Emir hasn't been murdered in your flat.' He paused. 'You know Rosie, this is just wrong what you've done. I'll talk to you when you get in.' He hung up.

When Tanya opened the door, Rosie gasped at the state of her face.

'Shit, Tanya,' she said, heading down the hallway. 'What happened?' She followed Tanya into the tiny living room, her mind flipping to junkie prostitute Mags Gillick the day she'd told her she'd got a dig from the bent cop who was using her.

Tanya sat down, lit a cigarette and inhaled deeply, the cigarette trembling in her fingers. She looked up at Rosie and sniffed. One eye was black and swollen and her mouth was puffed up and bloodied.

'Can I get you something, Tanya?' Rosie said, not really knowing what to say. 'Tea or something? Water?'

'Coffee, please.' Tanya jerked her head in the direction of the kitchen area behind her.

Rosie put the kettle on, searching in cupboards for the coffee and cups. She came back out and sat opposite Tanya.

'What happened, Tanya?'

'It was Josef.' She wiped a tear from her eye. 'He followed me last night from the hotel.'

'The hotel?' Rosie asked.

There was an awkward pause, and before Tanya took her eyes off the floor and looked up at her, Rosie knew what she was going to say.

'I am working as escort.' Her expression was flat, resigned.

'Oh,' Rosie said. 'I didn't know.' But she wasn't surprised.

'Only in the past few weeks. I needed to get some more money. I did it before. A couple of years ago, and at first when I come to England.' She blew out smoke and shrugged. 'What the hell. It is easy money.'

Rosie watched her as she dissolved into tears. It wasn't easy money. Never was. Not on any level. It was no easier for Tanya than it had been for Mags Gillick, or any of the women down the generations who had reduced themselves to hocking their bodies, whether it was for drugs, drink or any other reason.

Rosie got up, made two mugs of coffee and came back, handing one to Tanya before she sat down.

'So Josef followed you,' Rosie said, putting down her mug.

Through tears, Tanya told her about the beating, about how she had only let him in because she felt sorry for him, because there had been a time when he meant the world to her.

Rosie listened, saying nothing. Then Tanya stopped.

'He stole from me.'

'Your money?' Rosie assumed.

'Yes,' Tanya, said, swallowing. 'But that is not all.'

Rosie looked at her enquiringly.

'Do you mean the piece of paper you showed me, with the names of the refugees?'

Tanya shook her head.

'No. I have that in a safer place.'

'What then?'

Tanya swallowed. 'I stole two letters, Rosie. Suicide notes. From Tony Murphy, that day. I took them from his desk. One for his wife, and the second one was for Frank Paton.'

Rosie's stomach turned over.

'Christ, Tanya,' she sighed. 'That's serious.'

'I know.' She lifted her coffee mug, then put it back down without drinking. 'You know I told you I was Tony Murphy's lover. I was shocked, and also a bit angry that he left a note for her and for Frank, but nothing for me.'

Rosie couldn't believe what she was hearing.

'You mean you read the letters?' Rosie chastised herself for hoping Tanya had a copy of them. But she knew if she even as much as touched the letters she was crossing the line. Her heart raced as Tanya told her the contents of the letters.

'I send the letter to Tony's wife,' Tanya said. 'I went to the funeral and I saw her with Tony's children. I knew then that I was nothing. She deserve to have the letter. It is what Tony wanted.'

Rosie said nothing. 'But I kept the other letter, the one for Frank Paton. That is what Josef stole. It was in my bag.'

'Jesus.' Rosie said. 'Josef has that letter?'

'Yes.'

Rosie sat silent, pondering the problem for a moment. There was only one thing a scumbag like Josef would do with that letter. 'He will use it to blackmail Frank Paton, won't he, Tanya?'

Tanya nodded. Rosie rubbed a hand across her forehead and took a deep breath. 'Tanya,' she said, 'this has made things very dangerous. You do know that.' Tanya looked stricken but said nothing. 'Why did you steal the letter to Frank?' Rosie asked. 'I mean, I can see why you took the one for Tony's wife, because of the way you felt. But why Frank? Were you going to blackmail him?'

Tanya shrugged. 'I don't know, Rosie. That is the truth. I think maybe I thought of it at the time, I don't know. I just did it all very quickly, like I was shocked. Then after, I didn't know what to do with that letter.' She sighed and shook her head. 'Yes, I thought about blackmail, but that was before I took the paper from his office with the names of the refugees. Then I knew that maybe Tony and Frank were doing something bad with refugees, that refugees were going missing.' She looked at Rosie. 'I wasn't going to blackmail Frank, Rosie. I was going to give the letter to you to give to the police. It maybe help proving what they do to these people.'

'It would have certainly helped incriminate Frank Paton, Tanya. That's for sure. But it's not there any more, so God knows what will happen to it.'

They sat in silence, Tanya, sipping her coffee, touching her swollen cheek, Rosie watching her, her heart sinking.

'I wish you'd told me before,' Rosie said. 'But right now, that's not important. What's important is that you may be in danger. I think we need to talk about going to the police and what you do from here. You need to be protected.' She looked around the room. 'I don't know if you're safe here. Does anyone else know you live here? Frank Paton?'

'No. Only Josef.'

'That's dangerous enough.'

Tanya lit another cigarette and looked directly at Rosie. 'I have a copy of the letter to Frank,' she said.

Rosie hoped her face didn't show the naked excitement of the reporter she couldn't help being.

Tanya got up and went to her bedroom. She returned moments later and handed Rosie the letter.

Rosie read it, then she read it twice more, knowing she'd crossed the line yet, at the same time, not quite believing her luck.

'But there is a problem, Rosie,' Tanya said.

Rosie looked up at her.

'The letter Josef stole was folded up in my bag, but inside it was the business card you gave me.'

Rosie stood up. 'The card is gone?'

'Yes,' Tanya said. 'I'm sorry.'

'Shit,' Rosie said, and a shiver ran down her spine.

CHAPTER 19

It was a long time since Rosie had been this watchful as she drove into the car park behind her flat at St George's Cross. For months, after the night she was dragged out of her house and bundled into the boot of a car by big Jake Cox's hoodlums, she'd automatically paid close attention to anyone sitting in a car anywhere near the building. For the first few weeks, she'd been totally paranoid and seldom went into her flat at night by herself. If she worked late at the *Post*, McGuire had insisted that a taxi drive behind her to make sure she got into the building safely. But things moved so quickly in her job that the memory of one hellish night was often replaced by another. After returning from Spain and Morocco, safe only by the skin of her teeth, Rosie had almost forgotten the cold fear of that night they'd come to kill her. And with the memories of Kosovo still fresh in her mind, the terror in Glasgow seemed like a long time ago. But now, as she drove into the deserted car park, she looked over her shoulder as she jumped out of her car and trotted up to her front door.

Inside her flat, Emir was on his feet and looking terrified when she came through the door.

'It's okay, Emir.' Rosie smiled at him. 'It's only me.'

His face was pale, but he looked a lot better than he did last night.

'You okay, Emir?'

'Yes, thank you, Rosie. I just wait for you. I did not touch anything.' His dark eyes softened. 'I sleep very long.'

'Didn't you eat anything?'

Emir shook his head.

'You must be starving,' Rosie went into the kitchen. 'Let me make you some lunch.'

She took some eggs and switched them up in a bowl with milk. As usual, she had very little in her fridge, so she opened a tin of beans and emptied it into a pot. Then she stuck some bread into the toaster.

'Scrambled eggs and beans all right for you?'

'Yes please.' He smiled. 'I am hungry, but I did not want to touch anything.' He looked around. 'Is very beautiful house, Rosie.' He walked into the kitchen and stood watching her. 'You are very kind to let me stay here last night. But after I eat, I should go.'

Rosie put the scrambled eggs into the microwave and turned to Emir, leaning against the worktop.

'I'm glad to help you Emir, that's no problem for me. But we have to work out what we are going to do with you. You are a very important witness, and if there are terrible things happening to refugees, then the police will want to talk to you.'

Emir stiffened a little. 'Yes. But I am afraid, Rosie.'

'The police will give you protection, Emir. They will investigate your story of what happened to you and your friend, and they will make sure you are safe.'

Emir shrugged. 'But maybe they won't protect me, then what I do?'

'They will, Emir,' Rosie said. 'I will make sure they do. Because you'll be brought to the police by my newspaper, so they will know they cannot put a foot wrong with you – because we'll be watching. How do you feel about that?'

He nodded. 'I will do what you say, Rosie. You are kind. I know you care about people like me.'

They stood looking at each other, saying nothing. In Emir's hollow cheeks, Rosie saw a thousand young men just like him, displaced and bewildered. The microwave pinged.

'Right. Now you must eat, Emir.' She motioned him to the table. 'And afterwards, I have go to the office and talk to my editor, then I'll come back and see you. But you should just stay here and relax.'

He was already sat at the table with a mouthful of scrambled egg. 'Thank you. I will,' he mumbled.

At her desk at the *Post*, Rosie was going through her emails, conscious that McGuire had just breezed past her without making eye contact.

'Have you two had a lover's tiff?' Reynolds was his usual bitter and twisted self.

'Piss off, Reynolds,' Rosie said, without looking away from her screen.

'What you up to, Rosie?' He persisted.

'Not much,' Rosie shrugged, still not looking at him. 'Bit of digging around.'

'Still looking at the refugee stuff up in the Red Road?'

Rosie knew she'd have to talk to him. She sat back and flicked through her notebook.

'Yeah, I am. Might write a feature on this vigilante stuff. Don't quite know yet,' she lied.

Reynolds rocked back and forth in his chair, and planted his feet up on the desk.

'See that torso in the Clyde last week?'

'Yeah.'

'Word is that was a refugee.'

'Really?'

'Aye. But it's taking it a bit far for vigilantes to be cutting arms and legs off, is it not? Apparently someone pulled the lungs out, and the heart. That's what I heard, but the cops are saying nothing. Even my best detective contacts are keeping it tight as a duck's arse.'

Rosie tried to keep her face straight. The only contacts Reynolds had these days were brain-dead alcoholic cops who barely knew what day it was. His best contacts went when the crooked head of the CID, Gavin Fox, and two of his cohorts were brought down after Rosie's corruption exposé last year. Reynolds had been sneaking around briefing the cops against her all during her investigation, and McGuire never forgave him. He would soon be out the door for good.

'Well, I'm sure if anyone can find out what the cops are hiding, it's you, Bob.' As she went back to her screen, the phone on her desk rang. It was Marion.

'You've to come through, Rosie.'

'What kind of mood is he in?' Rosie asked.

'Not good.' Marion whispered. 'He's been biting heads off all morning.'

'Oh dear . . . I'm on my way.'

Rosie knocked on McGuire's half-open door and walked in.

'Hi Mick, I'm here,' she said, feeling a little sheepish.

He was studying some piece of paper on his desk and didn't look up. The body language wasn't encouraging.

'So you are. Sit down, Rosie,' he said, his eyes still fixed on the paper.

Rosie sat on the leather chesterfield a few feet away from his desk and fiddled with a pencil. Part of her was braced for a bollocking, but the bigger part of her, the part that always got her into trouble, was ready for a punch-up.

McGuire took his reading glasses off, sat back and clasped his hands across his stomach. He gave Rosie a look that was trying to be angry, but not quite succeeding. Then he shook his head and sighed.

'Fuck sake, Rosie! What am I going to do with you?'

'Listen, Mick.' Rosie sat forward. 'I know what you're saying. But . . .'

He put his hand up to interrupt her. 'No, Rosie.' His dark eyebrows knitted together. 'You listen to me. Just shut that mouth of yours for a minute.'

Rosie opened her mouth to speak, but swallowed her words, slumping back on the sofa.

'I cannot believe, after everything that's happened to you, after all the shit you went through last year with these tossers of Jake Cox's, plus the risks you took in Spain and Morocco, that after all that, you're still prepared to take fucking stupid decisions.' He slammed his fist on the desk. 'And not just stupid, by the way, but decisions that could get you killed. Are you off your fucking nut, woman?'

'I know what you're saying, Mick. But I ... I just felt for the guy after what he'd been through. I wanted to get him somewhere he could eat something and get cleaned up after his ordeal – Somewhere safe. I mean, we don't want to lose this Emir do we? He's the key to this.'

'No,' McGuire said, 'but we don't want to lose you either, Rosie.' He looked her in the eye and there was a little pregnant pause before he looked away, shaking his head. 'Why the hell, if you wanted to get him somewhere safe did you not just book him into a hotel? Why not just phone me and ask me what I think.' He stood up and came from behind his desk. 'I *am* actually the editor, Rosie. I make the decisions around here – not you.'

'You don't need to say that, Mick. You know I have huge respect for you.' She folded her arms and turned to him. 'But I didn't want to stick him in a hotel in case he'd freak at the first noise in the corridor and run away. The guy's jangling, Mick. I knew I could keep him safe in my house.'

'And what about the lowlifes who are looking for him? What about the guys who kidnapped him and were about to chop him up and sell his knees and his fingers in the open market? Do you think they've just gone back to big Al Howie and said he's done a runner?' He shook his head. 'They'll be more determined than ever to get him. And what if they had a stroke of luck and traced him back to your flat? Did you think about that, Rosie? You're not going to get a second chance with these fuckers. You had your chance that night on the Clydeside when your big Bosnian mate rescued you. That ain't gonna happen again.' He raised his hands in despair. 'Can you not see sense? Can you not see the danger signs all over the place?'

Rosie took a deep breath and puffed out her cheeks. 'Yes, Mick. I see the danger. I've got scars to remind me. I'm not fucking stupid. I don't do this job for a laugh.'

Silence. McGuire watched her for too long, and Rosie bit her lip to keep back tears that were a mixture of frustration, anger and cold fear – given what Tanya had just told her about her business card being stolen by Josef.

McGuire seemed to soften. He went back behind his desk put his feet up.

'Right. Okay, Rosie. That's your bollocking over.' He looked at her and half raised an eyebrow. 'I care what happens to you, all right?'

Rosie smiled, pushing back her hair. She was forgiven.

'Yeah. I love you too.'

'So,' McGuire said. 'Give me the full bhoona on what's going on.' He raised his index finger. 'And I mean every cough, spit and fart.'

Rosie began by telling him Emir's story of being kidnapped and everything he had seen at the slaughterhouse.

She filled him in on the trip to Manchester and what she'd learned about PD Pharmaceuticals. Then she told him about Tanya calling her earlier and everything that had happened in her house.

'Christ, Rosie,' McGuire said. 'First things first. This Josef bastard sounds like a right nice guy. You know exactly what he's going to do with that letter, don't you?'

'Of course. Blackmail Frank Paton.'

'Yep. Or maybe even try to sell it to a newspaper. Hey, maybe even us.' McGuire said.

'I wouldn't hold my breath.'

'Do you think he's got the wit to go through with the blackmail, if that's what he's going to do?'

'Don't know, Mick. But he's a bad bastard. He's been beating Tanya up for a while, and she left him a few weeks ago because he raped her after a drunken beating. That's the kind of guy he is. Who knows what he's capable of.'

Rosie stood up and handed the letter Tanya had given her. 'Tanya took a copy of Murphy's letter to Frank Paton,' Rosie said. 'She said she had initially thought of blackmailing Paton herself, but after the stuff she'd found in his office about the refugees going missing, she was going to give it to me to try and nail the story down. I think she's being honest about that.'

McGuire took the letter and held it away from his body.

'Fuck sake. It's burning my fingers. This is stolen property.'

'Well. It's a copy of stolen property.'

'Yeah. Tell that to the High Court judge,' he said, and read the letter.

'It's not exactly damning him on any specifics, but at the very least it would make the cops want to ask questions about what Murphy was getting at – the bit telling him they should stop, and see you in hell. You could read anything into that, but you can bet your ass Frank Paton won't want that letter going anywhere but in the ashtray.'

'Exactly. So we just have to wait to see what happens with that. We have no way of knowing.'

'We could doorstep this Josef bastard. But I don't know there's much point.'

They sat in silence, both trying to work out their next move.

'Mick,' Rosie said, knowing she was about to light the blue touchpaper. 'There's another problem.'

'Oh Christ, no!'

'Well . . . When I first talked to Tanya, I gave her my business card so she could get back to me. It was in her bag, inside the letter.'

'Oh, fuck!' McGuire put his hands to his head. 'So he's got that as well?'

'Looks like it.'

McGuire shook his head.

'This is not good, Rosie. Not good at all. This links you into just about everything.'

'I know,' Rosie said. 'If the cops get a hold of it, then they know I've been trampling around on what should have been their investigation. If anyone else gets a hold of it . . . well, I'd rather not think about that.'

McGuire put his pen in his mouth and drew on it as though it were a cigarette.

'I wish I had a fag.'

'You don't smoke any more.'

'I know, but I want one right now.'

'What about Emir?' Rosie asked. 'Is it time to get the cops in? I think it is, and soon. Obviously he can't stay at my flat for long, but I think I should call my cop mate Don and get them to see Emir. And we have to make sure that he gets protected.'

'Yeah,' Mick said. 'I don't think we've got an option any more, Rosie. This Emir is too hot to hold onto. Just being around him is a danger for you.' He paused. 'But handing him to the cops is going to cause all sorts of shit. They're going to wonder why we haven't done it before.'

'We'll just be economical with the truth,' Rosie said.

'Hmm ...' McGuire nodded. 'We also have to think about a story. How we're going to take it forward without alerting everyone. We need to start thinking about that, Rosie.'

'I know,' she said. 'I already have. Why don't I do a general piece on refugees being unaccounted for – given that the Refugee Council told me so many of them just disappear. We can say that in Glasgow alone in the past twelve months several have disappeared. Make it look like they've vanished into the black economy, but it might be enough to put the wind up Frank Paton. Maybe do that and see what it flushes out. Plus I'm also digging up as much as I can on this PD Pharmaceuticals mob. There's loads of cuts in them.'

'Good idea, Gilmour. Get working on that.' He stood up. 'Call the cops in and get that Emir out of your hair

– and make sure we get him photographed and taped. Go back to your house and do that now, then offload him to the cops.' He rolled his sleeves up. 'We'll deal with the flak from them as and when it happens. If they were on top of their game, they might even have as much information as we have. Refer them to me.'

'Okay,' Rosie said, turning to leave. 'But Mick, I think we should hang onto Emir for a day or two, just while I'm looking at other things. Because if we hand him over, we're kind of restricted, and cops might start wading into Paton's office.'

'Right. Okay, two days. And Gilmour . . .'

Rosie stopped.

'Keep in touch. Be at the end of the phone at all times. I might even think about moving you out of your house again.'

'Mick, I can't be arsed with that.'

'I don't care what you can't be arsed with. I'll be the judge of what needs to be done. Now piss off.'

CHAPTER 20

Frank Paton was sick with nerves. He'd already thrown up twice before he left the office in a taxi to meet Josef and hand over the five grand. Now he sat on a bench in Kelvingrove Park, dwarfed by its vastness, staring gloomily at the lush greenery rolled out in front of him in all its summer splendour like a painting by one of the old masters.

He swallowed his queasiness, one hand firmly on the hold-all he was about to part with, and looked at his watch. It was 7.30 in the morning. Any minute now ... The park was deserted, except for the occasional glutton-for-punishment jogger who didn't even look in his direction as he sat reading the *Post*. The story on the front page about refugees disappearing, coming on top of everything else had put the wind up the already unnerved Frank. At least the article wasn't suggesting any of the stuff he was involved in. It was merely floating the line that many refugees were unaccounted for, hinting that they could have disappeared into the black economy. One line suggested that vigilantes may be behind their disappearance. None of it should have troubled him too much, if he hadn't been such a jumpy wreck. The paranoia made him wonder if the newspaper had any more, or if they were just flying a kite with the story to see what reaction it would get.

In the distance, Frank saw the stocky figure of Josef walking briskly towards him. He had only met him a couple of times when he'd come to collect Tanya at the office after work. He was a torn-faced little bastard, Tony had remarked, as Josef had barely grunted when they tried to make conversation with him. Both Frank and Tony couldn't figure out what a beauty like Tanya was doing with a knuckle-trailer like him. Tony was always talking about how sexy their cleaner was – he'd obviously been giving her one, Frank thought. Perhaps that's why Josef was so mean-looking. Maybe he'd suspected.

As he approached, Frank shifted on the bench, and clutched the hold-all a little tighter. He'd had to pull in some markers to get five grand cash out of the firm's business account at such short notice. But his bank manager owed him a favour since he'd managed to get a case buried for him a few years ago, when he'd been caught naked in a sauna, a teenage hooker sitting astride him administering the 'extras' that were always on the menu.

'You got the money?' Josef said, standing over him.

'Sit down, for fuck's sake. I don't want to look suspicious.'

Josef sat down and turned his body towards him. 'You got it?'

'Yes, I have it.' Frank looked at him with contempt. 'Let me see the letter first.'

Josef went into his pocket and took out a folded piece of paper. Frank recognised it as their company headed notepaper. Nice one Tony. Why not leave a trail of incriminating fucking evidence? He felt sweat on his back.

'You can look at it, but you cannot hold it until you give me the money in my hand.' Josef unfolded the paper.

Inside the note was a business card for the *Post*, with the name Rosie Gilmour. Frank knew Gilmour by reputation more than acquaintance. It was her name that was on this morning's story in the paper about missing refugees. Now she'd been sniffing around and had perhaps talked to Tanya. That fucking bitch Tanya ...

Josef held the letter with both hands, and leaned in towards Frank. 'Read,' he said.

Frank read the words slowly, then again, then one more time just to make sure. His lawyer's intuition told him there wasn't anything specific to incriminate him or Tony, but there was no doubt that in the wrong hands – cops' hands – it would cause all sorts of problems. Some of it Frank may have been able to explain away, saying Tony had never felt good about some of the high-profile gangsters they'd been defending. But he couldn't afford to take the chance that the plods might decide to weigh in, especially after that refugee story in the paper. The last thing he needed was any close attention being paid to the lawyers who were handling most of the asylum cases in the city.

'You see enough?' Josef's mouth was a snarl.

Frank didn't answer.

'You want the letter, you give me the money now.' Josef eyed the hold-all.

Frank looked around him, then handed Josef the hold-all. Josef unzipped the bag, and his eyes lit up as he looked inside.

'Bundles of twenty,' Frank said looking straight ahead. 'The way you wanted it.'

He put out his hand and Josef gave him the letter and the business card. Frank put them in the inside pocket of his jacket.

Josef reached inside the bag and pulled out two wedges of twenty-pound notes. A little triumphant smile spread across his booze-addled face, then he said, 'Your partner, Tony, was fucking my woman.' He spat on the ground.

'Can't say I blame him,' Frank said, without looking at him.

Josef put the money back in the bag and rummaged around, peering inside, as though he was making sure there was plenty more.

'It's all there,' Frank said. 'Most money you've ever seen, I suppose.'

'This my compensation,' Josef grinned, looking at Frank. 'For my woman being such a whore.'

'I hope it fucking chokes you.'

As Frank said it, Josef's head was jerked back as a leather strap was looped over it from behind. Frank watched the disbelief in Josef's face as the strap was pulled tighter and tighter. Josef made desperate grasps at the ligature, clawing the flesh at his neck, but Clock Buchanan stood behind him, yanking it tighter as Josef's whole body struggled and fought for the last few seconds of his life. Frank stood up as Josef's face turned blue and his bulging eyes stared wildly at him for a time before he finally stopped struggling. Clock pulled the strap away, leaving him to keel over on the bench, then slip onto the ground.

'Now you know what it feels like, you little cunt.' Frank said, stepping over him. He lifted the hold-all.

'You've to come and see Al,' Clock said. 'He wants a word.'

Frank's legs felt weak as they walked towards his car.

Big Al Howie was far too buoyant for this time of the morning as he greeted Frank and Clock. He was at least two lines ahead of the game, and was buzzing around his office and bawling someone out on the phone as they came in the door.

'Just get it fucking sorted,' Al barked. 'Or you'll get sorted. Now, do you get my fucking drift, wee man?' He put the phone down, and threw himself onto his chair. 'Fucking numpties I've got to work with. No wonder I lose my patience.'

Frank stood awkwardly, as Clock took off his jacket and sat down.

'Sit down, Frank, for fuck sake,' Al said, lighting a ciga-rette. 'You look like you've seen a ghost. Anyone would think it was you who got choked to death.' He chuckled. 'By the way, I thought that wee method of getting rid of that fucker was a bit of genius on my part. Nice wee touch. I mean, after the way Tony killed himself, it felt like the right thing to do. Thought you'd like that. And you did the right thing, Frank, letting us take care of it.'

Frank sat down. His arms felt heavy with stress. He looked at Al. He didn't know what to say, but he knew he was expected to say something.

'Yeah. Little bastard got what he deserved.' Frank tried to look nonchalant.

'Exactly,' Al said. 'Who the fuck did he think he was? Some wee Russian farmer, coming over here and trying to blackmail the likes of us? He must have thought he was a gangster. Well, at least he saw how real gangsters do business before he popped his clogs.'

'Yeah,' Frank said, wondering what else to say.

'So, let me see the letter then.' Al stretched his hand across the desk.

Frank took the letter out and handed it to him, along with the card.

'By the way, Al, that business card. Rosie Gilmour from the *Post*. Looks like she's talked to Tanya, or at least has made an approach. Josef stole the letter out of Tanya's bag, and the card was there too.'

Al nodded slowly. 'Gilmour. She's fucking dangerous, that bitch. Big Jake should have dealt with her right the first time, but the boys fucked up.' He narrowed his eyes. '*And* she was all over that stuff in Spain as well, when

Jake got shot last year.' He licked his lips. 'She needs sorting big time, she does.'

Al read the letter aloud: 'We were the wide-eyed law students who were going to change the world . . .' He made a sarcastic face at Frank.

'Was that you and Tony one time, Frankie? All high-minded with dreams of changing the world?' He shook his head. 'Fuck me! The only people who change the world and make things happen are people like me. Crooks. It's crooks who run the world, Frank. My da used to say that to me, and by the way, he was a man who read a paper every day. He knew his stuff. He said the real crooks were the politicians and the bankers, but they were legit crooks, and got away with it. Fucking stealing from the rest of us. The gangsters – people like me and big Jake – just punched and slashed their way through because we couldn't be bankers or politicians. Well, they call us gangsters, and that's fine by me, but we're no different from them. Only difference is if we want something we go out and take it. Make it happen. We don't put it to a fucking vote.'

Christ almighty, Frank thought. Social studies, Al Howie-style. If it wasn't so serious it would be funny. He felt the urge to make a joke, but he didn't dare. Howie was a paranoid nutter with a coke habit who was making a speech, and who had a gun in his desk drawer. The last time Frank saw him take it out, he'd shot Tam Logan in the chest with it. You don't interrupt a man like that when he's on a wired-to-the-moon rant.

'Yeah,' Frank said, trying to sound enthusiastic. 'You're right.'

'I know I am.'

Frank flinched as Al went into his drawer. To his relief he only took out a wrap of coke, emptied it onto his desk and snorted a line.

'By the way, Frank, I'll tell you this. Guys like you? You're crooks the same as me. Don't get me wrong, I like you, and I liked Tony. But I don't think you're any better than me, for all your university high ideals. When it comes down to it, you're just a fucking gangster.'

Frank didn't like where this was going. Al was winding himself up. He wanted to get out of the office, but he knew better than to say anything that might put him over the edge.

'I think some people get the breaks in life, Al. And some don't. I was quite lucky.' Frank said. He wanted to tell Al that he was a piece of shit, and that he and Tony both grew up in a council housing scheme alongside guys like him. But they had studied and educated themselves out of the mire, while others robbed and went to jail. But what the fuck was it with all this philosophy? Frank looked at his watch.

'Al,' he said, hesitantly. 'I've got a client to meet in about twenty minutes. I need to get a move on.'

'Aye, right.' Al sat back and stroked his chin, looking again at the letter. He lifted it, flicked his lighter under it and held it as it burned. 'That gets rid of that then.' Then he held up the business card. 'This one might take a bit longer to destroy.' He set it alight. 'But as you see, Frank. It does burn.'

Frank stood up.

'I'll give you a call later, Al.'

'Frank?' Al said, looking up at him. 'I need at least two more bodies in the next couple of days. They're running low up there. It's like a fucking factory.' He chuckled.

'Okay, Al. I'll get it arranged and let you know.'

'Oh, and Frank?' Al said as Frank opened the door, 'say hello to your family for me.'

Frank didn't turn around. He had to get out of the room before he suffocated.

When the door closed, Al gave Clock a perplexed look.

'He can't handle this much longer, Clock.'

'I know, boss.'

'And that makes him dangerous to the rest of us. I can just imagine how quick his bottle would crash if he got his arse felt by the cops.' He sighed. 'He's getting to be a bit of a fucking liability.'

CHAPTER 21

PD Pharmaceuticals was one of the largest drug companies in the world, with various smaller subsidiary arms mostly based in Germany and Holland, some of which were involved in ground-breaking research into genetics. But the main thrust of PD's work involved the manufacture of medication for heart disease and hypertension, and they supplied the generic drugs, under various different brand names, across Europe and the UK.

Rosie had spent most of the afternoon in front of her computer screen in an office off the main editorial floor. She didn't want anyone looking over her shoulder as she ploughed through reams of newspaper cuttings. After nearly two hours' trawling, she finally came across a piece from five years ago by a German reporter, which kickstarted her radar. It was an exposé across two pages, claiming to have uncovered links from one of PD's smaller companies based in Belgrade to the illegal trade in body tissue. She skimmed through it, sat back, then reread it slowly and carefully.

'You beauty!' Rosie said, taking a note of the reporter's name. She went to the newspaper's website and dug out the direct telephone number of the newsroom.

'Sorry,' Rosie began when the German voice barked "Schmidt!" down the phone. 'I'm afraid I don't speak German. Do you speak a little English, please?'

'Yes. I do.' The male voice said. The Germans weren't big on small talk.

'May I speak with Gerhard Hoffman, please?'

Silence. 'Hello?' Rosie said.

'Hello,' the same male voice replied. 'Who is this please?'

Rosie told him who she was.

'Gerhard Hoffman no longer works here.'

'Oh,' Rosie said. 'He's left then?'

'He has.'

'Do you have a telephone number where I can contact him?'

'Hold on.'

Rosie couldn't make up her mind if the voice was just being cagey or it was simply that brusque, no-nonsense manner that didn't endear Germans to a lot of people across Europe. Especially the Brits.

'Hello?' This time it was a woman's voice. 'My name is Eva Muller. I am the deputy news editor. I understand you are looking for Gerhard Hoffman.'

'Yes, I am, Eva. Do you think I could have a contact telephone number for him?'

'Can you tell me what this is about?'

Rosie was irritated at the question.

'No, I'm sorry, but I can't.' Rosie said as politely as she could manage.

'Well, I'm afraid I cannot help you.'

'Sorry?' Rosie said, trying to sound more confused than angry.

'I cannot pass Gerhard's number if you do not tell me why you want him.'

Christ almighty, Rosie thought.

'Well,' Rosie persisted. 'Can you perhaps tell me when he left, then? Has he gone to another newspaper where I can contact him?'

'He left over two years ago. He is not with another newspaper.'

'Okay,' Rosie said. 'I understand. Then could I possibly trouble you a little further by giving you *my* telephone number and asking him to give me a call? Would you be willing to do that?'

'What is your number, and I will see if I can contact him. But I cannot guarantee he will call you.'

'Of course,' Rosie said, curtly. She gave her mobile number.

There was a pause after Eva repeated the number back to her. Then she spoke.

'Can I ask you, how did you get Gerhard's name?'

Rosie couldn't believe the stupid question – and from a deputy news editor. She was tempted to say the tooth fairy left it on her pillow this morning.

'From cuttings,' Rosie played it straight. 'I was reading some cuttings on a German company, and I found Gerhard's name.'

'PD Pharmaceuticals by any chance?'

'Yes it was actually.' What the heck. She was getting nowhere with this fan-dancing.

'I thought so . . . I will ask him to call you.' Eva hung up without saying goodbye.

'Charming,' Rosie said loudly into the mobile. 'And, by the way, I still don't forgive your mob for Clydebank.'

Rosie went back to the screen. After a few minutes, she dug out another cutting: an apology from the newspaper to the company Gerhard Hoffman had exposed. So that's why they didn't talk. Rosie was now thoroughly intrigued. She sat back and hoped for the best.

It was mid-afternoon when the call came in from Gerhard Hoffman. He had been a lot more forthcoming than his old boss Eva Muller, once he'd established Rosie's credentials by checking the *Post*'s website for her articles while talking to her, and also calling the office to make sure she was genuine.

Gerhard had told her the story was true and one hundred per cent accurate. He'd been furious that the newspaper didn't back him when the pharmaceutical company challenged the facts and threatened to sue, but when it had come to the crunch, there wasn't the level of proof the lawyers required to take the chemical company on. The paper ended up apologising, and on principle Gerhard walked out.

He told Rosie his initial tip-off about tissue trade had come from animal rights protestors, and at first he was sceptical. It was far-fetched to suggest that a pharmaceutical giant making legitimate drugs and involved in genetic research could also be dealing in the illegal trade in body parts and tissue. The animal rights protestors always had their own agenda, Gerhard said, but once they started working together, he believed them.

One of the animal protestors had got a job in the plant and provided inside information. They had been looking for evidence of animals being ill-treated in experiments, but what they'd discovered was much more explosive. The company was using corpses from undertakers and material from one particular private hospital. Gerhard's contact had managed to get into the company lab and had seen body parts cut up in small pieces, some of which, he explained, wouldn't be identifiable without scientific investigation. So without actually stealing parts, he couldn't prove the story if the paper had been taken to court. The chemical company's lawyers had flatly denied the allegations, claiming the tissue was from animals. Gerhard's exclusive was then trashed all over the German media.

Gerhard told Rosie that even one body could rake in a fortune because almost every part could be harvested, sliced up into minute pieces, with each batch making big money in the illegal tissue trade.

'It is a massive industry,' he said. 'For example, body skin is used in cosmetic processes like plumping up lips of models. They can charge six hundred euros a time for a shot of that. And believe it or not, ground human bone is used regularly by dentists to treat their patients. One dead body can be worth almost a hundred thousand euros once it is processed. It's sold in ounces or in grams and it's worth a fortune. They use everything, from tendons to heart valves, corneas for eye transplants, and even veins. Every part of a dead body is money. The people who harvest the tissue sell it on to tissue banks anywhere in the world, and they in turn make millions. It is big business.'

'That's incredible,' Rosie said, impressed by his knowledge.

'I know. I will never give up on my story because I know it is true. I still work on it, even now.'

Rosie confided in him some of what she had found. Gerhard said if she needed help he'd be there. The company was rotten. He was now concentrating his investigation on one particular man, not German, but from Belgrade, who was on the board at PD Pharmaceuticals. He had been a boss in the smaller company that Gerhard exposed. Rosie found it breathtaking that the company would be that arrogant, but Gerhard said it was a clever double bluff by them as attack was often the best form of defence. His story had been trashed, so there could be no recriminations against anyone in the company.

Before he hung up, he said, 'I am building up some more information and I have been to Belgrade several times to look at this man and the background. I will help you any way I can. I'm going again soon to meet someone who can give me information.' He gave Rosie the name of the man he was investigating and she wrote it down.

When the call ended, Rosie checked the board of directors of the company, and sure enough, the man Gerhard had named – Goran Boskovac – was there.

Rosie's next phone call was to Adrian. They had only spoken on two or three occasions since he fled Spain last year in the midst of the shoot-out. He listened to her story and she gave him the names of Raznatovic and Boskovac. He would get back to her. Rosie knew it was in good hands. She told him she might go to Belgrade, and he said he would look after her.

By seven in the evening, Rosie and Matt were sitting at the the farm road, far enough away from the slaughterhouse, but close enough to see that there were no cars in the car park. They had Emir with them, the whole thing a rush-of-blood-to-the-head decision.

'If McGuire finds out what we're doing,' Rosie said to Matt, 'he'll hit the roof.'

'I know, but we'll not tell him till it's nearly in the paper.' Matt fiddled with camera lenses, sticking them into the pockets of his safari waistcoat.

Rosie had decided to go back because they'd be giving Emir up to the cops in the next couple of days. This would be the last chance they had of getting anywhere near the slaughterhouse for the kind of pictures they wanted. They'd gone to Rosie's flat and talked it over with Emir, promising that they wouldn't venture anywhere near the place unless they were sure it was empty. Rosie knew it was as reckless a decision as she'd ever made, and as the three of them sat, watching the sun slip lower into the fields in the distance, her stomach was churning.

'You okay, Emir?' Rosie turned her body around to face Emir in the back seat of Matt's sports car. He nodded. In the three days he'd been staying at Rosie's flat, he looked a different man from the hungry, terrified creature she'd encountered.

'I want to help get these people,' Emir said, clutching the iron bar he'd told Rosie he would need to force their way in. 'For what they did to my friend.'

'Then let's go,' Matt said. He opened his door.

'Be careful, Matt, for Christ's sake,' Rosie said. 'In and out. As quick as you can.'

'Don't worry Rosie. I don't want to hang around in there in case I end up on one of their slabs.'

'Right. Keep your mobile on. Any problems this end, I'll phone, and if I do it means there's trouble and I'm on my way down – and you've to get out of there smartish.'

'Come on, Emir. Let's go,' Matt said, opening the back door.

Rosie watched as they disappeared down the slope towards the gate. She could see Emir working on the wire fence towards the back of the building, and then they were inside the car park. She sat, chewing her fingernails as they went behind the building and out of sight. Her mobile rang and she nearly jumped out of her skin.

'Hey, Scoop. You still got your boyfriend staying with you?' It was TJ.

Rosie quickly composed herself.

'Hi TJ. Yeah. Just for another day or two.' She hoped she didn't sound as nervy as she felt.

'Where are you?' TJ said.

'Oh, just out on a bit of a stake-out. Listen, I can't really talk, TJ. I'll call you in a bit.'

'Okay, Rosie. Why not come over, and leave that poor Kosovan boy on his own for the night? You must have him worn out.'

'Aye, right,' Rosie snorted. 'I'll call you in an hour or so.'

'Okay, sweetheart,' TJ said. 'You're obviously up to something. I can hear the stress in your voice.'

'Yeah . . . I'll call you.' She hung up, but, as she put the phone back in her pocket, she suddenly saw a car heading down the path towards the slaughterhouse.

'Oh shit!' She quickly grabbed the phone and pressed the speed dial for Matt, her heart thumping in her chest.

'Quick, Matt, someone's coming. They'll be at the gate in about forty seconds. I'm on my way.'

'Oh fuck!' he said, hanging up.

Rosie switched on the engine. She watched as the car stopped at the gate, where one of the men in it got out and opened the padlock, then dragged the gate open wide enough for the car to get through – but neglected to close it. As the men disappeared into the building, she stepped on the accelerator and sped down the path towards the gate.

There was no sign of Matt when she got to the gate.

'Oh shit, Matt. Where *are* you . . .' Rosie muttered through gritted teeth, her hands trembling on the steering wheel. She tried to take a deep breath, but it wouldn't come. Then suddenly there was a loud bang from inside the building. Gunshot.

'Oh fuck, oh Christ! No!' she said.

Then another shot. Rosie felt her whole body shudder. Then suddenly Matt and Emir appeared from the back of the building, sprinting towards the gate. She sped into the car park, sending dust clouds as she spun the car around to face the way out. Emir threw himself into the back seat and Matt jumped into the front. Rosie raced out of the gate as they closed the car doors.

'Fuck me!' Matt tried to catch his breath. 'Get your foot to the floor, Rosie. These bastards were shooting at us!'

From the corner of her eye, Rosie could see Matt was white as a sheet. She glanced at Emir, panting in the back seat. Then she saw the car behind them.

'Jesus, Matt. They're coming after us.'

'Just keep driving, Rosie. Get the boot down. They'll never catch us in this.'

'God, Matt. I was shitting myself out here. I thought you guys were a goner.' Rosie sped over a bump and everyone jumped. She kept on driving, taking the hairpin bends like a racing driver, bouncing off the verge and trying desperately to control the car.

'Mind the suspension, darlin'. I'm still paying up this shaggin' wagon.' Matt grinned.

Rosie glanced in the rear-view mirror. The car was well behind them, and they were heading towards the main road that would take them onto the motorway in a few minutes.

'That's us, Rosie, we're nearly there.' He slapped her thigh. 'Christ. You can drive a bit – for a mere woman.'

'Nothing concentrates the mind like panic.' Rosie felt a surge of relief as they hit the main road. 'I'm just going to hammer it until we're into the city.'

Matt turned around to look at the back window. 'They're nowhere. They were driving a poxy wee Peugot or something. No match for my beast.'

Rosie glanced in the back. 'You all right Emir?'

'Yes, Rosie. Now I am ok.'

They drove in silence until Rosie was on the motorway.

'So. How did it go?' Rosie shot a glance at Matt. 'Any good?'

'Oh, yeah,' Matt said. 'And how!'

Rosie's mobile rang, and she could see from the corner of her eye it was Don.

'Hey, Don.'

'Rosie. Don't know if you know, but there was a guy found dead up in Kelvingrove Park this morning. Turns out he was strangled. You'll never guess who he is.'

'Don,' Rosie said. 'I'm driving. Don't keep me in suspense, man. Who is it?'

'Some Russian guy called Josef. We traced him to the address of that Tanya bird who worked at Murphy Paton.'

'God almighty!' Rosie jerked the car into the slow lane as horns honked behind her. 'You absolutely certain?'

'Well. Short of him admitting it, we are. But we can't find his bird yet. Apparently she moved out.'

Rosie didn't answer.

'Are you there?' Don said.

'Don. The phone's cutting out. I'll talk to you later.'

Rosie immediately rang McGuire's private number.

'Mick, it's me. Remember the guy Josef – you know the boyfriend of Tanya I told you about? That's who the body was in the park this morning. He was strangled.'

'Fuck me!' McGuire said.

CHAPTER 22

Rosie waited until she saw Frank Paton come out of his office, then she followed him at a distance until he went into the wine bar at the top of the street. She waited in a doorway on the opposite side, deciding to give him enough time to sink at least one drink. Hopefully by then he just might be more approachable. But she wasn't banking on it.

Earlier in the morning, she'd gone to the office first thing, bracing herself to reveal to McGuire what they'd found at the slaughterhouse.

'I know by the look on your face, Gilmour, that this is going to give me an ulcer,' he said, folding his arms as he sat behind his desk.

'There's no easy way to tell you this, Mick,' Rosie said. 'But we went to the slaughterhouse last night. Early evening, while it was still light.'

'You should have told me,' he said calmly.

'I know, but I figured, before we give Emir over to the

cops and they start getting all over it, that we should try to get a look at it.'

McGuire rolled his eyes to the ceiling and shook his head. 'Don't tell me you broke in there, Rosie.'

Rosie shifted on her feet and said nothing.

'Fuck me, Rosie! What in the name of Christ did you think you were doing? Did you not hear anything I said the other day?'

'Mick,' Rosie interrupted. 'Listen. It's not as if they're going to phone the cops if they'd found out is it?'

'No. They wouldn't call the cops. They'd just bloody put a bullet in you. It looks like they've just bumped off Tanya's man, so these guys don't mess about. Are you completely out of your tree?'

Rosie put her hands up to stop him.

'Listen, Mick, please. Listen. Just forget how we did it. What's really important is what Matt got.' She paused. 'He took a picture of a human finger. Christ, Mick. There was all sorts of stuff just dumped in a bin. Something that looked like a bit of a brain.'

McGuire looked at her, his eyebrows raised.

'Are you serious?'

'Yes.'

'Fucking hell. Where are these pictures? Let me see them?'

'Matt's about to ping them over to you any minute.'

McGuire dialled the picture editor's number. 'Pete. Get in here quick.' McGuire turned to his screen.

The picture editor came in and he told him to sit down, then relayed what Rosie had just told him.

'You're fucking joking,' he said.

'Here they are.' McGuire scanned his screen.

Pete went behind the desk with Rosie and they looked over McGuire's shoulder. As the pictures began to feed through, Rosie talked them through the images which she'd already seen on Matt's camera. The first few snaps he'd taken were just general views inside the slaughter-house, and it didn't look any different from a butcher's back-shop or a restaurant kitchen. Most of the long steel benches and worktops were empty. But he'd managed to take pictures of glass containers with what looked like bits of flesh or bone inside them. There had been several containers of varying sizes, filled with some kind of liquid they'd guessed could be some sort of preservative. Matt had said he only got a couple of minutes to look at them, and couldn't make out what was inside, but there were enough of them there to convince him that it had to be something crucial to whatever it was they were doing. Some of them looked like gristle or muscle. Others had spongy flesh in them, but they were cut into such tiny pieces it was hard to say what they were, or had origi-nally been. It was only when Emir took him to a room at the very back of the building that Matt knew he'd hit the jackpot. Inside two ordinary household bins were pieces of bone and flesh that were clearly human remains. He'd kicked the bin over, and photographed the contents that scattered onto the floor. Among them was part of a human finger. And to his horror, pieces of what looked like brain.

'Oh fuck,' McGuire zoomed in on the shots. 'I cannot believe what I'm seeing. It *is* a finger! Christ almighty!

What the fu—?' He turned to Rosie. 'Sit down, Gilmour. We need to work out where we go with this. But we're going to have to move on it quickly. Especially with this Josef murder. And now that you've been in there and they know someone's been rummaging around the place, you can bet their little operation is all going to go tits up – if you'll pardon the pun.'

The picture editor burst out laughing.

Rosie sat down, and the decision was made to start putting the heat on Frank Paton. Then they'd hand over Emir to the cops – but they wouldn't tell them everything they had. Not yet.

Rosie looked at her watch. Paton had already been in the bar fifteen minutes, so she crossed the road and braced herself for the showdown.

The wine bar was dark when she walked in out of the glare of the midday sun, and at first she couldn't see him. There were only two men at the bar, and one at the wall-seating close to the door, reading a newspaper. As Rosie walked towards the bar, she glimpsed Paton in the far corner, sitting alone with a copy of the *Post* in front of him. But he wasn't reading it. He sat staring straight ahead, and Rosie watched as he swirled the ice around in the whisky glass, then took a swig and winced. Whatever he was drinking it must be strong. She ordered a soda water and paid the barmaid, who immediately sat down and went back to her magazine. Rosie went over to Paton and stood in front of him.

'Frank ... ?' She knew he would recognise her from

years of dipping in and out of the courts, even though they'd never actually met.

In the dim light, Rosie couldn't see if his face had drained of colour, but she'd definitely caught him off guard.

'Rosie Gilmour? The *Post*?' Paton gave her an enquiring glance.

'Yeah.' Rosie said, thinking that he feigned the surprised-to-see-you-here look quite well. But not well enough. She waded in.

'I was trying to get you last night. About your cleaner's boyfriend, Josef, being found dead.'

He looked at her then at his drink.

'I'd also like to talk to you about refugees, Frank. Asylum seekers.'

'If you don't mind, Rosie, can you not see that I'm out having a bit of a break?' He lifted his drink. You can make an appointment with my secretary. I'll try to fit you in.'

Rosie saw his jaw tighten.

'Well,' Rosie sat down. 'You see, Frank, I think it's best not to talk in the office. That's why I came here.' She leaned across the table and lowered her voice. 'Frank. I want to talk to you about refugees going missing . . . And I'm not talking about vanishing into the black economy, the story that was in the *Post* the other day.' She paused for effect. 'I'm talking GOING MISSING, Frank,' she emphasised, fixing him with her eyes. 'I think you know what I'm saying here.'

Beads of sweat formed on Frank's top lip, and he swallowed nervously. Rosie could almost hear his heart beat. She watched as he tried to look bewildered.

'What?'

'You know, Frank.' Rosie took out the list of names. 'Here's a few names for starters, Frank.' She read out three names and addresses, glancing up to see his trembling hand come up and flick the sweat from his lip.

'Stop,' he said. 'What the fuck's going on here? These are clients of mine. Where did you get their names?'

'So if they're your clients, then where are they, Frank?' Rosie looked at him coldly. 'They're not at these addresses. Haven't been for months. But then you know that, don't you?'

Frank pushed his drink away from him and moved to stand up. A bit of bluster, Rosie thought, trying to put her off.

'Look,' he said. 'I don't know what you're talking about, but you have a list of some of my clients. I don't know where you got it or what nonsense you're talking, but I'm not listening to any more of this.' He stood up and stepped away from the table.

Rosie got up and stood closer to him, so he would need to push past her.

'That's why Tony hanged himself, Frank, isn't it?'

The words stopped him in his tracks.

'What?'

'You heard, Frank. Tony couldn't cope any more with what you two were doing.' Rosie kept going as he pushed his way past her. 'We have the story, Frank. We know it all,' she bluffed. 'And this Josef murder. Tanya's man. It's all connected, isn't it?'

He turned briefly and squared his shoulders.

'Well, go ahead with your story then. But you'd better have your facts right before you go around accusing lawyers of getting rid of their clients.'

Rosie couldn't believe he'd said that. By the look of shock on Paton's face, he couldn't believe he'd said it either. For a second, he didn't know what to do. Rosie had to bite her lip to stop her from smiling.

He turned on his heel and scurried out of the bar like the cornered rat he was. When he was gone, Rosie put her hand into her pocket, took out her tape recorder and rewound it just to make sure he'd actually said 'lawyers getting rid of their clients'.

The dinner invitation at Cameron House from Al Howie was at short notice, but Frank Paton knew it was an offer he couldn't refuse. There were a couple of business associates, who'd been playing golf at Loch Lomond earlier in the day and were staying over at the hotel, that Al wanted Frank to meet. Al told Frank it was a wee thank-you for his good work. He asked him to drive his own car down, but he could still have a few drinks, and Clock would drive his car back up to Glasgow. Frank's wife was furious when he told her he was going to be busy for the evening. It was school parents' night, and he'd promised he would go. She was still shouting at him when he put the phone down. He put on a fresh shirt he always kept in the office for emergencies, splashed water on his face, and headed for the dinner. He wasn't looking forward to it. Not by any stretch.

*

He drove up the sweeping driveway into the secluded country mansion hotel, a one-time retreat for old money and class but often now the haunt of chav footballers and their appalling entourage of birds and minders. But nothing, not even the drug dealers and thugs who had lowered the tone, could detract from the lavish hotel and splendid surroundings nestling on the banks of Loch Lomond. How the other half live, Frank thought to himself, as he pulled up outside the hotel where Clock Buchanan stood on the steps waiting for him.

'I'll put your motor in the car park, Frank.' He jerked his thumb to the building. 'Al and the boys are in the bar. You've to join them for a drink before dinner.'

'Cheers,' Frank said, tossing him the keys. He took a deep breath, climbed the wide stairway and pushed open the heavy stained-glass swing door.

'Frankie boy!' Al was leaning on the bar with a drink in his hand. His coked-out eyes were lit up like a Christmas tree.

'Hey, Al.' Frank nodded at the two other men standing alongside him and strode across the room.

'Frank, this is Milosh, our main man up here.' Frank turned to the squat man with the dark close-cropped hair. Frank guessed he was about the same age as him.

'How you doing?' Frank said, shaking Milosh's hand.

Milosh nodded and looked at Frank but said nothing. His expression was flat, and Frank could feel his dark eyes scanning his face as he gripped his hand.

'And this is Goran.' Al turned to the other man.

'Pleased to meet you,' Frank said to the tall, middle-aged,

weedy-looking man with the same deadpan look as his mate. They both gave him the creeps. He waited for some kind of explanation from Al as to exactly who they were. He'd heard the name Milosh before, and knew he was the guy in charge of things at the plant, but he'd made it his business never to ask questions about who was who and what role they had in this despicable operation that he and Tony had got themselves swallowed up in. Frank was well aware of what they'd become; he didn't need reminding by meeting the personnel at the heart of it.

'Goran's over from Germany,' Al said. 'Bit of golf, bit of business. He's been at a couple of places down south, just to see the supply lines.'

'Oh, right,' Frank said, not knowing what else to say.

There was an awkward pause, then Al ordered a round of large drinks from the young barman. Frank had to stop himself from downing his in one gulp. A bit of small talk continued, and Frank was glad when the head waiter arrived to announce their table was ready. He led them to a small private dining room with all the deference of a footman from the royal household. Frank looked at his watch and felt a sharp pang of remorse, thinking of Louise at her parents' night waiting for her daddy to turn up. He'd be glad when this night was over.

Two hours later, Frank was in the front seat, half drunk as Clock drove him out of Cameron House and down onto the main road. He'd been glad the waiter had continually topped up their wine glasses because at least it took the edge off his nerves.

The two men, he'd learned over dinner, were both Serbs from the former Yugoslavia, who were now businessmen working at the forefront of the operation Al was fronting in Scotland for Big Jake Cox. Frank listened, stealing the odd glance at Clock, who sat sipping mineral water while the Serbs knocked back wine, then brandies.

In their broken English they'd described the success of the international tissue trade, and how the spare parts industry was the way forward. They also made jokes about how it also solved two problems at once. Apart from making them money, some of the tissue, brains and torsos they supplied helped for medical research, while also getting rid of the refugees who were a constant drain on any country's resources. Nobody cares about them anyway, Milosh had said. Al, who kept popping out to the toilet and coming back more and more spaced out, was laughing as he drank a toast to Frank for his tireless work in the area of refugees and asylum seekers. Everyone around the table had burst out laughing. Except Frank. He felt sick to his stomach.

Now he sat staring out of the windscreen as Clock drove his car up the Glasgow road. He was so morose he didn't even notice Clock had turned off the main road until he spoke to him.

'I need a pee, Frank,' Clock said, getting out of the car. 'All that fucking mineral water.'

In his boozy state, Frank hadn't seen the car that was sitting at the edge of the lay-by with its lights off. He put his head back and sighed, closing his eyes, while he waited for Clock. When the back door opened he jumped, but he didn't get time to turn around. Even if he had, all he would have seen was the masked man with the gun in his hand.

'Say goodnight, Frank.'

Then nothing. Not even time to see the image of his little girl one last time. The gunman shot him in the back of the head and his brains exploded like a water balloon across the windscreen.

Clock came back into the driver's seat. 'You follow me, Marty.' He reversed the car, pushing Frank's slumped body out of the way as he turned the car around. 'You made a right fucking mess here, man.'

They drove along the single dirt-track road that led down towards the edge of the loch. Clock eased the car so it was off the road and onto the grassy bank that sloped into the water. He let the handbrake off and jumped out as the car rolled down and slid into the water. He watched as it slipped beneath the surface until all he could see was the roof, before there was a kind of bubbling sound as Frank and his car disappeared into Loch Lomond.

CHAPTER 23

Rosie was surprised at how emotional she felt when Emir suddenly threw his arms around her at the police station. She hugged him back, feeling the tension in his wiry body as he held onto her. She caught Don and his boss making a face at each other, and reprimanded Don with a look.

'You'll be fine, Emir. Sergeant Elliot and Detective Inspector Johnson will look after you.' She turned to the cops. 'Won't you, guys?'

'Of course we will.' The big DI patted Emir on the shoulder. 'Come on, son. Let's get you a coffee and we can get settled down for a chat.' He shook Rosie's hand. 'Thanks for your help, Rosie. We'll be in touch.'

Don walked Rosie to the door of the police station. 'The boy looks terrified,' he said, lighting a cigarette.

'He is,' Rosie said. 'Where will you put him tonight?'

Don gave her a slightly perplexed look and blew smoke out.

'Rosie, he's not your wee brother. Leave it to the professionals. Don't worry. We're not going to keep him in the cells. We have a safe house for him, but we need a longer talk with him first. Then we'll get him some grub and settle him in.'

'What do you think of what he's told you so far?' Rosie asked.

'Dynamite stuff, if what he's saying is actually true. And, of course, if we can get enough on these bastards to lift them.' He took a long draw of his cigarette and flicked it away. 'But we've a bit to go before we'll be ready to do that.'

'Yeah.' Rosie looked away from him. She didn't like holding out on Don by not passing all of the information she had to him.

'So what's your next piece going to be?'

'Don't quite know yet, Don. I'm working on a few lines,' she lied. 'But now that Emir's with you, we'll be doing something very soon. Things are going to start opening up a bit, with the cleaner's man being murdered so soon after her boss is found hanged. It's all too much of a co-incidence. Lot of intrigue. The rest of the press will be all over it now.'

'We need a chance to look at this ourselves, Rosie. If you go blasting it all over the place, these bastards will disappear.'

'Well, it's kind of out there now, Don.' She gave him a cheeky smile. 'You'll just have to get your arses in gear.'

'Everyone's been briefed. There's a team getting prepared to look at that slaughterhouse place. I think things will start to move pretty fast.' He turned to go.

'I hope you'll give me a heads-up so we can be on the ball, Don.'

'Course.' He winked. 'Stand by your mobile.'

Rosie smiled and walked towards her car. As she got in, her phone rang.

'Where are you, Rosie?' It was TJ. 'Is everything all right?'

'Just about finished, TJ. Took Emir to the cops. I've just got something to do very quickly, then I'll be over. I'm starving.'

'Good. I've cooked the best curry outside of the Punjab. I've got some decent wine as well. See you.' He hung up.

Before she drove off, she tried Tanya's mobile again, but it was still ringing out. She hadn't been able to get her on the phone since Josef had been murdered. She was beginning to get worried.

Rosie parked her car close to Tanya's flat and walked up to the door. She rang the buzzer, but there was no answer. She waited on the doorstep, looking at her watch. She buzzed another flat in the building and the security door clicked open. When she got to the top of the stairs, she was surprised to see the door of Tanya's apartment was slightly ajar.

'Tanya?' Rosie knocked on the door.

No answer.

'Tanya? You there? It's Rosie.' She pushed the door open a little more.

Rosie swithered as to whether to go in. Her stomach tightened at what she might find, given what had happened to Josef. She took a step forward, then stopped. Bad idea, she thought. She took out her mobile and was about to press Don's number when the door suddenly swung open and banged against the wall. Before she could even take in what was happening, she was grabbed by the hair and dragged into Tanya's hallway. A hand went across her mouth.

'Shut the fuck up. Scream and you're dead.' The voice rasped in her ear.

She was slammed against the wall, her head jerking back. For a second Rosie felt dizzy with the pain and shock, but then she was back. Her legs felt weak.

'Where is the fuckin' bitch?' He was wearing a balaclava, but she could see his eyes blazing. He kicked the door shut.

'I don't know,' Rosie managed to mumble behind his hand.

He punched her hard in the stomach and she doubled over, gasping for breath. He took his hand away from her mouth and grabbed her hair with his other hand. For a split second, Rosie thought one hand looked smaller than the other. Maybe the knock on her head had made her confused.

'I don't know,' she said, 'I've been trying to find her. She doesn't answer the phone.' Rosie looked at him. 'Please. Don't hurt me.'

He put his hand around her throat and squeezed.

'You're Rosie Gilmour. That bitch from the paper.' He sniffed. 'You're on the fucking list by the way. In fact I'd probably get a bonus if I did you over right now.' He slapped her again and she felt a searing pain in her cheekbone. It brought tears to her eyes.

'Please! Stop! Why are you doing this? I'm just looking for Tanya.'

'Aye. Fuck you.' He squeezed her neck. 'You're scum. You and the rest of them reporters, poking their noses into everybody's business.'

Rosie said nothing, just tried to breathe.

'See when my brother got jailed for murder? You cunts splashed it all over your paper. Said he was scum from a scum family in Easterhouse.' He paused, took a breath. 'My ma died of shame a fucking year later. Never set foot out of the house because the papers said her and her weans were scum.' He swallowed. 'Everybody pointed the finger at her. Can you imagine what that was like? Died of shame.'

His eyes were shiny now, and Rosie thought for a moment he was going to burst into tears. But she knew better. Angry men like this didn't cry. They lashed out at everyone in sight. They punched and slashed and raged their way through life, and they blamed everyone – from the system to the cops – for making them the dysfunctional toerags they were. Blamed everyone but themselves. It was just her unfortunate timing to bump into a psycho with a grudge against the press. He touched his face and from the corner of Rosie's eye she could see the crooked, withered hand. He noticed her glancing at it and squeezed her throat again.

'You see this?' He shoved the hand in front of her eyes. 'I was born like this. My ma said I was special. She made me special when I was wee and everyone laughed at me.'

Rosie didn't know what she should be saying to this damaged nutter, but it wouldn't be a good moment to offer him a hug. She stood perfectly still and silent, trying to swallow with his hand across her windpipe. But she sensed weakness. Whatever he was supposed to be doing to her, he wasn't focused on it.

Suddenly she found the strength to jerk her knee up and slam him hard between the legs. She watched astonished as he crumpled to the floor. Then she amazed herself even more by giving him another swift kick in the balls.

'Fuck!' he groaned, doubling up on the floor, clutching himself.

'Fuck you.' Rosie stumbled over him and grabbed the door handle.

In a flash she was downstairs, running towards the exit and out into the street. She didn't stop running until she got to her car and locked the doors. Her hands trembled so much she couldn't get the key into the ignition. She dropped it, then fumbled around the floor and picked it up, glancing fearfully over her shoulder.

'Come on Rosie . . . Come *on*, for Christ sake.' She finally got the key in and screeched away.

It was only when she was at George Square that she pulled the car in and looked in the rear-view mirror. Her face was red and her eye puffy. Her lip was beginning to swell. Her hands shook as she pulled her mobile out of her pocket and phoned TJ.

'Rosie. Where are you?'

She swallowed back tears, but couldn't speak.

'What's up? Rosie? What's wrong?'

'Oh TJ,' she managed to say. 'I've been attacked. Can you come?'

'Christ! Where are you?'

'George Square. Outside the city chambers.'

'I'll be there in ten minutes. Don't move.'

Back in TJ's flat, Rosie sat at his kitchen table with her hands wrapped around a mug of sweet tea and a packet of frozen peas against her swollen cheek. She'd declined his offer of a brandy. He sat opposite her, his elbows on the table with his hand supporting his chin. TJ watched her, with that look that had disarmed her from the moment she realised she had fallen in love with him. So much had happened since then, but the look was still enough to unnerve her.

'Don't stare at me like that, TJ,' Rosie said, only half joking. 'It weakens me.'

'Jesus, Rosie.' He sighed, shaking his head. 'What are we going to do with you?'

Rosie flinched a little as he reached across and gently touched her swollen lip with the back of his fingers. She took his hand and held it.

'Sorry I scared you, TJ.'

'Come on. Don't be stupid. You know I would go to the ends of the earth for you, sweetheart.' He smiled. 'But knowing you, Gilmour, by the time I got there, you'd probably be busy doing something else.'

Rosie smiled, touching her cheek and wincing.

'Sometimes I don't know where I'd be without you.

That's the truth, TJ.' Her throat felt tight with emotion. 'I missed you so much when you were away.' She shook her head. 'I wish I hadn't. But I did.'

TJ pulled his chair closer. 'You know what I wish, Rosie?' His voice was soft. 'I wish ... I wish you didn't do this shit any more.' He ran his hand through his hair. 'I know you hate me saying these things, but that's what I really feel.'

'TJ ...' Rosie didn't want to hear it.

He held his hand up. 'I know, Rosie. But honestly, this shit tonight. That guy. He could have killed you. That's obviously what he does. It's nothing to scumbags like him to squeeze the life out of someone. And then what? That's it. It's over for you.' He shrugged. 'Sure, the papers might say wonderful stuff about you, but people will be eating chips out of the paper the next day, and you'll be dead, Rosie. And for what?'

Rosie touched her neck, still tender from the grip of her attacker. She knew that nothing she would say could make him understand what she was, what drove her every day. She'd been knee-deep in other people's misery for so long, she didn't really know how to be anything else. She did everything on instinct, gut reaction. She didn't ever stop to think of the consequences, whether it was chasing the human traffickers who stole the kid in Spain last year, taking Emir to her flat to stay, or going out to Tanya's house when it was obvious that someone had bumped off her man. Sure, she was reckless. But through all the investigations where she'd taken risks, the only question she ever asked herself afterwards was: What if she hadn't? What if she hadn't stuck her neck out, taken the risk? It was irrational, and she couldn't even begin to explain it to TJ or anyone else. She just didn't know who else to be other than the person she was right now, even if her face hurt and her lip was raw. She pushed her chair back and stood up.

'I'd better phone McGuire,' she said. 'He'll go nuts.' She walked away from the table, lifting her mobile, then turned, smiling. 'And where's this curry you promised? I'm starving. Oh yes. and I'm ready for that glass of wine now, *garçon*.'

As she walked into the living room she was dialling McGuire's number.

'Gilmour. What's wrong? I'm at the back bench up to my arse in the splash here.'

Rosie looked at her watch. She'd lost track of time. It was 8.30, and McGuire would be putting the finishing touches to the first edition.

'Oh. Sorry, Mick. I'll call later . . .'

'No, Rosie. Something's obviously wrong. What's up?'

'I got attacked.'

'Christ. Where? Who? Are you hurt?'

'I got a bit of a slap. Black eye and a fat lip.'

'Fucking hell! What happened?'

'I nipped out to Tanya's house because I couldn't get her on the phone. When I got there the door was open and suddenly I got dragged by the hair into the hallway. Don't know who it was. Some guy had me by the throat, slapping me, demanding to know where she was.'

'Fuck sake. How did you get away?'

'I kneed him in the balls. He just collapsed. Christ knows where I got the strength or courage to do that, Mick. I've never done it before, but I hit him hard enough to make a run for it.'

'Shit! Remind me not to mess with you, Gilmour.' His tone lightened a little. 'But listen. Are you okay? Where are you now? Should we get the cops?'

'No, no, Mick. I'm okay. Honest. I'm with my friend TJ. He came and got me and brought me to his flat. I was a bit shocked though, but I'm fine.'

There was a pause, and Rosie knew what was coming next.

'Right, Rosie. Listen. Don't go back to your flat tonight. Just stay there. This is getting rough now. We need to take these fuckers seriously. I'm moving you somewhere with a bit of protection. A minder.'

'I don't need protection, Mick. What am I going to do with a minder? I don't want a minder. Honest. I'll go somewhere else to stay till it dies down. But no minder.'

'We'll talk about this in the morning. Just get yourself a rest and make sure that JT bloke takes good care of you.'

'It's TJ,' Rosie said.

'Yeah. Right. Just make sure he's looking after you.' He hung up.

TJ came in with two glasses of red wine and handed her one. He put on a CD, and blues music filled the room as he slipped onto the sofa beside her. Rosie took a mouthful of wine, kicked off her shoes and sat back.

'I'll have this drink, then a long hot shower. Then maybe we can eat?'

'Sure.' He leaned over and kissed her on the cheek. 'I'm crazy about you, Gilmour. You know that don't you?'

She smiled but said nothing as he brushed his lips against her bruised neck. Rosie was instantly aroused by his touch as he caressed her thigh, and closed her eyes as TJ's kisses moved down to her chest and he unbuttoned her shirt.

In the morning, Rosie awoke to the aroma of fresh coffee as the sun streamed in the window. The sound of the radio drifted through from the living room. She groaned in pain as she tried to lift her head off the pillow. Her neck hurt from the whiplash as her attacker had thrown her against the wall. She touched her face and could feel it still swollen, but at least she could see out of both eyes. The cut inside her lip still felt raw. She sat up and leaned across to look in TJ's wardrobe mirror.

'Christ,' she said aloud, as she saw the swelling round her cheekbone and eye. 'How am I going to explain this in the office?'

She pulled on one of TJ's shirts and went into the kitchen, where he stood at the cooker stirring scrambled eggs.

'Hi, pal.' She gave him a hug.

'Look at you,' he said, leaning back. 'You look like a prizefighter.'

'Feel like one too. Have I time for a quick shower? I've got to go into the office and talk to McGuire.'

'Course. Make it a quick one though.'

Rosie was finishing breakfast when the phone rang. It was Don. She looked at TJ and he shrugged as though he could have predicted it.

'Hi Don.'

'Rosie. Listen. Very quickly. We're moving on the slaughterhouse this morning. A team went up there at sparrow fart. No bastard in sight. So the forensic boys are going up now with a few of the lads battering down the door.'

'Really? Brilliant. Thanks, Don.'

'Listen. If you're coming up, leave it for at least an hour or two, because this has been kept really tight.'

'Will do. But, Don, how is Emir?'

'Fine when I saw him last night. They've got him in a flat in the West End. Don't worry. Look, I need to go.' He hung up.

Rosie sensed TJ watching her and she resisted the urge to get up and start rushing around.

'Cops are up at the slaughterhouse. They've already started. But there's nobody there. They must have done a runner. Maybe they felt the heat was heading their way.'

'Or maybe they got tipped off,' TJ said.

'Good thinking, Batman.' The idea of a snitch inside the cops was nothing new. 'You're pretty on the ball for a sax player.'

TJ smiled. 'So what you waiting for, Gilmour?' He lifted her plate. 'I know your arse is twitching to get in about it.' He stood up and ruffled her hair. 'Now bugger off to work and let me get on with my dishes.'

CHAPTER 24

The official version Rosie told about her black eye and
fat lip was that she'd pranged her car and hit her face
on the steering wheel. Anything else would have left too
many unanswered questions. So she was prepared for the
shocked expressions on the faces of reporters when she
stepped onto the editorial floor of the *Post*. She put on a
brave smile as one of them jokingly asked what the other
guy looked like. She was tempted to tell the truth: that
the last time she saw him he was writhing in agony on
the floor, clutching his balls. She headed straight for
McGuire's office.

'Bloody hell, Gilmour! What a state!' McGuire quickly
got off his chair and came round from his desk to greet
her.

Rosie looked at him suspiciously. 'You want a group
hug?' She said, attempting to smile through her puffy
lip and shrugging him off.

'Let me get a closer look, Rosie.' He stood close to her,
examining her face. 'Hmmm ... If his bollocks are as

bruised as your face, he'll not be doing much damage this weekend. What a bastard.' McGuire shook his head angrily. 'What kind of man hits a woman like that? If I had my way, Rosie, I'd put these fuckers up against a wall and shoot them.'

He gently touched her shoulder and motioned her to sit down. 'Want a coffee? Did you get some sleep last night?'

'Yes, to both questions.'

McGuire buzzed Marion and asked for some coffee, then sat on the armchair opposite Rosie. He stretched his legs out and examined the perfect crease in his pinstriped trousers. 'This is not good, Rosie. We can't have you getting slapped around like that. We've sorted a place for you in the West End. Very secure, but I'm still thinking of putting a minder outside all the time. Or even in the flat.'

'I told you, Mick,' Rosie said quickly. 'I'm not living with a minder. No way.'

'Well, we'll see how you get on. Play it by ear, no pun intended.' He grinned.

Marion appeared with a tray of coffee and some biscuits and set it down on the table between them.

'So,' McGuire said. 'We need to think where we go from here in terms of a story.'

She told him about her confrontation with Frank Paton, and about the slip-up he made about lawyers getting rid of refugees.

'What a plonker,' McGuire said. 'Imagine an idiot like him defending anyone if he's as stupid as that.'

'Yeah. Just shows you how much pressure he's under when he can't think straight. He just about shat himself when he realised straight away what he'd said.'

'I'm sure he did, but what can we do with it, Rosie? Is there a version we can write at the moment that will put more heat on him? I hope you've got it on tape.'

Rosie nodded, sipping her coffee, then said, 'We could look at doing a piece on the names of those refugees we know who have already gone missing. Just ask the question where are they, and say that we put it to Paton and he refused to answer. But once we do that, the whole thing will start to open up.' She paused. 'I'm also thinking we should go to Bosnia. Check some things out on this Milosh – or Raznatovic, to use his real name. The cops are up at the slaughterhouse and there's nobody there, so that could maybe mean they've shut it down and he's done a runner back to where he came from.'

Rosie was keen to push the Bosnia trip, after Adrian's call. On her way to the office, Adrian had called with information he'd dug up on Raznatovic and Boscovac.

'You know this other guy I told you about – the one from Belgrade who's on the board at PD Pharmaceuticals?'

'Yeah.'

'Well, my contact over in Bosnia has told me that Boscovac and Raznatovic go way back. They grew up together and both were involved in the political scene when they were at medical school. These two men are the key to this whole thing, and we've got to go over there and at least see if we can get a hold of them.'

'I wouldn't fancy your chances of tea and a sit-down

interview with any of them. You might come out without your fingers.' He gave her a cautious look.

'Yeah, but I'd still like to go. We're the only ones who have this much information, and we need to be in the right place if it kicks off.'

McGuire nodded slowly, looking thoughtful and steepling his fingers under his chin.

Rosie's mobile rang.

'Hey Don. How's it going?'

'Rosie, Listen. Frank Paton's car has just been pulled out of Loch Lomond.'

'You're kidding!'

'Nope. And he was in it.'

'Christ almighty! Seriously? Suicide?'

Rosie turned to McGuire and mouthed the name Frank Paton, drawing her hand across her throat. He mouthed back 'oh fuck', and punched the air. Rosie shook her head and rolled her eyes upwards.

'I can't talk long,' Don said. 'It's not looking like suicide, given that there wasn't much left of his head. His wife reported him missing late last night when he didn't come home and she couldn't get in touch with him, but it was all kept hush-hush. The alarm bells only rang when a couple of amateur divers were in Loch Lomond this morning and saw the car. They saw a body in it, took the number plate and got the cops.'

'My God,' Rosie said. 'He was under huge pressure, Don.' As she said it, she felt a pang of guilt about their recent encounter.

'Yeah, well not any more he isn't. Looks like he's been

bumped off and the car driven into the loch. I need to go.'

The line went dead.

Rosie sat back and made a whistling noise.

'I think we've got tomorrow's splash taken care of, Mick.'

'What the hell happened?'

Rosie told him what Don had said.

'So they've done him in,' Mick said. 'Maybe they thought he was a loose cannon. Too edgy and nervous.'

'I think so,' Rosie said. 'They wouldn't take any chances of him buckling if the cops got to him. Bad move on their part – because the cops will be all over it now.'

'And now they've got your man Emir.' McGuire stood up, rubbing his hands as he went back behind his desk. 'This is beginning to open up big time. I do love it when this happens, Gilmour.'

Rosie stood up. 'I need to talk to the cops. They'll be issuing some kind of statement shortly. It's not as if they can keep Paton's death a secret.'

'Right,' McGuire said. 'Once the cops tell us what's what, you can start writing your version. Let's have a bit of intrigue about two lawyers dead, and connect the refugees going missing. Nobody else will have that.'

'It will open up the story though, Mick.'

'I know, but I don't think we have an option any more. It's already wide open now, so let's get something in about it – not the stuff we've got from Matt at the slaughter-house, of course. Let's keep our powder dry on that. We'll drip the intrigue and mystery first, then see what comes out.'

'Okay.' Rosie headed for the door. 'I'll start putting something together shortly.'

McGuire didn't answer, just sat looking at the blank pages on his desk. He was already thinking headlines.

By the time Rosie had finished her story, Frank Paton's death was already the number one item on the six o'clock news. Police had confirmed it was a murder inquiry, and the word coming to Reynolds was that Paton had been shot in the head. Rosie watched the TV coverage from the office where she was working, away from the main editorial floor. There was footage of the area in Loch Lomond taped off as a crime scene, and of the car being loaded onto a lorry to be taken for forensic examination. Paton's body was already in the morgue. They showed library pictures of Paton leaving the High Court in Glasgow with one of his clients who had just got off on an armed robbery charge. There were also holiday snapshots of him with his wife and kids on some cruise liner a couple of years ago. Rosie pictured the misery and shock of the family right now and she felt sorry for them, but her own sense of self-preservation also made her glad he hadn't committed suicide – especially since she was one of the last people to see him and heap pressure on him. At least she couldn't blame herself. She remembered his face just before he left the pub, a mask of shock and fear. She told herself he got what was coming to him. Look what he did to the poor people who had come to him for help. People like Paton deserved no mercy – and it looked like he'd been shown none.

Rosie was on the landline phone to McGuire, who wanted to know how long before he got her story, when Don called her on her mobile. She told McGuire she'd call him back.

'Don. How are you?' she asked, but he didn't answer. After a moment's silence, Rosie spoke again. 'You there, Don?'

'Yeah. Where are you, Rosie?'

'In the office, doing up the Frank Paton murder for the splash tomorrow. Some story.'

'Uh ... Listen, Rosie ... ' He sounded nervous, even perhaps shocked.

'What's up, Don?'

She could hear him breathing heavily. He was struggling to talk.

'Rosie ... There's been an almighty fuck-up.' He paused. 'It's Emir. He's been shot.'

Rosie slumped in her chair.

'*What*? How can he be shot, Don? He was under police protection, for God's sake! He ... um ...What ... I ...' Rosie couldn't think straight. All she saw was the look on Emir's face as he hugged her before going off with the cops. 'Oh, Christ, Don. Tell me this isn't true.'

'I'm sorry, Rosie,' he said. 'He's in the hospital. It was a couple of hours ago. There's a huge rammy going on to find out how the fuck it happened. Unbelievable fuck-up.'

'Which hospital? Can I see him? Is he going to die?'

'The Western Infirmary. It's not looking good, Rosie. Shot in the stomach. Lost so much blood.'

Rosie was on her feet.

'Will I get in if I come up?' Rosie paused. She had to get in. 'Don. You need to get me in to see him.'

'I don't know, Rosie. I need to speak to the DI.'

'Don, you *have* to.' Rosie's throat was tight. 'I'm all he's got. The poor guy's got nobody. Do you hear me Don? You guys owe me that. I brought him to you, and you fucking let him get murdered.' She bit her lip, fighting back tears of anger and frustration. 'Sorry, Don. Sorry.'

'Just head up there, Rosie, and I'll talk to the DI. I'll meet you outside.' He hung up.

Rosie sat back down, sent her story to McGuire, then dialled his number.

'Mick. Story's in your desk. Listen. I just got a phone call.' She swallowed back tears.

'What's up, Gilmour? What's wrong?'

'Emir,' she said, her voice breaking. 'They've shot Emir.'

'Oh fuck. But how? He was under police protection.'

'I know, Mick. Don't know the details, just that it's really bad. He's in hospital, but he's not going to make it. Listen. I'm going up to the Western Infirmary now. That okay? You've got the story. I . . .' She paused. 'I don't want him to die on his own, Mick. He trusted me. Oh shit, Mick, he was just a poor innocent guy.'

'Christ, Rosie,' McGuire's tone softened. 'I'm so sorry. Just go up and be with him.' He paused. 'But Rosie? I want to know how the fuck this happened. It stinks. Call me if you need anything.'

'Thanks, Mick.' She grabbed her bag, and dashed out of the office.

Rosie blinked back tears as she drove to the Western as fast as the rush-hour traffic would allow. Her mind was a blur, veering from rage to shock to an overwhelming, choking sadness. Emir, a helpless, innocent young man who came here seeking help, had been picked off by these scum of the earth bastards who never did a day's honest work in their lives, who plundered and murdered and destroyed everything in their wake that ever had a chance of being decent. She gripped the steering wheel. Something was rotten at the heart of this investigation, and she made a silent vow that, no matter what it took, she would bury every single one of them.

She saw Don standing on the steps as she parked her car, and she walked briskly towards him.

'What a fucking mess this is,' Don said. Then he saw her face. 'Jesus, Rosie. What the hell happened to you?'

Rosie had almost forgotten about her bruised face.

'Oh,' she touched her cheek. 'Pranged the car. Hit the steering wheel.' They went up the steps. 'Never mind that. What in the name of Christ happened, Don? Any ideas? Talk to me.'

'Someone must have tipped them off, Rosie. One of our guys.' He puffed his cigarette nervously and shook his head. 'I don't know who or how, but only an insider could have told them where he was. It was as tight as a fucking drum.'

'Who knew?'

'Just me, the DI – by the way, he's fucking jumping on his hat with rage – the boss and the Deputy Chief Constable – plus the team they had watching Emir. Not sure exactly who, but when we're putting someone in police protection like this, especially on a big inquiry, and a prime witness that was given to us by the press, then the very top gets to know about it. They have to. Chief Constable's on holiday, so the deputy was in charge. Apparently they're all going crazy back at HQ. It's going to get out, that we fucked up. There'll be an internal investigation.'

'Don, listen.' She looked at him intently. 'I need your help in this. I really do. This is just wrong. What's happened here is so wrong, and if there's someone on the inside who's part of it, I hope I can rely on you to help me.'

'You don't need to say that, Rosie.' Don looked a little offended. 'I help you because I trust you. Whatever I get, you'll get. But somebody wanted this guy dead, and some bastard inside our place was prepared to accommodate them.' He tossed his cigarette butt away. 'We'll find them.'

'Can I see Emir?'

'I talked to the DI. He said he'll get his arse felt if anybody finds out, but you're to go in.' He turned to walk inside with her, then he touched her arm. 'Rosie . . . He's not going to make it.'

Rosie shook her head and walked behind him.

Going up in the lift, she was reminded of a few months ago, when she made this very journey to say goodbye to her dying father, who had been a virtual stranger most of her life. She'd held his hand while he breathed his last and said he was sorry. A picture of him lying in the bed flashed across Rosie's mind. The lift doors opened and as she stepped out in the corridor, the DI met her, his face ashen.

'Sorry, Rosie.' He shook his head. 'What can I say? I just don't know. But I'll find out.'

Rosie nodded. 'Can I see Emir?.'

'In there,' he pointed to the side room off the ward. 'He hasn't got long. Lost too much blood.' He looked beyond her. 'It's not fair. None of it.'

Rosie sensed she had an ally. Don had told her the DI had been born and bred in the Highlands, the son of a cop. He was old school, and straight as a die.

'I hope you get to the bottom of it.'

'Too fucking right I will.'

The door opened and a nurse came out. The DI said nothing and ushered Rosie inside.

Emir lay hooked up to machines monitoring his heartbeat, his eyes closed, his face even more sunken than it had been. Rosie stood over him. She took his hand, warm and soft.

'Emir,' she said softly. 'It's Rosie.'

After a second he squeezed her hand. His eyes flickered and opened.

'Rosie,' he whispered, his lids heavy. 'Why?'

Rosie leaned over him and automatically stroked his forehead and hair.

'I don't know, Emir.' She fought back tears. 'But I will find out. For you, and for Jetmir, and for the others.'

He squeezed her hand. 'I want to go home, Rosie,' he murmured. A tear trickled out of his eye as he looked at her. 'I want to go home.'

Rosie gently touched his face.

'I know, Emir. I know.'

'Rosie. I need you to help me.' His breathing was shallow. 'Can you go to my grandmother. In Macedonia. Tell her I am happy here. I have job and my life is good. Please. Can you tell her.'

'Yes, Emir. I will go and see her when I go to Bosnia. I will visit.'

His lips moved to a weak smile. 'Thank you, Rosie.'

'I'm so sorry, Emir.'

'No. You help me. Only you.' He held on to her hand, his eyes locked to hers, pleading. 'I'm frightened, Rosie.'

'Don't be,' she said, stroking his face. 'Don't be afraid, Emir.'

His grip slackened. Then nothing. Rosie watched, swallowing her tears, as the life drained out of him.

She came out of the room and saw Don and the DI sitting in the corridor. They jumped up and came towards her.

'He's gone,' Rosie managed to say.

Nobody spoke. Don patted her shoulder, then walked briskly to the nurse's station. Rosie glanced around for somewhere to flee to, because she knew she was about to break down. She saw a nurse coming out of a staff toilet, and made a beeline for it.

Inside, she bolted the door and burst into tears. She sat on the toilet seat with her head in her hands, sobbing.

Guilt, anger and sadness for a young man who would have been happy with so little. If only she'd left Emir alone, perhaps he could have taken his chances that they wouldn't find him. He could have done a runner, left Glasgow, started out somewhere else. He might even still have been alive if she'd never gone up to him that day when she saw him the first time, weeping outside the flats. But no. She had to plough in, take him into her confidence, promise she would take care of him. She had failed him, and for what? For a story. She pushed the palms of her hands against her eyes and sniffed, wiping her nose and trying to compose herself. She stood up, and went to the sink and splashed cold water on her face and dabbed it with paper towels. As she did, she looked in the mirror at the flushed, puffy face looking back at her. She stood for a few moments, staring at herself long and hard, wiping her eyes with the back of her hand.

Rosie kept on looking in the mirror, and as quick as the shame washed over her and she saw the images of Mags Gillick who had died helping her, her guilt turned to anger. Yes, it was for a story, she told herself. That's who she was. But it was more than that. Emir was one victim – just one of the many defenceless people just like him who were at the mercy of the monsters who preyed on them because they couldn't fight back. They were screaming in the dark. If she didn't tell their stories then this would just keep going on – the murder, the brutality, would continue. She took a deep breath and vowed that if she did nothing else for the rest of her life, she would find these people and expose them, no matter where the hunt took her. For Emir, for his friend, and for all the poor people on the list who had come here seeking refuge.

She opened the door and went back outside, knowing that Don and the DI would see she'd been crying. She stood facing them.

'I hope you find these bastards,' she said to both of them. 'You have to.'

She felt her lip quiver.

'We'll find them,' the DI said, looking straight at her.

'Yeah, sure you will.' Rosie turned and walked briskly away.

CHAPTER 25

O'Brien's bar was filling up with the usual champagne set who were there to be seen with the right people in the right places, where they could rub shoulders and mingle with other like-minded tossers. In the restaurant off the main bar there were still a few lunchtime stragglers, drinking liqueurs and laughing in that three-sheets-to-the-wind way you do if you're still having lunch and it's past six in the evening. Rosie eyed them a little enviously, part of her wishing she could just lose herself like that for an afternoon of carefree boozing and eating in good company. She promised herself that when this was all over, she and TJ would go out one day and just forget to come back.

She sat at the bar sipping a gin and tonic, watching the door, waiting for Don. She'd already explained about her bashed-up face to the silver-haired Donegal barman who'd known her for years. She'd told so many people she had crashed her car she was beginning to believe it herself.

As she turned to the bar and ordered another drink, Don came up behind her and squeezed her shoulder.

'Hey Rosie. You all right?'

She swivelled around. Normally there would have been instant banter, but today there was none. Don looked worn out, even for a man with his prematurely craggy features.

'I'm okay,' Rosie said. 'You look shattered, Don.'

He asked for a pint of lager and sat up on the bar stool next to her. He lit a cigarette.

'Can I have one?' Rosie asked.

Don gave her a sympathetic look. 'That bad, eh?'

Rosie put the cigarette between her lips as Don flicked the lighter. She took a deep draw. It felt good.

'Sometimes, a cigarette and a stiff drink is the only thing.' She sighed out a trail of smoke. 'What a mess, Don. Poor Emir. I can't get him out of my mind.' She shook her head.

Rosie looked at Don, then down at the bar. She didn't want to tell him she'd been awake half the night, and that every time she closed her eyes she saw Emir's face that first day, when he stood weeping outside the Red Road flats. A desperate, sad, frightened guy, too far from home. And when she did finally drop off to sleep from sheer exhaustion, her nightmares were filled with marauding soldiers slashing their way through Bosnian villages – and then the image of her mother being taken away on the back of a lorry, her arms outstretched and calling out her name. She'd woken up, her face wet with tears.

Don took a long drink of his pint, then said, 'There's a lot of shit hitting the fan up at HQ. They want to talk to you, Rosie.' He fiddled with his lighter. 'You might get pulled in for an interview.'

Rosie bristled. 'Stuff that, Don. Would bloody fit them better if they put their energies into finding who shot a crucial witness they were supposed to be protecting. That's what they should be doing. What do they want with me?'

But she knew exactly what they wanted – to grill her to see how much more she knew.

'You're right, Rosie, but I'm just saying . . . They think you're maybe withholding information.'

'Yeah, sure they do,' she said, bitterly indignant. 'They might start asking themselves that if I've got information, then how come they don't have it.'

Don shrugged. 'I know what you mean, but this is serious now, Rosie. Really serious.'

Rosie tried not to look cynical. You're damn right it's serious, she felt like saying. She could show him a list as long as his arm of refugees who Frank Paton and Tony Murphy had probably sent to their deaths. She took a gulp of her drink and told herself to settle down.

Don leaned closer and lowered his voice.

'Forensics have come back with samples they found at the slaughterhouse. It's human skin, Rosie. Tissue and bone fragments. Something fucking sinister has been going on up there. It's beginning to look like Emir's story of him and his mate being kidnapped was true.'

Rosie kept her face straight.

'Really? So what's the thinking?'

He spoke in a whisper. 'Well, with that torso that was found in the Clyde looking like it might have been a refugee, and with asylum lawyers Murphy and Paton both dead, and now Emir ... There's no way vigilantes are doing this. We might be looking at organs or something being sold.'

'Christ!' Rosie did her best to sound surprised.

'It's big business.' Don stubbed his cigarette out. 'Worldwide. We've got guys looking at that too.'

Rosie said nothing and they sat in silence for a while, till Don ordered another drink for both of them.

'So, what are you doing about Emir's murder?'

Rosie had already talked to McGuire, and they were making a decision tomorrow whether to go along with the story he told her. Throw the whole thing wide open, McGuire had said. No matter what the rest of the media might do, the *Post* would always be in front because of the information they already had – and the pictures.

'There's an internal inquiry underway. Boss released a statement today. That'll spark off a few questions, but they're not making any comment. Standard quote.'

'Somebody inside the cops must have blabbed about Emir. They obviously told whoever wanted him dead where he was being kept. You've got to find who that is.'

'We will.' He looked Rosie in the eye, his mouth curling a little at the side. 'You know more than you're letting on, Rosie, don't you?'

She said nothing.

'Your story today about Frank Paton's murder ... there

were a couple of hints in there about refugees and stuff, and the piece you wrote last week about refugees disappearing.' He paused. 'You do know more Rosie, don't you?'

Rosie gave him an insolent look. 'I'm a journalist, Don, not a cop. It's your job to catch the bad guys. I just expose them in the paper.'

Don shifted in his seat. 'Don't get me wrong, Rosie. I think you're right, but I'm giving you fair warning because you're my friend. They're coming to talk to you.'

Rosie shrugged. 'Sure. I'll talk to them.'

She excused herself and went to the bathroom, glad to find it empty. She took her mobile from her bag and phoned McGuire.

'Rosie? What's up? You make me nervous when you phone me at night.'

'Nothing, Mick. Just to let you know quickly that the cops are looking to pull me in to start questioning me. I know where this could go.'

'Fuck them.'

'Listen, Mick. I'm going to have to go to Bosnia anyway, then to Belgrade, see if we can track this Raznatovic guy down. Why not get me out there as soon as possible?'

'Hmm. You might be right. We'll talk about it in the morning.'

When Rosie came back into the bar, Don had almost finished his pint. 'One for the road?' he asked.

'No. Thanks, Don.' Rosie looked at her watch. 'I need to get a move on. I've got something on tonight.' She put her bag over her shoulder. 'But to be honest, I'm knackered.'

'Yeah,' Don said. 'Me too. But tell you what, Rosie. I think we're going to be a lot more knackered before this is finished.'

They headed towards the swing doors and walked out into the mild summer evening, standing silently for a moment and watching the dying light throw long shadows from the magnificent buildings around Royal Exchange Square.

'I love this city.' Rosie gazed around, feeling kind of choked. Then she turned to Don. 'I hope you find your traitor, pal.' She shook her head. 'Because if there's someone inside who's prepared to let a major witness get bumped off while under police protection, then you guys are fundamentally useless – present company excepted.'

Don looked dejected. 'I know. It's grim. But we'll get to the bottom of it. The DI's as straight as they come. I told you that.'

He gave Rosie a bear hug and kissed her on the cheek. 'Watch yourself, Rosie.'

She glanced at him briefly, wondering if she should read more into that. She watched as he walked away.

Rosie was walking up towards the Blue Note to meet TJ and finish the evening with him as arranged. She was close to the bar when her mobile rang. There was no number.

'Hello?'

'Rosie?'

'Yeah. Who's this?'

'It's Tanya.'

Rosie stopped in her tracks. Relief flooded through her. Tanya was alive.

'Tanya! Are you okay? Where are you? I went to your house . . . I thought . . . I was worried they'd . . .'

'I'm all right, Rosie. I ran away. They came for me, two men. They beat me and took me in their car, but I got out.'

'How? What happened?'

'Rosie.' Tanya interrupted. 'I have no money in my phone. Can you meet me?'

'Of course. Where are you?'

'I am in a cafe. The one at the start of Woodlands Road. Is open late. It's safe here. There are always people.'

'Okay,' Rosie said. 'Wait for me. I'll be there in five minutes.' She hailed a taxi.

Rosie spotted Tanya through the big window at the Grassroots cafe. She went inside, giving her a wave from the door. The place was busy, mostly student types, and one or two lonely-looking people reading books. Rosie sat down on the leather easy chair opposite Tanya. They both looked surprised when they saw each other's bruised faces.

'People must think it's battered women's night in here,' Rosie said.

Tanya smiled through a cut lip. One eye was a little blackened, but her bruises were fading. 'Is nothing new for me, a punched face,' she said, resigned.

Rosie immediately regretted having made the joke.

'Sorry, Tanya. I forgot about what happened to you. I wasn't thinking.'

Tanya shrugged. 'No problem, Rosie.' She gave a long sigh. 'Is over now. Well, no more beatings from Josef anyway.'

'I'm so sorry, Tanya. I know he meant a lot to you at one time.'

Tanya took a cigarette from her packet and lit it. She was silent for a moment then blew out a stream of smoke and said, 'Yes. He did. But that was a long time ago.' She looked at Rosie. 'They killed him because he was trying to blackmail Frank Paton. I knew he would do that. I told you. He is so stupid. I mean . . . was.'

'I think you're right.' Rosie said.

'I know for sure, Rosie,' Tanya said. 'The men said it to me when they slap me. They said, "you'll get the same as your fucking blackmailing boyfriend." Then they hit me. They said was I going to blackmail them too.'

Rosie ordered a latte and another black coffee for Tanya. She told her about going to her house and the man who attacked her. Then, quietly, Tanya told her what had happened to her.

The men who burst into her flat had bundled her into the car and driven her towards the city centre. She pretended to be unconscious in the back; both men were in the front seat. When they stopped at the lights outside Queen Street station, she made a run for it. She smiled, saying they must be stupid because they didn't even lock the door. She ran past the taxi rank and up into the station, then downstairs to a platform. She had no idea where she was going, but she just jumped on a train that was about to leave. As the train pulled away from the station, she saw one of her attackers arrive at the bottom of the steps. But he was too late.

'You had a very lucky escape,' Rosie said. 'Good for you, Tanya. You are much tougher than you think.'

'I thought maybe they would come after me, but I know they wouldn't be able to find me. I stayed on the train for almost an hour until it went to the coast, a place called Helensburgh. I found a small guest house and stayed for a few days.'

'Where are you staying now?'

'In a small hotel in the city. Is okay for now.'

'You should really talk to the police,' Rosie said. She wanted to say the police could protect her, but she knew they couldn't.

'No,' Tanya said. 'I cannot do that. They maybe know I took the letters. I only going to stay here for a few days. I have a friend in London who will give me a room. I can go back to working with the escort agency there. It's money.' She stubbed her cigarette out and looked at Rosie. 'I will survive, Rosie. I came all the way from Ukraine for a better life, and one day I will find it here. If not here, maybe Spain, maybe Italy, or Amsterdam. I will work in anything until I get enough money. But these people won't win. They won't kill me.'

Rosie looked at her and her mind flipped back to Mags Gillick. She wanted a better life too, but she didn't get the chance. They sat quietly, and Rosie wondered if she was going to ask her for money.

'Is there anything I can do to help you, Tanya?'

'No.' Tanya shook her head and looked at the floor. 'I wanted to see you to say thank you ... for listening to me and understanding.' She put down her cup. 'I hope you find them, Rosie. The men who are killing the refugees. That is what they are doing, isn't it? That is why the refugees are gone?'

Rosie nodded slowly. 'I think so, Tanya, I am working on it. I will get them, but it's going to be tough.'

Tanya stood up, and Rosie walked with her out of the cafe, surprised and moved that she wanted nothing.

'Well,' Tanya smiled. 'Goodbye Rosie. Maybe we can keep in touch some time.' She took a step forward and put her arms around her.

Rosie hugged her back.

'Of course. Good luck, Tanya. Be safe.'

They parted, and Rosie saw that Tanya's tears had spilled onto her bruised cheek. She looked lonely, despite her defiance.

'I must go,' she said, sniffing and turning away.

Rosie watched until she disappeared up the road and turned off into one of the rows of tenement-lined side-streets where you could be anonymous in the melting pot of colour and cultures in the West End of the city.

CHAPTER 26

The flat where McGuire had moved Rosie to for safety was one of those fashionable minimalist jobs in the West End. Rosie sat drinking coffee at the kitchen table, looking around at the ordered, squared lines of pale wood furniture and pastel sofas – the kind of place where if you left a newspaper on a chair it would ruin the entire sterile karma. She wondered what kind of people would want to live in a place like this, and she was already missing the clutter of her own flat, where little remnants of what she'd been doing, wearing, reading were scattered around every room. But at least this felt safe – four solid bolts on the front door and double locks on every window. She'd joked to McGuire it was so secure it probably belonged to a drug dealer.

After a restless night, she had been up from the first signs of daylight, her mind buzzing with the phone call she'd taken from Mickey Kavanagh when she got home. It had answered a few questions.

Mickey told her that word had reached him from his Special Branch connections in London that there were already rumblings at government level over what was going on up in Glasgow. They'd had intelligence in the past that Raznatovic was involved with gangsters and that he may have gone to Glasgow, but the trail had gone cold some months ago and they did nothing more. He mentioned the name PD Pharmaceuticals and the deposed Environment Secretary Tim Hayman who was on the board of directors.

There was potential embarrassment for the government if anything dodgy was exposed about PD: not only because of the former Secretary of State's current involvement with the company, but also the fact that government had given them a five million-pound grant to come to Manchester – where they'd created four hundred jobs as part of their much-vaunted industrial regeneration programme. If there was something rotten, even if it did seem far-fetched, Mickey said, they wouldn't want it to get out. Rosie told him about Emir and how he'd been shot, but he'd already heard it on the grapevine. He told her to be careful, but the word was that Raznatovic had vanished.

Rosie was getting ready to leave the flat when her mobile rang.

'Rosie.'

It was Adrian.

'Adrian. Good to hear from you. You all right?' She pictured his face, always so serious, smudges of sleeplessness under his dark eyes.

'Yes, my friend. I can talk only for a minute. I have good information.'

'Great. What's happening?'

'He is here, the Serbian. In Belgrade, my people there tell me. He is hiding. Protected.'

Rosie's stomach tightened a little.

'Serbians tell you this, Adrian? But they were your enemies during the war.'

'Yes, Rosie, that is true. But before the war we were neighbours, friends. I still have contacts with some old friends who do not like what happened.'

'Do you think we could get to him?'

'He is a wanted man. War crimes. The authorities also will be trying to find him.' He paused. 'I think we can get him, Rosie, but is dangerous. I don't know if you should come.' He paused again. 'But I also think you may be in danger even in Glasgow. These people have many connections that can stretch across countries.'

Silence. Rosie remembered the last time she saw Adrian, and the shoot-out in the car park in the Costa del Sol as he'd rescued his sister from the people-traffickers who had trapped her.

'I want to come, Adrian.'

'Then come, Rosie. We will work together. I must go now.' The line went dead.

'Right, Gilmour,' McGuire said, as Rosie walked into his office. 'I've got a plan. Sit down.'

She sat down, saying, 'Before you start, Mick, let me tell you about a couple of phone calls I just took.'

She told him what she'd heard from Mickey Kavanagh last night, and about Adrian's call this morning. She left out what he'd said about the danger.

'Shower of bastards,' McGuire said. 'That explains a lot. They've obviously not been busting a gut looking for this evil bastard Raznatovic because of the potential embarrassment.' He took his reading glasses off and tossed them on the desk. 'How can they ever justify that? Well, fuck them, Rosie. We're going to give them it with both barrels.'

Rosie nodded, raising a finger in warning.

'Agreed, Mick. But if we just blast everything into the paper now, the rest of the media will be on us like flies round the proverbial, *and* the cops will be all over us.'

'I know. I've already thought about that.' McGuire got up and started pacing the room. 'Right . . . The big story of the day is Emir getting shot while in police custody. That's a live, running story and everyone is covering it because there's an inquiry. The cops know they look inept at the very least.'

'Yeah, at the very least,' Rosie said.

McGuire turned and faced her, spreading his hands as he explained.

'Everyone will be reporting the story straight. But nobody will have what we have – Emir's own story. So what I want you to do, Rosie, is get his piece written up. We tell the inside story of the murdered refugee. How he came to us for help, his claim about him and his friend being kidnapped and taken to this slaughterhouse. That will blow it open a bit. We don't say anything about what we did . . .' He pointed to Rosie, half smiling. 'Er . . . you did.

'We don't go in with what we know, what we saw inside the place, but we just pose the question: what happened to his friend who he never saw again? That's all provable, because his friend would be listed with the Refugee Council. Then we can print the list of the refugees taken from Paton's office who have also disappeared. We'll ask the question, where are they?' He paused. 'That might be a bit dodgy because cops will wonder how we got the list, so we'll just invent something for them if they ask.' He went back behind his desk, and stood looking down at Rosie. 'By the way, firstly we need to get you out of here, so you and Matt are off to Sarajevo in the morning. Once this hits the front page, the cops will be right in here with their jackboots on.'

'Definitely,' Rosie agreed.

There was a knock at McGuire's door, and Marion came in.

'Sorry to disturb you, Mick, but there's two detectives at the front door.' She looked at Rosie. 'They want to speak to you, Rosie'

'Fucking terrific,' McGuire scowled. 'With timing like that they should be on the stage. Get them to come up.'

Rosie took a deep breath. 'They're probably going to try to monster me.'

'Aye, that'll be right.' He dialled Marion. 'Get Hanlon down here, and give the coppers a coffee. Tell them Rosie's busy and she'll be with them shortly. Tossers can wait.' He put the phone down.

*

Half an hour later, when Marion ushered the two detectives into McGuire's office, he got up from behind his desk and greeted them, stretching out his hand. The company lawyer, Tommy Hanlon, seated with Rosie on the sofa, gave her a dig in the ribs with his elbow and they both stood up and shook hands with the cops. McGuire motioned them towards the long oak table in his office where he held his twice-daily news conferences.

The big detective introduced himself as DI William Craig, and Rosie made eye contact with the woman detective at his side, whom he introduced as DS Shirley McIntyre. She had a po-faced expression that said she'd be glad to bundle Rosie into the back of the police car by the end of the interview. Fat chance, Rosie, thought, glancing at Hanlon.

Hanlon opened a notepad, took a gold Mont Blanc fountain pen out of his inside jacket pocket and wrote on the page. Rosie smiled to herself. Who uses a fountain pen in this day and age? A maverick young QC like Tommy Hanlon, that's who. Someone whose self-belief in his ability and swashbuckling style in the courtroom made him the most sought-after brief in the business. When Hanlon strutted into court, he already knew he had his case won even before he cross-examined the first witness. Rosie felt safe.

The DI cleared his throat, and opened a folder he'd put down on the table. He glanced around at everyone.

'As you know, we are investigating the death of Emir Marishta, the Kosovan Albanian refugee.'

'The murder,' Rosie interrupted.

The DI reddened. 'The murder.' He nodded in Rosie's direction. 'We'd like to ask you a few questions, Miss Gilmour.'

He took a deep breath and was about to speak, when Hanlon interrupted.

'Detective Inspector Craig. I want to point out to you that my client will be very limited in what questions she will be in a position to answer today.'

The DI shifted in his seat and his face flushed even more. The words 'fuck you' were stamped on his forehead.

'I'm well aware of that, Mr Hanlon.' He glared at him. 'But if you don't mind, I'll proceed for the moment.'

Hanlon scribbled 'prick' on his notepad and turned it towards Rosie. She tried not to look at it.

'Right,' Craig said, addressing Rosie. 'So, Miss Gilmour . . .'

'Call me Rosie, please, Inspector. I am under fifty,' she said, deadpan.

He let her smart-arse comment fly over his head. 'Ahem . . . Rosie. So. I understand you had met and were in contact with the young man Emir. You had initially met him at the Red Road flats, I believe. During the demonstration?'

'Yes. That's right. I met him and we had been in touch. I've told your officers that Emir told me his friend Jetmir had been kidnapped.'

The DI nodded.

'And you didn't come to the police to report that information at the time?'

'Inspector, if I came to the police every time someone made an allegation or a claim, I'd never be doing anything else.'

'But you took it seriously?'

'I did. But then he didn't contact me again for a few days.'

'And when he did?'

Rosie lied. 'Well, you know the rest, Inspector. I handed Emir over to the police who listened to his claims and promised they would protect him.' Rosie paused. 'Which, as you also know, they clearly did not.'

The DI clicked his pen a few times.

'Can you tell me what else he spoke to you about, regarding the lawyers Frank Paton and Tony Murphy?'

Hanlon put his hand up.

'I'm sorry. My client can't answer that.'

The DI glowered at him. 'We are investigating a murder here, Mr Hanlon. It's very important that nobody is withholding information from any aspect that may assist the inquiry.'

McGuire cleared his throat.

'Then perhaps the first place you should be looking, Detective Inspector, is how a man who was assisting the police was murdered while he was under the protection of officers from Strathclyde's finest. Should you not be asking how this happened?'

'That's a matter for internal investigation.' The DI said, his mouth tight.

'And this is a newspaper, Inspector.' McGuire, leaned forward. 'We write stories. Our job is not to find murderers.

But I'll tell you this: we *will* find out how this man was murdered.'

The DI responded through gritted teeth. 'Withholding information from a police investigation is a very serious matter, Mr McGuire.'

'Yes. I'm sure it is.' McGuire pushed his chair back. This interview was over.

The DI got to his feet and the DS quickly got up and stood at his side. 'I don't think there's really much point in continuing with this interview,' Detective Inspector Craig said. 'I can see we are getting no cooperation.' He looked at Rosie. 'We'll be in touch.' He looked at the editor, now heading towards the door to open it, adding, 'And we may also have to speak to you in due course, Mr McGuire.'

McGuire held the door open for the cops.

'What a wanker!' he said when they'd walked out and closed the door behind them.

CHAPTER 27

'Your ears must be burning, Gilmour.'

Rosie took Don's call on the mobile as she made her way to the restaurant to meet TJ.

'What?'

'Big Bill Craig is calling you for all the bastards of the day after that interview in your office. Said he felt like a right prick.' Don was clearly relishing it.

'Well, maybe that's because he is one,' she said.

He laughed. 'He came in here like a fiend, kicking a bin in the corridor on the way into his office, saying you and the editor and that Hanlon made a right tit of him.'

'Well, it wouldn't have been his best interview.' Rosie chuckled. 'But what the hell did he think we would do? Sit down and compare notes?'

'Yeah,' Don said, 'know what you mean. But don't be surprised if he makes more of it. He'll be asking the boss if they can pull you in for withholding information. He knows you're holding out on him.'

'He knows bugger all, Don. If I'm holding out on him,

then he should ask himself how come he doesn't have the information in the first place?'

'I know, but he could make trouble for you, Rosie. Just saying. I'm marking your card.'

'Thanks, Don.' Rosie changed the subject. 'Any more word on the slaughterhouse or that Serbian guy?'

'Not really. Looks like he's done a runner. But the word is that there's a bit of political involvement and the cops will not be releasing any information about them hunting for a Serbian.'

'Wonder why.' Rosie was glad the police wouldn't mention the Serbian – it meant she had it all to herself and it gave her time to try to track him down.

'If I get any more, I'll give you a shout.'

'Cheers. Oh, and Don ... any news on who it was on the inside that gave Emir up to be murdered?'

He paused. 'Not yet, Rosie. Will let you know.' The line went dead.

Rosie was glad by the time dinner with TJ was coming to an end. They'd been making small talk, with her keeping him up to speed about the investigation and frisson with the detectives. But there had been an underlying atmosphere throughout the meal, and Rosie wasn't sure if it was just her guilty conscience because she was about to tell TJ she was off to Bosnia the following day, or whether there was something else going on with him. She watched him suspiciously as he split the remainder of the bottle of red wine between their two glasses. The waiter came over with coffees and they both declined liqueurs.

'TJ,' Rosie took a sip of her wine. 'I'm going out of town.' She paused as he looked at her over the top of his wine glass. 'To Belgrade. Well, going to Sarajevo first. Then to Belgrade.'

TJ took a deep breath and let it out slowly. He handed her a cigarette and flicked the lighter under it, keeping his eyes on her.

'To look for the Serbian?'

'Yeah, I'm told he's there. Adrian called me.'

TJ sighed, blowing out smoke. 'So you're going to hunt down a Serbian with a reputation for brutality and murder, who was over here hacking up refugees in Glasgow and selling their skin and tissue all over the world.' He paused, raising his eyebrows for effect. 'What part of the phrase "death wish" is it that you don't seem to understand, Rosie?'

'Oh, come on, TJ.' Rosie gave him a perplexed look. 'It's my job. You know that.' She pushed her hair back. 'What do you expect me to do? The key person in the story may be in a place that I have the chance to track him down and unmask him for what he's done; maybe even get him arrested. It's what I do. It will make it all worthwhile.'

'No, Rosie. It's not what you do. Hunting this guy down is for the authorities and the war crimes people. It's their job, not yours. You've got plenty on this story. More than enough to fill several days' newspapers.' He shook his head. 'Why do you always want to push it further and further? Why, Rosie?'

Rosie looked at him. She knew his reaction was motivated by worry about her safety. He was the one person in the whole world she totally trusted and believed in, yet even after everything he knew about her, he still couldn't see all of her. Deep down she knew he was right. She didn't need to go to Sarajevo to chase Raznatovic. What she'd already achieved in the story was more than enough. But it wasn't enough for her. She reached over and touched his hand.

'I know what you're saying, TJ, but you know me well enough now to know that I can't back off.' She looked beyond him and thought of Emir's last words. 'I have to go.'

'No, you don't, Rosie.'

'I do.' She sighed. 'Christ, TJ, why can't you just understand that this is part of me, part of what makes me who I am.'

'I try, Rosie, believe me. I love who you are and what makes you who you are. But sometimes . . .' He paused. 'Sometimes it feels there's just no room for anyone else. I'll never be the main priority for you.'

Rosie's heart sank.

'Please don't say that, TJ.' She touched his hair. The thought of losing him brought an ache to her chest. She looked into the softness of his grey eyes. 'Please don't say that.'

TJ was silent. He looked down at the table.

'When?'

'Tomorrow. From London. Matt's going with me.'

'Tomorrow? Christ, Rosie, thanks for the notice.'

'It was just last minute. You know how these things are. What difference does it make when I go?'

Silence. TJ finished his wine.

'Because I'm going away too, Rosie. To New York.'

Rosie's stomach dropped. She glanced at him then into her glass, trying to compose herself. Insecurity made her mind a blur of depressing possibilities. Christ, why had she never even considered he might leave her again? How stupid was that?

'Not for long,' TJ said, touching her hand.

'How long? Why?' She looked up at him, studying his face for any signs that he was about to finish everything.

'You know that place I told you about, the jazz place where I played with Kat and Gerry? Well, the resident band is going on a tour for about three to six months to Europe and they've offered us the gig – well for the first three months anyway. But it might be six.'

Rosie's gut burned with jealousy. She hoped it wasn't written all over her face.

'So you're going with Kat and Gerry?' she said. 'Nice and cosy.' She regretted it as soon as she said it.

TJ let go of her hand and gave her a petulant look.

'Don't be stupid, Rosie.'

She didn't answer, and they sat in long, heavy silence.

'When you going?'

'Just over a week.'

'Christ, TJ! When were you going to tell me? The day before you left?'

TJ put his hands up. 'I've been trying to tell you, Rosie. I was planning to tell you last week when you came to my house for the curry, but with you getting beaten up and stuff I didn't want to do it then. And then when

Emir got killed ... I just felt there was too much shit going on with you.'

Rosie said nothing. She let him hold her hand, but she didn't respond. She wanted to rise above all her anxieties and jealousy, but she couldn't. She stared into her wine glass, knocked back the remainder of it, then spoke.

'TJ. *Did* you have an affair with Kat? I mean when you were in New York?'

The words hung there for what seemed like an age. TJ kept looking at her and she held his stare for as long she could, seeing the hurt and anger in his eyes until she had to look away from him. She waited for his answer. Eventually he spoke.

'Rosie. Listen to me. Kat was and is a friend, and we were close. I won't answer that question. It's irrelevant. I love you, and I want to be with you. Look at me.' He touched her face and gently turned it so she was forced to look at him. 'I don't want to be with anyone else. I never stopped thinking about you. Even all the time I was in New York.'

There was another silence, then TJ got up and took some notes out of his pocket to pay the bill. Rosie got up and put her jacket on and they went out the door, the old restaurant owner giving them a discreet berth as though he sensed it was best to keep his distance.

Outside it was hot and sticky, and they stood looking at each other. Then TJ stepped close and took her face in his hands.

'Don't let's waste this, Rosie.' He kissed her on the lips, softly at first, then hard, pulling her into his arms and holding her tight as the sky opened up, first with heavy raindrops then suddenly in torrents.

They stood with the the warm rain streaming down their faces.

'Come on. Let's get a cab. I haven't seen your new place yet,' TJ said, and hailed a black hack as it came towards them.

CHAPTER 28

It was a short drive from the airport in Sarajevo to the mountain village of Olovo, where Adrian lived on the outskirts with his mother and sister. But the weighty silences in the car were making it seem longer. Rosie was glad Matt wasn't full of his usual banter from the back seat. On the flight over, she'd warned him that most of the area they were about to enter around Sarajevo was bound to be a place of deep sadness for Adrian, and they should both have respect for that.

From the front passenger seat, Rosie stole little glances at her Bosnian friend as he drove through places which still bore the scars of the Serb shelling and bombing that had all but decimated them during the Bosnian war – a war which had lasted over three years from 1992. It was always hard to tell anything from Adrian's poker-faced expression, but Rosie guessed that every time he did this journey, he could still see the lost souls murdered and butchered by the mindless thugs who rampaged through his homeland. The ghosts were everywhere, and even in the sunshine, blazing from a cloudless sky, there was an eerie backdrop aura about the landscape.

'Adrian,' Rosie said, leaning forward a little so she could catch his sideward glance. 'Maybe you could tell us a little bit about the area we're driving through here. We saw a lot of it on television at the time, and I saw a little when I went on the charity trip, but you were here. Do you mind talking about it?'

Adrian gave the kind of weary sigh that went with his hooded eyelids and tired pallor, but nodded and said he didn't mind talking.

He glanced out of the side window, taking one hand off the steering wheel to make a sweeping gesture. 'Here. Everywhere you see around here, is the story of killings and murder and rapes. I remember it always.' He turned to Rosie. 'Like you, maybe. The way you told me you remember many bad things you see in places.'

'No, Adrian, not like me. I wasn't part of it, like you were.'

He nodded and said nothing for a while as they continued along the isolated roads, driving between deep, rolling valleys and high mountains, lush and green valleys.

'Here, all around, is very beautiful,' Adrian said. 'For me is beautiful to grow up in this place. But is lot of bad memories now. I will take you to some places tomorrow when we are going to Belgrade.'

'Good.'

'But first, we will stop soon and drink coffee and we can talk about our work and the plans to find this Raznatovic. I have information for you.' He lit a cigarette and rolled down the window to blow the smoke out. After a few miles, he pulled into what looked like a panoramic picnic spot, and Rosie felt glad to be out of the car and breathing in the clean, crisp mountain air. Adrian told them to sit outside, and he headed towards the dilapidated timber cafe a few yards away, where the owner stood outside in his apron, smoking a cigarette. He greeted Adrian with a broad smile and a hug.

Rosie gazed across the sweeping countryside, struck by the absolute silence. She found herself remembering TV footage of these skies engulfed in smoke and gunfire, and of the endless streams of desperate Bosnians; she recalled the wailing at the mass graves, and the thousands of displaced people, their faces grey with shock and disbelief.

'It's awesome, isn't it?' Matt said, standing beside her. 'When you think how it was during the war, and how quiet it is now ... You could just disappear here, you know. Reinvent yourself, and nobody would ever find you.'

Rosie looked at him. 'I guess that's what a few of the Serb soldiers may have done while they were on the run for war crimes,' she replied, half smiling. 'Of course, if they were really smart, they pitched up in the UK and managed to pass themselves off as Bosnian Muslim refugees, then ended up in Scotland cutting up the bodies of real refugees for money.' She shook her head at how unbelievable it sounded when you put it like that.

'True,' Matt said, 'but I could really live here, you know. Just lose myself in this tranquillity.'

'What? You? In the middle of nowhere, with no night-clubs or pubs? Jesus! It's a bit early to be going native, Matt. We just got here.' Rosie grinned at him. 'You've not even had a drink yet.'

Adrian appeared with a tray of coffees and they sat down at the wooden picnic table.

Rosie put her spoon into the dark black coffee and she and Matt exchanged glances. Matt took a sip, then screwed up his face. 'I don't know whether to drink it or inject it,' he said. 'Christ, Adrian, what the hell is this!'

Adrian smiled, but not broadly. He didn't do broadly.

'It is Bosnian coffee,' he said. 'Very strong. Very good for you. By the time you leave, you will not be able to live without it.'

'Exactly,' Matt said. 'Maybe I should be injecting it.'

'So,' Rosie said. 'What's the situation with Raznatovic, Adrian? We didn't really get much of a chance to talk on the phone.'

'I know, Rosie, but I can tell you now.' He lit a cigarette and drew deeply. 'As I told you, he is here. He came three days ago. Very sudden.'

'Yes,' Rosie said. 'One minute the slaughterhouse was busy with cars and vans coming and going, and the next minute it was closed. They obviously got word they'd been rumbled.'

Adrian nodded. 'Yes, I suppose. But he is in Belgrade. He was first in one apartment in Belgrade, but now he has been taken to somewhere else . . . some other apartment in the city. But my friends are finding out for me, and I will know tonight or tomorrow.' He looked at Rosie.

'But tell me, what is your plan when you know where he is, Rosie? What do you want to do with him?'

'Well,' Rosie said. 'He's clearly not going to give us an interview. What I'd ideally like to do is find out where he is and how he is hiding himself – who is looking after him, protecting him. We'd want to get some kind of opportunity to snatch a picture of him. That would be the greatest thing, you know, a picture of the monster who kept on killing. And as much of the background detail as you've been able to get about him and Boskovac. That would put some real colour on it.' Rosie was imagining how the headline would look on a page. 'Along with all the rest of the material we've got, this would be dynamite. I know it won't be easy, but that's what I would like to do.'

'Then what?'

'Then I'd like to tip off the authorities. You know – Interpol, the war crimes people – tell them exactly where he is and how they could find him, and hope they'll move quickly and get him. But by that time we'll be on our way out of here.' She paused. 'Oh, by the way, Adrian, I have to go back through Kosovo. Well, Macedonia actually. I made a promise to Emir when he was dying that I would go to speak with his grandmother. They were taken to a town in Macedonia after their Kosovan village was invaded by Serbs. So I have to find her.'

'I will take you there. No problem.'

They sat in silence for a few moments, Rosie exchanging glances with Matt, sensing his discomfort when people weren't talking. So much for him wanting to live in tranquility.

'So it's going to be pretty dangerous then, Adrian,' Matt said. 'I mean, for me to get anywhere near this bastard.'

Adrian looked at Matt for a few seconds, as though studying him for signs that he had enough bottle.

'Is very dangerous. But once you decide to do it, you can only go forward. No going back. You must do everything I tell you when we are close to it. If you don't, you may pay with your life.'

Matt swallowed, then his face broke into a smile.

'Well, thanks for the heads-up on that, Adrian.'

Rosie laughed, and eventually, when Adrian got Matt's humour, he sat back and almost smiled.

'You are a funny guy, Matt. I remember from Morocco. But is not good if you are a funny dead guy.' He stretched his hand out towards Matt and they shook hands warmly then, coffee finished, Adrian stood up.

'Come on, not far now. We go to my house. You can see my sister. She is very different from the girl you saw a few months ago, frightened in the car in Spain that night. She is happy now. So is my mother. Then I take you to the small hotel in the town. We will have dinner tonight with my friend, and we can talk more of the plans.'

Outside the low timber cottage nestling at the foot of the hills, Adrian's mother was in the garden setting plates and cutlery on a wooden table. She looked up and waved, with a big, beaming smile, when the car pulled into the yard.

'My mother,' Adrian said, his expression softening. 'She

is very excited to meet you. She has been preparing lunch all morning. Always she is fussing,' he added affectionately.

Rosie and Matt got out of the car, as the woman came walking swiftly towards them.

'Welcome, welcome, my friends.' Then she said something in Serbo-Croat, her arms outstretched.

Rosie and Matt looked at each other, then at Adrian.

'She say she is happy to meet the people who helped to bring her daughter back to her.'

Rosie laughed. 'Then tell her thank you, Adrian, but that it was her son who did all the work.'

Adrian shrugged and said something back to her.

'Come,' he walked towards the table. 'Sit and we will have a drink before lunch.'

'Not more coffee, Adrian, thanks all the same,' Matt said, and this time even Adrian laughed.

'Okay, we will have tea.' He looked at Matt. 'We save the beers for dinner tonight in Olovo.'

'Sounds like a good plan, big man,' Matt said.

As they sat at the table, Adrian's mum disappeared into the house calling 'Fiorina, Fiorina' and shouting in Serbo-Croat. A few minutes later, she emerged from the house carrying a large teapot in both hands. Behind her, carrying some mugs and looking a little shy, was Fiorina. Rosie couldn't believe this tall willowy creature in the tight jeans and T-shirt was the same girl they'd seen, terrified and whimpering, clinging to her brother the night he rescued her from the whorehouse on the Costa del Sol. Rosie stood up.

'My sister, Fiorina,' Adrian said, proudly, as the girl put the cups on the table and wiped her hands on her jeans.

'Fiorina!' Rosie stepped forward. 'So delighted to meet you. You look wonderful. So different.'

'Thank you,' Fiorina replied. She pushed her blonde hair back from her face and looked at Rosie and Matt. 'And thank you so much for helping my brother to save me.' She threw her arms around Rosie. 'I will never forget you.'

Rosie found herself choked with emotion as she hugged the teenager. A raft of images from the Spanish investigation that could so easily have cost all of them their lives suddenly flooded her mind.

'Your brother did it all,' Rosie said. She turned to Matt. 'And this is Matt, you remember? The photographer who was working with us.'

Fiorina gave Matt a hug, and as she did, Rosie could see that Matt was bowled over by her beauty.

He made a face at Rosie over her shoulder.

'See. I told you I could settle down here.'

Rosie laughed and they sat back around the table, while Fiorina and her mother went back into the house and returned with trays of food.

For two hours they sat talking in the sunshine, Rosie and Matt listening while Adrian translated his mother's stories of her children growing up, of how their father died in an accident when they were young, and how much she had missed Adrian when he left. But she knew he had to go, because so many of the boys had not made it to their twenties once the Serbs came. She spoke of communities who had once stood together becoming torn apart by bullets and bombs.

Much to Matt's disappointment, Fiorina, they were told, had a boyfriend now and they were both working for the tourism area in Bosnia–Herzegovina; they'd decided that they would stay to help build the new country that was their future. Adrian, Rosie noted, was non-committal.

Rosie was fascinated to see how relaxed and almost normal he looked in the company of his own people. In all the years she'd known him, he'd always looked a little haunted, always on edge like the stranger he was in a land far from home, suspicious, ready to fight his corner at every turn. But here, he seemed more at ease, even though he wasn't a barrel of laughs. She wondered why he too didn't just stay here and make a life, like his sister was doing.

It was late afternoon by the time they rose to say their goodbyes, and Rosie meant it when she said she could easily have stayed on and enjoyed a few more hours in their company. It had been a glimpse at survival, and made her think of war-torn Kosovo she'd left a few months back, where the stricken refugees left homeless had been trying to pick up what was left of their lives. Here was a family who were testament to the fact that you could move on, rebuild and be strong and happy again.

'Thank you for bringing us to meet your mother and sister, Adrian,' Rosie said as they drove off. 'They are lovely people. You are so lucky.'

Adrian nodded. 'You can see how much it means to my mother to have Fiorina back. I cannot think how she would be if I couldn't find her in Spain. Now everything is much better for them.'

'And you, Adrian?'

He shrugged and said nothing as he yanked the car into reverse and turned back onto the road.

CHAPTER 29

Rosie heard her mobile ringing as she came out of the bathroom wrapped in a towel. It was McGuire. She glanced at her watch on the bedside table. It wasn't even 9.30 in Glasgow, so at this time of the morning it could only be trouble.

'Mick! Howsit going?' Rosie opened the wooden shutters on her window and sunlight flooded the drab bedroom.

'You might well ask, Gilmour,' Mick said. 'Has Interpol tracked you down yet?'

McGuire sounded chipper. Rosie was confused.

'Interpol? Why?'

McGuire chuckled. 'You're a wanted woman, Rosie. Cops are going nuts about today's paper. I blasted your interview with Emir all over the front page and inside, plus we ran the list of missing refugees with a big "where are they?" headline. We also made it clear that Paton and Murphy were up to their necks in something. Belter of a paper! I had the head of the CID on the phone before

I even got my arse on my chair this morning. They're more or less demanding to talk to you, said our story has compromised the investigation . . . demanding to know where we got the list . . . all that stuff.'

'Shit,' Rosie said, bracing herself to be summoned back to Glasgow.

'I told him to piss off – in the nicest possible way of course – but they're jumping on their hats, accusing us of withholding information. Especially you, Gilmour. You're for the jail,' he chortled. 'But on the bright side, we're number one on Sky News and we've twisted the nipples of every other paper chasing our story. As days go, it's shaping up to be a good one.'

'Sounds crazy, Mick.' Rosie was glad she was far enough away from the flak – especially flak from angry cops.

'Yeah, you're well out of it. I told them you were out of town on an investigation. I said you were incommunicado and would be for a week at least.'

'Oh, they'd love that.'

'I think they're gearing up to make a lot of trouble. I've got Hanlon coming in here this morning so we can circle the wagons. I hope I don't end up in the pokey.' McGuire was clearly relishing the moment.

'So what happens now?' Rosie asked. 'I mean they don't know where I am, so I just keep on going, right?'

'Yep. Just carry on. Are you in Belgrade yet?'

'No. Going up there today, but it could take a few days before we get anywhere close to this guy. It's going to be a bit dodgy. But when we get what we want, it will be in and out. We won't be hanging about.'

There was a pause, and Rosie knew what was coming next.

'Rosie, listen. I want us to get this Raznatovic bastard. Get a live picture of him, and the other guy if possible – but not at any cost. Am I making myself crystal clear?' McGuire's tone changed.

'Yes, I know, Mick. I won't do anything daft. My friend Adrian and his people are looking after us. I'll be safe enough.'

Another pause. 'Fine. But any sign of big problems, I want you out of there pronto. Understood? Plus at some stage you need to sit down and write everything you have about this PD Pharmaceuticals, and that side of the story. I want to be ready to go with the pictures Matt took inside the slaughterhouse, linking them to the illegal tissue trade – just in case we have to run it before you get back.'

'You mean in case you have to run it and I'm not there because I've been shot.' Rosie joked.

'Don't even talk that way, Gilmour. No, listen. Even if we can't say PD were part of it, we just have to say what we saw in the place and the stuff going to Manchester, then link back to the earlier stuff in Germany. We can be vague about it. That's going to take a bit of legalling, but I want to do it. Especially now, because the cops are so raging they might take some legal action to try and stop us using anything. I want to be ready.'

'Do you think there's political pressure being put on the police because of that ex-Environment Secretary's involvement – and they just want to close the investigation down?'

'Oh, yeah, they'll certainly want to close the investigation down, but that ain't gonna happen any time soon. Trust me on that.' He paused. 'Now get to Belgrade and keep your head down.'

'I will, Mick.'

Rosie sat sipping tea in the pavement cafe, close to the small hotel in the ancient town of Olovo where they'd stayed last night. It would be another hour before Adrian and his friend Risto would arrive to drive them to Belgrade. She opened her notebook and went over the information the German reporter had given her on the phone about PD Pharmaceuticals before she left. She'd write the piece when she got to her hotel in Belgrade later tonight, but she couldn't concentrate. Her head kept drifting back to last night, and the dinner with Adrian and Risto.

It seemed that Adrian knew everyone in the town, and wherever he went he was greeted with handshakes or a friendly slap on the back. He introduced Rosie and Matt as friends he'd met when he was in Scotland, so they were made even more welcome. Rosie was struck by the openness of the locals and could hardly get her head around their resilience after everything they'd been through in the war. Olovo had been one of the main targets of relentless bombardment by the Serbs and now, nearly five years on, some of the buildings still lay in rubble, while others carried pockmarks from the shelling during the march of the Serbian army towards Tuzla in the north.

Before dinner they were joined by Adrian's friend Risto, a thin, softly spoken man who looked to be in his early thirties, with the same pale and world-weary look that Adrian had. He'd been a teacher before the war, he told them in perfect English, but by the time it was over so much had happened that he had lost the heart to go back to it.

They all drank a lot of wine at the table, and on top of the beers at the start of the night, Rosie was beginning to feel more relaxed than she'd been all week.

'Once we get to Belgrade,' Adrian said, 'Risto will be your bodyguard any time I have to go to see people in the city. So you won't be on your own. He will be outside your hotel all the time and will keep in touch with you by phone.' He patted Risto's arm. 'We are old comrades, from our schooldays, until we had to carry a rifle here in this village.'

Risto did his best to smile.

'You will be safe with us.' Risto looked at Rosie and Matt. 'I know what you are trying to do here, and we will help you every way we can to find the Serb.' His expression grew dark. 'I wish I could get close enough to him myself. I would kill him with my bare hands.' He made a wringing gesture with his hands.

Adrian went to the bar and brought back a bottle of what looked like vodka and some shot-glasses. 'Now we drink,' he said, filling each glass. 'To justice.'

Everyone raised a glass. Rosie and Matt sniffed the drink suspiciously, but refusal wasn't an option. They knocked it back in one and Rosie felt it burn all the way down to her stomach.

'Strong stuff.' She blew her cheeks out.

'Is very pure vodka. Is better than the coffee, Matt, no?' Adrian clinked his empty glass with Matt, whose eyes were watering.

They had one more, and then sat smoking while Risto told his story.

'It was just over one year after the war began,' he said. 'Most of us were still in shock. All of a sudden, neighbours, friends – people we had worked with and known for years – were our enemies.' He glanced at Adrian, who nodded back in agreement.

Risto went on. 'Even now, when we look back, we can still hardly believe what happened to our country. We were being attacked by people we used to know. Terrible . . . So, like every other young man, we take up arms and fight to defend our villages and our families. We are all fighting together – Adrian, me, my brothers, all of the people we grew up with all along this area.'

He looked down at the table, reliving the nightmare.

'We hear stories of brutality, of murder and rape by Serb soldiers. And of massacres. But we almost don't believe them. Then in June it comes to our own door.' He sat back in his chair and took a deep breath. 'The Serb soldiers were transporting buses with people from villages around Visegrad, not very far from here. They were just beating and removing them from their homes and declaring it a Serb area. My brother was one of those people forced on the bus. They were bringing them here, to Olovo.'

Rosie watched him, his pale blue-eyes looking straight back at her.

'But before they got here, they stopped nearby to the area of Paklenik. They took around fifty men from the buses and put them on one bus. And everyone spent the night in a local town. But the next morning, they took the bus filled with the men and drove them to Paklenik. It is a place with a huge, deep gorge. At the edge there is a path leading to a big ravine in the mountains. So deep, you cannot imagine. It is a famous place here, and is known now as Hell.'

Risto paused, swallowed hard and bit his lip. He looked at Adrian, who reached across the table and squeezed his arm.

'Every one of the men, including my own brother, was executed and thrown into the ravine. We never . . .'

He stopped to compose himself, rubbing his hand across his trembling mouth. The rawness of his pain filled the room. Eventually he spoke again.

'We never got the chance to bury our dead brothers, or our fathers and sons. They took them from us and we never saw them again. Their bodies still lie there.' He slammed his fist on the table. 'Raznatovic was one of those soldiers. He was a captain, who commanded a section of the soldiers who took part in this atrocity.'

Rosie gave Adrian a look of surprise.

'We know this for sure, Rosie,' Adrian said. 'We have looked at Raznatovic and all the men responsible. There are several others and the Serb government knows their names, but nobody knows where they are. None of the soldiers who were part of this massacre have ever been found. They are all disappeared. But now, Raznatovic is back. That is his mistake.' He paused. 'And we know how to find him.'

They sat quietly for a while. Rosie felt anything she could say would be trite, so she said nothing. Eventually, it was Adrian who spoke.

'On our way to Belgrade tomorrow, we will take you there, so you can see this Paklenik hell for yourself, Rosie.'

Now, as she waited at the cafe for Matt and Adrian, Rosie looked around at the bustling town all these years on. She wondered just how many of the people were carrying around the same inner agonies and pain as Risto did every day. Yet it hadn't broken them. She thought of Emir and swallowed back the tears. He was just like these people. He had asked for nothing and harmed no one.

A rush of nerves tweaked Rosie's gut as the reality of what lay ahead of her in the next few days sank in. She was more scared than she'd been in a very long time. And she was ashamed to admit to herself that a significant part of her wanted to run away, back to the safety of Glasgow, and just write what she already had. Make do with it. Raznatovic was only one of the many Serb brutes who had taken part in those heinous atrocities. Why risk her life for one man? But the stronger voice inside her would not be silenced: to help bring one of these beasts to justice would make at least some amends to the poor innocent souls whose bodies lay rotting at the bottom of Paklenik gorge.

CHAPTER 30

Rosie waited for Gerhard Hoffman at the cafe closest to their hotel in the heart of Belgrade's Old Town. She looked intently at the faces of the people strolling in the busy main square, hoping she would recognise him from his old byline picture in the German newspaper.

The call had come soon after she'd arrived in the city and was about to go for dinner. She'd been taken aback to find that Gerhard was also in Belgrade, and Adrian had been immediately suspicious, suggesting he may be double-crossing her, but Rosie trusted her instinct. She told Adrian that Gerhard had said the reason he'd come to Belgrade was because one of his contacts had crucial information for him – information, he'd said, that she would want. That was enough for her.

'Rosie?'

The voice from behind made her jump. She turned around to face the short, stocky figure standing looking down at her.

'Rosie Gilmour? Gerhard Hoffman.' Piercing blue eyes

flicked across her face. 'I recognise you from the picture in your newspaper. I was across the street watching.'

'Gerhard!' Rosie pushed her chair back. 'How are you?' She smiled. 'How amazing we're both in Belgrade at the same time.'

The waiter appeared and Gerhard ordered a coffee for himself, and Rosie asked for more tea. He sat down and pulled his chair close to the table.

'You are not alone here, I trust?' He was watchful, eyes everywhere.

'No,' Rosie said. 'A couple of tables behind you is the photographer I'm working with, as well as two other contacts who are looking after me here.'

'They are not Serbian, I hope?' He almost smiled, but not quite.

'No.' Rosie didn't see the need to tell him who they were.

He turned his head around in the direction of where Matt, Risto and Adrian sat sipping beers.

'I see them.' He nodded slowly. 'I hope they are on the ball and taking good care of you, Rosie. This city is very beautiful, but these days can also be dangerous.'

'Especially for someone who's doing what we are doing, Gerhard,' Rosie replied.

The waiter arrived and put the cups down on the table. There was a little awkward moment when Rosie wondered if she should take the lead or let Gerhard talk. He stirred his coffee as though he were deep in thought. Finally it was he who spoke.

'I think what you and your newspaper are doing is very brave. I will help as much as I can.' He paused, drank a mouthful of coffee. 'These people are monsters.'

Rosie noticed the cup trembled a little. She was anxious to hear what information he had for her, but something in his demeanour told her he was troubled. She would have to let him talk.

He had a kind of crumpled, unkempt look, a raw, pink complexion with broken veins on his cheeks and heavy bags under the striking eyes. She couldn't put an exact age on him because what little hair he had was grey, but Rosie figured he wasn't as old as he looked. He'd been a boozer in his day, that much she was sure of, and she hoped the tremor in his hand wasn't for the want of a drink. The last thing she needed right now was a careless lush with a grudge.

'Not only are they monsters, Gerhard, but they are monsters who should have been in jail by now, after your incredible investigation,' Rosie said. She wasn't just buttering him up – she meant it. 'I was totally fascinated when I read your story about the company attached to PD Pharmaceuticals, then when I looked through the cuttings and saw the apology it was such a disappointment.' She shook her head and looked him in the eye. 'It's shocking that the paper didn't have the courage to pursue them.'

Gerhard nodded. 'They got away with it because they are powerful.' He looked at Rosie, then at the table. 'And, of course, they ruined my reputation as a journalist. Nobody trusts me fully any more. I am more or less finished in newspapers.' He clenched his fist in front of him. 'But I know I was right. One hundred per cent – as I told you on the phone.'

The awkward silence again. He took a deep breath.

'But I will be honest with you, Rosie.' He ran a hand nervously across his mouth. 'I had a drink problem back then. Well, I suppose as an alcoholic, I will always have a drink problem. But I haven't had a drink for four years.'

Rosie felt a little deflated. She sympathised with him, but he wasn't saying the right things to fill her with confidence.

'When I began the investigation,' he continued, 'I had just returned to work after being off – being in rehab. I was grateful to the newspaper for sticking with me. Then within a few weeks, this story came along and it just became massive, the deeper my investigation went. Suddenly we are exposing a major pharmaceutical giant for being involved in the illegal tissue trade worldwide.'

'So what happened?' Rosie asked.

'Well, once we published, the denials came thick and fast. There were the legal threats, and then the smear campaign by PD's lawyers, who were delving into my history and came up with the alcohol problem. They were intending to drag that into court, saying I wasn't credible as a journalist, but the drink problem should not have been a factor. It hasn't been a factor in my life for years, but it was used against me.'

'So the paper just buckled?'

'Yes. They didn't believe they could win it. Our paper's

lawyers advised them to settle, and they did. That was when I left, as a matter of principle. But I have never stopped hunting them down.' He leaned forward and lowered his voice. 'Since my story, other people came forward with information about the illegal trade in tissue, and how widespread it is – from Ukraine to Latvia and beyond, all across Eastern Europe, it is a web of corruption. But it is also huge all over the world.' He looked at Rosie. 'And also, these days, organised criminals are heavily involved.'

'That's exactly the area I am looking at, Gerhard. As I told you on the phone, refugees are going missing.'

He nodded. 'Yes. People-trafficking is big business, with gangmasters making money. But refugees? Nobody cares. Believe me, it's worth more for the criminals to bring in the refugees and then make money from their corpses. I am telling you, Rosie, there are companies across Europe who come to these people with a shopping list of body parts.'

'It's almost unbelievable, Gerhard.'

'But it's true.' He shook his head. 'People say I'm a little obsessed now.' He looked at Rosie. 'Maybe I am obsessed, but I am *not* some alcoholic nutcase, Rosie. I am right on this story. I know I am.'

Rosie nodded in agreement. 'I can see how hard it must have been for you,' she said, and thought how people-trafficking had just taken on a whole new meaning. She could see the story in the paper – Frank Paton and Tony Murphy . . . The Body Brokers . . . She shook herself free of her imaginings and turned to Gerhard.

'Gerhard. One thing I wanted to ask you: can you shed some more light on why a firm as massive as PD Pharmaceuticals would even allow any part of their empire to be involved in illegal tissue trade? I know it's big business worldwide, but why would they risk it? Why would they need it?'

'Greed, Rosie. Is all greed.' He shrugged and shook his head sadly. 'PD have several smaller subsidiary companies under their umbrella, and they would claim they are all autonomous in terms of management and that the parent company was unaware of what was happening. But that is just not acceptable. And anyway, even to be unaware is still a crime. They should have been more responsible, *somebody* must have known. And this man Boskovac I told you about. The Serbian. He was at the core of the company I exposed who were involved in the tissue trade, yet they now have him on their board of directors. It's so arrogant.'

Rosie screwed up her eyes a little.

'But why would PD put this Boskovac on the board? I mean, even if there was a whiff of scandal about the smaller company he was involved in. Why not just cut him loose? Ditch him? I can't get my head around that. Surely they would have to be seen to be whiter than white.'

Gerhard pursed his lips and raised an eyebrow.

'Unless the one man who could sink them needed to be placated in some way. Kept onside.'

'They could just have paid him off.'

Gerhard shrugged. 'Of course. But perhaps he knew

things that they could not put a price on. It could be that Boskovac knows where the bodies are buried, if you'll pardon the pun. What if he knows everything that went on, and how people in high places at PD turned a blind eye?'

'Are you speculating, or do you know that?'

Gerhard put his cup down. 'I'm working on it.'

'And what of his relationship with Raznatovic? Do you know more about that?' Rosie was fishing.

'I know they go back to when they studied together. They were both corrupt in the communist regime in the old Yugoslavia. I think the seeds were sown then. I am still tracking that.'

Rosie sat back, aware that Hoffman glanced fleetingly as she crossed her legs.

'You said you have important information for me, Gerhard.'

'I do,' he said. 'I should have it later today.' He lowered his voice almost to a whisper. 'I have been back and forth to Belgrade for a while, and I have my connections here and in Germany who assisted me at the time. There are still some people on my side. Listen. I have a contact here who has a photograph of Boskovac with the British politician – you know, the man Tim Hayman?'

'Of course,' Rosie said, dying to hear what was next. 'He is on the board of PD Pharmaceuticals.'

'Yes. But he was an associate and friend of Boskovac while he was still the Environment Secretary.'

Rosie raised her eyebrows. 'You can stand that up?' she asked.

'A photograph will stand it up, will it not?'

'What kind of photograph?'

'Both of them together.'

'Yes, but they're both on the board of PD now. Hayman's on PD's board in a consultative capacity, so it wouldn't be unusual for them to be photographed together.' Rosie's heart sank a little.

Gerhard gave a wry smile. 'Yes. But a picture of them while Boskovac was involved in the company I exposed, standing with his arm over the shoulder of the then Environment Secretary Tim Hayman. That would be unusual, would it not?'

'You have that?' She could see McGuire biting her hand off.

'I will have it later tonight. But it gets better, Rosie. Both Boskovac and Hayman are photographed at some shooting party in the Scottish Highlands. The picture, I'm told, is of them standing armed with rifles.'

Rosie's eyes widened. 'Seriously? You can get that?'

Gerhard gave a little chuckle. 'I see you are the kind of reporter who relishes winning the big fights.'

'Of course,' Rosie said. 'Especially when I might be able to bury the kind of low-lifes involved in this.' She paused, then looked right at him and said, 'It would be a real coup if you could get that picture, Gerhard. How will I know? I mean when?' Rosie could barely contain her excitement.

'I have known about the photograph for a few days. I wanted to tell you, but it was important for me to meet you first, to make sure you were the right kind of journalist for me to deal with.' He gave her a warm smile. 'And I am satisfied with what I see.'

'Thanks,' Rosie said.

'In a couple of hours I will be seeing my contact,' Gerhard said. 'I will call you later to meet you. If there is any problem and you cannot come, I will put it in your hotel for you. Where are you staying?'

Rosie told him. 'But I will meet you later tonight, Gerhard. That'll be no problem. I'll build whatever we're doing later around seeing you.'

Gerhard looked at his watch. He drained his coffee cup.

'Okay, Rosie. I must go now. I have something to do before I meet my contact later. Then I will call your mobile.' He reached across and shook her hand warmly. 'I am so glad to meet you, Rosie. When you called me that afternoon and told me what you were doing, I was elated. At last, perhaps we can nail these people to the wall.'

'We will, Gerhard. And I will write in my story of your part in the investigation – especially your earlier revelations that have led the way in this. You can take the newspaper when it comes out and stick it under the noses of your paper's bosses who lost their bottle.'

'I know where I will stick it,' he said, standing up. 'And it wouldn't be under their noses.' He smiled. 'I must go.' He turned and left.

The floating restaurants along the River Danube in Belgrade were a famous haunt these days for the gangsters and thugs who had established themselves in the new Serbia. Rosie, sitting with Matt in one of the corner tables where the surly waiter had put them, felt uneasy. Even though there were a few tourists scattered around, the place was full of shifty-looking Serbs flaunting their wealth and power.

'Look,' Rosie said to Matt, as one guy swaggered in with his jacket draped over his shoulders. He was followed by four burly henchmen and two equally burly Alsatian dogs.

'Christ,' Matt said. 'They don't look like guide dogs.'

Rosie glanced at them. 'No. The dogs are all part of the entourage with the gangsters,' she explained. 'You wouldn't just walk up to that table uninvited without getting your arm bitten off.'

Within a couple of minutes, two leggy blondes were brought to the table, and the guy who appeared to be the boss grunted to the Alsatians who were ready to pounce when the women came close. The dogs sat back down, vigilant, as one of the women sat on his knee, and the other put her arms around his neck and kissed his shiny shaven head.

'Hookers,' Rosie said, jerking her head towards the bar. 'There's at least another two of of them up there.'

Matt eyed them up. 'Bit different from the ones you see back in Glasgow . . . Yeah. I'd bet these birds have got all their own teeth.'

The waiter arrived and they ordered something that looked uncomplicated. He poured red wine into their glasses and left. Rosie leaned across the table, and gave a discreet nod to Adrian and Risto who were sat a few

tables away from them. Adrian lifted his chin in acknow-
ledgement. Rosie could see him eyeballing every table.

'I think it was a good idea of Adrian's for us not to sit
together,' she said. 'Even if I don't feel quite as safe
without him.'

'It's all right here, Rosie. There's loads of people. I'm
not worried.'

'I know,' she said. 'But it's just that they're all Serbs,
and you never know who's a gangster and who isn't. Plus
the fact that I don't think anyone who looks either British
or American is popular in Belgrade right now. I mean,
it's only months after Kosovo, when NATO was bombing
the shit out of this city.'

An image flashed across Rosie's mind of the sky over
Pristina, lit up with low-flying aircraft strafing targets
on the ground.

'You saw for yourself today, Matt,' she said. 'The bomb
damage in the centre of Belgrade, buildings in ruins.
There'll be no shortage of bitterness.'

'Well,' Matt gave her a cheeky grin. 'Not our fault if
these guys can't take a joke.'

Rosie looked beyond him and caught Adrian's eye. He
raised one finger, the signal they'd agreed earlier, to let
her know if and when Raznatovic just walked in at the
back of her.

'Shit,' Rosie's stomach turned over, and she whispered
to Matt. 'Look behind me. He's here. He's just walked in.'

'Fuck me,' Matt said quickly glancing up. 'So he has. I
hope to Christ he doesn't recognise me.'

'Don't even go there, Matt.'

The waiter arrived with their food, and Matt looked down at the table as Raznatovic and the three other men walked past, with the head waiter striding ahead of them. Rosie watched as he seated them a couple of tables to the right of Adrian. She was glad Raznatovic had his back to her. But she recognised one of the other men with him straight away.

'Shit, Matt. The other guy's here, the one I told you about. The Serb who's also on the board of PD Pharmaceuticals.' She whispered. 'Goran Boskovac. The Serbian.'

'Dancer! That's a result.'

'All you need now is to snatch a picture of the pair of them without getting us killed. How the hell are you going to do that, pal?'

'Well, it'll not be in here anyway, that's for sure. I'd rather keep my bollocks intact. We'll just wait and see how it pans out.' He reached across and touched her hand. 'Let's act like a normal couple. Maybe if the band strikes up a bit of Strauss, I'll take you up for a wee Viennese waltz. Should I lean over and kiss you?'

'Yeah, right, Matt. Just let's eat our dinner.'

Rosie kept an eye on Raznatovic's table. They were ordering dinner, with him leaning across and talking quietly to the man she recognised as Boskovac from the newspaper cuttings of Gerhard's original story. The other two who were with them looked like military types – minders by the cut of them. They didn't seem to take part much in the conversation, and both were sipping water, while Raznatovic and his friend drank beer.

'I can't believe that this bastard's just sitting there ordering dinner when you think what he's been doing in Glasgow for God knows how long, and what he did in Bosnia,' Rosie said, disgusted. 'Where does a guy like Raznatovic go when he sleeps at night?'

'Places you and me don't even know about, Rosie. They're subhuman.' Matt said between mouthfuls of food.

'Don't let it spoil your appetite, Matt,' Rosie said sarcastically.

'I won't,' Matt laughed. 'But seriously. Guys like that? I'd round them all up and shoot them.'

'Agreed. But I wouldn't say that too loudly in here.'

'True.'

'But you know what, Matt . . . If we can get to a stage where we can pinpoint where your man over there is hiding out, then alert the authorities and actually get him arrested, we'll have done something really worthwhile in our lives.' She saw Adrian get to his feet and walk towards her, discreetly pointing a finger to Matt when he got close.

'Adrian's coming. Not sure what he's going to do, but he won't stop and talk, Matt, and it looks like he wants you to go out. So you'd be best to follow him. He's trying to tell us something.'

'Okay. Maybe he'll go to the toilet.'

Matt waited until Adrian was almost out of the restaurant door then got up from the table and followed him.

Rosie had her phone on silent, but could feel it shuddering in her pocket and took it out. It was a missed call from TJ. She sipped her wine, thinking about how they'd parted a few days ago. She wouldn't say a proper goodbye, telling him she would be back by the time he left for New York in a week. She had been here in Belgrade two days now, most of the last two nights spent holed up in a hotel while Adrian gathered information from his contacts on Raznatovic's movements. He'd already established it wouldn't be possible to stake out the apartment where he was staying without being spotted. It needed to be more public, which also increased the risk of getting caught. The tip-off had only come this afternoon that he'd be eating in this particular restaurant on the banks of the river tonight.

Rosie sat back, looking out of the window at the moonlight on the Danube. At this rate, she'd be hard pushed to be back in Glasgow by the time TJ left, but she guessed that deep down he knew that.

Her mobile rang, but there was no number. She answered it quickly, not wanting to attract any attention.

'Rosie. It is Gerhard Hoffman.'

Startled, Rosie glanced around the room and spoke softly into the phone. 'It's difficult for me to talk right now. Can you call me back?'

'Yes. I have the photograph.'

'Brilliant!'

'I will come to your hotel later tonight. I will call you in a couple of hours.'

Rosie's heart did a little flutter as he hung up. She couldn't wait to tell Matt. Adrian walked past Rosie and back to his seat, followed seconds later by Matt.

'There's a plan,' Matt said, pulling in his chair. 'Adrian says there's going to be some chaos in a few minutes and we've to be ready.'

'Chaos?'

'Yep.' Matt was a little edgy. 'Wouldn't say what. Just said to be ready.' He put his hand in his pocket fumbling for his camera, making sure he was ready. 'Then, we've got to GTF out of here and away smartish.'

'Now I *am* really nervous.' Rosie finished her wine.

She saw Risto get up and leave the table, then walk past them and out of the restaurant.

When he didn't return after a couple of minutes, Rosie was about to ask Matt what he thought was going on, when suddenly the place was plunged into darkness. In the pitch black there were gasps of shock around the room.

'Oh shit, Matt.' Rosie blinked, trying to adjust to the dark. 'I guess this is the chaos.'

Then, suddenly, the sound of gunshot and a window shattering somewhere close by. Women screamed. Another shot and more windows breaking. Then the pinging sound of a bullet hitting something metal. The Alsatians started barking hysterically, and Rosie could hear people moving around her, making for the door. More gunshot and glass breaking.

'Jesus Christ, Matt. What's going on? Is somebody shooting holes in the bloody boat?'

'I don't know. But Adrian says to stay where we are until he comes to our table.'

Rosie's eyes were getting used to the dark, and around her she saw that people had dived below tables for cover.

Others were rushing towards the door, stepping over broken glass. She saw Raznatovic get up, and immediately Adrian rose to his feet. Raznatovic went past her, his minders barging people out of the way in the crush. Adrian came up to their table and grabbed Matt by the shoulder.

'Now. Go.' He leaned down and whispered.

Matt got up and pushed his way forward, and Rosie got up behind him. She could feel Adrian's arm firmly on her back as he steered her towards the door. From the light that was coming from outside, she saw that Matt had managed somehow to squeeze past everyone and was going down the gangplank to the quayside. Adrian kept close to Rosie, right behind Raznatovic and his henchmen. When they got outside, it was total chaos, people running around, rushing to their luxury cars. Others stood by bodyguards brandishing Kalashnikovs or handguns. The Alsatian dogs were hysterical and biting everything in sight as the bald gangster's minders surrounded him until he got to his nearby BMW. Raznatovic's minders, both carrying handguns made a path through the crowd for him. She watched as far as she could until Raznatovic disappeared into a waiting Mercedes with blacked-out windows. Dozens of people milled around the quayside in confusion, and somewhere in the distance was the sound of a police siren. Then Rosie saw Risto and Matt.

'Let's go,' Adrian said. 'You come in my car and Risto and Matt will follow.'

CHAPTER 31

The first two gin and tonics didn't even touch the sides, and, now on her third, Rosie was relaxed and smoking a cigarette, gazing around properly for the first time at the beautiful buildings in the Kneza Milahia in Belgrade's Old Town. In the bars and pavement cafes dotted along the cobblestone pedestrian precinct it felt just like any big European city – not a trace of the recent bloody history that would define the Balkans for generations to come.

'So, let's see what you got, Matt,' Rosie said. 'I can't believe you got away with taking pictures outside.'

'It was so mental, with everyone diving for cover in case someone was shooting at them, they didn't even notice me hosing them down,' he chirped.

He took his camera out and clicked on a few pictures, passing it over for Rosie to have a look.

'Perfect,' she said, as images of both Raznatovic and Boskovac face-on popped up. 'These are dynamite. I could kiss you, Matt.'

'Help yourself.' Matt opened his arms. He turned to

Adrian and Risto. 'You guys might want to look away. This could get really messy.'

Risto laughed, but Adrian was distracted by his mobile ringing. His eyes narrowed as he listened to the call, then he stood up and walked away from the table and disappeared up an alleyway.

'Something's wrong,' Rosie said, looking at Risto. He shrugged and said nothing, and she watched anxiously for Adrian to reappear. She breathed a sigh of relief when he did, but he was grim-faced.

'We have a problem,' he said, sitting back down. He lit a cigarette and inhaled deeply.

The others looked at him in anxious silence. 'They know we are here,' he said. 'Well . . .' He looked at Rosie and Matt. 'They know *you* are here.'

'Shit!' Rosie said, 'How the hell *can* they?'

Adrian spread his palms and shrugged. 'Because someone has told them, Rosie. Informed them. These people have many connections. Informants everywhere.'

'Jesus! Cops maybe?' Rosie gave Matt a bewildered look. 'Nobody knew we were coming here. Not even Don, my best cop contact. I didn't even tell him.' She shook her head. 'I can't understand it.'

'Is none of my people, Rosie. I can promise you that.'

Rosie looked at him. 'That goes without saying, Adrian.'

He shrugged. 'In Yugoslavia, we have always been so used to secret police when our country was communist. Won't be any different now. They will still be operating. I think maybe you have secret police in Scotland too? No?'

'Yes, we have Special Branch. People like that. But I can't imagine . . .' Rosie paused, and shook her head. 'No. Actually I *can* imagine how they would get involved, especially if Raznatovic is somebody they don't want to see on the front page of any newspaper because of the potential embarrassment. Plus the political implications of PD Pharmaceuticals' involvement.' She paused. 'It wouldn't be too far-fetched to think they may collaborate to keep it quiet.'

Adrian looked at Rosie. 'Then I think that is your answer, Rosie. Maybe they have been watching you.'

Rosie's blood ran a little cold. The idea that everything she had been doing in the past few weeks that led to Raznatovic had been picked up, was terrifying. It could only have been Special Branch. Rosie's mobile rang and she jumped.

'Christ,' she laughed nervously, glancing at Adrian who was watching her. She put the phone to her ear without looking at the screen.

'Rosie. Mickey.'

It was Mickey Kavanagh.

'Mickey,' Rosie said. 'You're freaking me out, reading my mind. I was about to call you.'

'Rosie, listen. You need to get out of there.'

The words sent another chill through her. Silence.

'You there, Rosie? Listen, I know you're in Belgrade. What the fuck are you doing there on your own?'

'I'm not on my own, Mickey. I'm being looked after. I have contacts.'

'Well, people know you're there. And if I already know,

then chances are that Raznatovic will know. You need to get the fuck out of there, pronto. What did you go there for anyway?'

'I heard he was here, that he'd done a runner, and I wanted to get him in Belgrade so we could use it in the story. I want to be able to say we tracked him down.' She glanced up at Matt. 'You know the sketch, Mickey.'

'Christ, Rosie, of course I do. I knew he was in Belgrade three days ago, but I didn't tell you because I knew exactly what you would do. Listen, sweetheart: these people will kill you. Are you listening to me? They will want you dead. Now whatever you're doing, put it down and get in your car and get out of there tonight. Just keep driving. Trust me, Rosie. You're a dead woman if you stay there.'

'Christ, Mickey! Now you're *really* freaking me out.' Rosie caught Adrian's eye as he was paying the bill. He gestured to her to hurry.

'Rosie . . . You know I don't fuck about with stuff like this. Now get moving, and call me when you're somewhere safe. Far enough away from Belgrade. Do you hear me?'

'I hear you, Mickey.'

Rosie put the phone back in her pocket. She tried to swallow but her mouth was suddenly dry. She lifted her glass and noticed her hand was shaking. 'We have to get out of here,' she said. 'That was my contact in London calling to say exactly what you've just told us, Adrian. They know we are here.'

'Come.' Adrian stood up. 'Let's go.'

CHAPTER 32

The dimly lit hotel foyer was deserted but for a few people sitting on sofas or at tables just outside the depressing-looking bar. The scene reminded Rosie of so many cities in the Eastern bloc where she'd been on assignment, the dreary bars and hotel foyers seeming to match the gloomy, resigned expressions of the people.

'I have a message for you,' the young man in the crimson waistcoat behind the reception said, as he handed Rosie and Matt their room keys.

Rosie made a surprised face to Matt. Risto hovered close by. Adrian had insisted he go into the hotel with them for safety as they picked up their belongings while he waited outside with the car.

The receptionist fished out a padded white envelope from the wooden pigeon holes behind him and handed it to Rosie without looking at her.

'Hope it's not a bomb,' Rosie joked to Matt, easing it open as the three of them walked towards the stairway to their rooms on the first floor.

'Bit late for that,' Risto smiled, as Rosie stuck her hand in the envelope.

She pulled out a photograph, and knew instantly who the package was from.

'It's from Gerhard.' She paused on the stairs and looked at Matt and Risto. 'You know, Gerhard? The German reporter.' All three of them stood looking at the photograph in Rosie's hands.

'Christ,' Matt said. 'It's some kind of shooting party. Look. It's Hayman! And Boskovac! Fuck me!'

Rosie couldn't believe her eyes. Hayman and Boskovac in overcoats and tweeds at the edge of a forest, posing with rifles over their shoulders, grinning triumphantly as they stood over a dead stag. The Serb had one arm around the cabinet minister.

Rosie flipped the photograph around and read the caption aloud: 'Environment Secretary Tim Hayman and company director Goran Boskovac on a shooting party in the Scottish Highlands in 1994'. She gave a low whistle. 'Christ! I don't believe this!' She stuck her hand inside the envelope and pulled out a piece of paper with a handwritten message scrawled on it:

This proves to you that powerful people were friends with evil long before they went to PD Pharmaceuticals. The picture is taken while the Serb was boss of the company I exposed. They were guests at an estate belonging to Lord Gennifer. Good luck.'
She pushed the photograph back into the envelope and put it safely in the pocket of her small rucksack, slinging it back over her shoulders.

'It's weird, though,' Matt said. 'Why leave it at the hotel if he was going to meet you?'

They both looked at Risto, and saw the muscle tighten in his lean jaw.

'Maybe like you he has decided to get out of Belgrade quickly. Perhaps he was afraid there may be no time.' He jerked his head towards the stairs. 'Come. We must go quickly now I think.'

Rosie followed Risto upstairs, still puzzled at the development. For a split second it crossed her mind that Gerhard had been betraying them, but she quickly banished it. Maybe Risto was right, and Gerhard was in a hurry to get out of the city. He did say he had been there before and was still investigating his story. It didn't feel right though, and she was glad they were getting the hell out of this place. She would call him and thank him for the picture as soon as she got to the car. But she wished she could have seen him.

Rosie watched as Matt went into his bedroom, leaving his door half open, then she walked the few doors down towards her room, Risto in tow.

'I come with you,' he said. 'Then we all go down together.'

The shock nearly knocked Rosie off her feet as she opened the door and stepped into the room. Facing her was a man tied to a chair with rope. A polythene bag was pulled tight over his head. The terror as he'd suffocated screamed out from his eyes, bulging like stocks. It happened so quickly, but in the split-second glimpse, she could tell that the purple face set to burst was Gerhard Hoffman.

Automatically, she swivelled her body around to Risto, but it was too late. She caught the slump of his body brushing against her shoulder as he fell to the floor. Before she had time to see what had hit him, she was grabbed from behind by the hair and a gun was shoved in her neck. A large fleshy hand was slapped over her mouth and nose and she heard herself trying to speak, choking for breath as she was dragged backwards. As she was pulled out of the doorway, there was just enough time to see Risto flinch as the bullet made a popping sound, ripping into his thigh and sending a splatter of bloodspots up the bedroom wall. The hand that was over her mouth let go, then she felt a hard punch on the side of her eye and went dizzy. But she was conscious enough to be aware she was being hauled in the opposite direction of Matt's room, towards the fire escape stairs. As her attacker pushed open the swing door into the darkness of the corridor, she prayed that Matt would come out of his room quickly enough to see Risto on the floor and would call Adrian. But as she was trailed downstairs and bundled into the back seat of a waiting car, she knew that this time she was on her own.

The gorilla in the back seat dragged her roughly around like a rag doll, and she looked up, trying to focus on his face.

'Wh ... What are you doing? Where you taking me?' Rosie saw him rip a piece of gaffer tape with his teeth. He cackled as he stuck the tape over her mouth, then got out of the car and into the driver's seat.

'You are going for a drive. Then I will give you the interview you want.' A voice from the passenger seat.

Rosie froze.

The passenger turned his body around and leaned across so she came face to face with him. Boris Raznatovic, his lips curled in a sardonic smile.

'You are surprised to see me.' Cold, dead eyes fixed her. 'But I am not surprised to see you. They said you would come. They said you are a brave reporter when you are chasing a story.' He wagged a finger. 'But you are also very stupid. And for that you will pay.'

Rosie lay still, desperately trying to contain the panic rising in her chest. She had to control her breathing, she told herself, as she struggled to pull in air through her nostrils. If she started hyperventilating, she would pass out. She could do this. She had to. She closed her eyes and prayed, inhaling gently, forcing every fibre of her body to stay calm.

The car pulled away slowly and Raznatovic turned back to face the front. She heard him sigh heavily.

'You people. You think it's clever to tell the world of our business in Glasgow and England, and of our business here. What are you trying to achieve? Are you so stupid you think you will stop us? You think anybody really cares about asylum seekers, refugees? You are very wrong. Nobody cares. You think anybody really cares about Bosnians or Kosovo Albanians, or someone from Africa? Everything is money, same as always. Politicians are not in charge in the new Serbia. We are. They were all criminals in the old days, just like us. Nothing has changed, only now we run the show.'

Rosie felt the sweat on the back of her neck as he turned around to face her again.

'I am going to prove something to you,' he said. 'Prove to you that nobody cares about you either. You think what you are doing is important, but it is not. We are going to a place and you will make a phone call to your editor, and tell him there is a price for your release. You see, everyone has a price. Refugees are worth more to us dead than alive, believe me. And you?' He half smiled. 'We will find out soon what you are worth, but I know it will be nothing. You can tell your story, but it will be the last one you will tell.' He turned away from her.

Rosie could smell cigarette smoke and listened hard as Raznatovic spoke to the driver in Serbian. A mobile phone rang and she heard Raznatovic talking animatedly. Very gently, she reached into her pocket and smuggled out her own phone, memorising the layout of the screen and how many taps of the keypad it took so she could send a message without looking. She knew Adrian's was the first name on her contacts, and she concentrated as she carefully picked out the the words, 'In car. Two men. Raznat . . .' Then she pressed what she prayed was the button to send the message to Adrian. She slipped the phone back into her pocket and strained her eyes to look up and peer out of the window. They hadn't gone far, so they must still be in the centre of the city. She could see the light of street lamps and hear the din of traffic. She thought of Tanya, and how she had escaped when Al Howie's men grabbed her in Glasgow. She raised her head a little and could see that the lock buttons on the door were up. Rosie could feel the adrenalin pumping through the veins in her neck.

Suddenly there was a deafening bang and she felt herself being shunted hard as her face banged against the back of the front seats. They'd hit something. A horn honked continuously and Raznatovic was shouting furiously at the driver. Rosie felt blood on the side of her eye from the thud, and eased herself up on one elbow. Outside, she could just see a man was striding towards the car shouting abuse at the driver, who was still being barked at by his boss. Rosie steadied herself as the man approached and hammered on the driver's window. She heard the click of a gun from the passenger seat. This was it. She had to be quick. She slipped her hand so it was on the door handle. In one, seamless movement, she pushed open the door, leapt out of the car and started running. A car swerved to avoid her as she raced across the busy road. She didn't look back to see if they were following her or shooting at her.

Rosie tore the tape off her mouth and ran for her life, crossing the street and running through the precinct and up a sidestreet. Her lungs were bursting and her heart pounding in her chest, but her legs were pumping like pistons as she kept pushing herself on.

The further she ran the more deserted the streets became, and she found herself up a quiet alleyway that looked like a residential area. She had no idea where she was. There were no bars, no shops, just the basic signs of life in the windows of the dark-grey stone buildings on either side. She stopped and leaned against a wall, bending over to catch her breath. From the corner of her eye she saw a long shadow coming towards her, and she jumped inside an open doorway, into the cold dark entrance to a block of flats and closed the door. Close by, a door opened on the ground floor and an old woman came out eyeing her suspiciously. She said something in Serbian and waved Rosie away. She thought she heard the word police. Her stomach turned over. She took a step towards the old woman, wiping the blood from her eye and mouth.

'Please,' she said, her lip trembling. 'Please. Help me.' Rosie looked at the door to the entrance, terrified it was going to burst open. 'Please let me stay for a moment.' She shook her head. 'No police.'

The old woman's eyes studied her.

'Please,' she joined her hands in pleading, tears coming to her eyes.

They stood in silence for a moment, then the woman spoke. 'You are English?' She stepped back in the doorway. 'You are in trouble? You are running away?'

'Please. Someone is trying to kill me. I am not a bad person. Please help me.' Rosie felt sick as she tasted blood in her mouth.

The woman looked as though she was going to close the door. Then she raised her hand and beckoned Rosie to follow her. 'Come.'

Relief flooded through Rosie as she walked behind her along the gloomy hallway. Through the living-room door, she could hear opera music. An image of her mother listening to an LP of Maria Callas on their old radiogram even as she was in a drunken stupor, flashed into her mind. She followed the woman inside and for a moment they both stood there in silence, with just the strains of the music from an old radio in the corner. Rosie swallowed and stood looking around her at the cosiness of the room, the crochet table covers and chairbacks, and dark wood shelves littered with ornaments. Old family photographs lined the mantelpiece – pictures of a safe normal life. And suddenly she couldn't stop the tears. She stood wiping them with the palms of her hands as they ran down her cheeks.

The old woman's expression softened.

'Sit.' She motioned her to the small sofa. 'I make some tea.'

Rosie sat down. Her mobile rang and she took it out of her pocket, struggling to hold it in her trembling hands. It was Adrian. She bit her lip and wiped her nose.

'Adrian,' she managed to say.

'Rosie, where are you? Are you okay?' He sounded breathless.

'I'm okay, Adrian.' She sniffed. 'I . . . I don't know where I am . . . I'm . . . In a house . . . Hold on.' Rosie turned to the old woman in the kitchen a few feet away, pouring boiling water into a teapot. 'Excuse me. Please. Can you tell me where I am?'

The old woman put down the kettle and turned towards her.

'You are bringing trouble to my house?'

'No. No, please. No trouble. My friend is coming for me. I will tell you what happened. Please. Just tell me the address.' Rosie went back to the mobile. 'Hold on, Adrian. Stay on the line.'

A few moments later, the old woman came in carrying a tray with tea, and a bowl of steaming water that smelled of disinfectant. She put it down on the coffee table in front of Rosie and reeled off the address.

'Tell your friend, go to the Kneza Mihaila and turn right at the top and left for two hundred metres, then after two right turns is my street. I am number twenty-seven. He must ring the bell twice.'

'Thank you.' Rosie sniffed, and relayed the information to Adrian.

'I will be there as soon as I can. Not long. You are okay, Rosie. Don't worry.'

Rosie felt the tears again and blinked them away while the old woman poured tea into cups. She spooned sugar into one and handed it to Rosie.

'For the shock,' she said. 'You have had a shock and the sugar will help you.' She smiled and Rosie saw the laughter lines around her eyes and high cheekbones on what had once been a lovely face. 'So. You can tell me what has happened to you. I see you are very frightened.'

Rosie stretched out her hand.

'My name is Rosie Gilmour. Thank you for helping me.' She paused, not really knowing what to say next. 'You speak very good English.'

The woman smiled. 'Yes. I travelled in Europe when I was young. My name is Katya. I played second violin in the national orchestra – when we were Yugoslavs. I meet many people from Western Europe – in Germany, France, Italy . . . and one time in England. London. In the good days . . .' She looked beyond Rosie at a photograph on the polished sideboard of a young woman with a violin and sighed. 'Before everything changed.' She looked at Rosie. 'But what happen to you? What brings a young woman with blood on her face to my house?'

Rosie sipped her tea, trying not to wince at the sweetness. Katya lifted the cloth out of the water and wrung it out, then dabbed it onto Rosie's face. She stiffened as the disinfectant stung.

'It will help. In case of infection.' Katya said. 'What happened to you?'

'I am a journalist,' Rosie said. 'I am in Belgrade investigating a story, and someone . . . some people . . . are trying to stop me. They came to my hotel tonight and they kidnapped me. I escaped because they crashed the car. I kept on running and I found myself here.'

Rosie decided not to tell her about Gerhard Hoffman. His face contorted in terror flashed through her mind and she blinked it away. He had come to help her and paid with his life.

The old woman pursed her lips and shook her head.

'So many gangsters these days. All criminals everywhere. Streets are not safe any more. In the old days, before this war with the Bosnian people, everyone was together. We were Yugoslavs, respecting each other. But now . . .' She sighed wearily. 'So much has been lost.'

'I know.' Rosie caught the sadness in the old woman's eyes. 'I am trying to expose bad people, Katya. When my friend comes, we will go back to Scotland where I live. And I can tell my story in the newspaper where I work.'

'Ah, but the British newspapers. The television. Always they tell stories about the Bosnian people. Always the Serbian people are bad it says.' She looked at Rosie. 'I am ashamed of so many of my people for what they do to innocent Bosnians. But I tell you . . . we have lost people too. Serbian people are destroyed by this war – Not only the innocent people who are killed. We are destroyed in our hearts.' She glanced at a photo on a table by her hearth of a young man squinting in the sunshine on a beach somewhere. 'I lost my son Jebril.'

They sat in silence. Rosie didn't want to speak in case she would say the wrong thing. Eventually she felt she had to say something.

'Was your son killed in the war?'

Katya took the framed photograph in her hand and gazed at it sadly. 'No. Not killed.' She brushed her hand over the picture. 'But he might as well be. He is gone now. Like so many other young Serbian men. He went away to avoid the terrible things they were being forced to do. He ran away, so he cannot come back. He is somewhere in Europe. Greece, the last time I heard from him.'

'Your only son?'

The woman nodded. 'My daughter, his little sister, she die when she was only seven. I was already a widow then.' She put the picture back on the table. 'I am alone now.'

'I'm sorry,' Rosie said.

Katya looked resigned and shook her head. 'Every day I wish my daughter could be with me,' she said. 'There is an old saying, maybe you also have it in Britain ... A son is a son till he takes a wife, a daughter is a daughter the rest of her life ... But sometimes is not the case. Sadly for me, it wasn't.'

Rosie watched her, thinking of her own mother and how she would have loved to sit in the warmth of a room with her as she grew older, telling her the stories of her work and her life.

They sipped their tea in silence. The purity of the music made Rosie want to cry again.

The doorbell rang twice, making Rosie flinch.

'Your friend is here.' Katya smiled at her nervousness. 'You are safe now.'

They both stood up and walked along the hallway.

'Adrian,' Rosie said, her ear at the door. 'Is that you?'

'Yes. It is me. Hurry. We must go.'

Katya and Rosie stood looking at each other.

'Thank you, Katya. You have saved my life.' Rosie's voice caught in her throat.

Katya smiled, again the wrinkles showing the fineness of her features.

'Maybe,' she said. 'But you must be careful. You should go home. Go away from here.'

'I am.' She squeezed her hand, then turned and opened the door.

Adrian stood in the hall, his face pale but relieved when he saw her.

'Rosie. You are all right?'

Rosie nodded, throwing her arms around him. He hugged her hard.

'Come. We must be quick.' He whispered. 'Risto is hurt. He has lost a lot of blood. We must drive now to Bosnia, because we cannot stop here.'

Rosie turned around.

'Goodbye Katya. Thank you.'

'Goodbye Rosie.' The old woman watched until they disappeared out of the main door.

CHAPTER 33

Rosie and Matt sat in a cafe close to the clinic where Adrian had taken Risto. It had been a terrifying journey from Belgrade, with Adrian driving at breakneck speed in the ancient Volkswagen Polo, which at one point had flames coming out of the engine, forcing them to stop to let it cool for a few minutes. Risto had lain in the back seat, his trousers saturated with blood. The makeshift tourniquet wouldn't have held up much longer, and he'd been drifting in and out of consciousness for the last twenty miles. Adrian had made a phone call to a contact, and the clinic was waiting for Risto by the time they arrived.

Rosie rubbed her face with both hands, and her eyes stung from tiredness and tears.

'You all right, Rosie?' Matt stretched across the table and squeezed her wrist.

Rosie nodded. She was conscious that she hadn't said much for most of the journey. Once the initial adrenalin had burned out after her escape from Raznatovic's clutches, the horror of Gerhard Hoffman's face kicked in. The reality of what he'd done to help the investigation haunted her, bringing back memories of Emir that first day they'd met at the Red Road flats. She thought of Mags Gillick, of Taha, of Tanya, and the people who had died or risked their lives to help her investigations. Guilt washed over her.

'To be honest, Matt,' Rosie leaned her head back on her shoulders and gazed up at the cloudless sky, 'I can't get Gerhard Hoffman out of my mind. It was me who contacted him. He didn't seek me out. Same with Emir.' She shook her head. 'If I had left these people alone, never gone near them, they would still be alive today.'

'You can't afford to look at it like that, Rosie,' Matt touched the back of her hand. 'Thoughts like that will drive you nuts. Don't even go there.' He poured some more tea into both their cups. 'Hoffman was already a marked man from what he'd done years ago. And the fact that he was back and forth to Belgrade, still investigating, it was only a matter of time before somebody took a pop at him. As for Emir ... That's just very sad, Rosie, but that's what happens. This is what we do. We're journalists, not missionaries.'

Rosie nodded, staring beyond Matt.

'Yeah, I know. We do our job, then we zip it up and move on to the next big story.'

'Exactly. It's how it has to be.'

'I just wonder what happened in those last couple of hours with Gerhard. The arrangement was that he would phone me and come to the hotel, and he obviously did come because he left the envelope with the picture. Somebody must have been watching him.'

'Yeah. Well, from what that bastard Raznatovic said to you, they must have known you were here. So they'd know he was here too. Maybe Gerhard got suspicious and didn't have time to meet you or think it was safe, so he came earlier and dropped the message off. But they got him at the hotel.' He paused. 'I don't suppose we'll ever know, Rosie, but you can't torment yourself with that.'

Rosie nodded. But she knew the thought of Gerhard's final moments would haunt her.

Her mobile rang. It was McGuire. Rosie looked at Matt as she lifted it off the table to answer it, mouthing McGuire to Matt, who gave her the thumbs-up as she answered.

'Gilmour! Where the fuck are you?' McGuire barked. 'Are you all right?'

'Hi Mick. Yeah, I'm fine. Er . . . I'm back in Bosnia. Had to get out of Belgrade fast.' Rosie grimaced at Matt.

'I'll say you did, Rosie. I've got fucking cops onto me from Interpol. They say there was a dead body in your hotel bedroom. What the fuck, Rosie? Is this true?'

'Er . . . well . . . Yes, it is, Mick.'

'What? Who?'

'Sadly, it was Gerhard Hoffman.'

'Who?'

'Hoffman. Gerhard Hoffman. The German reporter who exposed the company in the first place, remember? I told you about him.'

'What the fuck was he doing in Belgrade? I didn't know you were meeting him. Christ, Rosie!'

'I didn't know either, Mick. Listen, just calm down till I tell you. It's awful. Poor guy got murdered. They suffocated him with a poly bag, for Christ's sake. He'd come over to Belgrade to work on the story himself, and this is what happened to him. He was trying to help me, Mick. And now the poor guy's dead. I feel terrible.'

There was a silence. Rosie knew that in another time, another mood, Mick would be making jokes about dead bodies popping up every time Rosie left the office. But he refrained.

'Fuck me!'

'Yeah. It all went a bit mental, Mick. I got to the hotel this night, and there was a message from Hoffman. Actually, I'd met him earlier in the day and he said he was getting a picture for me from a contact, and I was to meet him at my hotel later. Next thing, I go to the hotel because we're preparing to leave Belgrade fast, and when I got there Hoffman had left a message – an envelope with a picture. And, wait for it, Mick. This will blow your socks off.'

'A picture? A picture of what?'

'It's a photo of Tim Hayman, and the Serb guy Boskovac I told you about. They're only at some bloody shooting party in the Highlands, brandishing rifles with their arms around each other like two best mates. And the thing is Mick, this was taken five years ago – while he was still Environment Secretary and while the Serb was with the company Hoffman exposed as exporting body parts and tissue.'

'You serious, Rosie?'

'You're damn right I am. And that's what happened to poor Hoffman after he came to help me. I went to my bedroom to get my bag, and there he was right in front of me, Mick. Tied up and suffocated. I just about had a heart attack. Then some bastards kidnapped me at gunpoint. Took me to Raznatovic.'

'Kidnapped you? Fuck! You met Raznatovic?'

'Yeah, but I got away. Sure, I'm here now, talking to you, Mick. It's a long story. Save it till I get back.'

'I want you home, Rosie. Tonight.'

'Mick, I'm safe now. I'm in Bosnia.'

'No. I want you back here, Rosie. Don't make me say fuck again.'

Rosie puffed, frustrated. She knew they had done just about everything they came to do. As soon as she'd got into Adrian's car last night, she phoned Mickey Kavanagh, knowing he would tip off Interpol where they could find the Serbian. The war crimes people and the police would already be hammering down Raznatovic's door, and even if he'd gone, there was a better than ever chance they'd track him down. Her work was finished here, and she'd managed to escape Serbia without the cops dragging her in about Hoffman's body in her hotel room. All she had to do now was go to Macedonia to keep her promise to Emir.

She told McGuire all of this, and waited while his brain ticked over.

'Christ almighty, Rosie. Raznatovic is after you. The cops are after you. If you get arrested anywhere over there by any Serbian authorities you could be there for years. It's safer to come straight home. And I want to see this story as soon as possible.'

'I know, Mick. Just give me two more days, that's all. Let me go to Macedonia. I owe it to Emir. Then I'm home. I'll get the story done tonight around the picture we have, and as much background as I've got on the Serb. You can get Vincent in Westminster to front Hayman up over the picture. It's a belter of a line and we're miles ahead of everyone. We're nearly there, Mick. Nearly there.'

There was a pause while Mick digested all this, then, 'Right,' he said. 'Okay, Rosie. Two more days. Now make sure Matt and that big Adrian bloke are looking after you. Two more days, then you're out.'

'Okay, Mick.'

'And get to a hotel tonight and get that story over to me.' He paused. 'Are you sure you're all right?'

'Sure, Mick.' The line went dead.

CHAPTER 34

The next morning they were geared up and ready to go by eight. Rosie was a little groggy as she loaded her bag into the boot of Adrian's car. A mixture of exhaustion and relief had contributed to all of them drinking more than they should have over dinner in the restaurant in Olovo last night. Now she had that jet-lag feeling that always crept up on her when she was working out of town. Risto had been kept in hospital, and she and Matt had said their farewells at his bedside, hugging like old comrades, promising to meet again, even though they knew they probably wouldn't.

'It will take almost a day and a half to get to Kosovo and then to Macedonia,' Adrian said, as Rosie got into the front seat beside him. He turned his body so he was facing her. 'But there is something I want to show you before we go.'

Rosie looked at him curiously. He hadn't mentioned anything last night.

'Fine.' She assumed he'd be taking them to another landmark illustrating the area's tragic history.

She fiddled with her mobile as they drove out towards the edge of the town. She looked at last night's text message from TJ. He was leaving for New York in two days. He'd joked about her getting a move on if she was going to see him. She knew it wasn't going to happen, and pushed it to the back of her mind. She didn't have time to think about that now.

Rosie looked out of the windscreen as Adrian took the car off the main road and up a twisting road away from the town. As they neared the brow of the hillside, she could see what looked like a graveyard. She glanced at Adrian from the corner of her eye, but he stared straight ahead in silence.

They drove up the narrow path towards the gated cemetery and Adrian stopped the car. He turned to Rosie.

'I show you something.' He switched off the ignition and opened the door.

Rosie looked at Matt and shrugged. They both got out of the car. An old woman wearing a headscarf and a coat that was too heavy for the sunny day came out of the graveyard, dabbing her eyes with a handkerchief. She stopped for a second, shook her head as her pitiful expression acknowledged them, and walked on.

'Come,' Adrian took a deep breath and walked through the wooden gates, Rosie and Matt following behind him. They walked past some ancient gravestones, weathered and overgrown with weeds, some toppled on their side. Others were so old they didn't even have markings. When they climbed to the top of the rise, they suddenly stopped in their tracks. Ahead of them were endless rows of small white marble pillars, close together like a column of sentries frozen to the spot.

'Jesus, Matt. Look at this.' Rosie gazed at the gravestones as Adrian walked ahead. 'There's so many. War graves.'

'Kind of brings it home to you, doesn't it, when you see it like this.'

They stepped closer to the first row and looked at the inscriptions. Some had flowers, trinkets, children's toys. All they could understand were names and what must have been ages. Eight, ten months, twenty-five. The lifeblood of future generations buried side by side.

'Come on.' Rosie said, and they went to catch up with Adrian.

Adrian kept going until he was close to the last row, then he stopped at a gravestone near the end. It was ringed by a little wooden fence. Fresh flowers bloomed in a metal vase. He stood looking at it, his big square shoulders suddenly sloping.

Rosie and Matt came slowly closer but stood behind him, saying nothing. He turned around.

'Come closer.'

They shuffled beside him. Rosie read what she could understand from the inscription. Marija, February, 1994. Then the name Adrijan. There were more names and words she didn't understand, until she saw the name Adrijan again. She turned to Adrian.

'My fiancée, Marija. Our unborn son, Adrijan.' He swallowed. 'She wanted to name him after me.'

'I'm so sorry, Adrian.' She didn't need to ask what happened.

'The Serbs. They came to the village and took everyone out of it. Marija was in the field helping her mother. They killed them both. Butchered them. The baby, who was torn from her stomach, lay by her side when they found her.' He shook his head. 'I was in the next village doing some work, and when I came back I was met at the edge of town by my friend Risto who was waiting for me. He told me.'

'I'm so sorry,' Rosie said, again, not knowing what else to say.

Adrian nodded. 'I wanted you to see. I never told you anything about my life before, because it is just for me.' He touched his heart with his hand. 'I keep it here. I want to keep it inside me and never let it go. But I know one day I must.' He looked at her, then back at the grave. 'I just wanted you to know. You are my friend, Rosie.'

They were silent for a moment, then Rosie asked, 'Did you leave here after everything that happened?'

'For a while I stay and fight. Then my mother said one day they would come and round us up on the buses and take us away, maybe to Paklenik gorge like the others. She told me I must go.' He gazed around at the landscape. 'But I have never really left.'

They stood in the stillness, Rosie trying to imagine the slaughter and the wailing as each family buried their hearts.

Eventually, Adrian spoke. 'We must go now, Rosie. We have a long drive to Macedonia.'

CHAPTER 35

They had stopped in a little Kosovan town in the early evening so that Rosie could find a place to put her story together. They also needed to rest for the night, having driven all the way from Olovo south to Kosovo – or what was left of Kosovo, Matt had remarked. Every bombed-out town and village they drove into was still raw with the same depressing story of communities and lives ripped apart by war. Houses and mosques had been razed to the ground by rampaging Serbian soldiers who left behind a trail of destruction. Most of the streets were deserted and only the drone of the patrolling NATO vehicles broke the silence. Soldiers from KFOR, the United Nations force, were posted around, armed with rifles to keep the peace since the ceasefire a few months earlier. But in most of the areas south of Pristina there was nobody left to fight, and anyone who hadn't fled from the bloodbath had little fight left.

'If we stay here for the night,' Adrian said, as he pulled

up to what might once have been a smartish small hotel, 'we can head straight for Kacanik tomorrow early, then it's only a few miles to Macedonia. It should only take a morning to get to where we're going.'

Kacanik. The name flashed up a blur of faces and horror stories as Rosie recalled the refugees spilling across the border post of Blace into Macedonia a few months earlier. Many of them had walked from Kacanik with nothing but the clothes they stood up in. Nobody had been prepared for the mass exodus of desperate refugees fleeing from the Serbs into their nearest southern neighbours. In the beginning it had been a trickle of fifty or a hundred a day coming across – old men and women with bruised faces telling waiting reporters how they were dragged from their homes and beaten with rifles. Frightened families had recounted seeing neighbours and friends with their throats cut lying at the roadside as Serbian paramilitary gangs showed no mercy.

'Come on boss, you've got a splash and spread to write.'

'I'm here, I'm here,' Rosie shook herself back from the dark reverie as Matt rapped on the window.

She pushed the door open and got out, gazing around at the quiet streets, the narrow roads, still strewn with rubble from bomb-blasted buildings. A military truck flying the Dutch flag came trundling up the road, and the soldiers seated in the back with the canvas pulled across like curtains on a stage, waved cheerily. One of them whistled, and Rosie smiled at them.

'Come on. Let's go.' She slung her rucksack on her back

and dragged her hold-all out of the boot, then followed Adrian up to the hotel entrance.

The call from McGuire to tell her they'd arrested Raznatovic in Belgrade had come as no surprise. Mickey Kavanagh had tipped Rosie off about half an hour earlier, and it was then she'd made the decision they'd stop at the first place that looked reasonable so she could fire up her laptop and get started. She was glad of Mickey's tip-off, because she was one step ahead by the time McGuire phoned, reeling off suggestions to her. This was boots and saddles time – McGuire had used his favourite phrase when he was rolling out a big story. He wanted every cough and spit.

In her earlier stories, they'd held off on any mention of Raznatovic and his background, because McGuire agreed with Rosie that they had that all to themselves. They'd do it when the time was right, when they could blast the whole story on the front page. Having the picture from Hoffman of Goran Boskovac and Tim Hayman was the icing on the cake. Nobody else would even have a sniff at that.

'We'll keep the story of your kidnapping till you get back, Rosie, and then we can milk it for all it's worth. But right now, I want you to write chapter and verse of what we know about Raznatovic – everything about his early years, his part in the Bosnian massacre, and how he managed to dupe the authorities here and come in as a Bosnian refugee. Everything about the slaughter-house and his life in Glasgow with the hoodlums. Right up to his arrest in Belgrade . . . And how it was us who tracked him down,' McGuire had said. 'And the stuff about him working as a GP in London is brilliant. The Home Office will shit themselves over that!'

Now, in her hotel bedroom, Rosie read her copy for the final time, making sure there were no loose ends as she would be on the move by the morning, until they got to the Macedonian town to try to find Emir's grandmother.

Rosie rubbed her face vigorously with both hands. She could do with a drink and a cigarette. She'd been smoking more in the last couple of weeks than she'd done in months, and vowed to cut it down to the occasional one with a drink when she got back home. She looked over the second story for the spread, which she'd written around the photograph of Boskovac and the minister.

McGuire had told her the story of Hoffman's murder was on the wires and the foreign pages of the broadsheets, but it hadn't made the main TV news in the UK. A German being bumped off in a hotel bedroom in Belgrade could be anything. But he couldn't conceal his delight that the *Post* would be the only paper that could reveal the truth behind his murder. He said he'd get a decent tie looked out for the TV cameras when they came to interview him about the *Post*'s groundbreaking exclusive. This is what he lived for.

This was what Rosie lived for too, but right now it didn't feel that way. She thought of Emir, and how frightened he was as he'd gripped her hand in the hospital. She thought of her meeting with Hoffman, and how troubled he'd seemed. She knew the image of him in the bedroom was sure to haunt her for years to come. Part of her wished she didn't do this any more, that she was back in Glasgow, seeing TJ off to New York and planning a trip to see him. But a bigger part of her couldn't wait to see this story in the paper. She looked out of the window into the blackness. Her mobile rang.

'You nearly finished, Rosie?' It was Matt. 'There's a gin and tonic with your name on it at the bar.'

'I'm on my way.' Rosie pushed back her chair, stood up, and pinged the story over to McGuire.

The sunburst red-and-yellow Macedonian flag fluttered high on the border post at Blace. Rosie was glad to see it, even though the very sight of it brought back disturbing images. The garish flag was known as the sun of liberty, and it had meant safety and refuge for so many fleeing Kosovans just a few months ago. Right now, for Rosie, it meant they were almost home. By this evening, they would be on a plane from Skopje airport to London, and in Glasgow the following day.

'Can you stop here for five minutes?' Rosie asked Adrian as they crossed the border. 'I just want to look at something.'

He glanced at her curiously and pulled up at the side of the road.

Rosie got out and crossed over to stand closer to the edge of the sprawling field. It was on this very spot she'd witnessed human suffering on such a huge scale that, even weeks after she'd returned home, she couldn't look upon an empty field without seeing a seething mass of desperate refugees living in the muddy squalor they'd been abandoned to for days. Now the vast field at the foot of the rugged hillside lay empty and silent. But even though fresh grass had grown over the mud and slime, Rosie could still hear the noises in her head. The crying of children, the coughing and hacking of people ill from sleeping rough and lying in the rain with nothing but the clothes they'd been wearing when they'd been burned and battered out of their homes days earlier.

With the sound of the rushing river at the far side of the field, an image came into her head of the morning she'd seen an old woman limp to the edge of the river. She'd hitched up her heavy coat and skirt to urinate in public, because there was no option, and Rosie had watched as the woman wept at the sheer indignity of it all. She swallowed her tears as she remembered walking among the people one chilly, smoky dawn, and finding their stories of mutilated bodies in the streets they'd left behind almost too far-fetched to be believed. It was only days later, when the people were finally bused to refugee camps around Blace that she'd gone behind the wired fences to speak to them and realised that so many of them told the same stories, they just had to be true. But it was over now. And as she looked at the row of tall, skinny poplar trees that separated the border from Kosovo, she was glad she'd returned to see for herself that it really *was* over. Perhaps now her sleep would not be so haunted.

'Okay.' She turned to Matt and Adrian who were standing at the car watching her. 'Let's go.'

In the car, Matt squeezed her shoulder. 'You all right, Rosie?'

'Yeah. I'm good, Matt.' She took a deep breath and read the piece of paper she'd pulled out of her bag. 'There's no address,' she told them. 'Just the name of the grand-mother and the name of the town of Tetovo. We'll just have to wing it, guys. I've been in Tetovo before when I was here during the war, and I remember there were a couple of centres set up where refugees could go to find each other. So many of them had been split up in the chaos after they came over to Macedonia that it took months to hook them back up together.'

'Is that what happened to Emir's grandmother?' Matt asked.

'That's what he told me. He said she was taken in a bus from here on the border with one of his aunts, and that they'd been in touch a couple of times to say they were now living in Tetovo until they could go back home. So let's hope she's still there, because a lot of the Kosovans did go back home in recent weeks once the NATO forces had made it safe for them.'

'If she is old, I think she will still be there,' Adrian said.

'I hope so.' She looked at her watch. 'Because we only have one shot at this.'

They reached the outskirts of Tetovo after a couple of hours' drive through awesome scenery, past sweeping fields and lakes, surrounded by the skyline of snow-capped mountains. The town was sprawled across the grassy plains at the foot of a mountain, and the closer they got to it, the more crammed together it seemed to be. Down the ages, Tetovo had always been an Albanian enclave and Muslim town. After the Bosnian war, it took several thousands of the fleeing Bosnians, and when the Kosovo conflict kicked off, at least a hundred thousand people flocked there. As they drove through the bustling town, it was clearly still a little chaotic from the massive influx of refugees, with people milling around in the main square, or outside centres that looked like aid shelters.

'Phrases like needles in haystacks are coming to mind, Rosie,' Matt said.

'Looks like it. But let's see if we can find a centralised place – if there is such a thing – to ask some questions.'

Adrian pulled the car over to the side of the road and got out. He went into a cafe and spoke to some men sitting at a table playing a board game with matchsticks.

'I'm glad Adrian's here,' Matt said. 'My Macedonian is shite.'

'What, like your Spanish?' Rosie grinned at him.

'I thought my Spanish was actually muy impressive, by the way, señorita.'

'Yeah, right,' Rosie said.

After a couple of minutes Adrian came back. 'There are some aid agencies still working in the town. They have given me a couple of names. We must go up past the main square, and the centres are close to a mosque up at the edge of the town.' He got into the car and they drove off, winding their way through the traffic in narrow, busy streets.

'This reminds me a wee bit of that shithole in Morocco – Sale – we drove through that time with Adrian last year.'

'Yeah,' Rosie said. 'But without the body in the boot.'

All three of them laughed, recalling the tension and danger of the last big investigation that had brought them all together, hunting for the kidnapped toddler stolen from her parents on the Costa del Sol.

'Let's hope we don't have the same trouble getting out of the country as we did at the end of that trip,' Adrian said, lighting a cigarette.

They managed to find a place to park close to the mosque. All three of them got out of the car. Rosie knew she and Matt stuck out like sore thumbs among the Muslim women and men. A few months ago, towns like this were heaving with press and TV cameras, filming refugees arriving in buses, and interviewing displaced persons before they were shunted to neighbouring towns and villages that were all trying to cope with the sudden influx.

All Rosie had to go on was a photograph of Emir's grandmother and aunt and their names. He'd told her about them the night he stayed in her house and said they were now living in Tetovo. When he died, Rosie had insisted that Don and the DI quietly gave her a copy of the photograph and his old address that was in his belongings. It was the least they could do, she'd told them.

At the makeshift reception area in the hall next to the mosque, Rosie asked the weary-looking man at the desk if he spoke English. He answered her in French. Rosie's grasp of the language gathered that they needed another part of the building. He took them to an office close by where a woman sat behind a desk. Rosie showed her the name and the photograph. The woman looked at the names and went down a list. She looked up and shook her head.

'Is not here.'

'You have never had a record of either of the two women?'

The woman shook her head. Rosie gave Matt a frustrated look. The woman watched them, then stood up.

'You can try across the road in the shelter for the old people. They may know. But I have nothing here.'

They crossed into the shabby building which looked like it had been a clinic or small hospital ward, with rows of beds and a waiting area. Rosie went up to the main desk and spoke to the woman, who shook her head, not understanding. Adrian arrived at her shoulder and spoke in what Rosie guessed was Macedonian, or some kind of variation of Serbo-Croat that most Slavs understood. He took the piece of paper from Rosie and showed it to her. She got out a huge book and opened it, muttering something to Adrian. Rosie watched as she scanned her finger down the list of names, then she stopped and smiled up to Adrian, and spoke.

'Is here,' Adrian said. 'She has the name on the list.'

The two of them spoke again, and Adrian thanked her.

'Let's go,' he said. 'She gave me an address, but she isn't supposed to. It is close by. The woman is living with an Albanian family.'

The address was on the far side of the town, through a warren of blocks of flats and up narrow little streets that led to rows of ramshackle houses. Rosie's throat felt tight with emotion as they drove past people who were clearly poor refugees, idling through their days, waiting to find out what the future held for them. She wondered where they would end up – would they ever go home? Would they ever be able to find something of the life they had when so much that was precious to them had been lost? If Emir hadn't ended up in Glasgow, he might have been wandering around here, caring for his grandmother, clinging to the only family he had left. She was dreading meeting them, afraid they would see through her story that Emir was happy.

When they stopped the car outside the address, half a dozen people gathered, eyeing them suspiciously as they went towards the houses. A middle-aged man approached them and they stopped. Adrian gave them the names of the two women. His face showed nothing, but he immediately disappeared inside a house and, moments later, a woman, came out looking confused. She was not old enough to be Emir's grandmother, and Rosie assumed from the picture she must be the aunt.

'I am Besa.' She put her hand on her chest. 'You are looking for my aunt?'

'Yes,' Rosie said. 'I'm sorry to trouble you. You speak English?' She smiled, gratefully.

'A little. From the hotel I am working in many years ago.'

'I am looking for the grandmother of Emir. I am from Scotland. I am a journalist. I would like to talk to you about Emir.'

The woman's face lit up, then fear registered and her eyes grew dark.

'Ah! Emir is okay?' Her expression pleaded for reassurance.

Rosie steeled herself as the woman studied her face. She took a deep breath and opened her mouth to speak, but the woman intervened. 'Emir is hurt?' She shook her head, touched her lips. 'You come to us with bad news.'

Rosie glanced at Adrian and Matt, then nodded. 'Yes. I'm sorry. Emir . . . Emir was killed.' The tears came without warning, spilling out of her eyes. It was all she could do to stop herself from breaking down.

Her words hung there like a cruel blow. In this far-flung little corner of the world where people had seen too much sorrow, a stranger now came to break more hearts.

The woman's face fell and she kind of crumpled, seeming suddenly unsteady on her feet. Rosie stepped forward and reached out an arm, but a woman standing behind her supported Besa who was now in tears.

'Emir,' she whispered and buried her face in her hands, shaking her head. 'No Emir. He is a good boy. His mama . . . His papa . . . murdered by the Serbs. Please. No Emir.'

'I'm so sorry.' Rosie, sniffed and wiped her tears, but they just kept coming. 'I'm so, so sorry,' she said again.

The people close by looked on disconsolately as Besa dabbed her eyes with her apron and tried to compose herself. 'What happen?' she asked.

'It's a very long story,' Rosie said, 'but he was killed. He was murdered, and the police in Scotland are investigating.'

'Why killed? Why Emir?' Besa looked bewildered.

Rosie knew she would have to give more. Besa deserved to know more.

'Emir was helping me with a story for the newspaper, because bad things are happening to refugees in the UK. They are being kidnapped and killed. He was one of them who was attacked. They tried to kill him.' Rosie paused. 'They killed his friend.'

'Jetmir?' Besa looked shocked, then mumbled something in Albanian.

'I'm afraid so.'

Besa shook her head again. 'Please . . . Please. Why you come here? You come all this way to tell us this?'

'Because . . .' Rosie swallowed. 'Because I promised Emir in the hospital before he died. He asked me to come here and to tell his grandmother that he is fine and is happy. I made a promise to him.' She bit her lip. 'Emir was a very brave young man. He was helping me to find the people who were killing the refugees. He wanted to find out what happened to Jetmir. We were working together.' She shook her head. 'I feel bad because I was the only friend he had, but . . .' Rosie choked. 'But I couldn't save him.'

Besa's hand trembled as she wiped a tear from her cheek.

'You were with him?'

'Yes. He was not alone. I held his hand.'

Besa looked at her, and Rosie waited for an angry outburst of emotion blaming her for his death, but it didn't happen. Besa stepped forward and put her arms around her. They both stood there, hugging each other and crying on each other's shoulder. Eventually, Besa let go, and she jerked her head in the direction of the house behind her.

'Emir's grandmother – my aunt. She is an old woman. She is sick. Please do not tell her the truth. Tell her what Emir say – that he is happy.'

Rosie nodded. 'I will.'

In the little kitchen, the old lady sat near the window in a wooden armchair. She was dressed in black, with her silver hair pulled back neatly in a bone clasp. When Besa introduced Rosie as a friend of Emir's, she opened her toothless mouth in a joyful smile, and took both Rosie's hands in hers. Her eyes were milky with cataracts.

'Emir,' she said, happily. 'Emir.' She nodded and spoke in Albanian.

Rosie looked at Besa.

'She is asking is Emir happy. Is he living in a good country.'

Rosie glanced at Matt and Adrian, then at Besa. 'Tell her yes, he is very happy. He is in Glasgow in Scotland and he has a job. And he is very happy. He has a nice apartment. He told me to tell his grandmother not to worry, that he is happy.'

The woman relayed the message and the grandmother broke into a smile. Then she gazed out of the window, and spoke again.

'She is asking will he come to see her some time. Will she see him.'

Rosie paused. She looked at the grandmother's face, the deep wrinkles on her papery thin skin. For a fleeting moment, Rosie thought she saw a look in the old woman's eyes that knew none of what she was saying was true but that she was playing the game like everyone wanted her to. She saw the woman's eyes fill up.

'Yes,' Rosie nodded. 'Tell her she will see him some time.'

Besa relayed the message and the old woman smiled. She took Rosie's hand again and held it tight.

'Thank you,' she said in English. Then she spoke to Besa.

'She says you are very kind to come all this way to bring to her the love of her grandson.'

And once again, Rosie felt that somewhere behind the fading, weary eyes, the old woman knew that the reason this stranger had come so far to see her, could only be because Emir was gone. She just didn't have to say it.

'And here we are at last, Rosie,' Adrian glanced at her from the corner of his eye, as he took the slip road off to Skopje airport. 'Soon you will be home.'

Rosie thought she detected a trace of sadness in his expression.

'I'm going to miss you, Adrian.' She gently patted his

shoulder, letting out a long sigh. 'It's been some journey – in more ways than one.'

Part of her was desperate to get back to Glasgow, not just to feel safe in her own country, but to shake off the heaviness of these past few days, revisiting the scenes that had haunted her since she left Kosovo. But the crazy part of her – that she could never really explain to people – didn't want to leave. There was something about living on the edge like this, so far out of her comfort zone, which gave Rosie such an adrenalin hit that she felt more alive than she did in any other area of her life. She wished she didn't feel that way, but she did, and as long as she did, she knew her life would always be pretty much a mess. She looked at her watch. The flight to London was in three hours and they'd be too late for the last flight to Scotland. TJ was going in the morning to New York. No way would she make it on time. She'd already resigned herself to that.

Her mobile rang. It was McGuire.

'Gilmour? You're a star! Take a bow! We're all over Sky News today.'

'Oh. Hi Mick. We've been on the move all day. Did it say much?'

'Not a whole lot. Just that they'd arrested the Serbian army commander wanted for war crimes, who had been on the run in the UK. They also flashed up a copy of our front page yesterday, with the picture of Hayman. Fucking marvellous news! He's stood down as an MP, by the way, after our revelations. Downing Street is covered in shit over it. They've launched an immediate investigation into

PD Pharmaceuticals. If I didn't have a paper to put out I'd be opening a bottle of champers.' He paused. 'But I'll keep it till you get back, Rosie. Tell Matt I said well done. Both of you. I'm so proud of you, I'm even saying it out loud.'

'Don't you go crying on me now, Mick,' Rosie joked. 'I hate when you do that.' She was feeling better already. The gloom had lifted.

'What time are you up here tomorrow?'

'Should be there by midday. I'm catching the flight out of here in around three hours – unless there's some kind of stop on me by Interpol.' Rosie was only half joking. Her stomach knotted at the thought of it.

'Christ, don't say that! You should be all right coming out of Macedonia, but you might get your backside felt in the UK. If not in London when you arrive, then maybe when you get back here.'

'You think so? In the great scheme of things, now that they've arrested Raznatovic, the fact that I left the scene of a murder that he had obviously instigated is a mere detail is it not?'

'Don't bank on it, Gilmour, but I've got Hanlon standing by just in case. Keep me informed.' He paused. 'You and Matt can have an extra Kit-Kat on your expenses when you get to London tonight. But get some sleep because I want you fresh for your story on the kidnapping when you get home tomorrow.' He hung up.

'Your editor is very happy,' Adrian said, as he pulled the car into a space at the departures area.

'Yes. Ecstatic by the sound of him. Raznatovic will

probably lie around jail for a while now before they set a trial date, but the good thing is they got him,' Rosie said, getting out of the car as Matt dragged their bags out of the boot.

He hooked his camera bag over his shoulder. 'We'd better get a move on, Rosie. I just want to get through security and lie low until it's time for the flight.' He extended a hand to Adrian. 'Big man. You're some turn.' Adrian shook his hand, and Matt stepped forward and gave him a hug. Adrian looked a little surprised, but hugged him back.

Matt turned and walked a few steps ahead, leaving Rosie and Adrian standing together. She smiled at him, suddenly recalling the haunted young Bosnian refugee she'd first seen in the cafe in Glasgow when they first met. It seemed like a lifetime ago.

'I wish you were coming with us, Adrian,' Rosie said, and meant it.

'Me too, Rosie.' He shrugged. 'I will be here for a little while more, but then I move on again. Is always the way with me now. Home is not the same for me.'

'I know,' Rosie said, thinking of the cemetery. She could see Matt standing at the doors waiting for her. She didn't really have any words for the way she felt right now – not any that would do it justice.

'I better get going.' She wrapped her arms around Adrian and he kissed her on the cheek then held her tight. Tears stung Rosie's eyes.

'I'm so grateful for everything you've done for me, Adrian.'

He let go of her, and his pale eyes scanned her face.

'You are a good woman, Rosie. I do miss you. I see you again I hope.' He kissed her again, this time softly on the lips, just for a moment.

She was a little taken by surprise and hugged him again. 'Goodbye Adrian. Take care.' She let go of him and walked away, turning back to see him still standing by his car, watching her disappear into the building.

CHAPTER 36

There was something about the sight of the lunchtime canteen rush that gave Rosie a ridiculous sense of comfort. She was home. She stood in the foyer of the *Post* as the lift doors pinged open and the various staff spilled out, full of their usual banter and gossip as they headed for the canteen on the ground floor.

'Good holiday, Rosie? Where's your tan?' The big cheery receptionist grinned at her.

Rosie smiled back, her eye still a little swollen and bruised.

'Yeah. Brilliant, Liz. Laugh a minute.'

Some things never changed. It didn't matter whether you'd been shot at, kidnapped or beaten to a pulp by some thug – the good thing was you always got the same patter when you came back into the office. It was as reassuring as outstretched arms.

She went upstairs and stood for a moment, gazing around the expanse of the editorial floor, half empty as it usually was at this time of the day before the afternoon buzz built up. It was good to be back. She could see McGuire talking to Marion outside his office, and when he looked up and caught sight of her, he beckoned her across.

'Welcome back, Rosie,' Marion said. 'I hope you're putting that black eye on your expenses,' she smiled.

'Oh, you bet I will, Marion.' Rosie winked and went into McGuire's office and closed the door.

'Christ, Gilmour, I feel I should hug you.' He came towards her. 'In fact, I'm going to hug you.'

He put his arms around her and gave her a squeeze. Rosie felt a little choked – a mixture of exhaustion, and gratitude that she'd actually made it in one piece.

'Don't get all weepy now, Mick. At least wait till you see my expenses.'

'Are you all right Rosie? I mean with the bloody kidnapping and stuff?'

'Yeah,' Rosie said, as casually as she could manage. 'I'm okay. At least I'm here to tell the tale.'

McGuire looked at her, shaking his head. He motioned her to sit down on the sofa, then went to his desk and picked up two copies of the *Post*. He held them up to her like a trophy.

'Fucking brilliant! We stuffed everybody! In fact we've been stuffing every other paper from day one on this story. Sales are up a right few thousand in the last couple of days.'

Rosie gave him a sarcastic look. 'Yeah, never mind the poor bastards getting their bodies sliced up and pickled – as long as we're selling millions.'

'Oh you know what I mean, Rosie. We've set the agenda big time with this. Fucking resignations all over the place.' He opened the paper. 'Look.'

Rosie saw the headline: 'Hayman Stands Down', and below, the story of his dealings with the company at the centre of international illegal trade in human body tissue.

'And not just him.' McGuire turned another page. 'A detective has been suspended pending an investigation into the death of your pal Emir.'

Rosie brightened. 'Really? Who is it?'

'Some guy named Nicholson. Not even a DS, just a detective who was on the job of looking after Emir. He must have given them the whereabouts. My spies tell me it turns out he's been on the take from Howie's mob for a while. He's for the high jump anyway, the bastard, but you have to wonder why it took them so long to fucking realise he was bent.'

'Shocking,' Rosie said. 'And you'd think they'd be able to hand-pick a crack team to look after a protected witness.'

'Yeah. I also hear the Deputy Chief Constable is getting his arse kicked big time. The Chief was on a week's holiday, and Emir was murdered on the DCC's watch. So there's a view taken that the buck stops with him.'

'Good. Deserves all he gets. I need to find out a bit more about it. We should just keep hammering them. We shouldn't let them get away with being so completely inept.'

McGuire gave her a perplexed look. 'I thought you might say that. But give yourself a rest, Rosie, you just

got back. Take a couple of days to bask in the glory –
well, after you write up your kidnapping piece today.'

'I will, Mick. I will. But I need to make a call.' She pressed
Don's number. It answered after two rings.

'You still on the run, Rosie?'

It was good to hear Don's sarcastic voice. 'I'm in hiding
– behind the sofa. Less said about it the better.'

'Are you back though?'

'Yep, only just. Tell me: what's the craic with the cop
suspended. I just heard.'

Don lowered his voice. 'Can't talk right now. Why don't
I meet you in O'Brien's for a quick drink . . . about six?'

Rosie rubbed her face. She was tired. She would take
a couple of hours to write up the kidnap story, and she
needed to go back and reacquaint herself with the safe
flat.

'Okay, Don. I'll be there.' She hung up, then turned to
McGuire. 'I might have a bit more intelligence on the
cop situation later today.'

The door opened and Marion came in carrying a tray
with coffee and some sandwiches.

'Thought you might be hungry,' she said, setting it
down on the coffee table.

'Great, Marion. I'm starving.'

McGuire's phone rang on his desk and he answered it
impatiently. When he hung up he came back and took
a mouthful of tea without sitting down.

'Listen, Rosie. I've got to go up to a directors' meeting.
Some bean-counter crap, but I've got to be there.' He put
his cup down. 'Are you all right to do the kidnap story?

I mean how *are* you with it? When I come back down I want to hear all about it. You're a bit bashed up.'

'I'm okay. It was scary, but I'm fine. I'll tell you about it over a bottle of something stronger than this.' She held up her teacup.

'Deal.' He headed for the door.

Rosie settled down and read over the newspapers she'd missed while she was away. Her eyes rested on the picture of Emir that Matt had taken at her flat before they took him to the police station that afternoon. His drawn expression and dark eyes were full of fear and apprehension. She remembered him sobbing like a lost child that morning at the Red Road flats, and then how much more relaxed he'd been as they'd sat in her flat the night before she handed him over to the care of cops. He'd talked to her about growing up in Kosovo, about the murder of his parents, and how he and his friend Jetmir were full of hope for the future. She reflected on the look in his grandmother's eyes . . .

She sat back and flicked through the other stuff she'd sent while she was on the move – the full story behind the Raznatovic involvement. She looked back at the Frank Paton revelations, thinking of his ashen face that day she'd confronted him. One of the other reporters, young Declan, had written a good piece about a government probe into refugees in Scotland. There was a photograph of the woman Rosie had spoken to from the Scottish Refugee Council and an interview with her declaring how shocked they were at the revelations. But she claimed that government cutbacks prevented them from checking the whereabouts of every refugee every single day. Some things never change.

It was, as McGuire had said, a groundbreaking investigation, and the entire media was a country mile behind them in the chase. Rosie wished she felt as triumphant inside as the bravado exterior she was putting on. But the truth was that all she could think about was Emir and Gerhard Hoffman. She noted there had been no arrests as yet. Both Al Howie and Clock Buchanan had vanished, probably to the Costa del Sol. But they would get their day . . .

Her mobile rang and she looked at it, confused. It was TJ.

'TJ?'

'Hey Rosie.' His tone was light. 'Where are you?'

'I'm back, TJ. Just a couple of hours ago. I'm in the office. Where are you? You in New York already?'

'Nope,' he said. 'Put it off for a couple of days. I'll catch up with the others.' He paused. 'I couldn't go without seeing you, Rosie.'

She tried to speak, but her throat was tight.

'You there, Rosie?'

'Yeah . . . I . . . I'm just . . . Can't believe you did that.'

She heard him sighing. 'Just didn't feel right, not seeing you. Cost me my first week's gigging money, by the way. Are you okay? They didn't shoot you or anything?' he joked.

'Not quite,' Rosie managed to say. She took a deep breath. 'I'm so glad you're here, TJ. I . . . I thought you'd be gone. I had just resigned myself to it. There's been so much going on over in Bosnia and stuff that I tried not to think about it, but when I got to London last night, I felt . . . Well I felt like shit, just knowing that I'd miss you by a few hours.'

'Well, we've got a couple of days. Then I'm off. Why don't I come to your place tonight? We can get a take-away.' He paused. 'Or are you too knackered from the trip?'

'No. No way, TJ. I'm okay,' Rosie said quickly. 'But . . . er . . . I have to see someone at six. A cop. I'll be there by around seven.'

Rosie felt a little sluggish as she sat on a bar stool in O'Brien's, sipping a mineral water as she waited for Don. It had been a busy afternoon, writing the spread on her kidnap ordeal, then dashing up to dump her bag in her flat before coming out to meet Don. More than anything right now, she longed for a large gin and tonic to straighten her out, but she resisted, knowing that mixed with the exhaustion and stress she felt, it would hit her between the eyes. The last thing she wanted was to turn up to meet TJ half sozzled.

She watched as Don came through the swing doors and automatically looked over to the bar. He came towards her, his craggy expression even more wiped out than usual. He glanced at Rosie's bruised eye as he eased himself onto the bar stool.

'You've been getting on some Serbian tits, I see. You're not fussy who you fuck about, Rosie, are you?' He offered her a cigarette and flicked the lighter under it. 'You're lucky they didn't cut your ears off.'

'They're just not fast enough,' Rosie gave a little swagger to her shrug.

'What happened to you?'

'I got kidnapped.' Rosie drew on her cigarette and looked beyond him. 'Long story. But as you see, I got away.' She swirled the ice in her glass. 'So what's the score with the bent detective? And I hear the Deputy Chief is getting pelters.'

Don took a long drink of his pint and looked confounded.

'It's all gone fucking mental. The detective was on the take. He's been on the force for years. In the CID for about nine, but one of these guys who was never going anywhere. Bit of a booze bag. We're also hearing he's been tipping them off on drugs busts. Can't believe nobody had an inkling.'

'Bastard! Is he not locked up?'

'He will be. He's being watched. The word is that they're going to arrest him in the next twenty-four hours. They're trying to get footage of him getting pay-offs.'

'From Howie?'

'Yep. And Clock Buchanan. He's a hit man for Howie's mob.'

'I know who he is.' Rosie remembered him writhing in agony from her kick. 'But I thought they'd gone missing, disappeared to the Costa?'

'That's just a smokescreen put out by the cops. We know they're still here. We want to get them all together. We've got a grass in their mob who's hopefully going to stick them in.'

'How come the grass couldn't have stuck them in before . . . before poor Emir got shot? Or any of the other shit that went on up at the slaughterhouse?'

Don shrugged. 'He didn't know. Nobody had a sniff about what was going on up at the slaughterhouse – if you'll pardon the pun.' He smirked at his wit.

'You're a comedian, Don.' Rosie said, deadpan. 'But is the detective daft enough to go out and get a pay-off from them in this climate?'

'We'll soon see. Anyway, he'll get ten years in the poky for this.'

'That all? I hope somebody does him in.' She drained her glass and slid off the stool. 'Will I get a shout when you're going to move on him – considering it was me who gave Emir to you in the first place, not knowing I was sending him to his death?'

'I'll talk to the big DI.' He winked at Rosie. 'He likes you. I'd say you'll be in with a shout.'

Rosie decided to take the tube to the West End and make the short walk to her flat. It was a warm summer's evening and she wanted to relish being back home, feel the Glasgow ground beneath her feet walking up to the train station. The walk would refresh her.

On the way up to Queen Street station, she stopped at an off-licence to buy a bottle of red wine, hoping she had another one at home. As she browsed the shelves, she became vaguely aware of a man standing at the other side of the doorway outside, and she thought he was looking at her. She dismissed it, hoping the paranoia and constantly looking over her shoulder would soon pass.

At Buchanan Street underground platform, it was eerily quiet compared to what it would have been an hour earlier. The rush hour was over and there were only a few people standing around, mostly students or tourists on their way to the West End. The distant rumbling of the tube approaching sent a gust of stifling hot air through the platform, and Rosie was thinking she would be glad to be out of this and back into the freshness of the evening. When the tube arrived, she stepped in and sat down, her eyes automatically looking up at the overhead tube map. She did it every time, obsessively checking she was on the right train, as though she suffered from some kind of short-term memory lapse. It was even worse whenever she was in London, when she could spend half a morning like Rain Man, reading the tube map, memorising the different routes. The control freak in her was terrified of getting lost – even though she knew that all you had to do was cross the platform and get back to where you came from. She smiled wryly to herself at her Obsessive Compulsive Disorder. A shrink would have a field day if they ever got her on the couch.

She settled down and looked around her. A little brat with a posh accent was running up and down the carriage making a racket, slamming his fist on the windows. Rosie wondered how much private education it took before you got to the part that told your kid to sit on its arse on the train and behave. She noticed a guy a few seats up from her, sitting staring at the floor.

Vicious-looking bastard. She flicked a glance at him again. Suddenly, a chill ran through her. His hands: one was larger than the other.

Panic surged through Rosie, catching in her chest. She tried a deep breath, but it wouldn't come. She looked around at the other passengers, then kept her eyes on the floor, squinting from behind her dark glasses to make sure. The big hand and the wee hand. Shit! It was Clock Buchanan! She hadn't seen his face that day, but could feel his hand around her throat when she left him in agony on the floor after booting him in the balls. She looked up at the tube map. One more stop to Hyndland Road. Her heart was pounding.

Rosie stood up before her stop and moved closer to the door. From the side of her eye, she could see the guy with the mad psycho look was still staring at the floor. Maybe it was her imagination. Paranoia. He could be anybody. Calm down, she told herself, but her gut told her it was him. She felt her back damp with sweat. She needed air, but she knew one more attempt at a deep breath would make her lightheaded. Just hang on for a few seconds more, she told herself, then open the door and dive upstairs. She wouldn't walk home even though it was only a few hundred yards. The tube stopped and she banged the button with her fist to open the doors. She got out and took the stairs two at a time not even looking back. At the top she phoned TJ.

'Where are you, TJ?'

'On my way up to yours. Why? It's not seven yet. You home?'

'No.' She could feel her voice shaking. 'TJ . . . I think I'm being followed.'

'What? Where are you?'

'I just got off the tube at Hyndland.' She walked briskly out as she spoke. 'There was a guy on the tube. I think it was the nutter who attacked me at Tanya's house that day. Remember? The guy with the big hand and the wee hand?'

'What? Was he on the train?'

'Yeah. But I think maybe I saw him, just before that, TJ. Outside the off-licence in Renfield Street. Then on the tube. I think he's followed me.'

'Right. Okay. I'm in a taxi. Just go into the nearest busy place and wait for me. Just stay there. Any shop. Just get off the street into somewhere busy.'

Rosie figured Clock was only a few yards away if he'd got off the train. She jumped into the Costa cafe and hid behind a pillar so she could see outside and still be concealed. Then she saw him. He was standing on Byres Road looking up and down. He was looking for her. It *was* him. Shit! He turned around and started to walk towards the door of the coffee bar.

Rosie made a beeline for the toilet. She was shaking with fear. She stood waiting inside, hardly breathing. Surely he wouldn't sit down in the cafe. He'd been following her and he'd lost her. Hopefully, he would just go away. Her mind was a blur. How the hell had he known where she was? Or had it just been sod's law that they happened to be in the same street at the same time and he got lucky? After a few minutes, she decided it might be safe to go out. She took a deep breath and opened the door into the corridor. But as she did, she came face to face with him. He grinned like a maniac and shoved her back into the toilet.

'You cunt.' He punched her face and knocked her against the tiles. 'You'll not get away this time. You made me look like a prick.'

'You are a prick,' Rosie heard herself saying as she instinctively lashed out at him.

'Fuck you!' He tried to punch her, but she jerked her head swiftly and his fist hit the wall. 'Bastard!' he rasped.

She swung a punch at his face and heard it connect on the flesh, but it just made him worse, and her hand hurt.

'You think you can fight me, you wee bitch?' He shoved her against the wall, his forearm pushed hard against her throat. 'You're dead meat, Gilmour. History. Big Jake's doing his nut over in Spain that you fucked up our operation here. I hope you enjoyed your big story, you bitch. Because it's your last.'

'Fuck you.' Rosie tried to punch him again, but felt her head knock against the tiles. Then she let out a gasp at a searing pain in her stomach. Her hand automatically went to the pain, as he backed off with a mad smile on his face. She saw the knife in his hand. Blood trickled through her fingers. Her legs buckled.

'Fuck you,' he spat on her as she began to slide down the wall. 'That's for my ma.'

She could see him disappear out of the door as she hit the floor. The phone. Shit! So much blood now, seeping in a pool onto the floor.

'Oh God, no! My phone, my phone! Where is it?'

She kept a hand on her stomach to stem the blood bubbling out as her other hand fumbled for her phone. Her hands trembled so much she couldn't hold it. She managed to press the last number she called.

'TJ . . . TJ . . . I've been stabbed. Hurry. Costa cafe. Hurry. Hurry, TJ . . .'

She was dizzy but could hear noises in the distance. She was aware of the door opening and someone screaming. Then seconds later room the swayed and she saw double. People were coming towards her. She thought she saw TJ, but maybe it was a dream.

'Rosie. It's me. You're okay. The ambulance is on its way.' It was TJ. 'Stay with me, Rosie. Stay with me, sweetheart.' She saw the tears in his eyes as she passed out.

CHAPTER 37

By the fourth day, the consultant finally gave Rosie the all clear to leave hospital, stressing that she was to do nothing strenuous until the wound healed. The knife had nicked a vein in her stomach and she'd had to have emergency surgery to repair it. She had lost a lot of blood. She was ordered to have at least two weeks off work and complete rest.

McGuire had come to visit her in hospital, waving the *Post* with the front-page headline that Clock Buchanan had been arrested and was in custody, facing a string of charges. Stabbing Rosie was only one of them. Howie, unfortunately, had disappeared. Police continued to probe the illegal tissue trade story blasted wide open by the paper's exclusive investigation. Rosie was disappointed that she'd missed out on the big story – not being there when Buchanan was arrested making the pay-off to the crooked detective. But McGuire told her to forget it – it would have been worse if she'd missed her next birthday.

Rosie had given her statement to detectives from her hospital bed, and so far it didn't look like they were going to pursue her or the paper for withholding information from the police prior to her initial story. Hanlon had tipped her off on a visit that they were too covered in crap from their own ineptitude to go chasing the reporter who had cracked the case for them.

She had even got a card from Christy Larkin, congratulating her on the story and wishing her well. He'd chucked his job and was going travelling, the card said. The dinner she'd promised would have to wait.

TJ had changed his flight again, postponing another week to look after her. And the *Post* would pick up the cost of the flight for 'that banjo player boyfriend', McGuire had told Rosie.

'He plays the sax,' she'd insisted.

'Well, whatever. At least he was in the right place at the right time.'

Now Rosie watched from the sofa as TJ got his bags organised and was preparing to go.

'You know something, TJ,' Rosie said. 'The past couple of days have been just about perfect. Maybe I should get stabbed every week.'

'Yeah, attention-seeking. I've seen it before with you.'

It was going to be tough to say goodbye. He brought mugs of tea for them and sat beside her.

'I'm going to miss all this, Gilmour,' he said, ruffling her hair. 'Life's never dull around you, that's for sure, but I miss these little times together, listening to your patter and stuff. It's been great these past few days.' He leaned over and kissed her. 'Happiest I've been in a while, if I'm honest.'

'And you didn't even have to take a bullet for me this time.' Rosie snuggled down into the sofa with her feet on the coffee table.

Her mobile rang. McGuire.

'Howsit going, Rosie?'

'Fine, Mick, but you already phoned me this morning. What's up?'

'Have you seen the news?'

'No, I haven't.' Rosie flicked on the telly and went to Sky News as she spoke.

'The Raznatovic bastard has gone missing. Can you fucking believe that?'

'You're kidding me, Mick. Missing? I thought he was being taken to a jail in The Hague to await trial. Christ almighty, how can he be missing?'

'That's what everyone thought. The news is sketchy. It just came up on Sky saying that he escaped on his way to hospital for some heart scare. Must have been an organised job.'

'Bloody Serbs. They probably fixed it. There'll be so many of them among guards and the military who were supposed to be watching him, maybe some of them were from his old command or something. What a bastard. They'll never get him now.'

'Exactly. I've just been saying as much in an interview with Sky News and the BBC. They wanted to talk to you as the reporter who blew the lid off this whole story and tracked him down to Belgrade, but I told them you weren't fit. Hope that's okay. I just thought you'd want to know.' He paused. 'Has your man gone yet?'

'That's okay about the interview. I don't want to do that. TJ's going shortly.'

'Right. Well, I'll get Marion to phone you, see if you need anything, and she'll get some grub in for you. And on Friday, if you're up to it, I'll take you out for lunch. I'll get you picked up.' He paused. 'But I'll be having the whole restaurant checked out for bombs and hit men before we go. Take care.' He hung up.

'What's up?' TJ asked, leaning forward.

Rosie shook her head. 'The Serb, Raznatovic. He's escaped. Christ! It's unbelievable. After everything we've done.'

'Inside job. It has to be.'

She nodded. 'That's what McGuire said. Have to agree.'

Rosie thought of Adrian and wondered how he'd be reacting to the news. She was itching to phone him, but she wanted to give TJ her undivided attention for his final few minutes.

They watched the item come up on Sky News and saw McGuire ranting about the ineptitude of the Serb authorities and floating various conspiracy theories.

'You're dying to get back into this, aren't you, Rosie?' TJ turned towards her.

'No. I'm not,' Rosie said, and most of her meant it. 'I mean, what's the point of knocking my pan in nearly getting killed in Belgrade if the bloody authorities let the bastard go? Makes a mockery of the whole thing. All seems suddenly pointless.' She let out a sigh of frustration.

TJ sighed and gently massaged the back of her neck. 'That's how it is, Rosie. It's not worth getting yourself killed over. How many times have I told you that?'

'I know.' Rosie felt deflated, but she didn't want to hear that. 'I know.'

TJ looked at his watch. 'Right. I'd better get moving. Taxi will be here in a second.'

On cue, the buzzer on the intercom went and he answered it, saying he'd be right down.

Rosie got to her feet very gingerly, trying not to stretch.

'Well.' She looked up at TJ. 'Should I say, 'so long' or something suitably American?'

TJ put his arms around her and held her close, her face pressed against the warm softness of his neck. Rosie felt a sinking feeling in her stomach.

'Don't do that, TJ.' She sighed.

'What?'

'Make me want you so much, then leave me.' She felt a little catch in her throat.

'Not for long though.' He kissed her face and her neck. 'When you're fit in a couple of weeks you can come over, and we'll have the best time of our lives. You know you'll be able to take a few weeks off after everything that's happened to you.' His eyes scrutinised her face. 'You just have to want to.'

'I do want to,' Rosie said. 'I really want to, TJ.' She opened her mouth to say something else. She wanted to ask if he would still feel this way in five weeks' time when he was up to his eyes in work and New York bars and surrounded by women, especially Kat. But she couldn't. He wouldn't let her. He kissed her again.

'Then make sure it happens.' He hugged her one last time as she walked him to the door. Then he picked up his sax case and pushed his suitcase into the hallway. She watched as he walked downstairs.

'I'll call you tomorrow. Once I get into the digs and get some kind of phone sorted out.'

'I'll miss you, TJ. I will. I really will,' she called after him, as though trying to convince him.

'Sure you will, sweetheart. See you soon. I love you. Remember that.' He blew her a kiss from the bottom of the stairs, then turned and left.

Rosie went back into the flat and stood for a moment with her back to the door, the emptiness instantly oppressive. She missed him already. The television blared with the Sky News update on the Serb war criminal, and she went across to the sofa and turned the volume up loud, glad of the distraction.

For three days after TJ left, Rosie had been mooching around the flat, reading, watching videos, talking to old friends on the phone for hours at a time. She'd also talked to TJ, who sounded happy and full of excitement about the jazz club. He had lots of plans for them when she came over, he told her. She was even beginning to look forward to the trip, and over lunch when she'd ventured into town, McGuire told her the paper would pay for her flight and throw in some expenses as part of her convalescence. It was all positive, but none of it felt right, just sitting around doing nothing.

Now, she came out of the shower and flicked onto Sky News. Football and sport dominated as it always did on a Saturday morning. She was in the kitchen when the news bulletin came on, and her ears pricked up when she thought she heard the name Raznatovic. She came back in quickly.

'Serbian war criminal Boris Raznatovic, who escaped while in custody has been found dead,' the news reader said. She turned up the volume on her remote control.

'The body of the 45-year-old feared commander, also wanted in the UK in connection with missing refugees being sold as part of the illegal international trade in body tissue, was found in an area in the north of Bosnia known as Paklenik Gorge.'

Rosie watched open-mouthed as the pictures moved to the mountain gorge, with the voiceover describing that this was the notorious spot where Serb soldiers massacred more than fifty Bosnians during the brutal ethnic cleansing that was one of the most lasting images of the war. She listened as the story continued.

'Raznatovic, believed to have played a central role in the atrocity, was found hanging by his feet over the mouth of the 400-foot gorge, where the bodies of the dead Bosnians still lie. His throat had been cut.'

For the next two hours Rosie watched the footage over and over again as it came up on every Sky bulletin. She kept trying to phone Adrian, but his number rang out.

Then, early in the evening, as she was cooking dinner, her mobile rang. It was Adrian.

'Adrian! Have you heard the news?'

'Of course I have, my friend.'

'Raznatovic. They found his body. He was hanging by his ankles or something. Swaying over the gorge, they said. I saw it on television. They had pictures of Paklenik.'

'Yes. I know.'

Silence. She knew Adrian didn't burst with excitement about anything, but she'd expected a bit more than this.

Finally, he spoke, his Slavic tones rich and thick, as he seemed to choose his words carefully.

'It was important before he died that he feel the fear that my people felt when he and his men executed them. I know for sure that he felt it.' He paused. 'Risto and me could see it in his face.' He paused again, and Rosie held her breath. 'We wanted him to die looking down at the people he murdered.'

'Christ, Adrian!' Rosie couldn't believe her ears. 'But how? I mean how did you find him?'

In the pause that followed, Rosie could picture Adrian's understated expression.

'Remember, Rosie . . .' His tone was measured. 'Remember we told you that before the war, we are one people, Serbs and Bosnians – we are Yugoslavs, all friends, before all this happen? Well, some friendships last forever. I have friends who are Serbs, who are sickened by what Raznatovic and his men did to our people. Raznatovic's own people organise his escape on the way to the hospital, but my friend who is with the guards knows about this, and he tells me where I can find him.'

'My God!'

She heard Adrian take a deep breath and waited for him to speak.

'Now, whatever happens to me in my life, Rosie, I did one good thing. For my people. For my country. For my Marija and Adrijane.' The line went dead.

'Adrian? You there?' But there was nothing.

Rosie stood for a moment trying to take it all in. Her mind was flooded with images of their journey across Bosnia to Belgrade and back through Kosovo to Macedonia. She thought of Emir and of Gerhard. She went across to her window and opened the balcony doors and stood outside watching the afternoon traffic. Just another Saturday.

Her mobile rang. It was McGuire.

'Have you heard the news, Rosie?'

'Yes, Mick. I heard.'

ACKNOWLEDGEMENTS

Much of what I've written in this novel is based on the many tragic souls I enountered in refugee camps in war torn countries from the Balkans to Somalia to Rwanda. I was humbled by the resilience of the masses of innocent men, women and children scattered to the four winds because of the brutality of others. I often wonder if they ever made it back home, or if their lives are still filled with the same uncertainty of those dark days. I hope this is an honest tribute to them.

I want thank the following people: My sister Sadie for her rock solid support every day, as well as my brothers Arthur, Hugh and Desmond. My talented nephews and nieces who keep me young and make me laugh. Great friends Mags, Anne Frances, Mary, Phil, Helen, Donna, Louise, Jan and Barbara. In Kerry, everyone in Mhurioch and Ballydavid who make me feel at home, especially Paud and Mary Kavanagh. Friends, Simon and Lynn, Thomas, Annie, Mark, Keith and Maureen, for the many shared happy hours and problems solved over Glasgow dinners and copious amounts of wine. On the Costa del Sol, thanks to Rosalind McCabe, who is a great support at book launches. And Franco Rey, for being there for me since this adventure began. My agent Ali Gunn who helps make dreams come true. Jane Wood, my fantastic editor at Quercus for her guidance and continued support, and her assistant Katie Gordon. Lucy Ramsey, Director of Publicity, and all the brilliant team at Quercus. Also thanks to Dr Bernadette Higgins for her expert medical background, and George Parsonage junior at the Glasgow Humane Society for giving me the benefit of his knowledge and experience.

Sign up to find out more about Rosie Gilmour at:

quercusbooks.co.uk/anna-smith

Join the conversation:

#screamsinthedark

As good as Martina Cole . . .

or your money back

We're so sure that you'll love *Screams in the Dark*
as much as Martina Cole's books that we'll give you
your money back if you don't enjoy it.

If you do wish to claim your money back, please send the book, along with your
receipt and the reasons for returning it to:

Anna Smith money back offer

Marketing Department

Quercus Books

55 Baker Street

London W1U 8EW

We'll refund you the price of the book, plus £1 to cover postage.

Offer ends May 2014.